IRRESISTIBLY BROKEN

J. SAMAN

Cover Design: Lori Jackson

Photographer: Michelle Lancaster

Model: Mitchell Wick

Editing: My Brother's Editor & Emily Lawrence

✳ Created with Vellum

1

The headline was all anyone cared about. It was all that was repeated over and over and over again ad nauseam across every news network, entertainment magazine, and blog. "Suzie Ward, manager of the hugely successful pop band, Central Square, and girlfriend of Zaxton Monroe, found dead in the shower."

The headline was followed by mass speculation because even though there were some leaks and a few statements here and there, no one knew what actually happened except for us. And even then, I'm the only one who knows the truth. A secret I will take to my grave. A fucking heartbreak that has turned me into the delightful mother-fucker I am today.

Especially today.

Eight years ago, I lost the love of my life.

And it doesn't seem to get any easier with the passing of time. Maybe it's because I lost more than just her that day. I lost a piece of myself I haven't been able to retrieve.

My phone vibrates on the seat beside me, but I don't bother checking it. It's either one of the guys, my brother, or work. None of which I want to deal with right now. I should have stayed home today. I shouldn't have gotten out of bed this morning, but today we have a photo shoot for a few pieces in the new women's fall line, and I have to be in it, and who gives a shit?

Bed and whiskey for breakfast were a much better option.

My driver, Ashley, sits quietly and patiently up front, staring straight ahead and allowing me this moment. He knows. He's been with me long enough to know I'll get out when I'm ready and I'm just not there yet.

Will I ever get past this? Will the hurt ever dissipate?

"What happens if I call in sick?" I mumble under my breath and notice Ashley stirring up front. I'm not asking him, but I wouldn't mind if he answered me all the same. He's the closest thing I have to a fatherlike figure in my life even though I pay him to be here because my actual father is a world-class piece of shit. He's the reason I'm the CEO of Monroe Fashion instead of him.

"May I suggest, if you talked about that day, it might help to unburden your soul."

"One has to have a soul for it to be unburdened."

He breathes out a mournful sigh in a way that tells me he's not amused.

"Talking about it won't unburden me. It will only burden others." The truth shall not set me free. It shall ruin someone who is already suffering more than he should.

"You know—"

"I know. And thank you. If I ever do want to talk about it, you might hear more than you ever wanted."

He chuckles at my wry tone just as a flash of whitish-blond whisks past my window, snapping me out of my miserable thoughts. Inadvertently, I follow the trail it makes, transfixed by the unique color and wavelike flow as it bounces and plays in the summer sunshine and breeze. That is until it drops from my view in a sudden swish and swoop along with the body it's attached to. Then there's the scream.

"Shit."

Snatching my phone, I fly out of the car and race up the three cement steps to the first landing where a woman is yelling and fighting with a man trying to snatch her purse. Gripping the leather handle, he gives a solid yank, managing the upper hand with the purse while simultaneously shoving her to the ground. Hard.

Without thinking twice, I collide with him, the full force of my size and weight knocking him back. The purse slips from his hand, skidding on the steps, but before he can catch himself from falling or right his body and flee, I grab him by the shirt and haul him up. Feet dangling from the ground, I get a better look at him.

"Jesus," I hiss in dismay. "What the hell are you doing snatching purses at your age?"

The kid, who can't be any older than seventeen, sneers at me, all punk-ass bravado despite the fact that I have him dangling like a proverbial worm on a hook. "Fuck you, man. The fuck you care what I do? You don't know me."

I set him down, but I don't release my hold on his shirt. "You think stealing from women makes you tough? Makes you a man? Do you know what being tough is?" I get right up in his face. "Tough is being a man even when the odds are stacked against you. It's doing the right thing when the wrong thing is easier. Grow up. Get out of your shit and do better. Now go before I call the cops."

I shove him away but make sure he sees me staring after him. For a second, he falters, his gaze snapping down at the woman who is still on the ground, then back up at me before he runs off.

I turn, taking in the now-seated woman swearing under her breath and staring incredulously at a high heel clutched angrily in her fist. The long, narrow heel of the shoe hangs limply from the black stiletto, having snapped.

"You're not supposed to do this," she bemoans. "Not today! Your job is to carry me from point A to point B without snapping like a twig. Don't you know what this means for me? Now look." Her hands fly about her body. "I'm a bloody mess. Literally." She threateningly shakes the shoe. "I'm gonna tell Marie you did this to us, and she won't be pleased. Not at all."

Marie? I take a better look at the shoes. Marie Marcato. Exclusive and expensive. But clearly, she's speaking in jest and ire because no one knows or speaks to Marie directly. Not even me and I've been trying for longer than I care to admit. Still, I can't understand how she's more upset about her heel snapping than she is about the fact that she was almost *mugged*.

My shadow looms over her, blocking the blinding summer sun. "What were you thinking fighting with him? He could have been armed or seriously hurt you. Are you okay?" The cuts on her knees are dripping blood down her shins and onto the concrete steps, but she's more focused on her broken shoe.

Alarmingly bright cornflower-blue eyes snap up and glue themselves to my face. And the moment they register me, they grow round as dinner plates, her plump pink lips parting. "Shit," she breathes harshly.

"Now you're catching up. That's what I said when I saw you were struggling with him. Are. You. Okay?" I repeat, my annoyance dripping through into my tone now that she's staring at me like, well, like everyone else does. Starstruck, awed, and terrified. "Do you not know how to answer questions or is English along with common sense a difficulty for you?"

She scowls at my sharp, curt words. "Did you honestly just ask that? Do you have any sense of how insanely rude and condescending that is after what just happened?"

My lips bounce, attempting to curl up into a smirk, but I beat it instantly away. "Whatever gets you to speak."

She blinks away from me, staring down at her knees that are bleeding and oozing everywhere. "He shoved me, and my shoe broke," she shoots back. "Obviously, I'm not having the best of mornings."

"Obviously," I deadpan, mocking her snarky, sardonic tone. "And now you're hurt. For the third time, are you okay?"

"Um. I don't know," she admits with a shaky breath. "I'm pissed. And hurt. And annoyed. At so many, *many* things right now."

"Can I help you up?"

"You might be the last person on earth I should ever ask for or accept help from."

Okay. I'm not sure what to do with that. "Do you work here?"

"Probably not for much longer. I'm a design intern. First day." Regret immediately strikes her features, and she frowns, shaking her head violently. "I seriously wish I hadn't just told you that."

I chuckle and with the sound of my laughter at what she inaccurately assumes is at her expense, she scathingly glares back up at me with those arresting eyes. Then there is her hair and those sexy lips and those entrancing pinpoint freckles on the bridge of an adorably petite nose and across the upslope of her perfect high cheekbones and shit.

I can't stop looking at her.

Though I know I've seen her face before, I'm struggling to place where exactly. Even so, my stupid cock stirs in my pants. Not the most opportune time for that, given her vantage point of me from the ground.

Slowly, she starts to stand, albeit awkwardly because she can't roll onto her knees to help herself up and the pencil skirt she's wearing is restrictive around her thighs.

"That's not a good idea," I tell her. "You're bleeding. Your shoe is broken. Not to mention, you just admitted you're not sure if you're okay."

"I'm fine." She hisses out a shocked breath as her knee scrapes the ground. "I can't exactly live here and besides, I don't want to be late on my first day."

"I'm sure they'll understand when they see you."

She rolls onto her side, attempting to use her elbows, and this is just ridiculous.

"I don't know what that move is, but you're only going to hurt yourself more," I admonish. "Was your purse really worth this? Here, take my hand."

"No, thanks." She shoves my proffered hand away, her pride getting the better of her.

Or maybe it's because you're being a dick to her after she was just attacked. I push that thought away.

"Do you know who I am?" I ask coolly, annoyed she's brushing me off when I helped her with the mugger and am offering to help her again.

She strikes me with a look. "You mean other than the jerk standing over me, making fun of me? Yes, I know who you are."

"Then I'm shocked you're still speaking to me like this." She's an intern. That means she works for me whether directly or not. So her talking back to me like this?

"Me too. Must be all the blood loss and adrenaline making me loopy. I take it no one talks back or insults you?"

"Not if they have any sort of natural self-preservation instincts, which I think we already established you don't."

"Wow," she mocks. "You're a real prince amongst mortals, there, *Zaxton*." She snorts. "What kind of name is Zaxton anyway? Paxton, Jaxson, Saxton even, but I've never heard of a Zaxton."

My eyes narrow into menacing slits. I can be terrifying when motivated. "A none of your business, *intern*, name. Speaking of names..." I raise my eyebrow expectantly at her.

"Nuh-uh. I'll be fired for sure if you know who I am."

I have no idea what that means, but I don't care enough right now to fish for more answers. I can't stand watching her flounder about another second whether she wants my help or not. Bending down, I loop my arm around her hips, pulling the majority of her weight up to spare her knees. I do my best to ignore the way her body feels against mine. And how good she smells. Perfume, shampoo, body wash, or her natural fragrance—whatever it is, if I could bottle it up and sell it, I'd be richer than I already am.

Once she's upright, albeit a bit wobbly, I take a step back, releasing her as fast as I can without her falling back to the ground.

"Thank you," she murmurs. "And thank you for saving my purse. Maybe I shouldn't have tried to fight him for it, but I've had enough of people taking from me and walking all over me to let it happen with some kid." Turning away from me, she starts hobbling one-heeled up the steps, anxious to get inside and away from me. Is she for real?

"You're dripping blood everywhere," I call after her, hating how quick she was to dismiss me. Hating how I want her eyes back on mine. "Will you stop? You can barely walk like this."

She emits an exasperated sigh because she knows I'm right. Blood is running all down her legs and across her heelless foot and even into the other remaining good shoe.

I'm fed up with this game.

"I don't remember asking for your—ah!" She belts out a half-scream as her legs are swooped out from beneath her and I lift her body into my arms. "What are you doing?"

"Carrying you in. You're bleeding all over my steps and were just attacked. I have to make sure you're okay."

I hold her tightly against me while I carry her bride-style up the steps. She's tall and thin, but with perfect fucking curves in all the right places. Her hair kicks up in my face as I adjust her, assaulting me with her delicious scent. I pull her in closer, liking the way she feels against me a little too much. What is that fragrance? A goddamn summer afternoon in the country with wind, wildflowers, and sun? It's killing me not to bury my nose in her silky hair and breathe it in deeper.

"I can walk," she protests, completely oblivious to what she's doing to me.

"I beg to differ. Stop squirming."

"I'd stop squirming if you put me down."

"We're almost there. Now stop. Squirming." My hand on her thigh clenches in warning, and she gives up the protest.

"I'm trying not to get your suit sleeve covered in my blood."

"Appreciated, but I'm going to be changing suits in a few minutes anyway."

She laughs bitterly at that. "That your standard practice, Mr. Monroe? Just how many wardrobe changes a day do you have?"

My head tilts down. My eyes, dark and hooded, lock with hers. I smirk at how brazen she is with me. "You've got quite the mouth on you for an intern speaking to her boss on her first day."

She shrugs against me, trying to keep her face hidden since people are absolutely staring at us. I can't exactly blame them either.

Of the many, many things I'm known for, carrying damsels in distress up the steps and into my building isn't one of them.

The door opens, a blast of frigid air making her shiver when it hits the blood on her skin. I press her tighter. "You all right there?"

"I'm fine. Totally great. I mean, considering it's my first day and I was nearly mugged, the heel of my shoe snapped, and I'm bleeding like a bad bitch out of hell. Oh, and I'm swearing at my boss, who just so happens to be you of all people." She claps a hand over her mouth, murmuring, "Sorry," through her fingers. "I just." A heavy sigh. "I didn't want to see you like this. I didn't think I'd ever have to see you at all. That's what he said and then you swoop in to save the day and I... I'm done talking now."

I'm not sure I understand anything she's saying. My confusion must be evident because she gnaws on her lip and shakes her head, indicating to me she's not going to clarify.

"Mr. Monroe, what happened?" The lobby security guard walks briskly by our side as I carry her over to a bank of seats along the wall between the elevators and floor-to-ceiling windows.

"She got hurt outside on the steps. Do we have a first aid kit down here, George?"

"Of course, sir. I'll go fetch it right away."

George scurries off just as I place her upright on the cushioned leather. Then I'm kneeling before her, tugging my white silk handkerchief from my breast pocket and pressing it against the cut that's bleeding the most.

I know it has to burn. Her chin wobbles and she sucks in a sharp breath as her pretty blue eyes glass over.

"You know his name." It's a half whisper as she stares down at her knees, refusing to meet my eyes.

"Yes. I know his name." My tone is terse. "I know his wife's name as well as his children's names. He's been working here since I was a kid and he's a good man."

Her head bobs up and down. "Didn't mean for that to come out as judgmental as it sounded." She tilts her head. "Or maybe I did. Sorry." She touches the sleeve of my suit coat. "My blood is on you."

My eyes stay locked on her pretty face. "Should that bother me?"

"Doesn't it?"

Does it? It feels like it should be gross, yet it's erotic in some strange way.

"No."

She peeks up at me through her long lashes, a coy smile curving up her lips, and the air leaves my lungs like someone just drove a knife right through my chest. She's easily the most stunning heartbreaker I've ever encountered.

"Does everyone hop to do your bidding the second you snap your fingers?" she asks, ignoring everything but my sour attitude while dropping her broken shoe to the floor and checking her watch. She's late or getting there. So am I, for that matter, but I don't care all that much right now.

I like her attitude. I like that she fought back even though it cost her her shoe and knees. I like her snapping at me and calling me out on my shit while asking me bold questions no one ever has the balls to ask.

"Yes," I answer flatly, still crouched before her, unable to so much as shift away from her.

"You're quite the intimidating man."

I grunt in dismay at her cheeky tone and mockingly flirty expression.

"No, I mean it," she insists. "You are. I bet you can feel it every time you touch me."

My eyebrows bounce in surprise and my grip on her calf tightens while my other still presses in on her wound. I intimidate her, but she's not afraid of me.

"What exactly does my touch do to you?" Thumbs on both hands brush back and forth along her skin and goose bumps erupt in their wake, her pupils expanding ever so slightly.

Fuck.

That's what my touch does to her. I'm not the only one feeling this. I shouldn't be reacting to her—she is an intern, and this is *not* what I do—but it's as if my brain and body are on disconnect.

Because I recognize her elegantly radiant face. I never catalog a woman's features anymore. Not beyond the scope of professionalism and necessity of business.

But I know her face from somewhere.

"Repulses me," she whispers, still half-smiling at me.

"Is that so?" My thumbs brush again, dragging a longer trail on her skin, and her breath skitters in a sharp hiccup. I smirk arrogantly. "Are you always this much of a brat to people who help you?"

"I think it's just with you. You seem to have a strange effect on me."

"What if I like having this effect on you?" Not words I should be saying to her, but again, I want to see how she reacts to me if for no other reason than my own perverse need.

Mercifully and before this can go any further, George returns, proudly carrying the first aid kit. "Sir, you're needed upstairs."

"Tell them—"

"I can take it from here," she interrupts, snatching the kit out of George's hand. Swinging her legs out of my grip, she places them up on the seat and pops open the white top of the large box, effectively dismissing me.

I stand, pocketing the blood-soaked handkerchief when I should throw it away.

"Thank you for your help," she tells me, forcing a weak smile that doesn't reach her eyes. "I'm sorry if I was short or even insubordinate with you. It's obviously already been a day for me and hopefully, you can pretend I was nothing but respectful and polite."

I scowl, annoyed with everything. Her. Me. The way I want to clean her wounds and bandage her up. How I want more time with her when I shouldn't.

Without another word, I'm gone. The tap of my perfect, nonbroken shoes on the marble floors echoes through the lobby that is progressively growing more and more crowded as the official start of the day approaches. The elevator is already there waiting, but before I step on, I glance back in her direction.

Our eyes lock for the briefest of seconds, my pulse jumps, and then I'm on the elevator alone. No one else dares to step on while I'm in here. I press the button for the top floor and curse under my breath as the doors close. What the fuck did I just do with that girl and why do I want to do it all over again?

I scrub my hands up my face. I never should have gotten out of bed this morning.

2

AURELIA

I stare at the closed elevator door for a moment, trying to figure out what just happened. I was nearly mugged, shoved to the ground, and hurt. Oddly, that's the furthest thing from my thoughts at this moment. I saw Zax. The one and only person I had been hoping to avoid while working here.

And then I was rude. And he touched me. And we might have flirted a bit? I don't know about that last one for sure.

I forgot how gorgeous the man is and simply put, magazines and internet shots did not do him justice. Tall, broad, and visibly muscular even beneath his charcoal suit and navy button-down. Intimidating, serious dark eyes matching thick, slightly unruly hair, and a chin dimple that rivals Henry Cavill's.

He's impossible not to stare at and drool over.

A man who has never shown me an ounce of kindness before. I understood it. Even back then. I knew why he hated me, but it didn't make the pain of it any better just as his kindness—*could that be construed as kindness?*—this morning only makes this worse.

He didn't recognize me. A lucky break.

Hopefully, he will forget about me, but at the very least that's over and I don't have to see him again. I blow out a sigh of relief at that and remind myself it's only one year. One year to prove myself again and put what happened in New York behind me. I need this. Lord Jesus sleeping in the manger, I need this. I don't even care that I had to ask for the favor of a lifetime from a man who may in fact be worse than my new boss to get it.

He owed me as far as I was concerned, and we promised neither would tell Zax anything.

Then I run into Zax before I even make it into the building.

Quickly, I dig my phone out of my purse. Just as I send a text telling my new boss what happened, I hear a screech. "Here you are. We've been waiting upstairs for you for the last half an hour. You should already be in hair and makeup and oh my motherfucking God, what the hell is this mess?"

I glance up to find a tall, handsome, impeccably dressed Black man with trendy clear-framed glasses standing above me, gaping at my wounds in revulsion.

"Um. I'm sorry. Are you talking to me?"

"Are you being ironic, Robert De Niro? Of course I'm fucking talking to you. Who the fuck else would I be talking to when I'm literally standing here, staring at you? You're not only late for the shoot, but your knees are a bleeding fucking mess."

I blink about ten thousand times, half thrown off by the number of F-bombs he's dropping, and half—wait. "I'm sorry. Who are you?"

"Who am I?" He places a manicured hand against his chest, gaping at me incredulously. "You have the fucking audacity to ask? I'm your fairy godmother, bitch, and you should consider yourself damn lucky I don't fire your tall, skinny ass right here on the spot. I do not do diva model shit, and you showing up all kinds of late for your shoot is just that."

"Did you just say model?"

He brings his forearm up to his forehead like he's been stricken. "Lawd give me strength to get through this fucking Monday." He bends down so we're at eye level. "Hi. I'm Lamar. Is English your first language?"

Why does everyone keep asking me that today? "Yes."

"Then what the fuck is there to question?"

My heart stops and starts, confused about how I should proceed. I've already pressed all my luck today considering Zax miraculously didn't fire me as I thought he was going to. "I'm not here to be your model. I'm a design intern, already late for my first day after nearly being mugged and then sprawling ass on your front steps."

He stands back up to his full height, pursing his lips. His eyes thin in speculation as he examines every inch of me, and then it's like he's having a eureka moment because I see it all flash across his face. "You're Lia Sage. You're that model from fashion week who walked in that fucking gown that still makes me hard whenever I think about it."

Great. Here we go with the gown.

My face drops before he can read just how incredible and how awful those words make me feel and I go about cleaning up my bloody skin and bandaging my wounds.

"Right?" he persists when I don't answer. "Don't tell me I'm wrong."

"You know what you think you know," I tell him as I plaster Band-Aids on my knees.

"I know the truth, you know? Since we're saying you know about sixty times."

My head shoots up faster than a rocket, ignoring his teasing lilt. "What?"

He gives me a, *yeah, sucks to be you*, look. "I know what that bitch Vermicelli or however she pronounces her name did to you."

"Valencci," I correct, but he ignores me.

"It was buzzing all through the back of the shows and not just hers."

I shake my head. "You can't know and that can't be true. If you know, then everyone would know and then I wouldn't have lost out on my internship and every other internship, only to be forced to call in a favor to the last man on earth I'd ever want to call in a favor to and wind up here. After you already rejected me once."

"Sorry to break it to you, sweetums, but I know and so does

everyone else. Just because we know doesn't mean shit doesn't turn bad for you. No one wanted to start a fucking battle with Valentisha because that bitch throws down the way Mike Tyson did when he bit that dude's ear off. She doesn't fuck around and you're a model and an intern. Disposable and replaceable. See what I'm saying?"

I frown, not even bothering to correct him with her name again since I'm too busy feeling like I'm being sucked into a black hole. "I know exactly what you're saying."

Part of me wondered at this. I should feel better that people know the truth about what happened, but I don't. Because it's still everything he said. Disposable and replaceable. It makes me so insanely angry. And I hate that I'm like this. I've never been like this even when I've had more reasons than most to be.

Being like this means they took more than just pieces of my life from me. They took my spirit, and I can't—*I won't*—allow that to happen.

I mentally shake myself. I just need to get through this morning. Through this day. My therapist when I was a kid used to say that life happens no matter what and ninety percent of that is out of our control. What is in our control is how we choose to respond to it.

"Fabulous," he says, oblivious to my inner battle. "Now that we've cleared this all up, come with me."

I bend and grab my shoe off the ground, hoisting it up for him to see. He gasps in horror and yeah, take a number.

He snatches it from my hand, holding it hostage. "Well, you won't need these upstairs, and I'm sure someone can glue that or something."

"Hey. I need that." I swipe up to grab it back, but he holds it out of my reach.

"I just said you didn't." Somehow he manages to roll his eyes, shake his head, and purse his lips all at once. "Now come on, model. We're already late."

I chase barefoot after him as he hot-trots it to the elevator, impatiently pressing the button about sixty times.

"I'm not a model," I protest, staring at his profile while he glares at the metal doors of the elevator.

"Liar."

I throw my hands up in the air. "Fine. I'm not a model anymore."

"Liar again."

"I'm not," I state emphatically. "I graduated top of my class from FIT (Fashion Institute of Design) with a degree in fashion design. I want to be a designer."

He grabs my arm and drags me onto the elevator the second the doors start to part. "Fine. Whatever. I get it. Who cares? This morning you're a fucking model because that's what I said you are."

I open my mouth to protest, when he cuts me off.

"You're an intern, which essentially means you're a company bitch. That makes you my company bitch, and since I outrank practically everyone in this building unless your last name is Monroe, you don't have a choice other than to quit, which we both know you won't. This is literally your last option if you ever want to do anything in the fashion industry again."

"Thanks for the brutal honesty," I murmur sardonically. "Monday mornings aren't always real enough."

"Sweet pea, I never sugarcoat shit because no matter what, it still stinks. My model DNSU'd and I need someone perfect for this and you're it."

I'm afraid to ask. "DNSU?"

"Did not show up. But you've got tons of modeling experience and you will fit into the dresses we have set up for the shoot and will look incredible beside Zaxton when we shoot you with him because you're tall."

My stomach drops. "You're shooting me with Zaxton?"

Lamar grins evilly at me, showing off each of his whiter-than-white teeth. "Welcome to Monroe Fashion. But don't worry, Zaxton Monroe is everything you've heard him to be and then a hell of a lot worse."

Don't I know it.

We ride up silently while Lamar has his face glued to his phone, typing on it a million miles a minute. The doors open and without a word, his hand snaps out and grasps my forearm. He drags me along at light speed, which if I had to guess is likely how he does everything.

"Sit. Stay. Don't move." Lamar snaps his fingers at a salon chair.

We're on the twentieth floor, which is big and wide-open and I'd say at least two floors high. Very industrial with concrete floors and giant windows. It's obviously where they do the majority of their photo shoots. I didn't get much of a tour, only a few things Lamar called out as we passed them like the sample closet (drool), where we'll be shooting, and now this chair.

"I'm not a dog," I grouse but do as I'm told anyway.

"No, honey, you're not. You're a model, which means you're used to people telling you exactly what to do and doing it. Now come heel."

I harrumph, but he ignores me. "That's annoyingly true. Maybe if I had more backbone and put my money where my mouth is, I wouldn't be here."

"No. You'd still be here," he states, only to reconsider. "Or maybe not since Valentina would have gutted you like a fish and tossed you in the East River as chum for whatever the fuck lives in there." He shudders. "This is why I like Boston so much better than New York. Can I ask why you stopped modeling?"

"I'm twenty-three."

He gives me an impatient look as he pushes up the bridge of his glasses. "And?"

"And I want to be a designer. I love modeling. I do. It's fun for the most part. It's why I delayed going to FIT for a year. I met some incredible people and traveled around the world and earned nice money, but it's cutthroat. It's being told you're fat and to lose weight when you're not and you shouldn't. And unless you're on the top of everyone's A-list, you burn out fast and young."

He gives me a crooked smirk.

"What? What's that look?"

"You're smart and see things for exactly what they are. I like that in my interns and models."

"Smart people don't make as many mistakes as I've made."

"No. Smart people learn from those mistakes. Young people who trust the wrong people make the kinds of mistakes you made."

Gulp. This is why people need people in their lives who are ride or die and always have their backs. I have a bestie, but who couldn't use more people? "I think I like you."

"Don't. I'm a fucking asshole." He grabs my chair and spins me around to face the mirror and the pre-loaded trays of makeup and hair-styling equipment. I'm also greeted by two women, one small and curvy with short fire engine red hair and the other average height with pin-straight brown shoulder-length hair and heavy bangs. "These goddesses are two members of our in-house style team. Sonia (the redhead) does makeup and Eloise (the brunette) does hair. Ladies, this is Lia—"

"Aurelia," I correct.

He shakes his head. "No. The modeling industry knows you as Lia Sage, so that's who you are today. Anyway, as I was saying"—he dismisses me, turning back to them—"ladies, since our original model DNSU'd, *Lia*," he emphasizes my name, "is standing in for her, though she's technically now an intern in our design department."

"Welcome," they say together.

"Hi." I return their enthused smiles. "It's very nice to meet you both."

"We're already running late, and we all know how much Zax loves being behind schedule, so let's get this going." Lamar snaps his fingers and then both ladies come at me as he goes off to do God only knows what. My face is cleaned of any makeup I was wearing and then it's cream and foundation and concealer and contouring and the works. My hair is brushed and blown and curled and played with.

All the while I sit here, letting them do what they do best.

"I'm sorry I didn't come in clean for you. I wasn't expecting to model today."

"Oh pish." Both wave me away. "You're perfect and a lot less work than the other woman who was supposed to be where you're sitting."

"So true," Sonia agrees, spraying the back of my hair with hairspray. "She's a nightmare. Do you want anything to drink, hon?"

"Am I allowed anything other than coffee or water?"

"Jesus, I don't want to know," Eloise says, grimacing. "Yes. You can have whatever you want, but if you ask for alcohol at"—she checks her watch—"nine fifteen in the morning, we're going to have an intervention."

I giggle lightly. "No. I was going to ask for a Diet Coke, but I know carbonation isn't something a lot of photographers and shoot directors like their models to drink prior to a shoot."

"Honey, no one is seeing your stomach and as long as you don't burp on Mr. Monroe, you should be fine."

The three of us laugh. "No gas on the boss. Got it."

"I'll go fetch you a Diet Coke. With a straw and nothing after lips!" Sonia warns and I nod, already knowing that drill. No ruining the makeup or messing with the hair.

"I can't get over your hair color," Eloise exclaims, running her fingers through my long strands to work out some of the curls into loose waves. "This color is just stunning."

"Thank you," I murmur through thin lips so as not to disrupt my makeup.

"It's natural, right? If not, I'm going to have to have sex with whoever did these highlights to learn their secrets."

My smile is uncontainable and I'm so glad for it. I needed some of this after the near-mugging, Zax, my broken heel, and bleeding-knees fiasco of the morning. "It's natural. No kinky favors required."

"Thank goodness for that." She gives me a wink.

"Her skin is just as incredible. Here, hon." Sonia hands me a Diet Coke in a can with a straw. I hate drinking it this way, but it's all you get when you're not allowed to move your head all that much. "We never get to see the models walk during the shows because we're always backstage. But we know who you are and have followed your career, so we're really looking forward to getting to see you work this morning."

"Wow. Thank you." I'm flabbergasted. I had no idea people knew much of me beyond what happened at fashion week this past spring. "I don't even know what kind of shoot I'm doing," I admit.

"This is round one of five for hair and makeup," Sonia informs me, putting the finishing touches on my eyeshadow. "It's for the fall line. They have you in the blue dress first because that's the dress they want in the shoot with Mr. Monroe."

"Oh goody."

They both snicker at my sarcastic tone, tossing each other meaningful glances. "Not a fan of his?"

"You mean like everyone else in the world is? Not exactly." This morning notwithstanding, my reasons are better than anyone else's.

"He's... rough," Eloise agrees diplomatically, tapping a hairbrush against her thigh. "I mean, never rude. At least not to us. But brusque and sharp and a total perfectionist. As you'd expect for someone in his position."

"I still love him." Sonia places her hand over her heart, her expression dreamy. "I can't help it. Central Square was my absolute favorite band ever. I went to see them in concert ten times and that includes multiple cities. I was devastated when they broke up."

"You and me and everyone else on the planet." Eloise half-laughs before growing somber. "After what they all went through, after what *he* went through losing Suzie, I don't blame them for calling it quits and for him being... grumpy."

Central Square was the perfect mix of boy band pop and fierce rock band. Five guys from Central Square, Cambridge, who hit it big as teenagers after a YouTube video of them went viral. They were the equivalent if Bieber and One Direction had a love child huge. I met them about two seconds after fame hit and they were set to travel the world. Overnight they became undoubtedly the world's biggest band and that's how they stayed for four years. Global travel and playing to sold-out stadiums. Zaxton was the eldest and played bass, whereas his younger brother, Greyson—who is still a hugely successful rock star—was the front man.

Then their manager and Zax's girlfriend, Suzie, died in the

shower. It was tragic, and after that, the band couldn't go on. They officially broke up within weeks of her death, all of them going off in different directions, doing different things, though they are all rumored to still be very close.

But eight years later, Zax has never been photographed with another woman. He doesn't date. And he's a notorious, well, grump as Eloise put it.

Ping. Both Eloise's and Sonia's phones chime, snapping all of us out of our reverie.

"What's that?" I ask as the two ladies fly for their phones.

"Company chat. They're ready for you."

Speaking of the company chat, I slip out my own phone as I stand, making sure my boss and Iris, my best friend, who works here as a marketing intern, got my message about where I am. They did, which is a relief. My boss wrote that she was glad I was able to pitch in where needed, so clearly she's not angry about me being late or missing my first day as a design intern.

Iris is a different matter and she's already asking for full details.

Later, I text her, slip my phone back into my purse, and take a look at myself.

"Wow," I half-whisper. "Ladies, just wow."

My long whitish-blond hair is in thick glossy waves, coasting down my back and over my shoulders with a few soft pieces framing my face. My makeup is simple yet smoky, playing up my blue eyes and making the color truly stand out and pop against my creamy, pale skin.

"You made it easy for us. Now get going before Lamar comes out here to find you. He's back in the closet."

"Thank you."

Quickly, I scoot across the room, my bare feet slapping against the cool concrete. The door to the 'closet' is open and I enter the palatial space that is filled with rack upon rack of clothing, shoes, handbags, coats, lingerie. Whatever you can imagine, it's in here.

"Lamar?" I call out, unsure where to go in here.

"Lia! Ass back here now."

I follow the sound of Lamar's voice until I'm by a three-way mirror with a large octagonal platform in front of it and a series of open stall dressing rooms. He scrutinizes my hair and makeup and gives me a firm nod.

"Perfect. This is your dress." He points to a royal blue silk midi dress—thank God because it will cover my bandaged knees—that has thin metal, gold woven straps, and a matching belt. "If you're not wearing a tiny nude thong, there is one in the dressing room for you. And yes, before you ask, it's brand-new. No bra. Shoes are in there as well. You have two minutes. No fucking joke."

He points to the stall, and I race in there, ripping off my clothes as I go. Any modesty you ever have as a woman is gone within a week of being a model. Most of the time, it's large, open changing rooms where we go from outfit to outfit and there are usually staff as well as other models around at all times. Not to mention half the time our clothes are moved and partially removed during shoots. That said, Lamar is kind enough to have his back to me to give me some privacy.

"When am I shooting with Mr. Monroe?" My heart is beating so fast, my hands clammy at the thought of seeing him again. Not just seeing him, but shooting with him.

I can only pray that after this, I won't have to deal with him again. It's one shoot and then he'll be up on the executive floor, and I'll be down with the other interns, and our paths won't cross. He'll forget about me, and my anonymity will remain safe.

If I can keep my mouth shut.

But for now, it's trial by fire and I've already been burned today.

"We shoot you first and then with him. He fucking *hates* modeling. Like to the depths of his Monroe soles hates it. You should know that now because whatever you've heard about his rosy disposition drops another ten points to less than zero when he's forced to do these shoots."

I get on the dress, which fits perfectly since it's a standard sample size, and then I slide into the shoes that are matching blue patent leather with a peekaboo toe and add on another four inches to my already five-ten height.

I exit the dressing room, spinning around so Lamar can zip me up.

"If he hates modeling and doing shoots, why does he then?"

Lamar laughs as if the answer should be obvious. He twists me around and places me in front of the mirror, doing a quick loop around me to make sure it's the way he wants. "Matches your eyes beautifully. I can't believe I'm fucking saying this, but I'm so glad that other hag didn't show up. This dress was made for you. Move."

He does it for me, guiding me by the shoulders out of the closet and back into the main space that is now set up for the shoot, complete with a white bed, a large white cushioned lounger, and photography equipment everywhere.

Just when I think he won't answer my question, Lamar leans in and whispers in my ear, "He's the CEO and face of the company. He's also ridiculously famous in his own right, both for better and for worse. His face is half of what sells the fashion for this company and though he loathes it, he's a savvy enough businessman to understand that and make the necessary sacrifice. Modeling time." He thrusts me forward. "Franco, this is Lia, our model for the day. Make beautiful things happen."

"Ah, Lia. We've met before." Franco takes my hand and walks me toward the lounger. "It was years ago in New York. You probably don't—"

"It was my first shoot when I was sixteen for *Teen Threads*. I remember. You were patient and kind when I didn't think that was possible in this industry after what I had been told. It's a pleasure to see you again."

Franco smiles kindly. "You as well. You have grown into a beautiful woman. Are you ready?"

Not like I have much of a choice. "As I'll ever be."

Franco gives me an indulgent wink that reminds me of one my grandfather used to give me and then an assistant is helping me onto the lounger, placing me how Franco wants me as flashes go off all around as they test the lighting.

I learned early on in this business that the sexiest thing a woman can wear is confidence. Even if you don't initially feel it, fake it until you do. Still, my stomach is up in my throat as it is every time I've ever done a shoot. But this is worse. I don't care how attractive Zaxton is or how much I hate him. This is my second chance at a career and a life that wasn't just taken from me, but stolen. Lamar might have been joking about Valencci's name earlier, but he wasn't kidding about who she is versus who I am.

That woman ruined my life. Or at least tried to.

But I'm here now. And despite my less-than-happy past with Zaxton being kicked up into my face, this is make-it-or-break-it time for me. If I do a bad job here, I'm out. I have no illusions about that. No one cares how well I design if I'm a shitty model today.

Worse, I have to pose with Zaxton and after our encounter this morning, I have no idea how that will go. He wasn't happy with me, but he did stop to help when no one else did. Hell, the man scared off my mugger before freaking carrying me up the steps and getting me medical attention.

And his touch... His eyes...

It almost felt like there was more—

"Lia, I want to start with you sprawled on the lounger," Franco says, cutting through my thoughts. "I want your hair cascading around you, and I want your eyes on me unless I tell you otherwise."

I nod and get myself in position, taking a deep breath and shifting my mind to focus solely on what I'm here to do. I don't allow it to wander. To question whether or not Zaxton is here or if he's watching me now. And I certainly don't acknowledge the kick in my pulse or the thrill through my blood at that errant, useless thought.

No. Zaxton Monroe is the last man on earth I should be thinking about or allowing my body to respond to in that way. He can never find out who I am. He can never know the strings I had to pull to get myself here. If he ever does, that will be the end of me in this business for sure.

3

ZAXTON

"**P**erfect, Lia. Now arch your back and allow the dress to drape the same as your hair is over the end. Yes. Like that." *Click. Click. Click.*

"How long are you going to hide back here and watch?"

"You're running late," I shoot back, ignoring the teasing lilt in Lamar's voice. He's the only one I allow to get away with that shit and that's simply because he's one of maybe six people on the entire planet I can tolerate.

"Our model DNSU'd."

"How did this one get up here?" I ask, unable to remove my eyes from the girl. The one whose blood is upstairs in my office all over my custom-made suit jacket and silk handkerchief.

"I found her bleeding in the lobby and recognized her instantly. She's also an intern here, which makes her mine to do with as I please whenever I need her."

My molars gnash together before I even comprehend what I'm doing. Why do I care if he calls her his and claims he can have her whenever he wants her? He's not even being sexual necessarily, though knowing Lamar, he might mean that both in a professional and personal way. Even if that's wishful thinking on his part.

"Does Jacob know you're trying to fuck a model?"

He laughs at my tone, and he should. I'm a fucking mess today and not all of it has to do with the gorgeous blonde sprawled out on my chaise like the ultimate sexual temptation.

"Jacob knows I like everyone, but she's a little young for me. Likely for you too."

Now it's my turn to laugh because, yes, she is young for me, but more than that, I don't date or fuck women in the light of day and Lamar knows it. Any women I fuck, I do so under a cloak of total anonymity. As far as the press and the world are concerned, I've been a monk since Suzie died, and if my dick and brain didn't require sex on a somewhat regular basis to make it through the goddamn day, I would be.

Exclusive clubs are the only way I can breathe some days. And even then, I feel nothing. No thrill. No excitement. Sometimes I think I'm so dead inside that if I cut myself, I wouldn't bleed. Speaking of bleeding...

"We met this morning," I admit. "I helped her. Some punk kid was trying to snatch her purse and then he shoved her. She fell and started bleeding. I recognized her from fashion week this past February."

It took me some time to remember where I knew her from, but it hit me quick and it hit me hard when I did. I watched her walk for eighteen seconds and I stared like a stalker the entire time, knowing if anyone saw me, they'd believe I was taking in the gown she was wearing—I was doing that too because that gown... fuck!—but her face owned me.

Then after that show, she was all anyone was talking about. Her beauty and that dress she wore, yes, but it was the drama and gossip that surrounded her and the designer she walked for. I saw her before I knew everything else. She caught my eye when models never do. They're too tall, too skinny, too into themselves.

But fuck did I want her.

Which is why I never looked her up beyond hearing her name. Lia Sage.

"Interesting," Lamar drawls, a perceptible lilt to his voice.

"Don't start."

"I simply said interesting. You're the one staring at her like she's candy-coated crack."

Probably because she is.

"Intern. Young. Model. Not interested."

"All of that I believe. Except for the last one. No one is not interested in a woman who looks and smells like that."

She does smell good.

The scent of her this morning had my dick hard before I even noticed her face. Then there's her hair color. It's natural. I had my doubts because no one has hair that color naturally, but this girl does. Her face is art.

My stomach squeezes tight. I want this woman. Impertinent mouth and all.

She knew who I was and yet she mouthed off to me anyway. No one, I mean *no one*, does that. Not even Lamar or my asshole friends or my fucking brother. Okay, maybe my friends and my fucking brother, and yeah, likely Lamar too, but the rest of the world treats me with kid gloves and practically jerks me off anytime I enter a room.

She didn't seem to care.

I lean against the wall, folding my arms across my chest as I continue to watch her, already busted, so I don't even bother trying to hide it. "She has a mouth on her that rivals yours. Did you know she asked me what kind of name Zaxton is?"

"It's a seriously legit question I'm positive everyone who meets you wonders. I sure as fuck do. It's a weird name."

I throw him an unamused side-eye that doesn't faze him a bit. "I should have fired her then and there."

A Cheshire grin lights up his face. "Ah, but you didn't, did you?"

No. I didn't.

"Okay, Lia," Franco calls out, snapping me out of my trance. "Sit up now. I'm going to ask you to just do your own thing. Feel how beautiful and sexy you are in this dress. You want the guy you've been crushing all over to notice you in it. Your hair is gorgeous, and your makeup is stunning, but you want him to see that extra, special something about you. Am I right?"

Lia laughs, her smile erupting across her exquisite face and *hell*.

A dozen more clicks capture it, and I can't even blame Franco for that.

She sits up, kicking off her shoes and bending forward, practically in half. Her fingers graze her feet and slowly, oh so fucking slowly, she glides up, a pure come-hither expression all over her face. One hand daintily finds her collarbone, the other tucks in along her waist as one gold strap falls seductively off her shoulder. The curves of her full breasts peek out, playing with the neckline of the dress.

"Yes. Holy shit." Franco starts to go nuts, snapping about a million pictures a second. "Look right at me. Don't move. That. That right there. Hold it, Lia. That pose. Now look at me like you want to fuck me. Like I'm the only man in the world you want. Yes! Yes! Keep going."

"Fuck!" Lamar jumps forward, itching to get back out there. "That's going to sell this dress and every piece in this fall line. Look at her."

I'm looking at her.

I'm also thinking about the fact that I have to shoot with her next.

"That's it. Tilt your chin and then glance up at me. Give me a sexy smirk. Perfect, honey." *Click. Click. Click.* Franco checks the screen on his camera. "I've got it. That was beautiful. Such good work. Come here so you can see." Lia stands and skips over to him, and I turn around, staring out at nothing as I mentally get myself ready.

"You know what today is," I grumble. "Why the hell do I have to do this now?"

Lamar is beside me, hand on my shoulder. "Because life goes on even when we don't want it to."

"Remembering how my life goes on when hers doesn't makes me more of a dick than I typically am. You want to subject everyone to that right now?"

"That's your own shit. No one else's. Fashion has no patience for heartbreak. It's the antidote to it. It's why they call it retail therapy. I could coddle you, but that's not my style nor will it fix a fucking thing. I know today is hard for you, but you have work you have to do and this is the job."

He's right. I know he's right.

Tapping a rhythm against my thigh, my eyes close and I picture Suzie's face right before she stepped into the shower. I should be focused on her and nothing else. And yet I haven't stopped thinking about the woman who has occupied my entire morning. What it is about her that has me so fascinated, I have no idea, but it stops now. A model and an intern. A pretty face and a hot body. None of these things are a novelty in my world.

She's nothing to me and that's how she'll stay.

With that mental declaration, already wearing the suit they want to shoot me in, I walk into the room, the tap of my shoes cutting through the chatter, and everything comes to a standstill.

"How are we doing, Franco? Everything ready?"

"Good morning, Mr. Monroe. Yes. I was just showing Lia some of her photos." He flips the camera around so I can see one of the images he just took. I don't take the bait. Nor do I so much as acknowledge the woman standing beside me, staring up at my profile.

"Fantastic. Can we do this and do this quickly so I can get back to my day?"

"Of course, sir," Franco acknowledges before speaking louder so the whole room can hear him. "Let's get set, people. We're shooting in two minutes."

"Wow. So you're this unpleasant to everyone and not just me."

I roll my eyes at the intern, who is bending to put back on her shoes. That motion shouldn't be sexy, but damn it if it's not. I grit my teeth and walk away from her, allowing the assistant to place me by the window that has some sort of dark screen covering it. Above me are twinkling lights that cast a warm glow as the overhead lights are dimmed ever so slightly.

"You sure you should be wearing heels that high?" My tone is filled with sarcasm as my gaze drops to her dress-covered knees. "You clearly have an issue with keeping them intact."

"Aw, are you worried about me?"

"More like my shoes with you in them."

"If they're made the way they should be, then the heels on these won't snap. Mine only did because I was getting mugged and then thrown like a rag doll." She does a twirl, the skirt of her dress fanning out around her. "See. Look at that. Perfect."

No kidding.

"Mr. Monroe," Franco cuts in. "Take her hand and spin her once before bringing her into your body. It's a date night and you're both out at some fabulous party. Smile. Have fun with each other. Be in love."

Be in love? He can't be serious with that?

Begrudgingly, I extend my hand and she places her small, cool one in mine. It's annoyingly soft and fragile against my larger one and judging by the way her eyes widen and pupils dilate ever so slightly, she feels it too. The way I felt it downstairs when I touched her legs. Crackling energy before the lightning strike.

I spin her to an applause of clicking cameras. She tosses her head back, allowing her blond, blond hair to fly along with the dress, and then I give her a tug, pulling her to me. Her body lands firmly against mine and I stare down into her eyes, the bluest I've ever seen. They match the dress as if it was designed just for her.

Head tilted back, chin pointed up toward me, she gives me an adoring smile, placing the hand I'm not holding on my chest.

A dozen more clicks even as they start to fade away the longer I look at her.

"Lia. What kind of name is Lia?"

She smiles coyly up at me as I place her hand around my neck, drawing her body firmly into mine. Her scent floods my nostrils, making my pulse thrum and my cock twitch.

"The none of your business kind."

I resist the urge to smirk at her for throwing my words back at me. She has fire, I'll give her that much.

"Ah, but you work for me, so I think it is my business."

"Can't we just pretend it isn't?"

"Pretend?"

"Yep. You know. Fantasy. Imagination. I'm simply a model here to make your clothes look good. Later, I'll be something else, and if you're still interested in my name, I'm sure you have ways of discovering it. Even if I hope you won't."

My eyebrows bounce in confusion. "You hope I won't?"

"You repeat a lot of my words."

"Because you speak in riddles and codes when you're not openly contemptuous toward me."

"True. I'm playing defense and not well. Something about you gets under my skin." She shakes her head, her teeth catching her lip until she realizes she's meant to play a part with me and looking vulnerable and nervous isn't it. A dazzling smile reconstructs her face, one hand up around my neck, the other now toying with my blue tie that matches her dress.

She gives me a tug, jerking my head down until our faces are inches apart, mine still hovering slightly above hers.

"Forget about all that," she urges. "Put your hands on me."

"What?" I practically choke.

"We're in love, remember? Lovers touch. You want to be done with this shoot and frankly, so do I. So put your hands on me, Mr. Monroe. Show them with your body and your eyes all the dirty things you want to do to me. Place one hand on my bare skin so the cameras can see it. The other on my lower back so my body is arched toward yours."

"Now you're telling me how to do my job?" I cock an eyebrow.

Her fingers twirl into my hair, playing with the ends, and fuck, why does that have to feel so damn good? I resist the urge to close my eyes.

Her gaze is so warm and so cold all at once. It no doubt matches my own and now we're both fighting smiles.

"Maybe I'm better at it than you are," she counters, returning my raised eyebrow. "We both know you hate modeling and I've been doing it for seven years. I know how to design and sell clothes you want someone to peel off your body."

Fucking hell.

With the fire of challenge and desire shooting through my veins, and wondering if she'll balk under the pressure, I inch in. Closer. So close I can see every fleck and shade of blue in her eyes. My hand flips her hair up, finding the smooth skin between her shoulder blades. The other goes to her lower back as she instructed, only I don't stop there. I continue to slide lower. So low I catch the bony prominence nestled at the crest of her ass cheeks.

My already hard cock jerks between us, but there is nothing I can do about it. She'll either feel me or she won't, though when she shivers ever so slightly and her breath catches, I can't fight my victorious smirk.

"That what you're after, model?" *To feel how hard you make your boss*, I don't add.

"Mmhmm. Much better. Who knew you had some seriously hot seduction in you? Now smile for the cameras, Mr. Monroe," she whispers against me, her sweet breath fanning my lips.

"I don't smile, and I never seduce," I reply with no hint of amusement, fighting the battle to keep my eyes on hers instead of dipping down to her glossed lips.

Her fingers glide up my chest, catching on the lapel of my jacket. "I noticed," she says. "Maybe you just haven't found anyone tempting enough to use them on."

Until now, I think. The thought catches me off guard and I tip my head down to hide it.

"It's a shame," she continues, oblivious to my inner struggle with her.

"What's that?" I reply in an emotionless tone, playing with the long, silky strands of her hair as they tickle my fingers. Praying this will be over any second so I don't have to continue inhaling her alluring fragrance and torture myself with touches that are not nearly enough.

"Think of how much happier you'd be if you did both—seduce and smile."

I stiffen, the accusation in her words hitting me all wrong, a penetrating slice through my armor. "Who says I'm not happy?"

A frown mars her pretty face. "Everyone. The world." Her frown deepens and I see it in her blue eyes. The pity. The headlines as they dance through her brain. She shakes her head. "I'm sorry. I'm so sorry. I shouldn't have said that. It was careless and insensitive. It's not as if you don't have your reasons for being this way."

She knows nothing of my reasons nor does anyone else.

I practically shove her away, taking a step back and breathing hard. "I'm done here," I announce and storm off without so much as a backward glance at anyone. Not today. Today I'm allowed to hurt as much as I need to hurt.

The model can fuck off right along with everyone else who gives me that look. I'm done with her. An unwanted diversion, I should have fired her this morning when I had the chance. I won't make the same mistake twice.

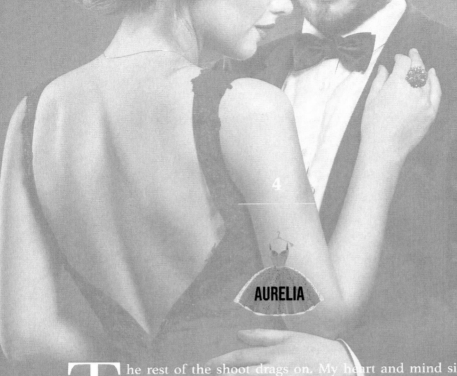

4

AURELIA

T he rest of the shoot drags on. My heart and mind simply
aren't into it, stuck in the worst sort of tailspin as I replay
what happened over and over again, berating myself harder
and harder each time I do. I got carried away. Swept up in the
moment. In the way he was staring at me and how he felt against me.

I don't know why I said that to him. I don't know why I said any of
that to him. It's as if the second I get near him, I grow angry and
snappy. He rubs me the wrong way and I know I'm biased. I know I'm
holding onto old grudges I should let go of.

The hatred that plumed off him like smoke, the scathing look he
gave me... all the heat and fire of our touching and flirting instantly
extinguished. My big mouth went and threw his trauma in his face.

What sort of person does that?

After what feels like an eternity, I'm dismissed, sent to find my
way to the design floor and over to my desk. One of the closet assis-
tants glued my heel, but the damage has already been done. I'd love
to imagine I can put this morning and the accompanying disasters
behind me and get to what I'm actually here to do. Design.

But I can't help the plaguing thoughts. The guilt.

I should hate him.

And while I certainly don't like him, it's impossible to hate him fully. Maybe it's what he lost that excuses all his current sins. Or how he helped me this morning. Who knows. Whatever it is, it has me pulling up my intraoffice chat on my phone and typing his name into the message block. My fingers tap on my screen as I debate what, if anything, I should say.

Then I think better of it.

Having him keep his distance while hating me is for the best. If I message him, he'll know exactly who I am—if he doesn't already. Lia has a different last name than I do because I wanted to keep it all separate. It was my agent's idea, and it was the right one.

I stare at his name, only for a message to come in from Iris.

> Iris: Heard about your morning upstairs with Monroe. Your shoot with him is all anyone is talking about.

> Me: Great. Do they know I'm Lia?

> Iris: Don't think so. They're saying Lia or model, but how long before they connect the dots? Your boss Gretchen knows so it's only a matter of time.

I figured that, but I had been hoping word wouldn't have spread. I was hoping for just another shoot and for my name to remain separate. I've managed to screw everything up in just a few hours.

> Me: What are they saying about the shoot?

> Iris: That you two had enough chemistry to blow up a lab and then he stormed off. No one has seen the pics yet, but I hear they're hot. Is it true? I need all the details and I need them now.

I glower, tapping my fingers on the screen once more. They're not wrong. I just wish there wasn't already gossip about me. Especially with Zax. No way he doesn't find out who I am now. I start typing, so angry with myself.

> Me: There was no chemistry, only acting. It was a shoot like any other I've done with a male counterpart except Monroe was Monroe. Cruel, cold, and dismissive. To me and the staff. I have to imagine that's how all his shoots go.

I likely shouldn't write this on a company message, but I want her to quiet the rumor mill on her side of things and hopefully this will do that. The less talk about it, the better. Besides, it's not like I'm saying anything about him people don't already know.

I hit send, put my phone down with a bit more force than I intend, and pull out the lunch I brought with me. I have a meeting in ten minutes, and I haven't had a second to spare to eat anything. Scarfing down my peanut butter sandwich and chasing it with my Diet Coke, I check my emails and get myself situated.

"Hey." A voice over my shoulder startles me and I spin around in my chair, only to bang my already banged-up knee directly into the side of the cubicle partition.

I wince, my teeth clamping down on my lip to stifle my whimper.

"Oh, damn. Sorry," a cute, hipsterish boy with a plaid button-down, black suspenders, and gray slacks says with a wince of his own. "I didn't mean to startle you. Are you okay?"

"Nothing a vat of tequila won't cure."

He laughs, his green eyes sparkling. "I'm Howie. Like *Howie* did it, I don't know. Not like *Howard the Duck*. My parents were cruel, but they weren't that cruel."

I cover my mouth with my hand, laughing lightly. "Oh my gosh. You just quoted *Airplane* using your own name as the joke. Please tell me we work together."

"We work together. I'm one of the designers on the women's line team and I've been paired with you for the first six months of your internship. Do you go by Lia or Aurelia?"

"How do you—"

"Know your modeling name? I know. Everyone on the floor knows. Gretchen announced in our staff meeting that you were going to be late because Lamar pulled you in to cover for the shoot. You're already famous around here and you were famous even before that."

My shoulders slump, unamused by the hyperbole. Everything in me deflates at once. "Fabulous."

"Hey. That's a bad thing?"

"Probably. Definitely."

"Shit. I didn't mean to upset you."

"It's not your fault," I tell him, attempting to offer a weak smile. "It's my own."

He leans against the side of my cubicle, looking miserable. "I'm not getting off to a good start with you. I just meant no one knew you were Lia Sage until the shoot this morning, but we had all heard about Lia Sage, if you know what I mean."

"Unfortunately, I do."

"Crap. I'm making it worse now, aren't I?"

"You're fine. I promise, Howie not Howard. Are you going to this meeting with me?"

"Yep. I came to get you. Gretchen wasn't sure if you were back from your shoot yet."

Gretchen, our boss, so far seems great. Then again, I've been fooled by bosses before, so maybe I should reserve judgment for now. Not to mention, I doubt she'll be my boss for much longer now that word has gotten out about who I am.

I stand, wrapping up the remains of my lunch and stuffing them back into my bag. "I was worried everyone would be pissed I missed my first morning."

We start to walk toward the conference room on the far side of the floor.

"Nah. What were you going to do? Say no?" He chuckles, throwing me a sideways glance. "I don't think anyone has ever said no to Lamar and certainly not to Mr. Monroe, but it hasn't been all that necessary either. Both are very good at what they do and even though we're in Boston and not New York, they seem to have their fingers right on the pulse point of fashion."

I nod in concession. "The fall line I was shot in today was incredible."

"I can't wait to see the pictures. Everyone has been—"

A body slams into me, knocking me back a step. "You scag. I haven't seen you since you got to town and then all this madness happened on your first day, and I had to hear about the juicy bits from my fellow marketing people and not my best friend? How are your knees?" Iris hugs me fiercely, then pulls back and hold me at arm's length so she can examine me. "Oh, lovebug, you did a real number on yourself."

"They'll heal."

"How about the rest of you?"

"The jury's still out on that, I'm afraid."

Her face creases with worry and I subtly shake my head before she can say anything else about it.

"I see you've met Howie." She switches gears, catching my hint. "Isn't he adorable? If he didn't have a girlfriend already, I would have totally shipped the two of you."

"I'm right here," Howie says, though there is no bite to his words.

"Yes, darling. I see that plain as the freckles on your handsome face. Promise if you ever break up with your leading lady, you'll take mine on."

"Iris, I'm right here too."

She laughs, waving us both away. "Come. It's a fun marketing design meeting. I can't wait." She links her arms with both of ours, walking between us. "I still want details. The good. The bad. The absolutely gorgeous. I hear Mr. Monroe smells divine, fact or fib?"

"Fact," I begrudgingly admit.

"I knew it. How was he to work with and what happened in that shoot? You never replied to my last text. The rumors are wild."

"I told you how it went," I tell her as we approach the edge of the conference room. She gives me a funny look, only for me to be swallowed up by everyone else in the room. Gretchen takes a few minutes and introduces me around. Everyone on the various teams, both interns and regular employees, seem nice. No one asks about my photo shoot with Zax this morning, though they clearly all know about it.

Then we sit down, getting to some of the fall marketing plans they received from upstairs management as we head toward the end of summer and dive toward fashion week, which takes place at the end of September this year.

Just before the meeting begins, Iris's pen taps my hand. "You never replied about what happened with Zax during the shoot," she whispers, swiveling in her chair so our heads are close.

"Huh?" I whisper back, my eyebrows knitting, though I'm keeping my focus straight ahead on the woman setting up the presentation. "Yes, I did."

"No. You didn't."

Now she has my attention. "Iris, I texted you back almost immediately after you texted me."

She bites into her lip as she shakes her head, her eyes wide. "Honey, no." She pulls out her phone and opens up our text stream, holding it under the table so no one else can see. And sure enough, there is her last text talking about the shoot and the chemistry, but there is no reply from me.

A sick sort of dread fills my stomach, the back of my neck growing hot. "I must not have hit send." Only I'm nearly ninety-eight-point-six percent positive I did hit send. "Or maybe it didn't go through."

Please, God, let that be the case.

"Check your phone. Have you been texting with anyone else?"

I shake my head, sucking my lip between my teeth and gnawing on it like a starved animal tossed a bone. "Only Gretchen and she didn't mention anything. Iris, I trash-talked Mr. Monroe."

"What do you mean when you say trash-talked him? You never say shit about anyone even when you have a mouthful of it."

"Shit."

She rolls her eyes at me. "I'm being serious."

"So am I," I argue. "The man ruffled my feathers, and I ruffled his right back and... ugh!" Sliding back a little, I grab my phone and set it on my lap, pulling up the office chat app followed by my chat with Iris. "I don't see my reply. It's not here."

"No kidding. We've already established that. Go to your dashboard. Check to see if you sent it to someone by accident."

"Oh God," I groan under my breath. If I sent it to my boss, that would be the best-case scenario and the best-case scenario is not something I'm known for. Only in my gut, I know she's not who I sent it to. "Wait. I can't. You do it for me."

"For real?"

"Iris!"

"Fine. Give me your phone." She takes it from me before I can hand it off and the second she clicks back to the dashboard, her expression sinks.

I fly out of my seat, garnering everyone's curious gaze in my direction. "Sorry. Gas bubble." And yep, I totally just said that. I immediately sit back down and cover my face with my hands, hyperventilating into them without caring who is watching me lose it. Bile races up the back of my throat and I think I'm two seconds from throwing up. Or passing out. Adrenaline shoots through my veins, hyping up my panic mode. One thing after another, I can't catch a break. "Tell me what I saw isn't what I saw."

"Ehhhh."

The world tilts, my vision fuzzy. "I sent it to Zax. Mr. Monroe. I sent it to him." Fuck. Motherfuck. Motherfucking tity-sucking ass-kicking bitch, I am screwed with a capital S.

"Why did you have a message window up with him in the first place?" she hisses, her gaze locked on the SMART board ahead as mine should be, but I can't do anything but stare at my phone, as I take it back from her. And yep, bright and shiny is the message I sent to Zax. And the small four-letter word beneath the message that says, READ.

So now he not only read the horrible things I said about him, he knows exactly who I am.

"It doesn't matter why. All that matters is that I sent it to him and not you. I'm done, Iris. That's it."

"Oh, nonsense. What did you write? It can't be that bad." She snatches the phone from my lap and glances down at it, then frowns. "Damn. You're fucked."

"What do I do?"

She gives me a *how the hell should I know* look. "There's nothing you can do, right? You sent it to him and not me. He's read it. Best shot is he ignores it and doesn't care since everyone has said something similar at least once in their lives after meeting him."

"And worst?"

"Worst is you're out on your ass by the end of the day."

"I can't lose this job. It's my last chance after Valencci blackballed me. I opened my mouth then and this is where it got me. I opened my mouth again and it could end me. When will I learn to keep my damn mouth shut?"

"What are you going to do?"

I suck in a shaky breath, my hands trembling. What will I do if Zax fires me? Or more aptly *when* Zax fires me. I take another deep breath, this one calming, thinking this all through. I used to believe everything in life happens for a reason. That what doesn't kill you makes you stronger.

But have I been stronger these months since all this went down? Or have I been made weak and scared by the people who have sought to do just that? One day this will be a memory and how do I want to look back on it? As the moment that finally sank me, or the moment I seized my life once and for all, even when it felt like it was crumbling around me?

"You know what?" I say, taking another breath to settle my heart. "I'll be okay. I'm just freaking out as I've been freaking out since fashion week back in February." Since I was a sixteen-year-old kid, left to fend for myself. "I can't keep living like this anymore. I'll do what I have to do," I declare. "I'll model and design on the side. I'll find a smaller design house and try to get in there. All else fails, I'll move abroad and figure my situation out there, away from New York and now away from Boston."

He knows who I am. There is no way I stay. No way.

He's hated me from the moment he met me and today, all these years later, even with him not recognizing me, he still hated me.

"Why do I have to have such a mouth on me?"

Her hand grasps my forearm. "Because you are entitled to one as we all are. No one questions Zax's mouth or even Valencci's. Why? Because they have more power? Fuck that. You had a designer steal your dress and not only claim it as hers, but when you attempted to speak out about what she did, she blackballed you against every possible internship out there. So now you're here. And maybe you said some things you shouldn't have. You were disrespectful and I get it. He's the boss. But fear of speaking up is what has consistently placed women in the dark ages and had us not viewed as equals. Be bold. Be strong. And if this is where it ends for you here, remember you are brilliant and talented. Carve your own path without requiring the aid of anyone else."

My heart swells. "Thank you. I needed that. More than you'll ever know. Can I have your children?"

She covers a snicker as a cough when people turn in our direction. "No. Children are for women who are better, less selfish humans than I am. I am not meant to be a mother and that's simply the laws of nature. Some of us aren't."

I hold up a hand. "I have no judgment on that. My mother was never meant to be a mother. Lessons I learned the hard way more than once."

"No joke. Instead of birthing my children for me, how about I buy you drinks this week? We'll find some Boston pub and try to ignore the beer breath and sports jabber of the locals. My dear, Dorothy, we're no longer in New York, and Boston seems to be a different breed."

"The Fritz family lives here."

She fans her face. "Lord, I know it. But those gorgeous billionaire doctors are all unfortunately taken now. Anyway, we're stuck with the

Central Square crew, who are all single as luck would have it. You think if I went and stalked a few of their doorsteps, they'd let me in for a snuggle?"

"Um. Not likely. But then again, it's not like I know them. That well."

"That well?"

"Please don't ask."

"I'm asking. Just not now."

"Aurelia Whitlock?" A woman walks into the room, calling out my name in front of everyone. I blush seven shades of virgin red.

Here we go. That didn't take long.

"That's me."

I stand, putting all my things together, separating my personal from my work belongings without sparing Iris or Howie or anyone else a look. I can't bear it.

"Please come with me. Mr. Monroe has requested you for a meeting in his office in three minutes."

Oh, I'm sure he has.

5

ZAXTON

My eyes have been glued to my window since shortly after I got back up here and read her text. Words, so many words along with so many memories on repeat through my mind. The first time I met Aurelia Whitlock, I hated the sight of her. Or more aptly what she represented and brought into my life. Yet another mother figure who would pretend to give two fucks for exactly two seconds before growing bored and deciding her time was better spent spending my father's money.

Her mother wasn't the first stepmother I had nor was she the last.

Aurelia, as I recall, was a young girl covered in two sizes too big glasses, braces, and nerves. She was a lanky thing, all arms and legs with a stick figure for a body. She defined all things evil in my mind and I knew she wouldn't be in my life longer than a year, two tops.

And I treated her accordingly.

Greyson was the same way, I think, though I'm not positive about that nor did I pay much attention. I was twenty and dating Suzie and attending college, and our band had just hit it huge. Not to mention, Grey and I had been down this wealth seeking, pretending to give an actual fuck while dragging my kids along for the ride road before.

My father got off on them being young, pretty, and helpless. He treated them like expensive bottles of wine, something delicious to savor and enjoy, but when you're done, that's it and you move on to the next bottle.

We had just recorded our first album and were all over the radio. Our label had us set up for a six-month world tour that we knew was going to be the adventure of a lifetime. Truth, back then, I assumed we'd be a flash in the pan. I didn't think Central Square would stay as big for as long as we did.

Greyson was the voice. I was bass and occasionally backup vocals. Lenox piano and keyboard. Callan drum. Asher guitar. Suzie our manager. We grew up together. Bounced around between each other's houses, we were never apart despite our age differences. It all just clicked. Still clicks, even without Suzie.

I had made arrangements to do my college classes online and I had a tutor set up for Grey and Asher since they were both still in high school. Callan, Lenox, and Suzie were just eighteen, but Callan was taking the same route I was and starting college online.

Our father hated it.

He had a new wife he already regretted and a new stepdaughter he didn't want to deal with and there Grey and I were, leaving to go live big rock star dreams. Well, more like Grey's dream, but I wasn't letting him go off on his own like that at the age of sixteen, and someone had to be the adult of the group.

Greyson was the real talent in that. Still is. Man pumps out album after album and they're all fucking platinum.

Grey shines like the sun, and back then, it pissed our father off that his children were more talented, loved, and worshiped than he was. Whereas our friends' parents were happy and excited for us, my father was jealous and resentful. It made me hate him more than I already did for the things he used to say to Grey.

In truth, I don't remember much about Aurelia other than her hair. It's the same color and maybe that should have tipped me off, but how could it? This woman looks nothing like the girl I met back then and frankly, after those couple of months where she lived in my dad's house, I left and then our parents subsequently divorced. I never gave her much consideration after that.

Like I said, she wasn't the first one to come along.

But it bothers me. All of it.

Me not recognizing her. Me being drawn to her. Me wanting to fuck the woman who was once my stepsister. It fucking bothers me.

And then there was her text. A text that was blatantly not meant for me to read but was about me all the same. She wasn't wrong in what she said about me, but it still grates on me that she said it. Who was she lying to when she said there was no chemistry between us and that it was just any other shoot for her?

I exhale through my nose, my gaze sightless as I replay this morning with her. She felt it too. Right? She smiled and flirted and shivered. The woman shivered at my touch. Was that in fear or lust?

Does it even matter? No. It makes no difference if she felt it along with me or if it was all an act. Wouldn't it be better if every lick of desire that I perceived as mutual was just that, perceived? She knew who I was all along, which brings up more issues.

Since the moment I lost Suzie, nothing in my life has made sense. Nothing has felt right.

My world has been... gray. Gray and monotonous, but other than my bad temperament, no one has challenged me. No one has dared to call me unhappy.

Till her.

Unhappy. It's such a basic word. One a child would use. But its meaning resonates.

A knock comes on my door, but I don't bother to turn around as I call out, "Come in."

It's her. I know it's her and I need another minute to get my head back on straight before I fire her.

The door opens. "Mr. Monroe, I have Ms. Whitlock for you," my assistant, Thalia, announces, speaking in that gentle motherly tone she uses when she's afraid I'm at my wits' end. She's not wrong.

"Send her in and shut the door behind her, please."

"Yes, sir."

The soft tap of heels on hardwood floors. The click of the door closing. And there it is. The buzzing energy as it fills my office, making the air thicker, more stiflingly, and yet somehow easier to breathe as I take a deep inhale through my nose, searching for her fragrance. I thrive on antagonism and this girl is wrapped in it where I'm concerned.

"I received your text," I start, still not bothering to turn around, which is more self-preservation than being a dick, but it serves both purposes.

"Yes. I know you did, though I didn't mean to send it to you."

"Was your boyfriend accusing you of having a moment with your boss?"

She laughs, though there is no humor in it. "My boyfriend? Is that your way of fishing?"

I don't reply because yes, it was, and the inane jealousy it breeds only fuels my rancor. What is wrong with me? Where is all this coming from?

A deep sigh that tells me she's as exhausted with all this as I am. "My friend Iris was. She heard about the shoot this morning. Everyone did evidently."

My lips form a straight line. "I see. Well then, I hope you set her straight on exactly who I am the way you did with me."

"I'd apologize for it, but I'm not all that sorry. If you're going to fire me, then I'm glad you know what I think of you."

Ballsy fucking woman.

I suppress my grin. "Do you feel I should keep you on as an employee after everything that's happened today? After the way you've spoken to me?"

I turn, curious to see her expression when she answers. She's glaring contemptuously at me, venom flowing so profusely from her I'm shocked it's not dripping on the floor and pooling around her shitty, broken shoes. I return her withering stare and for a moment, that's all we do. We stare, eyes holding, locked in a voiceless battle.

But the longer this goes on, her animosity slips into something else I can't quite name. It's not humor, though her lips are quirked ever so slightly as if she's ready to smirk or smile no doubt at my expense.

She looks as she did this morning when I found her sprawled across the steps. Her makeup is nothing more than eyelashes painted in black mascara and pink gloss along her lips. Her hair is down and still has that tousled by a man's hands appeal it had during the shoot, but she's attempted to tame it back behind her shoulders.

It's clear she doesn't want to be seen as Lia here. She wants to be Aurelia. But try as she might, there is no hiding beauty like hers. If anything, it shines brighter with the lack of makeup and styled bouncy waves. No longer the girl who didn't quite fit into her body, I admit she's the sweetest thing I've ever seen.

I cock an eyebrow, growing impatient for her answer.

Shoulders squared, back straight, eyes dead on mine. "Yes. I feel you should keep me," she finally says, her voice firm.

"Why?"

"Because I'm very good at what I do, and I think I can be a valuable asset to your team."

Slowly, I walk back over to my desk, keeping my gaze on her even as I sit down. She remains standing as I tap my keyboard, causing both my monitors to spring to life. Her face and bio are right there for me, but it's generic. It gives me no details about her life after our parents divorced.

"Did you really design the dress you walked in at fashion week?"

"Yes."

I wave for her to sit, but she ignores me.

"Tell me about it. About what happened with Valencci. The truth." The itch to know about her, about her life in between the years I knew her, to learn about all that's happened with her is pervasive. It annoys me to no end, but not enough not to press for answers.

She puffs out a breath, her hands going to her narrow hips as her rigid posture subtly slips.

"My last year at FIT, I was interning part-time for Valencci," she starts.

"Were you still modeling then?"

"Yes, but not as much. I was taking mostly print work in the city to help pay for school and living expenses."

"Your mother wasn't helping with that?"

She gives me a look that tells me there is a lot I don't know.

"No," she says and leaves it at that. "Anyway, it was late, and I was exhausted. Valencci kept me there because we were waiting on a delivery of some gowns that she personally wanted to oversee. I was doodling in my sketchbook to pass the time and she saw the dress I had been working on as part of my senior project. She loved it. Went crazy for it and told me that she didn't want me to use it for school. She told me she wanted it for her fall line and that if I did that, she'd give me full credit for it, and I could walk in it as the final piece in her show during spring fashion week."

"Which you did."

She nods. "Which I did. I immediately agreed. That was my shot. No other student got anything even remotely close to that. Only when Valencci saw how everyone reacted to the dress during rehearsals, she pulled the credit away from me. I didn't discover this until after the actual show when she told the press, who were raving about it, that it was her masterpiece. I confronted her and she essentially told me that the dress had been worn at her show, not mine, and that I had agreed to make it for her label.

"We had no contract. No signed agreement that would hold her to her word. When I threatened to go public about what she did, she laughed. She told me no one would believe me or care, and then proceeded to have me blackballed. My internship for this year with her company was pulled—obviously. But more than that, I couldn't acquire another one."

I lean back in my seat, appraising her. That's a variation of what I heard. Whether Valencci intended it or not, word about what she did spread. Valencci isn't just cutthroat, she goes straight for your jugular. Not only that, she has dirt on everyone in the fashion world. She makes it her mission to know everyone's darkest secrets so she can use them as leverage when needed. Lucky for me, I have no secrets she could possibly unearth, and I don't give a fuck about that woman enough to play her games.

Fashion, for all its beauty, is the ugliest business around.

"How did you get here then?" I ask, leaning back in my chair with my hands folded across my stomach.

"If you're firing me, Zax, there is no point—"

"I haven't decided what I'm doing with you yet."

With a loud exhale, she slides onto the chair on the other side of my desk, her skirt riding indecently high as she adjusts herself and crosses her legs. The urge to place her on the edge of my desk, shove her skirt up to her waist, and spread those longer-than-long legs wide for me is agonizing. I close my eyes for a moment to steady my breathing and realign my pulse.

Why does it have to be *her* my dick is so eager to play with?

"I can't tell you how I got here."

That has my eyes snapping open. "Yes, you fucking can. This is my company, Aurelia. I am the CEO and if you have any wish or prayer or hope of staying here as an employee, you will be honest and you will tell me everything."

"Zax..." She slumps forward, placing her face in her hands. For such a strong, quick-witted, and smart-mouthed woman, she's incredibly broken. I wonder if others see it too or if her beauty hides all her cracks. Maybe it's a takes one to know one sort of deal. It occurs to me now that things haven't been easy for her, her world less than the perfect it appears. The cliché hits me hard. You can't judge a book by its cover. Don't I live and breathe and die by that?

"Tell me."

"I had been rejected from everywhere, including here. I had nothing left, and the moment presented itself, so I asked for a favor," she murmurs into her hands.

"A favor?" I shoot up in my chair, my forearms landing hard on my desk. "From whom?"

Hands plummet to her lap, her head going back, eyes fixed on the ceiling. "It will only make this worse. Not better."

I assume she's speaking for both of us now. "Don't care. Tell me," I demand, my tone growing harsher.

She shifts ever so slightly, her head turning toward my bookshelf as she whispers, "Your father."

That motherfucker. I grip the edge of my desk, leaning my weight against it as I pin her with my hard stare. "Tell me you're joking."

Her teeth catch her bottom lip as she sucks it into her mouth and shakes her head.

"Do you know what you've done by calling in a favor with him?"

She doesn't answer.

"Jesus, Aurelia." Agitated, I drag my hand through my hair. "How the hell does he still have those types of connections here?" I shoot out of my seat, pacing to the window and then back, standing behind my chair, my hands fisting at the leather. "He'll use you. He'll hold this over your head, and he'll use you as leverage to get whatever it is he's after."

"I know."

My eyebrows hit my hairline. "And you agreed?"

"No. Not to that. I... I was desperate." Her hands fly through the air. "I never agreed to that, and he never said a word. Frankly, in the moment, I didn't think about it. My dream, my life had been stolen from me because I trusted the wrong woman. Story of my life there," she says bitterly. "I was out of options and your father... he came to my graduation."

"*He what?*"

"I didn't invite him," she rushes, holding up a placating hand. "I hadn't seen him since our parents divorced when I was still a kid, but there he was. He told me he was in that part of the city for a meeting and saw me walking into the auditorium in my graduation gown. After, he took me to dinner."

Christ. This just keeps getting worse. I'm in front of her before I even know how I got here, my hands gripping the arms of her chair as I get right up in her face. "Did you fuck him?"

"What?" Hurt flashes through her eyes as a blush storms up her face.

"He attends your graduation. Takes you to dinner. Somehow gets you an internship you had already been turned down from. Did you fuck him?"

"No. I didn't fuck him," she snaps at me, her tone eviscerating even as her eyes glass over. Her hands press into my chest, attempting to shove me back, but I don't budge. "I didn't suck him off either if that's where you're headed next. And fuck you, Zaxton Monroe. You presumptuous asshole, sitting high up in your ivory tower. I'm not a whore, despite what you think of me. I don't do that. I don't fuck men for power or personal gain."

Shit. My accusation wrecked her when I think she was already wrecked. I can't stand that look on her face. "I'm sorry." I soften my voice and posture, kneeling before her as I did this morning. "That's not... I don't think you're a whore. It's just that you wouldn't have been the first beautiful young woman my father set out to seduce for all the wrong reasons."

Her voice catches. "No one came to my graduation. My mother was off somewhere with husband who knows what number, and even if she wasn't, she wrote me off a long time ago. I have no family and any friends I had were graduating with me. I was alone, like I always am, and he was there. He listened as I told him what had happened with Valencci."

A grand says he already knew and that's why he was there.

"And he offered to help?"

She shakes her head. "No. He didn't say much other than how sorry he was, and I let it drop. Then he called me last week in New York and asked if we could meet for dinner. I did and then he brought it up again, asking a few more questions, but that was it. Then he asked if I had tried getting a position here and I told him yes. I asked if there was any way he could get me in as an intern here. I was half-joking. I knew he was no longer the CEO. But he said yes. Then he got up and made a phone call and by the time he returned to the table, he told me I had an internship with Monroe Fashion. The following morning, I received an email to that effect from a woman named Beth, and a week later, here I am."

Beth? She's our head of HR and in charge of our interns.

"That was it?"

"That was it," she confirms. "I don't know who he spoke to or what was said. All I know is that I got the internship, and I didn't question it beyond that."

She gives me another shove and this time I move away from her without going far. I sit on the edge of my desk, my legs wide on either side of her chair, with hers crossed between mine. I should go back to my seat. I should distance myself from this woman, who is growing more and more dangerous by the second, but I can't seem to force the action.

"You didn't reach out to me."

She laughs. But it's not just any laugh. It's a head thrown back, loud enough to be almost considered a cackle, sarcastic and lacking in humor laugh.

"Okay. I get it."

Sitting back in her chair, she pins me with a look that I'm positive has lesser men falling at her feet and begging for mercy. "You hated me."

"I hated what you represented," I counter. "I hated your mother. Everything about her." Aurelia was the girl I... I was awful to. I treated her like she was nothing. I know I did. I was angry and spiteful and resentful, and I wanted to ruin her mother when she pretended to care.

I never considered the daughter beyond the mother's scheming.

"The sins of the mother are not those of the daughter. Your father played the same games as she did. Where your father married for youth and beauty, my mother married for wealth and comfort. You were stuck in the middle of that, but so was I. Only it was worse for me. I was a child. You were an adult by that point. You left to travel the world and become a famous rock star. I was stuck with them."

She said her mother wrote her off a long time ago. I need to explore that, but not yet.

"You still could have... I don't know. You could have called me."

"And you would have been nice and given me an internship here?" she challenges, her tone mocking.

"No. Likely not," I admit, gripping the edge of my desk and tapping my fingers on the wood. A nervous habit and a calming tempo as it's the opening chords to my favorite song our band ever played.

"Exactly," she says with a look that indicates I'm finally starting to catch on. "You were awful to me. Cruel at first and then indifferent, which was worse than you being cruel. I knew you hated me. You never attempted to hide it. There I was, stuck with our parents, but suddenly, I had two older stepbrothers. At least Greyson was nice to me."

"He's nice to everyone."

"A character flaw, no doubt." A hint of a smile returns to her face. "But an admirable one. Especially to a lost and lonely young girl."

I smirk. "Are you trying to make me feel guilty?"

"Is that an emotion you're capable of?"

"Certainly more than empathy."

She snorts out a laugh and I shift, wanting to be closer to her, sliding so I'm barely perched on my desk.

"Well, I'm not trying to make you feel guilty. I'm explaining why I don't like you all that much and why I didn't reach out to you and why I didn't tell you who I was this morning. I assumed the second you knew and learned how I got here, you'd fire me. And lo and behold, here I am." She pans her hands around my office. "About to get fired. All on day one. I had hoped this would at least last a little longer."

I stare at her, thinking all of this through. My father placed her here for a reason. A reason he doesn't want me to know about. Either he thought she'd fly completely under my radar or he knew I'd learn about her being here.

"Did my father ask you not to tell me who you are or that he helped you?"

"Yes. But I was grateful for that. I didn't want you to know I was here either."

For that reason alone, I should fire her. She represents far too many troublesome variables. Not to mention there is that other not-so-minor issue—I'm insanely attracted to her. But looking at her, this woman who has been plowed over time and time again by people and life and yet is still fighting. Fighting with a smile on her face and a laugh in her voice.

She is Persephone battling the darkness and monsters of the underworld.

I don't want her around, and most days I don't care about being labeled an asshole, but I'm not sure I have a choice but to keep her here.

"Go and come back tomorrow."

Her eyes widen. "You're serious?"

"Are you trying to change my mind?"

"No." A giggle. "Holy wow. Thank you." She flies out of her chair, her arms wrapping themselves around my neck as she hugs me to her, and my grip on my desk tightens so I'm not tempted to do something stupid. Like hug her back.

Lord, I never pray because you and I aren't on speaking terms after what you did to Suzie, but if you could make this woman smell like dog shit instead of heaven and feel like razors instead of everything right, I'd be forever grateful.

"Are you done?" I quip, though I'm saying the words through gritted teeth. "This is hardly what I'd call professional or appropriate for the workplace."

She laughs, and it makes her soft breasts bounce against my chest. I stifle my groan.

"Yes. Sorry." She pulls back and straightens my tie. The same blue tie on the same suit that I never bothered to change out of earlier. Then again, my other one is covered in her blood. "I'm going to go before you do change your mind. Thank you, Zax. I won't let you down."

"Email me your portfolio and hopefully I won't have to see you again."

She smiles, those rare blue gemstone eyes of hers dazzling as the sunlight filtering through the window catches them. "From your mouth to God's ear on that." She winks at me and then she's gone, and I can breathe again. Even if this new tightness in my chest doesn't feel like it's going anywhere anytime soon.

6

ZAXTON

"Our father is a real motherfucker," I say to Greyson right as I sit on the couch, tossing one arm back along it while taking a sip of my scotch.

His dark eyes meet mine over the rim of his glass. "What did he do now?" Tossing back the tail end of his drink, he holds his glass out to Callan, who does the duty of refilling it with another two fingers. All five of us are here—hiding at Callan's since as an emergency room doctor, he's the least conspicuous of all of us now—drinking to Suzie. Even Lenox, Suzie's twin brother, is here, and that bastard never leaves the wilderness of Maine where he's been hiding out since her death.

He checked out when she died.

I think part of all of us did. She was our glue. Our guiding light. The crazy adorable tomboy who loved nothing more than hanging out with the guys and being with me. We would have followed her to the ends of the earth and back and for a while, that's exactly what we did. We played and toured and made albums with her leading us every step of the way.

When she died, all of us lost the will to go on with it. We couldn't be Central Square without Suzie. There was no way. Not to mention, I had decided I was already done and leaving the band, and I know Callan and Asher were damn close to that point too. They had other dreams, as did I. Only mine were never realized. At least not the ones I had at that time.

Other than Grey, who is my brother, I've known these guys since infancy and trust and love no one in the world the way I do them. It's the only reason I was ever in that band to start with. I play decent bass, not great bass.

I proceed to fill the guys in on my eventful day, sparing no details about Aurelia or our father's involvement with her coming on at Monroe. The only thing I gloss over is my ill-placed infatuation with her and that thanks to her I was sporting an uncomfortable chub for most of the day. I finally succumbed and took care of that in my office bathroom once everyone was gone for the day before leaving and coming here.

Not my finest moment.

"Aurelia Whitlock is a model by the name of Lia Sage?" Grey muses, rubbing a finger along his bottom lip, his gaze unfocused as if he's trying to picture her. "Damn. I haven't thought about her in a hundred years. I wouldn't know her if I hit her with my car."

Good thing you didn't, or she'd own your ass too. "Obviously, I had the same issue, and I did a full photo shoot with her. I haven't seen her or thought about her since she was eleven or so." Which only serves to make me feel like more of a dirty creep than I already do with the nine-year age gap we have.

"I always felt bad for her," he continues. "Her mother was a real piece of work."

"So's our father."

"This her?" Asher asks, dropping his elbows to his knees and flipping his phone around for me to see.

I glance quickly at the screen, not allowing my eyes to linger on the close-up of her smiling face. "That's her."

"Damn." He whistles through his teeth, turning his phone back around and studying her image. Then he starts swiping and I can only imagine half the images that come up. "You got to do a photo shoot with *her* today? I might be in the wrong profession."

"Like you don't get enough model action," Callan teases. "You're a championship winning quarterback in the NFL. You have women who look like that falling all over you."

"So says the doctor. You have patients throwing themselves at you. Oh please, Dr. Barrows," he mocks a woman's voice. "I'm so ill. You must help me. And touch me here"—he places a hand over his groin —"while you're at it."

Callan rolls his eyes and smashes a pillow to the back of Asher's head. "Shut up, dickhead, or I'll tell the press about when you begged me to write you a prescription for a certain blue pill because you were positive you had ED when in reality, it was just a case of whiskey dick."

We all start cracking up, remembering that night.

"Hey! That wasn't my fault." Ash throws the pillow back at him. "I didn't realize taking a muscle relaxant and a few shots would result in that."

"Lesson learned," Callan quips. "You were also likely dehydrated considering that was after you won the fucking Super Bowl."

"Yeah," he says with a wistful gleam in his eye. "That was a great night. Other than the droopy fellow down below, of course. He cost me a bad performance with the hottest woman I've ever seen. Remember that girl? Wouldn't mind getting a second chance to make a better first impression."

"Speaking of hot women," Grey cuts in. "Let's get back to Aurelia because this is actually something we need to figure out. A woman you'll never see again, Ash, is not."

"What is there to figure out about her? She's trouble. And a headache. And you can't fuck her." I point at Asher, who gives me that devilish grin he knows pisses me off.

"Neither can you, it seems," he retorts. "Though she certainly appears to be under your skin already. How adorable. Zax has a crush on a girl."

"Not true."

"True," Grey hoots, laughing at my expression. "Shit, she is under your skin. Wow. I feel like I should snap a picture of you to commemorate this monumental moment in time. Zaxton Monroe likes a girl. When was the last time that happened?"

I flip him off. Dumb fucking question to ask, especially today.

"I don't like her and she's not under my skin. She's a nuisance."

"With a face and body that turns you on."

"Grow up, Asher. A pretty face and a nice body are nothing new. What she represents, on the other hand..."

"What is your father after with her?" Lenox asks, standing off to the side, leaning against the wall of windows, and pushing us back to task.

"I don't know," I admit, meeting his eye. "But it has to be something, right? No way he was at some random meeting and saw her walk into her graduation. No. He had to know who she was, where she'd be, and what was going on in her life."

"That's some stalker bullshit if you ask me. He's preying on her for sure. But to what end?" Callan questions, just as the doorbell rings with our dinner. He jogs over to answer it, his question hanging heavy in the air, leaving the rest of us silent.

"Maybe I should have fired her." My head falls to my hands and I stare at the floor.

"No," Asher murmurs, his voice pensive. "No, you did right by keeping her on. Life, or more accurately people, haven't been the kindest to her. So she's there since you already told her she should stay. Now you have to create a game plan."

"A game plan?" Grey parrots, swirling the liquid in his glass around.

"She's an opponent, right?" Asher continues, his gray eyes gleaming as he works all this out. He scoots to the edge of the couch, angling his body forward like he's about to call a play in the huddle. "She's working for your company, but she's also likely in communication with your father. Who knows if everything she told you is true or not. For all you know, your father might have coached the whole thing. She was mugged by some random kid, and you were the one to find her and intervene. Then you helped patch up her broken knees. She's a model and the one you hired for the shoot with you today just so happens not to show up. It's—"

"Suspicious," Lenox finishes for him. "A hell of a lot of coincidences that may or may not add up."

I fall back in my seat, thinking about our interactions today. Could all that be true?

"You're just paranoid," Callan accuses, setting the bags of food down on the large coffee table. We all dig into our Thai feast, Suzie's favorite, and something I never eat except this one day every year. For a few minutes, silence ensues, likely all for the same reason. Suzie.

She was something different to each of us. Her death did something different to each of us. Changed us in irrevocable ways. We each bear the scars of her loss. We just wear them differently.

"Happy birthday, Suz," I whisper, staring down at my spring roll.

"Thirty doesn't feel the same without her turning it with me," Lenox says, his voice laced with pain.

Eight years. They have no idea all that we lost and never had in those eight years.

"Do you remember that time she got trashed in Berlin and stood on a table, singing "99 Luftballons" in German only to get the entire bar in on it with her?"

I inwardly smile, remembering the night Asher mentioned. He's never one to dwell on the misery and heartache the way Lenox and I are prone to do. Everyone reacts differently to loss, but true loss affects everyone the same way. That's why it's so hard to get over. Because once you lose someone, they take some of you with them. You're never quite whole again and the rest of you is constantly trying to compensate for that missing piece.

"We made the German papers for that," Grey muses with a laugh in his voice. "She got so drunk she fell off the table doing one of her crazy dance spin moves and fell right on top of me. Broke my finger. I couldn't play guitar for a month. Couldn't play well for at least two."

"You're still shit at it, so you can't blame her for that."

Grey flips Lenox off. "Better than you are at piano and keyboard, old man."

Lenox folds his tattooed arms, pinning Grey with a stare that makes lesser men piss their pants and cry for their mommies. He doesn't say anything, but he rarely does anyway, so it's not from lack of a solid retort. Lenox doesn't speak a lot on a good day and today is clearly not a good day for any of us.

"It's today," Callan bursts out, dropping his fork on the side of his plastic takeo-ut box.

"What is?" Grey asks.

"Today is Suzie's birthday and the anniversary of her death. *And* today is the day that this Aurelia woman started as an intern."

I blink, my fork paused in midair loaded with Pad Thai. "What do you mean?"

"She started today, Zax. This girl, this ex-stepsister of yours who is seemingly placed in your company—your father's old company— started today. Why did he call her last week after not seeing her for over a month and suddenly decide to help her? Why did he go out of his way to meet her for dinner and then have her start today when all other interns started weeks ago? If he was going to help her all along, he could have done it the night she graduated. He waited."

"Fuck," I hiss, dropping my fork the way Callan did and shooting out of my seat, pacing over to his floor-to-ceiling windows and staring out at the Beacon Hill night.

"He knew you'd be vulnerable today," Greyson states.

I nod at that. He wasn't wrong in that assumption either. He pushed Aurelia at me today, knowing any man with a pulse—even the emotionally dead inside ones—wouldn't be able to resist her. Is that why she mentioned I was unhappy? Was she hitting me at my worst, digging the knife in deeper? I feel like the ultimate sucker. She seemed so genuine and fun and scared and real.

And I fell for it.

"I should have fired her."

"No," Asher jumps back in, building up speed on his earlier argument. "But you need to treat this like football. Like chess. Like a game you can't afford to lose against an adversary who's already more skilled and two steps ahead."

"The question is, is she being played the same as you are or is she doing the playing?"

Callan's words hit me hard. Did she want me to see that text so I'd call her to my office and then she'd set me up even more? I reacted to her, dammit. Physically, I reacted to her. I teased and flirted and was hard for her.

"I hate this." I fucking hate everything about it because I *was* vulnerable. I was weak. I wanted that woman more than I've wanted anyone since Suzie and now look where I am. Out skilled and already two steps behind as Asher said.

"Bring her on to be your intern."

"What?" I spin around, staring at Grey.

"She's an intern," he says as if it should all be obvious. "A design intern. The design team falls directly under you right now, right? Your design intern left a few weeks back and you have yet to replace her?"

"Yeah. So?"

"So make Aurelia your executive design intern. Bring her upstairs. Tell her you were impressed with her portfolio or some shit. That way you'll be able to keep an eye on her at all times."

"Right," Asher agrees. "Friends close and enemies even closer."

Lenox gives a grunt, which is his way of saying he's in agreement with that. And while it sounds like a solid, smart plan, I have no idea how I'll manage working that closely with her. I barely made it through today. Having to see her, breathe in her fragrance, listen to her laugh and sweet fucking voice.

How will I survive wanting this woman the way I do while working with her?

Even when I don't trust her and am starting to hate her once again for putting me in this position. My father might be pulling the strings on her, but to what end? Is she a victim or an accomplice? Unsuspecting or fully compliant?

I have to know.

For more than just Monroe Fashion.

I have to know for me.

"You're right. You're all right. I'll do it."

LATER THAT NIGHT, after what is likely one too many drinks, I sit in my office in my quiet penthouse and stare at my phone. I could call my father. It would be the first time I've spoken to him since I took over his position at Monroe three years ago. Not that him shouting at me like a toddler throwing a temper tantrum is what I'd call a conversation.

I could toss a what the fuck at him and see where it lands.

He'd likely deny it. Say he was simply helping one of his former stepchildren as if he'd ever given a crap about anyone other than himself before. He's spiteful and angry that he got tossed out on his ass the way he did. He seduced a young employee, which is why I went a little too harsh—or maybe not—on Aurelia. The woman lodged a formal complaint against him, and he paid her off to keep quiet. Not to mention he was also single-handedly bringing the company down. Shitty marketing choices, poor designs, cut-rate manufacturers and fabrics, you name it, he did it in order to cut corners and skim off the top to pad his own bank account.

The board was only too eager to hire me on as CEO, keeping the Monroe name and brand but bringing a celebrity in as the new face. In addition to me coming on and modeling our lines, Greyson and Asher do as well along with Oliver Fritz, a famous billionaire celebrity, not just in Boston but all over the world. In the past three years, the company has once again become one of the largest and most prestigious luxury design houses.

My father obviously has someone on the inside. Someone who was able to secure Aurelia a position she had already been turned down for. Beth. Aurelia mentioned an email coming from Beth.

I don't call my father. I have no plans on tipping my hand.

Instead, I shoot Lenox a message about this piece of information, asking him to silently look into it for me. Lenox is a quiet hacker. A computer genius, who likely wouldn't mind a bit of a challenge.

Then I text Aurelia. Hell, she started it anyway.

> Me: Looked over your portfolio. Tomorrow you report to my floor, to me, as my design intern.

The bubble with the three dancing dots appears almost instantly and I can't stop my pulse from jumping and my lips from quirking upward like a fool. *I shouldn't be smiling at you. I should hate you and I do.* Then I glance down at my hard dick straining against my slacks, asking the question, *who the fuck are you kidding*? Right. I need to realign my thinking and stop wanting this woman.

Or maybe acknowledgment is better? Isn't that what they say? That acknowledging there is a problem is the first step in working to overcome it?

> Aurelia: Um. Yeah. That's not what we discussed at all today. What happened to we hoped to never see each other again?

> Me: Things changed.

> Aurelia: Riiiight. Sure. Suddenly you want to work with me? I'm not buying it. We nearly came to blows and I most certainly had bloodshed. Besides, I am part of the design team on the twelfth floor.

> Me: Now you're part of the design team on the twenty-sixth floor. Wasn't that your goal by designing and wearing that dress for Valencci? You've got the talent, Aurelia. I can't keep you on the intern team with a portfolio like this.

Truth? I did review her portfolio. And truth? It is incredibly good. She does have talent. Real talent and creativity. So giving her this promotion isn't completely without merit and no one will accuse me of favoritism once they see it. As Grey said, the design team right now reports directly to me and I'm down an executive intern.

> Aurelia: You want me to work for you? You know that comes with my mouth, right?

> Aurelia: Crap, I know that sounded dirty, but it wasn't meant to be. I didn't mean to insinuate that my mouth works for you or does things for you.

> Aurelia: And yeah, wow, I just made that a whole lot worse. I swear, that's not what I was thinking about. I'm nervous about this. You make me nervous.

I chuckle, rubbing my finger along my bottom lip, rereading her words.

> Me: What do you have to be nervous about with me?

> Aurelia: Um, how about the fact that you openly dislike me and are a notorious grump? Plus, you're impossible to please. Or so I've heard.

And just like that, all her talk about her mouth and pleasing me has my mind going to images of just how she could please me. On her knees. Blue eyes on mine. Mouth wrapped around my—I shake my head, growl, and force myself to push all that away.

> Me: Are you afraid you don't have what it takes to deal with me?

> Aurelia: Ah! Don't throw down the gauntlet. Yes. I have what it takes. I said you make me nervous, not scared. But why are you doing this? With me?

> Me: I already told you. You're talented.

> Aurelia: Thank you. That means a lot coming from you when we both know compliments aren't your strong suit. Is this on the level or is it some first-day in the big leagues hazing thing?

> Me: This is on the level.

Sort of.

> Aurelia: Okay. I'll report to you tomorrow. I'll try to be polite and professional. In fact, if we could put today and our past aside and start with a clean slate, I'd appreciate that. This shot means everything to me, and I am very grateful for the opportunity.

I pause here, reading this again and again.

The jaded rock star, CEO, son of a piece of shit in me doesn't trust anything she's saying. Especially after the way Callan and Lenox laid the timing of everything today out for me. I've been told bullshit by such skilled liars they could have passed a polygraph.

But there is a part of me that doesn't want to believe she's involved in something sordid and underhanded with my father. As childish as it sounds, I want to believe she's genuinely a good, honest person who got herself stuck in a bad situation and used the only avenue she had to get out of it.

Brutal realization grips my throat, restricting my air and causing my body to seize up.

That's why she's so dangerous to me.

It's more than she's under my skin. I care.

I care about her. I care about whether or not she's playing me. I care about her past and the horrible things that have happened to her. I want to know all of them so I can fix each of them one by one. In one day, she got me to care.

Maybe it's our past or the way I treated her back then. I do feel guilty about that—she was only a child. Maybe it's how she got me to smile and laugh and turned me on to the point of madness.

Whatever it is, it can't happen. None of it.

> Me: See you tomorrow

I leave it at that, and I shut off my phone.

First step in dealing with Aurelia Whitlock is admitting I am attracted to her. Second is believing I am strong enough to restore myself to sanity and treat this attraction for what it is—a flaw I can ignore and overcome. How hard can that be?

7

AURELIA

"**Y**ou're sure this is on the level?" Iris questions as we step onto the elevator bright and shiny early on this lovely Tuesday morning. I didn't sleep. Hardly a freaking wink and whenever I did fall asleep, I had wild dreams about my new boss. Half of them had to do with me bleeding on his suit and him telling me if I didn't stop doing that, he was going to put me over his knee and spank the naughty girl out of me.

Not the best dreams to have before you start working for someone you categorically don't like all that much.

"You know, those were the exact words I asked him. He said yes."

People start piling onto the elevators, shoving us to the back.

"Explain to me how you know him again?" Iris leans in, speaking in a low voice so only I can hear. "Because we've been best friends for four years since we started at FIT together and I know nothing of this." Ironically, Iris is the main reason I wanted to intern here. My boss is the last.

"I can't. Not here and not now."

"I heard his last design intern quit after a week of working for him, moved to Montana or someplace and became a professional fly fisherman. Fisherwoman? Whatever. I didn't even know that was an actual profession. The point is the woman is working with live bait and fish instead of humans and fabric swatches. She didn't just leave the job or this company, she left the industry because of him. Not to mention you only make it up to the executive intern pool once you've done a full year as a basic intern and they select you."

I toss my hands up and bang into a guy's coffee, nearly spilling it all over his white shirt. He gives me a terse look.

"Sorry," I mumble sheepishly before I turn back to Iris. "This is exactly my problem. Why am I being given this position when I shouldn't be? What am I missing?"

"Don't know, sugar, but it's yours now and you need to ride that bull till he's ridden hard and put away wet."

"Huh?" I wave her away because this is Iris and Iris doesn't always make sense. "I'm a mess with this job. When in my life have I ever been clumsy? Never, Iris. Never. I can parade down a runway in dental floss they call a bikini and six-inch stilettos in front of spectators and photographers without so much as a misstep. Yesterday, I fought with a mugger and smashed up both my knees. Last night, I burned my hand and my tongue on my bowl of pasta. And now I'm nearly spilling coffee on strangers. This isn't me."

The elevator stops on Iris's floor, and she drags me past the other elevator patrons, down the hall and into the ladies' room. After checking to ensure we're alone, she turns to me, grasping my shoulders and twisting me to face the mirror.

"Look at yourself and tell me what you see."

"Iris, I seriously don't have time for—"

"Tell me what you see," she demands.

"I see myself."

"No. You see a talented, badass bitch who doesn't take shit from anyone even when they come at her full-on. You see a woman who has risen to the top like cream when all odds were against you. You see a woman who does not fail and does not allow someone else to make you question who and what you are. Know your value and whatever you do, do not let Zaxton Monroe and his sexy, evil mouth derail you."

I think her words through, giving myself a good, hard look. She's right. That is me. Or more appropriately who I want to be. "I've got this."

She gives my shoulders a squeeze. "You've got this. Now get your adorable ass upstairs and show those executives precisely what you're made of. And while you're at it, give your boss a rub and suck."

"Iris!" I blush seven shades of Hades.

"What? Lord knows the man could use a good blow job and a few well delivered Os to get rid of the perpetual pinched brow and scowl on his far too handsome face."

"Well, those BJs and Os won't be coming from me."

She purses her red lips to the side. "Pity. I bet he has a pretty dick to match his pretty face and I'm curious to know if he still remembers what to do with it. Now get." She smacks my ass toward the door. "You can't be late on your second first day."

"I love you," I tell her and leave the bathroom, but instead of taking the elevator up the remaining eight floors, I decide on the stairs to help work out some of these jitters. By the time I reach the executive floor, I'm panting for my life, I might have pit stains from sweat, and my feet ache in my heels, but at least my muscles have stopped vibrating. Opening the door from the stairwell, I stare across the vast floor and give myself a second, "I've got this."

"Are you talking to me?"

My head flies to my right and I find a petite pregnant woman juggling a stack of papers in one hand and a coffee in the other. "I'm sorry?"

"You said you've got this and if you were talking to me instead of giving yourself a mental pep talk, I won't complain."

"How about both?" I offer and a smile peels her lips apart.

"Sounds great. Do you mind taking the papers? I get one small coffee a day with this thing growing inside me and I don't want to ruin it by having it go cold."

"Not a problem." I shuffle the stack of papers teetering precariously from her hand into mine, reorganizing them and pressing them against my chest. "I'm—"

"Aurelia Whitlock a.k.a Lia Sage. Yes, I know. I'm Beth, the one who emailed you about your initial position here. I'm the HR person in charge of interns for Monroe Fashions. Now that you're on the executive team, we'll be working closely."

"Oh." My eyes startle wide. "It's so nice to meet you in person. Uh. Thank you for having me up here?" Yeah, that came out as weird as it sounded, question mark and all.

She gives me a knowing grin as we walk through the polished executive floor. "Don't worry. I know all of this seems a bit sudden and unorthodox. Frankly, it is." She takes a sip of her coffee and practically moans after she swallows. "Sorry. I was a three large coffee a day person and now I'm down to this pathetic thing."

I hold up my hand. "Zero judgment."

"Fantastic. So, as I was saying, we don't typically get executive level interns until your second year and those positions are few and far between. But as luck or fate or whatever you want to call it would have it, Mr. Monroe's last design intern left shortly after accepting the position and he has yet to refill it. I don't think they had... good working chemistry."

I snort under my breath. "You don't have to sugarcoat the situation. I worked with Mr. Monroe yesterday and have heard the rumors of his... temperament."

I follow her into an office where she sets her coffee down and takes the stack of papers from my hand, putting them on the edge of her desk. She signals for me to shut the door and I do. "Have a seat for a minute."

I take a seat on the other side of her desk while she lowers herself into her own chair, rubbing at her belly. She lifts her coffee and rests it on the arm of her chair, holding on to it like it's her lifeline. I'm not a coffee drinker. I'm a Diet Coke drinker, which I know is gross in the morning, but we all have our kinks and vices. When I was working solely as a model before I started at FIT, some of my fellow models would start their day with a diet pill, a Red Bull, and a cigarette.

My Diet Coke feels like a kale smoothie by comparison.

"Mr. Monroe is tough," Beth continues. "I won't lie or sugarcoat it as you said. He's a perfectionist, which is not a bad thing at all in this field. Perfection is the image we sell. But he does not tolerate anything less than what he puts out."

"I understand and I plan to give this new role everything I've got."

She nods, seemingly mollified by that. "I will admit, I was skeptical about his motives for bringing you up on only your second day."

"Yes. I was... surprised," I admit to her.

"We all were. But after reviewing your portfolio, I understand better. You're very talented and I think if you can stick it out working with him, you can pretty much write your own ticket."

"Thank you," I say, a bit floored by that. Frankly, part of me still thought Zax was playing me somehow. He said it was legit, but why me when I'm positive this company is filled with dozens of equally if not more talented designers? I don't trust him. He has to have an angle because a man like him seems to be all sharp edges with no smooth lines.

"Do you mind if I ask what your relationship with Mr. Monroe is?"

That takes me aback. "I don't have one."

"I saw some of the images from the shoot yesterday."

"I'm not following."

She gives a disbelieving look.

"Anything you saw in the photos was modeling. Acting," I tell her emphatically, hoping the part of me that doesn't fully believe that doesn't leech through. "Mr. Monroe is my boss. Nothing more."

"Excellent. I'm sorry if that seemed crass, but I had to make sure. A few years back, this company nearly came to a large scandal, and we do everything we can to avoid that now."

"I understand." Sorta. I imagine the scandal she's speaking about is Zax's father. I don't know what happened here in the company or between them, but Zax certainly flew off the handle when he discovered his father's involvement in my being here and his father didn't hide the animosity that lives between them.

Maybe I should disclose that I'm Zax's ex-stepsister, but why bother? I barely knew him then and he hated me. It's not exactly as if we had a warm and cozy relationship and he's made no effort to hide the fact that he still doesn't like me or my mouth all that much. And honestly, that's not how I want to be seen here. If Zax didn't feel the need to clue people into that fact, why should I?

"Perfect." She sits up, setting her coffee down beside her keyboard. "I think we're good to go then. Yours is the empty desk in the open space outside of Mr. Monroe's office. Thalia, who is his assistant, can direct you. I'll check in with you later today or tomorrow morning. Best of luck."

I stand. "Thank you."

"Can I give you a piece of advice?" she calls out to me just as my hand hits the doorknob.

I roll my head over my shoulder and meet her dark brown eyes. "Sure."

"Focus on your work. Not on him. You're young and very beautiful and judging from the shoot yesterday, despite what you say, there is some chemistry between you and him. But women have been trying to win over the dead heart of Zaxton Monroe for years to no avail. I'm not saying that's your interest or intent, but he's gruff and has no problems letting everyone know it while firing people at the drop of a hat if he so chooses. If you're serious about fashion design, then use this as your leg up in the industry and do your best to work around him."

Interesting. I wonder if she's speaking from personal experience. "Thank you for that advice. That was always my plan."

Another nod and then she dismisses me by moving her focus to her computer. I shut the door behind me and steal a breath, glancing left and right. It's a massive open floor with gray hardwood alternating with gray carpet. The walls are windows, letting in a lot of filtered light. All around me, people are hustling about, doing their jobs with a definite sense of urgency. I wonder if that's what Zax imparts to them.

There is no denying the power he wields. Both here and in the fashion world.

Even for a Boston-based company. Not exactly known as the

fashion Mecca of the world. He's a rule breaker. A trendsetter. Is very successful at what he does. And clearly has zero fucks to give if anyone doesn't like the way he runs things.

Weaving my way to the other side of the floor, I find Zax's office and the empty desk in a partially partitioned cubical that I assume to be the executive design intern's. Thalia, the woman who came and fetched me from my meeting yesterday, is nowhere to be seen, so I set my bag down on the desk and look around.

Zax's office has a direct sight line to mine, and I wonder if that's intentional. Not for me necessarily, but so he can keep a close watch on his interns.

Just as I unzip my bag to pull out my laptop, the door to Zax's office opens and out comes Thalia, but it's Zax who catches and holds my attention. He's wearing a dark blue suit with a crisp white button-down shirt and no tie. His thick, dark brown hair is a tousled disaster as if he's already been running agitated hands through it. The man is seriously too tense for his own good.

Maybe Iris was on to something when she said the man could use a few good Os.

Aside from that, he looks sexy as hell. What is it about tall, dark, and handsome with a chin dimple? I'm used to beautiful men, but never once felt weak in the knees from any of them like I do now. His is the sort of handsome I'm not quite accustomed to. If I didn't just promise Beth and Iris that I'm not here to nail the man, I'd swear my vagina would take it upon herself to climb his face before impaling herself on his dick.

His eyes lock on mine, a smoldering fire begging to be unleashed pinning me where I stand. It's a look that either says I'm picturing you in several different positions naked or I hate you so much I want to pitch you out the twenty-sixth floor window and watch you fall. I honestly can't tell which.

Either way, he's visibly worked up. A live wire anxious to electrocute all within his sight, and right now, that's me.

Zaxton Monroe is rich, powerful, infuriatingly gorgeous, and thinks I'm here to ruin his life. Problem is, he might not be wrong. Even if it's not intentional.

He doesn't speak and neither do I, even as his gaze does a slow perusal of me. The air crackles with the intensity radiating off him, the temperature of the air rising as he lingers on the hem of my dress. His jaw locks tighter than a drum as his now narrowed eyes find mine once again.

I smirk, giving him a small wiggly finger wave. "Morning, Mr. Monroe."

Without a word, he slams his door shut, and I blow out the breath I didn't realize I was holding.

"Your boss is intense, Thalia. How ever do you manage that?"

The mid-fifties woman who resembles a librarian says, "My son is in prison for running gangs and first-degree murder."

"What?" sputters past my lips.

She laughs at my expression. "Only kidding, but that's how. With humor, motherly patience, and reminding myself that it could always be worse. And when all that fails, wine. Lots and lots of wine."

"Smart woman." Taking a seat at my desk, I open my laptop to get going on my emails and any assignments I haven't seen yet.

And of course, the one right at the top...

To: Aurelia Whitlock
From: Zaxton Monroe, CEO
Subject: Appropriate Workplace Dress
Miss Whitlock,

I have taken the liberty of attaching the segment from the HR documents you signed upon hire. While we don't have a dress code here at Monroe Fashions per se, we do have a certain level of professionalism we require from our employees at all times. Especially on the executive level. This means we do not allow skirts or dresses above midthigh.

Prior to your first official meeting as an executive design intern, I expect you to go to the closet and acquire either a longer dress or skirt or even better, pants.

Zaxton Monroe

IT TAKES me two read throughs before I feel I can digest what he just threw up at me. I glance down at the hemline of my dress. It's not above midthigh. Well, I mean. Maybe when I'm sitting, it is. But with the inch and a half of lace at the bottom, it looks longer. Doesn't it? Then again, the fucking audacity of this man.

"Is he freaking joking with this?"

My email pings with an incoming message.

To: Aurelia Whitlock

From: Zaxton Monroe, CEO

Subject: Appropriate Workplace Dress

No, I am not joking.

MY HEAD FLIES every which way, but Zax is nowhere to be seen. Does he have a microphone somewhere out here? Yeesh. Scary world, I totally wouldn't put that past him.

But I did warn him.

To: Zaxton Monroe, CEO

From: Aurelia Whitlock

Subject: RE: Appropriate Workplace Dress

Mr. Monroe,

While I appreciate your concern over the length of my current dress, I can assure you per the HR guidelines excerpt you sent me, my dress is fully within compliance with what humans would consider professional workplace attire. Even on an executive level. Add to that, it's my own design and frankly not your place to comment.

I look forward to my first executive intern meeting.
Happy morning,
Aurelia

To: Aurelia Whitlock
From: Zaxton Monroe, CEO
Subject: RE: RE: Appropriate Workplace Dress
Is this your way of resigning from your new position? Because if you don't change prior to that meeting, you're officially out the door. Same if you ever say happy morning to me again.
Zaxton Monroe

To: Zaxton Monroe, CEO
From: Aurelia Whitlock
Subject: RE: RE: RE: Appropriate Workplace Dress
I officially don't like you. How's that for official? And my happy morning was ironic. I hope your morning is spent with bitter, two-day-old coffee, undercooked eggs that leave you with food poisoning, and people finally telling you exactly what they think of you. I'd be more than happy to go first. I will change, but I can't promise you'll like it.
Aurelia

I HIT send and then slam the top of my laptop closed, refusing to read or acknowledge any reply. Yes, I likely just went way overboard with how I spoke to him just now, but man, the asshole, has a knack for finding my every hot button and pressing it until I explode. Plus, he went there first with demanding I change. What kind of messed up, patriarchal, sexist ass shit is that? Change? I bet he has never asked any of the men in this company to do that. I should report him to HR. Only didn't Beth, my HR person, just warn me about the chemistry thing and that I should keep my distance and focus on my work? Not to mention, I'll be out on my ass and back where I started, which is stuck between screwed and royally fucked.

"Problem?" Thalia asks without removing her eyes from her monitor.

"Evidently, I have to go change."

She snickers under her breath and then drags her eyes over to me. I get a quick once-over and then she's back to whatever it is she was doing before. "Now I understand the morning I just had."

I sigh, staring down at my dress. I'm used to New York and in New York, there is no such thing as too short. "Do you think it's too short?"

"I think your legs are longer than a giraffe's and a floor-length gown on you will be too short. Other than that, I refuse to answer because I'm guessing you've already been told it is."

Another sigh. "I've also been told I have a mouth that gets me into trouble." In fact, I know it does. I'm shocked he hasn't stormed out of his office to yell and then fire me before having security escort me out.

"Good. He needs a bit of trouble to shake things up here. If he's going to be even more of a grump than he typically is, at least let it be for a purpose."

"I guess I'm the right woman for the job then," I deadpan. "So long as I change."

Thalia pushes up the bridge of her horn-rimmed glasses. "Honey, he's on the last stitch of his sanity as it is. I'd change. For everyone's sake."

"Because I like you." I wink at her, then storm past his office, making sure to peer through the glass window and glare at him. He glances up at the perfect moment and catches me in my childish act of defiance. I so wish I could flip him off to seal that deal, but I don't. I'm not that crazy.

Even so, I don't miss it.

The way his dark eyes sharpen as they watch me. The buzz humming through the air, even with a closed door separating us. The way my heartbeat and blood pressure shoot up at the mere sight of him. That damn sexy, irritable scowl he loves to wear so much.

Beth referred to his heart as dead and that's certainly been the word on the street.

Soulless. Broken. Dead inside.

The man beneath that cool exterior is anything but. The pent-up beast living inside him is very much alive, raging, and barely contained. He hates it and he fights it, but one of these days, that beast will escape. The question is, when it does, will it be what finally sets him free or destroys him for good?

8

AURELIA

The meeting starts in approximately fifteen minutes. That doesn't give me a lot of time to wade through the closet that is roughly the size of an entire Boston city block and since city blocks in this city aren't laid out the way they are in New York, some of these blocks are long and wide as fuck. We're talking racks and racks and racks and yes, they are divided into seasons, and yes, I am a sample size, but I also want to make my new boss eat his words.

Or emails rather.

Which means whatever I find, while it needs to be an appropriate length and likely demure, I want it to be knock-your-heels-off sexy. You know, to prove a point. I'm calling it a modern form of revenge for the required costume change, but the man sets my blood from room temperature to boil within seconds and I'm nearly positive it's the same for him with me. Not to mention—and please keep this to yourself—I might, just a teeny, tiny bit, get off on our back and forth.

What can I say, it's been a lonely few years where men are concerned and something about texting and sparring and emailing with him is addicting. And yes, I completely understand it's in a totally unhealthy way. I don't want nor expect anything to happen with Zax. Maybe that's what makes this all safe in my mind. It's a go-nowhere sort of play.

Meeting normal men when you're a model is difficult. Even when I didn't tell them that was my job outside of school, they guessed it easily. Tall. Blond. Skinny. Decent-sized rack. It was New York and I was living in the garment district. Plus, my face was in magazines and on billboards. Not exactly a stretch.

So guys saw and heard that one word. Model. After that, anything else zapped from their mind. All they wanted was to be able to tell their friends they fucked a model. The fact that I have brains and a personality was superfluous. I was the book people only admired the cover of without bothering to flip open and read.

I know, wah, poor me, I'm pretty. Big shit. If I didn't need it to survive when I was younger, it wouldn't have mattered to me. Beauty is fleeting. It's skin-deep. It's misleading and dangerous. Ted Bundy was considered charming and handsome and look at what he did. And no, obviously I'm not a serial killer, but I'm tired of people only taking the outside of me as my true value.

So I pretty much gave up on love and lust in New York. Plus, frankly, I didn't have a lot of time for that particular extracurricular. In a normal universe, where Zax wasn't my boss, emotionally broken, my ex-stepbrother, or scary, intimidatingly hot times ten, maybe I'd see what all this swirling energy between us was about.

But that's not a possibility.

This isn't about me trying to get in his pants. This is war on some strange level I don't quite understand. But at least it appears to be mutual. He's playing the game just as much as I am. I think.

Turning down one of the summer aisles, I groan. "So many good options."

"I thought I saw your miss thang clickety-clacking in here," Lamar says, startling me so badly I jump and emit a small unladylike screech that he graciously pretends not to notice. "What on earth are you doing in here when we're expected in a delightful spring/summer meeting?"

"I've been forced to change due to a dress code violation."

"*Dress code violation?* What in the fuckity what?" He pushes down the bridge of his glasses to give me yet another scrutinizing once-over. That makes at least three today. He pushes his glasses back up his nose and frowns. "What's wrong with it?"

"Too short."

"Hmmm." His lips purse to the side as his gaze drops to my thighs. "Your knees look good. Hardly a visible scrape on them, so that's clearly not it."

"Nope."

"Hmmm."

"I don't know you well enough to know what your hmmms mean."

"Probably for the best. Let's find you something and find it quickly so we're not late to this meeting. I'm protesting that colorful solids will be *it* for next spring/summer while Martina is all about the florals. I can't let her win this. Florals are so two years ago."

"Agreed."

He clucks his tongue as he twists me around, shoving me down the aisle by the shoulders. "I know. It's why I'm a god in the closet."

"Are you in the closet?"

"Honey, that is the lamest way to ask if I'm gay. No, I'm not in the closet. I never was and I never shall be because one should never be ashamed of who they are. I fuck everyone without discrimination. I'm an equal opportunity lay. With a committed boyfriend, but the mindset is there." He stops me, pivoting me to the right. "Here. This. It will look fabulous with your skin color and really set off the vibe I'm hoping to push for next year. Change."

"In front of you?" I toss a quirked eyebrow over my shoulder as I take the pale pink summer dress from him. It's playful and oh so girly with a sweetheart neckline that clings to the bust, flaring out into a version of a vintage nineteen-fifties skirt. I'm in love.

"You did yesterday."

"That was before I knew you liked what I carry."

He snorts. "Everyone likes what you carry whether they eat your type of sashimi or not. Change. We don't fucking have time for this, but I will go and find you the best fucking shoes ever to go with this while you get naked."

With that declaration, he marches off, a man on a mission, and I quickly slip out of my beautiful white lace dress and into this one. But the second the soft chiffon is on my skin, I hum in delight. Zax may be a douche, but the man does make some premium threads. I feel gorgeous and feminine, and I haven't even seen myself in the mirror yet.

"Ah, stunning. Love it. Shoes." He tosses a matching pair of pink heels at me that have black poke a dots on them to play up that nineteen-fifties vintage feel. I slip them on quickly, gathering up my stuff in my hands. "Hair and makeup stat."

"I don't have time."

"Shush it, woman. I need two fucking minutes." He rushes me back to the entrance and then he's diving into my hair, pushing up strands and twirling them around his fingers and pinning them all behind my head, making sure a few key strands are down, playing with my neck and shoulders and framing my face. "Pink gloss. Now."

I swipe it across my lips while he dabs a light bronze shimmer on my upper cheeks.

"Perfect. Now let's go."

Taking my hand, we sprint out of the shoot area and back onto the elevator.

"He's going to fucking die when he sees you."

"Who?"

I get a look that says don't bullshit a bullshitter. "Really, bitch?"

"That wasn't my goal."

"Really, bitch?"

I roll my eyes at him while pursing my lips, annoyed I'm so readable when I pride myself on being anything but. "Not for the reasons you think. I was just angry he made me change and wanted to cut off his nose to spite his face."

He holds up a hand. "Fine. That I'll buy. Mission accomplished. I bet he'll never make you change again."

With a smirk on both our lips, I quickly dispose of my stuff, grab my laptop, and head down the hall toward the conference room the meeting is being held in. I slow my stride, pressing down my dress right before I enter. I don't glance in Zax's direction even if I'm acutely aware of precisely where he is and the *exact* moment his eyes land on me.

The air stirs, priming with energy. If he were Zeus and capable of shooting bolts of lightning from his thunderbolt, I'd be... pregnant? Crap. No! I can't finish that thought because now all I'm thinking about is his thunderbolt and the lightning that shoots out of it.

In fairness, I'm not the only one.

Everyone is staring at him with dumbstruck awe, even half the men in here. He may be a coldhearted, intolerable jerk, but there is something irresistibly broken about him that ensnares everyone within his radius.

I take a seat, setting up my laptop and saying good morning while introducing myself to the people on either side of me, who are both interns as well. Nate works for Lamar and Hope works in makeup. Finally, when I can put it off no longer, I plaster a sugary sunshine smile on my face and find my boss, who is across the room, looking like someone kicked his thunderbolt until he electrocuted himself.

Still, I feel a tingle in places I won't mention when his gaze licks a murderous path over me. My hair. My lips. My neck. The sweetheart neckline that clings perfectly to my breasts. I give him a *you told me to change* flutter of my lashes. He's not amused. Not even a tiny bit, and while this was my goal—evidently my past of being tossed about like I'm nothing has made me spiteful—I suddenly realize with his blatant ire that I might be fucking with my endgame.

The shame of it?

I like his ire. I like his attention. I like his dark eyes narrowed in on me. I love the way I piss him off because that means I get a rise out of him, whether good or bad. I frankly don't care which right now, because honestly, both are good in some twisted way. If he's attracted to me, he hates it and wants to destroy its very essence within him. The problem with that? I am its very essence, and that means I go down with the ship.

I'm playing stupid games I have no business playing.

I told him I was going to be professional and right now, I'm being anything but.

Clearing my throat, I uncross and recross my legs, focusing on the slides both on my screen and on the SMART board by the front of the room. I ignore the man who simply put is impossible to ignore. But I make one hell of a valiant effort at it. And as person after person drones on and Lamar argues with some woman over florals versus solid colors, I get better at it.

Or it's that he's doing the same with me and I'm not feeling the pressure of our volley.

"Maybe add some textures instead to give the colors more depth and movement since that's what you're afraid you'll miss by not doing florals," is out of my mouth before I even realize I've spoken.

"What was that?" Zax sharply cuts in, even though I am speaking to Lamar and Martina.

It's so silent in here, you can hear a pin drop. I'm getting the impression interns are meant to be seen and not heard. Slowly, I glance up from the screen and over at Zax, who does not look pleased to find me speaking.

"Texture," I reiterate, refusing to cower under his withering stare. "We're talking about solids in pale and bright colors and that's beautiful. But it has to be on the right fabric to really make it pop and with texture, you can take it to the next level. High-sheen satin, crepe silks, crinkle finished cottons, and even some suede or leather accents without making it appear too autumn/winterish. The Monroe dress I'm wearing right now is a simple chiffon and it's stunning, but the texture makes all the difference. Things like that will allow the colors to stand out more and add an extra element to the designs."

"Yes! Thank you," Lamar says, waving a hand in my direction while staring at Martina, only to slam it down on the table like a judge's gavel calling the final verdict. "That's what the fuck I've been saying. Solid doesn't have to be boring when done right. Texture and design. That's what we do, bitches. We fucking design."

The room erupts into more discussion, and I do my best to participate. Only, I note I'm the only intern who does. A point proven when Nate leans over to me and whispers, "I give you so much credit. His last intern had a nervous breakdown and quit after she spoke up in a meeting like this."

My eyes bug out of my head, and I turn to face him. "What do you mean?"

"You heard about her, right?"

I nod.

"Well, I think she was trying to be a shark in a pool of clownfish, but she sat here for five minutes, telling everyone how wide-leg pants make all women look fat and that we need to be trendsetters and return to skinny jeans so women can stop hating themselves."

"Wow. That's a serious argument. I will admit, I miss the skinnies like an empty nester. They were my babies. But I'm loving the high-waist and how it gives beautiful curvature to women's hips. I think wide legs have their place with the right top and I disagree that women of all shapes and sizes don't look fabulous in them. Plus, I legit hate the word fat."

"Agreed and I think we'll see a resurgence of the skinny in the form of not so tapered at the ankle, but anyway, she argued with both Lamar and Mr. Monroe for those five minutes and then Mr. Monroe chewed her out privately in his office after the meeting. She up and moved west after that."

"Damn. So you're saying I'm about to get my ass chewed out by the big boss?"

"Possibly. Just remember, mama said there'd be days like this. You wouldn't look good in plastic overalls or whatever those things are the fisher-people wear."

I giggle under my breath, springing back to the room as the sound of a piercing whistle cuts me off.

"It's solids," Zax announces, his sharp voice slicing through the room and the growing argument. "Enough of this back and forth. Sweet. Fun. Playful. Sexy. All of that for the next spring/summer women's line. But we're done with flowers."

Martina pouts but wisely keeps her mouth shut.

"I want final mockups showing colors and textures by next week. We're on limited time to get them done before fall fashion week."

Textures? Did he just say textures?

"Andrew, where are we with our men's line?"

The meeting continues on. The entire next spring/summer line for both men and women is hashed over and weeded out. It's an ongoing, never-ending process because the spring/summer items are worn at fall fashion week the year before. There is a six-month gap between when the clothes are walked on the runway and revealed to the world and when they're released to the world as purchasable items unless you're a celebrity and then you can make any request you want to the designer, and they'll pretty much have it made for you since that draws in publicity.

Fashion has been the only constant in my world since I was a teenager.

I was discovered in a Boston Starbucks, sipping on a hot chocolate, killing time before school when I was approached. I signed a contract with a big modeling agency and then within weeks, I was walking runways and being photographed for websites and magazines.

That's when my mother dumped me.

She cosigned an apartment in New York for me, told me I had to finish high school—a new freaking high school at that since we had been living in Boston—and then she was gone.

I was left to myself, living in New York where I knew no one, going to school, doing my homework, traveling when I was told. I was sixteen and parentless and alone. I constantly lied about my age to other models and designers. But it was all I had, my only love and passion. I can't let it go. Not without the fight of my life.

Which is why when Zax calls me into his office for a second day in a row, I enter ready to give him the fight of *his* life. Until he hits me with a blow I am not expecting.

9

You know the worst part of attraction? It's how insidious it can be. How Machiavellian when it infiltrates. A leech, slowly sucking your blood until you're powerless against it. The way it alters your basic brain chemistry is alarming, filling your mind with dangerous thoughts and desires. A need so fierce, you'd give anything to stop it.

I came in here this morning with a battle plan. A solid mindset I had zero plans of allowing to be derailed. I set this in motion. I brought her up here. I know there was solid, logical reasoning behind that. But one look at her in that dress she was wearing, one email exchange, one dress change, that smart fucking mouth, and I've been... *this*.

I don't even know what this is other than not me.

Christ, I'm so fucking screwed. This woman...

She picked out that dress simply to be the world's biggest cock-tease and prove her point. The way that pink fabric clung to her gorgeous tits. A dress I designed. *My dress*. She was wearing my dress and she looked fucking delicious in it. Cotton candy, I could lick her until she dissolved on my tongue.

I agreed to textures. Openly. I said the words in front of the whole damn room.

At the time, I told myself it was because she was right. That it would make the colors pop—what self-respecting CEO uses that term?—and add an extra layer to the designs.

But now that I'm not looking at her in that sweet as spun sugar dress with her hair all up and playful and begging for my hands to do—

Any other intern. Any other intern. Any other intern.

I've been impossibly hard. All morning. Since I woke up and even before that. But it's not just any other hard-on. It's a hard-on with purpose. With imagery to back it up. It's my traitorous appendage saying *hey, we did this yesterday in your office bathroom, so why not make this a new trend since we like it so much.* It's fantasies of her hair running through my fingers and her quickened breath against my lips and her soft tits pressed to my chest and her needy fucking moans searing a path straight through me.

And the best part? She'll do anything I want her to. Anything I want to do *to* her. Because it's fantasy. Toxic, sick, dangerous fantasy. And so fucking good.

Mentally, I shake myself. This has to stop. Indulging in these fantasies is dangerous. I'm not a horny teenager and certainly not one who loses his head at the hands of a woman. A woman who, admittedly, hates me. Who I don't trust and should hate in return.

I have self-control. I'm a master of it. I'm all fucking self-control all the fucking time.

I clear my thoughts the moment the door opens.

Nothing has ever distracted me from work before. For that alone, I should have fired her. My father and his scheming be damned. The scary part? Lenox determined that the email to Beth ordering Aurelia an internship position here came from me. As in from my email account. As in someone hacked my email. Beth confirmed this when I challenged her on it. With wide eyes and a hand on her pregnant belly, she looked impossibly confused.

"You, Zax. You told me to hire her."

Right. Only I didn't.

Then fucking Aurelia walks in with her longer than long legs everywhere. Maybe this is my father's ploy. Death and ruination by a woman.

Any other intern. Any other intern. Any other intern.

"Interesting dress choice," I say as I hear her sit down. My body, once again, is facing the window and the gloomy Boston day beyond the glass.

"Is it not the appropriate length?" she questions with a feigned innocence that has me grinning.

"I didn't bother examining it on you."

I can all but hear her mentally calling me a liar.

"Are you going to chew me out the way you did your last design intern? Because if you are, I can tell you, it won't have the same outcome as it did with her. I don't like fish."

I spin around, staring at the impossible woman perched on the edge of my desk instead of in the chair opposite my desk as she should be.

"Is that what people are saying about why she left? That I chewed her out for some reason, and she fled?"

She tilts her head, studying my expression with a question in her eyes. "Isn't it?"

"No."

"What did happen then?"

I fold my arms over my chest.

"As your intern, don't I have a right to know why my predecessor left?"

No. She doesn't. But for some reason, it pisses me off that she thinks so little of me. Did I not help her when she was nearly mugged and then injured? Did I not keep her on when every instinct I had was to fire her?

"She was body shaming the models we had picked to showcase wide-leg pants and jeans for a spread in *Vogue*. Two of the four models were full-figured curvy women. She argued with Lamar and me over the pants during our meeting and then followed me in here after, demanding I replace the pants altogether *and* replace the two models with skinnier ones. I told her no. I explained how those women were beautiful and that they looked beautiful in the clothing, which they did. She became irate over this and stormed out."

Her eyebrows shoot up to her hairline. "Seriously? That's what happened?"

I stare blandly at her. It's not my place to tell her that the girl had an eating disorder and couldn't tolerate curves on any woman, much less herself. I can only hope she's in a better mental state out of the world of fashion. Despite preconceived notions of me, I like it when people challenge me as long as they're doing it in a productive, constructive way. Business is business.

The only thing personal here is the woman staring at me as if she's never seen me before.

"Huh." She blinks at me. "Okay then."

"Are you done being a brat and demanding answers you aren't entitled to? I'd like to actually get down to work."

"Yes." Standing, she flips open a notebook and then finally sits in the chair, crossing her legs at the knee. The end of her pen is delicately nestled between her lips as she peers up at me, patiently, quietly—for once—waiting on me to begin. She looks like a version of a woman modeling a nineteen-fifties secretary.

The image is so startlingly sexy, I immediately sit down.

I clear my throat. "You mentioned telling Marie about her shitty shoes. Is that real? Do you know her?"

The pen falls from her lips, eyes startled wide, likely because she hadn't realized I overheard her yelling at her shoe yesterday morning. If she's embarrassed, she doesn't indicate it. "Yes. I know her. I was one of her favorite models. She gifted me those shoes, but now I'm wondering about that being her favorite model thing considering the heel snapped. Why are you asking?"

"Because word on the street is that she's thinking of selling off her business and that includes her warehouse in New York. I'd like to buy it, all of it, but she's impossible to get in touch with. Or was until I dropped your name this morning."

The very edge of her sexy mouth tips up into a smirk. "She doesn't like other humans."

"So I've surmised and frankly, I respect that about her since peopling isn't my favorite activity either. That's why you'll come to New York with me in two weeks and attend the meeting I tentatively managed to set up with her. Plus, I have a meeting with the visual designer to go over layouts for fashion week."

"Really? I get to travel with you to New York?" She scrunches her nose.

I lean back in my chair, my fingers tapping out a rhythm on the edge of my desk. "Is that a problem for you? You are my executive design intern, are you not? That requires you to travel with me when I have important meetings."

"It's fine. It's just..."

"It's just what?"

"Nothing. It's nothing."

"Aurelia," I warn dangerously.

Her hand goes flying up in the air, the pen along with it. "Oh. Crap." She shoots out of her chair, bending over to grapple for the pen.

Her dress goes up, showing off the backs of her toned legs with her pert ass in the air. My cock jumps in my slacks, and I groan, covering my face with my hand. Wondering if I'll ever catch a break with her.

"Sorry," she says and then I hear a bang and then another, "Crap," and then I think she's finally sitting again. "God, I've never been clumsy a day in my life before yesterday. What are you doing to me?"

I could ask you the same question.

"I know I said I wanted us to pretend like today is our first day and that yesterday and our past never happened."

My hand falls to the arm of my chair. "That not working for you?"

She smiles, her lips sweeping wide, showcasing her perfect white teeth. "I'm struggling, but I'll get over it. You're just surprising me up, down, and sideways today and part of that is I didn't think you'd want to travel with me."

I bite back a grin, forcing myself to focus on the main reason she's here and why I'd bring her with me, other than it is technically part of her job to do so. Per Lenox, my father is in California at the moment, but he lives in New York, and I'm curious to see if he'll contact her or try to see her.

"It's not a vacation and it's not personal. This is business."

She holds up a consolatory hand, her pen dangling precariously between two fingers. "I know."

"And yet you're still staring at me like I have three heads."

"It's nothing." She shakes her head, continuing to give me that smile. "I'm great, and I look forward to joining you to help do whatever I can with Marie and with set design for fashion week."

"Fantastic."

She's still smiling at me, giving me a look I can't quite read.

"Why are you still here?"

She laughs in a self-deprecating way. "Right. Sorry." She stands but pauses another minute. "Can I say something? One last thing and then I swear, I'll put all this nonsense behind us and be totally professional?"

I grunt, giving her a bored expression. "If you must."

"You're not as much of an asshole as you try to be."

That takes me aback for a second, though I quickly recover.

"You don't know me well enough to make that assumption."

"Maybe not," she concedes. "But it's still a hunch I've got. Sure, you're rough and callous and generally a dismissive asshole of everyone around you—"

"Glad you're not holding back for me," I interject, still trying to maintain my blasé tone and posture.

"You didn't let me get to the good part. I wasn't finished. I was going to say that I think there could possibly be a suggestion of a living, breathing, decent human beneath all that..." She waves a hand around in the air, gesturing at me. "Exterior."

I quirk an eyebrow. "Exterior?"

She nibbles on the corner of her lip as if she's trying to hide her smile. "I won't flatter you by saying you're hot if that's what you're searching for. *That's* unprofessional."

"And calling your boss an asshole isn't?"

"Maybe. Sorta like demanding someone change their dress for a perceived 'dress code violation.'" She puts air quotes around the words.

And because I can't resist flirting with her, I say, "I was merely searching for clarification on what you meant by exterior. You're the one who called me hot without prompting."

She giggles, thunking the butt of her palm against her forehead. "So I did. Pretend I never used that word."

"We're doing a lot of pretending with each other." Me pretending I'm not attracted to you and enjoying that you think I'm hot and human. You pretending we have no history and that you don't think about me in any way beyond this job.

"We are," she agrees. "I've been told we have chemistry, but I'm thinking it's more like a lab experiment gone wrong. But that doesn't change the fact that I don't think you're as much of an asshole as you'd like to be seen as."

I roll my eyes, sitting up and tapping on my keyboard, dismissing her. "Save it for someone who cares, Pollyanna, and get the hell out of my office before I fire you."

She twirls around like a ballerina, causing the skirt of her dress to flare up and giving me yet another indecent view of her endlessly long legs.

"You won't fire me," she says in a sing-song voice. "You need me for Marie. And you don't scare me, Zax. But you do still make me nervous." She gives me a wink, then practically skips out of my office in those goddamn poke a dot heels.

Zax. She called me Zax. Not Mr. Monroe. "That's not being professional," I call after her.

"I'll work on it," she promises. "You're just so much fun to rile up. Like playing with an irritable bear after hibernation." She closes the door behind her.

I scrub my hands up and down my face. Bears are hungry after hibernation. Doesn't she realize what riling me up and playing with me will get her? Attacked. Pinned to the fucking floor and devoured.

Standing, I head for my bathroom to splash some cold water on my face. Only when I catch my reflection, I pause. I'm smiling. But it's not just any smile. It's an amused smile. And she doesn't think I'm the asshole everyone else—including myself—thinks I am.

My smile slips, and I turn on the faucet, pooling water in my hands and then splashing it across my face. I do this two more times and dry myself off with a fresh towel. It's been one day. Aurelia has no idea who I am, and she never will.

10

ZAXTON

I watch as the summer sky crawls from bright sunshine to glimmering lavender and pink to muted dusk. I've been sitting in my office all fucking day, one call after the other. One fire drill quickly followed another. That's all this week has been. Whereas most industries shut down over the summer or at least slow, fashion never does.

Summer is our busy time heading into fall/winter and winter is our busy time heading into spring/summer.

So as I press end on my last call and stare out the window, knowing I have a night of not fucking much ahead of me because that's how I've planned it, I breathe out the tired breath that's been living in my lungs since I first came on here. Peeling myself up and out of my chair, I cross the room and open my closet.

My bass, Belle—gold and shiny, named by Suzie—is in here and I slip her out and on, tickling the first few chords of "Come Together" by The Beatles, only to need something edgier and morph directly into "Come as You Are" by Nirvana.

This is how I survived high school and likely middle school before that. Music. Playing. Callan, Lenox, Suzie, and I used to get so fucking stoned and spend hours jamming, listening to music and mocking whatever in our lives felt like bullshit. Then when Grey and Asher got older, they joined us, Greyson on his acoustic and then electric, singing along.

And his voice. Fuck, his voice is so good. He made us become real. That holy shit, this isn't a joke and we could become something incredible sorta thing. He did that. He's still that.

And somehow, the five of us guys just coalesced with Suzie running our show.

We wrote songs and performed them and fucked around and it was all so much fun.

We'd just jam. And forget our lives. Grey and I would pretend our mother wasn't dead and our father cared about us and what we did with our time.

Then a video Suzie recorded and randomly decided to post online went viral.

That's all it took.

One thirty-second video for our lives to change. Calls from record labels started pouring in. We hit six million views on that one video, so Suzie started posting others and our stardom blew up past everything else. Tour and record contracts. Top of the charts albums. Award shows—that we won. Fans. Millions of them. We were stalked and followed and obsessed over.

We were compared to Bieber and One Direction with a pop, alternative sound like Silversun Pickups and The Cure. We were a vibe. Our own. And it was fun. So much fun. Grey and Asher had tutors and then got their GREs. Callan and I did our online college thing. Lenox and Suzie wanted it all to last forever.

Then one Friday morning, it all changed. I was flying so high. I had it all. The girl. The music. The life. A father who was no longer part of my life nor Greyson's. Suzie and I had made the choice and I was ready for it, even if she wasn't.

Staring down at Belle, I finish the song and immediately go into "Hear You Me" by Jimmy Eat World. It's what I played at her funeral since words weren't going to be possible. I don't know what it is about today that has me breathing so heavily, but I can't stop it. The flashes. The memories. The hurt. The way I miss her.

I begin to sing the lyrics, but then I'm lost. Lost in that day.

"You're sure about this?" she asked me. "It's a big deal, Zax, and I'm sure we can figure something else out."

"I'm positive," I replied, wrapping her around me and kissing her forehead. "Grey isn't a baby anymore. Neither is Callan or Ash. They don't need me like they used to."

"Maybe."

"No. No maybe. It's time, Suz. This was never going to be my thing. Not forever."

She pushed up, her green eyes on mine. "I wanted it to be forever."

My lips pressed into her nose, and I hugged her tighter. "It still can be. Nothing says you can't continue to manage them. I told you, I'm fine with that. We're a team and if that's what you want, that's what you should do. I'm the one who's done."

"No. I know. I thought that's what I wanted too, but now..." She sighed. "I have to think about it. I'm not sure what Lenox will do or how he'll take it if I leave."

I nod because what we're talking about doing is no small thing. It's been our lives for the last four years. "We'll tell them everything tonight at your birthday party. It'll be fine. It'll be great. I'm so fucking excited about this. This is the next chapter of our lives."

"I know. Me too. First, I need a shower."

"Agreed. You stink."

She laughed, smacking my shoulder. "So do you. Come shower with me. It's my birthday. You can't say no to me."

I started to kiss her, my hands in her hair, holding her to me. "We could do this first."

"We have a busy day."

"Fuck our busy day. You're my day. I want you first."

She kissed me back and we made love. Quick, but sweet because that's all we had time for. I watched as she walked to the shower. I watched as she winced and rubbed her temple, then covered it all with a smile that didn't reach her eyes when she noticed I saw. And something hit me. Hit me hard.

A strange sensation I couldn't make sense of. Like I was watching every-thing from outside my body. Watching her that way.

I hesitated. My gut and brain were screaming at me. They were telling me something wasn't right about that. That something was off. And deep down, I think I knew it. I just brushed it off. Told myself I was overtired and overthinking and nervous about everything that was happening because it was all big. Because that's what you do.

You brush things off. Especially when you're twenty-four and everything in your life is perfect.

"I love you," I called out to her as if that would assuage every ounce of anxiety I was suddenly feeling.

"I love you more."

The shower started in our hotel room and I sprang up and went directly for my suitcase. My hand closed over the box, and I opened it up. A smile lit my face as I stared at the diamond ring I'd wanted to give her for weeks but was waiting for her birthday to surprise her with.

Then I went to the bathroom. That's when I heard the thud. That motherfucking thud. The one that still reverberates through my skull.

Compressions. Shouts. Sirens. Lights. Me holding Lenox back. Grey holding me back. Asher and Callan losing their fucking minds. *"She's gone."*

She's gone.

She's gone.

She's gone.

A stroke at twenty-two. And only I know why it happened.

A soft tap on my door jars me out of my thoughts and my eyes snap open. "Yes?" My voice sounds like my soul, dead.

The door opens and in walks Aurelia Whitlock. Her long, plat-inum hair swishing around her narrow shoulders and down her back. Her face—more luminescent than a renaissance painting and more radiant than the morning sun.

"I thought I heard you still in here. I'm sorry. I hope I didn't bother your playing." She eyes Belle and my fingers still on the strings and frets.

She did, but thank God for that interruption, even if it's her.

"It's fine. What do you need?"

She shifts her weight, her gaze getting in on the motion.

"What?" I bark.

"Dinner?"

"Huh?"

A smirk. "You haven't left your office all day and Thalia was out. Did you eat lunch?"

"No."

"It's nearly eight. Can I order you something or are you leaving?"

I stare at her for a very long few seconds. Wondering if this is part of an agenda or her simply being the sweet, thoughtful woman everyone here thinks she is. It's not hard to see how she's already friends with everyone and they adore her.

Was this something my father asked her to do? Cozy up to me?

"I'm an adult, Aurelia. If I want food, I'll order it or make it. What are you still doing here this late on a Friday? Isn't everyone else already gone? You trying to win intern of the month?"

Was she waiting for me to leave so she could snoop around in my office?

She blinks at me and musters some pissed off strength that's such a turn-on it's almost fantastical as she saunters into my office like she owns both it and me.

"You've been avoiding me all week and here it is Friday," she accuses. "And yes, I stayed for a reason. I've emailed you and you respond through Beth or Thalia. I've been going to Lamar, but there are a few key design things I don't want to brush off. I wanted to discuss them with you, but since you were on the phone all day with your door closed and weren't responding to my emails, I had no choice but to wait for you."

Oh. Well then. Maybe not trying to stay late to snoop? I hate that I think this way about her. I hate that I care about her motives. I hate that she's working up here with me and that I have to watch her because I don't trust her.

"You plan that speech?" I'm being a dick and I know it. But being a dick feels good and wrong and right, and I want her to call me out on it. I want her to tell me I'm being a dick and open that smart fucking mouth at me. I tug Belle up and over my head, placing her gently back into her case and locking it up. Aurelia follows my every move while trying to stay fierce. She's merely a sweet kitten with soft claws playing in the lion's den.

"I might have."

"What's your issue?"

Another step and she closes the door and I hate that she did that. Even if it's likely just us left here. A closed door is asking for sin and ruin and sucks for her, but both of those are my middle name.

"Are you in too much of a mood to do this?" she questions. "I know it's late, but we need to have the final drafts of this by Monday morning. I was going to offer to order in dinner and show you my grievance, but if you'd rather do it first thing Monday morning…"

I'd smirk, but I don't have the desire. "You trying to read me now? How about you just say what you came in here to say and save the theatrics for someone who gives a fuck."

A head tilt and I'd swear she's grinning at me. "Fine. You wanna do it like this, we'll do it like this. I hate the colors Martina picked out to go with the approved fabrics and designs. Especially for the women's casual wear line. She's pushing them to press but…"

"But what?" I challenge when she falls silent, hands on her hips.

"Listen, I know I'm new. I know it's my first week and I know you not only don't like me, you likely don't give two shits about what I have to say. But… you're not fucking Lily Pulitzer."

"Meaning?"

"Meaning you don't do vibrant pastels, Mr. Monroe. You agreed on colors and textures for these fabrics, and she's been fighting with all of us all week. She said you signed off on it."

I did no such thing and why am I just hearing about this now? *Because you've been hiding in here and ignoring her.*

"Does Lamar know she's pushing vibrant pastels?"

"Yes. And he flipped. She downplayed it in our last meeting he was in, but then this morning she was all about it, saying you approved it after Nate and I challenged her. She said if we didn't do it like this, it would be the biggest fashion mistake since Hammer pants."

"Hammer pants?" coughs past my lungs.

"Yeah. You know—"

I hold up my hand, stopping her. "I know what they are. But I didn't think anyone still referenced them."

Aurelia throws her hands up, then sits on the arm of a chair on the other side of my desk. "Well, what can I tell you, boss? She did. Hammer pants because that's likely what she wore in the early nineties. She swore not using pastels for this line would be an even bigger mistake, but I'm pretty positive using pastels would be. This line is not for that color scheme, and I need to know if you actually did sign off on this. Because if you did, I'll try and shut my mouth. Maybe." Her head bobs the other way. "Likely not. But if you didn't..."

Is Martina the one my father called to get Aurelia in here? She has pull. She could access my email if she snuck into my office. And she's done shit like this before. One other time she tried to circumvent Lamar and me on something. We didn't catch it in time, and it was a disaster we had to scramble around and fix. I ripped into her, and she was furious with me about it. Told me I needed to trust her judgment on things more than micromanaging everything and everyone.

Hmmm. Motive? Only my head is spinning with going through all the options. Yet another name to shoot over to Lenox for him to check out when so far no one has come up dirty.

"I didn't approve that."

She blows out a breath. "Thank God. I'm not complimenting or kissing your ass, but every other piece for this line is fantastic. Those colors would destroy them. I saw the swatches this afternoon and they're terrible."

Today she's wearing an emerald-green skirt that hits her knees and a pearl-white sleeveless silk blouse that reveals a hint of her lacy bra beneath. I know Lamar fashioned her into it this morning because that motherfucker sends me pics of his redesign every goddamn morning to make sure I 'approve' of the length of her dress or skirt.

Yet another thing I wish I could go back in time and change.

I've done a fantastic job of ignoring Aurelia while not ignoring her at all. The amount of time I've spent watching her from my office without her knowledge or during meetings is borderline stalker territory. I tell myself I'm doing my due diligence. That I'm keeping the close eye that is the reason she's up here in the first place.

I tell myself it has nothing to do with how Lamar has taken to making her his own personal model, complete with daily wardrobe changes as well as hair styling and makeup alterations. The staff loves her. Thalia raves about her and my assistant raves about no one. Aurelia brought in homemade grain-free, gluten-free blueberry-lemon muffins for the shoot yesterday—sounds like tasteless hockey pucks to me—that even a few of the models ate after she promised them they were loaded with fiber and low on fat. Nate, Lamar's intern, follows her around like a puppy, doing everything he can to make her smile and laugh. She spends most of her time with him, along with two other people. Howie, a designer downstairs, and some female marketing intern I don't know. They all eat lunch together most days.

I know all this. Because I watch her compulsively. Obsessively.

And here she is, tracking me down after I've stayed in my office working all day. She's right. I fucking hate pastels.

"Show me."

"Yes, sir."

And what the fuck is that? Yes, sir. It makes my dick hard every damn time she says it. It's as if she knows I want to command her. Own her. Possess her pleasure. Her looking at me with those pretty eyes and saying those words? I don't even command women into submission. Not typically. I never did that with Suzie. And it's not something I seek out now because that's a whole other production. I go to the club—not that I've done that in a few months—and I find someone available and easy, and that's all I've cared about.

But that *yes, sir* from her lips...

I stand and I don't even know why, so I shift over to the window, so I don't have to look at her. "Should we order food? Since you feel I'm nutritionally deprived."

"I. Ah..."

I spin back around. "Is there a problem?"

"I was actually going to drop that bomb, tell you that you needed to eat, and flee."

I laugh. A real laugh. One that hits me hard and fast and is uncontainable. I lean back against the window and fold my arms. "Is that so?"

She's smiling back at me, playing with a piece of her hair in a move that isn't meant to be seductive, but sure as hell is anyway. "I didn't think you'd want to eat with me, and I wasn't trying to insinuate myself into your Friday night dinner plans. I just figured you had to be hungry after not eating all day."

"I don't have Friday night dinner plans. But if you do, feel free to show me whatever Martina did to my clothes and go."

"My big plans are going to be spent with pizza, the remaining boxes I have to unpack, and watching a true crime documentary with a glass of wine. I only have one real female friend in this city and Iris is visiting her parents this weekend."

My body pulses with an idea. An idea to order in food and spend the night here with her, eating, talking, hiding away from the world... Then there's the other idea. The idea of what comes after all that.

I shut it down and change the subject. "Do you regret that you're here and not back in New York?"

She giggles lightly under her breath. "I didn't have a lot of friends in New York either."

Only she knows that's not what I'm asking, so I wait her out, wanting a real answer.

Her gaze drops, staring sightlessly at my desk as she contemplates my question. She stands, walking over to my bookcase and adjusting a picture I have on there of me with the guys that was taken back in February after Asher won the Super Bowl. Fingers glide over my smiling face as she takes it in, then she turns back to me.

"No. I don't regret that I'm here. Iris is here and she's my person. My only real person. Plus, I grew up in Boston and it's always sort of felt like home in a way, even when I never exactly had a permanent home here. I'm grateful, Zax. I like being here. I like your company. The people and the designs and the fact that input is valued. I like that you're honest with me. I haven't had a lot of that in my life and I appreciate it more than you know."

I have so many more questions about her just from that. I'm tempted to ask them all because I want her to keep talking. I want her to keep looking at me as she does. She'd answer them for me. I know she would. She's not someone who is meant to be so alone. She's meant to be surrounded by people. People who are good to her and would take care of her.

I'm not those people. I'm not those people for anyone anymore.

"Are you here because of your dad or because you like this?" she asks, snapping me back.

I falter. She sees it. "No one has ever asked before."

She doesn't so much as twitch a muscle.

"I don't know," I admit truthfully. "I went to business school and got my MBA and dicked around with investing in some startups that did well. Then my father pulled some shit, and I was asked to step in and take over."

"And here you are."

"Here I am." Looking at you. Thinking about you. All your complicated mess that has somehow become my complicated mess. Only it's now that I realize looking at her and thinking about her has become the best part of my day. I spent a week doing little else. For better or worse, she's the first thing to wake me up in eight years.

"You're good at it," she tells me as if it's a promise. A vote of confidence in case I was thinking of quitting it all now.

"I hire the wrong people."

She laughs, treating me to an expression that stirs my blood as she joins me at the window, peering out at the darkening sky. "You didn't hire me."

"Who did?"

A heavy sigh. "I don't know. I wish I did and I'm sorry I don't have more of the information you need because I know you need it. I haven't talked to your father since that dinner in New York. I know you're wondering about that too. You're the CEO and my boss, and I hope you trust that I'm not here to hurt you or this company. I'm here for a fresh start."

Her words along with her scent and proximity slither along my skin and seep into my pores. The need to believe her is piercingly strong. She affects me so acutely. It's why I've physically avoided her all week even if I never took my eyes off her.

Thoughts spin through my head. Is she as tangled with need as I am whenever I'm near her? What would happen if I leaned in and kissed her? If I pressed her up against the glass, slid up her skirt, and fucked her right here in my office?

I go crazy at night. Thinking about the color of her nipples and how they would taste on my tongue. Wondering what her pussy and cum would feel like on my cock. Is she loud? Quiet? Would she prefer my fingers or tongue or both? Is she the close her eyes or stare into your soul when you're inside her type?

Somehow I'm closer to her. Somehow I'm nearly touching her.

She doesn't turn to look at me, but I can see what this is doing to her. Her breathing. The rise and fall of her breasts in her blouse. The slight parting of her lips. The way her fingers are now pressed into the cool glass as if she needs something to ground her. This woman has a hold on me unlike anything. And after my long day and my thoughts of Suzie...

I lean into her ear and whisper, "Go home, Aurelia. Email me everything you think I need to see, but for fuck's sake, go home. Now." Before I carry out everything that's tearing through my mind. Before I rip everything, the only thing, I have a strong hold on apart.

A hard swallow. And then her eyes are on mine, staring straight into me from less than a foot away. "Good night, Zax." Without another word, she spins on her heels and flees my office, and I wonder how long my self-control with her will hold before it snaps.

AURELIA

"**D**id you hear?" Nate comes rushing over to me as I'm setting my things down Monday morning, quickly glancing around to make sure we're alone. "Martina was fired."

"What?"

He nods, still searching around, but it's relatively early and most people haven't arrived yet. "Lamar texted me this morning. We have a big all-hands meeting at nine. Do you think it's because of the pastels?"

"I don't know," I murmur, feeling bad that I might have possibly gotten her fired. That certainly wasn't my intent, even if she wasn't the nicest. And had zero fashion sense.

"I'm not complaining. She was a b to the itch. And a liar since we all know Mr. Monroe didn't sign off on anything. When I told Lamar she said that, he went batshit on the phone with me for an hour. He must have called Mr. Monroe over the weekend and told him. Clearly, since she's now gone."

"Right. Um."

"What?"

"I told Mr. Monroe Friday night about the pastels. Do you think this is my fault?"

He snorts. "No, Aurelia. I think it's Martina's fault. You know, since she was the one doing the lying along with the pastels."

My phone chimes with a text and I pick it up to see it's from Lamar.

CLOSET NOW!

"Wow," Nate muses, reading over my shoulder. "Those are some shouty caps."

"I'm assuming this is for my daily wardrobe change."

"You should start showing up to work in yoga pants and a T-shirt. Might make your mornings easier." He eyes my eyelet white capri pants, lavender billowy blouse, and up twisted hair.

I laugh. He's probably right. "Eventually, Lamar will grow tired of playing Dress-Up Daisy with me, right?"

"Nah. You're Dress-Up Lia. He gets to prove a fashion point with you while living out his jealousies and desires through you. Besides, I don't think he does this for you, if you know what I mean."

"Actually, I don't know what you mean?" I quickly challenge as I stand, hoping he's not inferring something about Zax. No one knows about our past and I don't think anyone knows about the strange undercurrent sizzling between us since we both go out of our way to hide it and ignore it. Especially whenever we're around anyone else.

"Aurelia, he's flipping off the visual marketing team who never seem to hire a model up to his standards. You're the first and they didn't even hire you. He stumbled upon you in the lobby."

"Lamar never mentioned that to me."

Nate takes a sip of his coffee and gives me a *well, now you do* shrug. "I've been here two years. You look fucking hot in everything he puts you in and he wants to show that off." Nate scoots off the corner of my desk—practically spilling his coffee—just before I can shove him off. His hand flies out toward me, warning me off. "Don't shoot the messenger. I'm just saying, you're a beautiful woman and model, Aurelia. Nothing wrong with that."

"There is when that's all people see of me," I counter.

"Fine. Maybe there is more to your story than your pretty face. Maybe your pretty face is a smoke screen few choose to look beyond. But if it helps sell some of our clothes?" A shrug before he spins. "I'll see you at the meeting. Let us pray we make it out of there with our jobs!" He crosses himself and then is off to his desk on the other side of the floor.

"You're Jewish," I yell after him.

"We need all the help we can get. Jews don't have a symbol like that, and Jesus was a Jew until he wasn't."

Man might have a point.

Begrudgingly, I head for the elevator, pressing the call button and staring down at my phone as I type one-handedly back and forth with Iris. Taking a sip of my Diet Coke, the elevator doors open and before I can take my first step, I'm knocked back completely. So hard I fall flat on my ass and back. My can of soda shoots out of my hand, flying high in the air and landing on the carpet beside me. Liquid immediately spills out, seeping along the fibers and into my hair. That's when everything else hits me.

Donuts.

An entire box of them.

Covered in frosting and sprinkles and sugar glaze. Filled with jelly and custard.

All of them on me.

"Fuck!"

A voice I don't recognize. I blink up at the ceiling. *What the hell, Mondays?!*

"Holy fuck of fuckers."

"Agreed," I grumble.

"Are you okay?"

I blink and then scowl.

"Shit. Right. Of course you're not okay. You're covered in donuts and Diet Coke. Silver lining? At least I didn't drop the coffee. Think of the burns."

I half sit, only for someone to grasp my hand and help me the rest of the way up. A face in my vision as the donut assassin crouches before me.

"For real, I'm so sorry. I didn't see you there. Are you actually okay? Did I hurt you?"

"I've never been so wet and sticky in my life. And before you go there..." I start cracking up. "Hell, I just said that, didn't I?"

He's laughing too. And his smile is so damn cute. Boyish and loaded with dimples and sparkling, crazy-colored eyes. "You did. I won't even pretend my mind didn't go straight to the gutter with it. That's classic." I feel a finger swipe something that is likely frosting from my face and watch as he pops the digit into his mouth, licking it clean. "Delicious."

I'd blush if I did that sort of thing. "That's a total player move."

"It might be. That bother you?"

"You mean the fact you're flirting with a girl who has pink frosting and Diet Coke making a love child in her hair? I'm a total catch right now. How could you not flirt?"

He falls onto the clean side of the floor beside me, clutching his chest. "And I'm dead. Like right here."

"Death by donuts and caffeine. I think I'll join you."

A handsome smirk against his gray, sparkling eyes. "I've been told there are worse ways to go."

"Me too. But I think I win for today."

"Nah, babe. We both win. You're all wet and sticky, and I'm the one who made you that way."

My hands cover my face as I start laughing uncontrollably. "Oh, you went there, Mr. One Upper."

"I did and it was bonus round material. Can I help you up, Lia?"

"Aurelia," I correct.

"Ah. Okay. Do you know who I am?" Before I can stop him, he's pulled me upright, dragging clumps of confections from my hair and knocking them off my shoulders.

"Asher Reyes," I answer, still half-laughing. "Championship winning quarterback for the Boston Rebels. I met you once upon a time before we were this."

"I remember, Cinderella." He gives me a wink. "You're far more stunning now, though. May I say, age and puberty have made you a knockout?"

"Stop flirting."

"Against my basic nature. Where were you headed before I derailed your morning?" He bends down, flipping open the white with pink and orange writing box and combing the remains of the donuts off the floor and back into it.

"Costume change."

He peeks up at me through his thick, black lashes. "Is it time for the ball already?"

I smile down at him. This man is incorrigible. "So it seems. But Lamar likes me to wear Monroe couture he personally picks out, and for once, I'm not going to complain." I stare down at my ruined blouse and then wince at the chocolate frosting and red jelly stains on my white capri pants. These were my favorites and no amount of praying or Jesus is going to get those stains out.

"May I join you?" He stands upright, walking over to the large waste bin in the corner by the elevator and dumping everything in it. "I was coming to find Zax, but I'm supposed to be where you are, I think, since today is my fashion model day. Not to mention nothing will piss him off more than if I'm somewhere flirting with you, and half my life is spent trying to get a rise out of that man."

"I never agreed to the flirting."

He takes me by the arm, pressing the button for the elevator that dings and opens for us immediately. "That's because you haven't been flirted up by the right man." He guides me on.

"Is that so?"

"More than so. It's fact." We turn to face the front and there is Zax, scowling at us like a madman. "Morning, bro. I'm escorting your lovely Aurelia down for a costume change. You missed it. We just had the best meet-cute we'll tell our grandchildren about one day. I guess it's true what they say about the early bird." He winks at Zax. "Wouldn't you agree?"

The doors shut and then we're shooting down to the twentieth floor.

"Did you see his face?" He leans in and whispers to me, though, we're the only ones on here.

"He doesn't like me very much."

Asher stares incredulously at me for a moment and then a knowing smile peels his lips wide. "Doll, you know that's not true, right? Zax's problem is that he doesn't *want* to like you. You're his intern and his ex-stepsister and frankly, an unknown. But now that I see you in the donut-coated flesh, I get what all the fuss is about."

I shake my head at him. "I'm not sure I'm following."

"Maybe that's for the best. But I'll bet you my Super Bowl ring he'll be joining us on the shoot floor in less than ten minutes."

The doors open and Lamar is right there waiting for us. "You're late—Ahhh!" he screams. "What the fuckity fuck is this disaster?"

"This is Asher Reyes," I introduce, waving a hand toward Asher and making him crack up again. "But I don't think it's fair to call him a disaster."

"Woman, do not test my patience right now." Lamar fingers a piece of my hair, then drops it just as quickly with a shudder, his expression one of pure, abject horror. "Do I want to know?"

"Donuts and Diet Coke. Please don't ask. But can I take a shower before you beauty me up?"

"Yes. Please. Now. I can't stand this sight for another second. The showers are in the back of the bathroom. Go and I'll have something waiting for you when you get out. But move quickly because we're on the clock. We cannot be late for this meeting."

"So I've been told. Bye, Asher." I give him a wave. "It's been interesting."

"Bye, Aurelia. I certainly hope I get to see you again soon." He takes my hand and kisses the back of it.

I head for the ladies' room, anxious to get clean since I feel nothing short of nasty. I shower quickly, wrapping a towel around myself as I go searching for whatever Lamar said he was going to leave for me, only there's nothing here. No clothes other than my sticky, wet, soiled ones. Clutching my towel tightly to my chest, I tiptoe out of the bathroom, peeking left and right.

"Lamar?" I call out and then spin around when I hear the soft tap of men's shoes. Only it isn't Lamar. "What are you doing here?" I ask Zax, blinking up at him.

"Delivering your clothes." He holds up the garment bag and stops directly before me. His electric gaze, charged like the sky right before a thunderstorm, is all over me. My neck. My bare shoulders. The point where the towel meets my chest and the slight swell of my cleavage above it.

"You're staring," I tease, only it's not a tease. It's a truth and a dare all in one.

Suddenly, I feel like I'm melting from his heat, the drops of water still clinging to my skin instantly evaporating. I've never reacted this way to anyone before and I certainly never expected it to happen with Zax, but now it feels like no matter what I do, there is no getting around it.

A muscle twitches in his jaw, the fingers on his hand hanging by his side, tapping out a rhythm against his thigh. Something I've noticed him do often. He doesn't speak nor does he hand me the bag. I could take it from him and go, but this look... this look is too good to let go of.

"What's the outfit?" I ask when I can't take this another second.

I expect him to say something crude. Something brusque. Like, how the fuck should I know or what do I care. But instead, he shocks me with, "It's a fitted white midi dress with a square neckline and red belt accent."

"Oh." I swallow thickly at his gravelly voice. "Sounds beautiful."

Another long once-over, his eyes snagging on my hand that's holding my towel up and then back up to my eyes. "I have no doubt it will be."

Jesus. He keeps this up and I'm going to drop the towel just so I can see those eyes darken further, that expression grow hungrier. I was two hot seconds from falling to my knees for him in his office Friday night. I'm like a chick in a porno with him about to ask him to come inside and fix my cable box.

Then it hits me. What Asher said about him being down here within ten minutes after seeing us. How he doesn't want to like me but that doesn't mean there isn't something still brewing beneath the surface. I'd have to be dead not to see and feel it. Hell, I can practically taste it.

But that doesn't mean it's safe or sane or smart. If anything, it's the opposite.

"Thank you, Mr. Monroe," I say, reaching up and grabbing the bag from his hand, making sure our fingers don't touch. "I appreciate you delivering my dress for me. I should get changed. I don't want to be late for your big meeting." I turn to go but then think better of it and twist back to him. "You fired Martina."

It's not a question, but he nods all the same. "She wasn't trustworthy."

Simple as that.

"Okay."

Now I turn to go when his voice stops me. "And, Aurelia? Stay away from Asher. You're not his friend and you're sure as hell not modeling with him." With that, he walks off, practically storming, though his pace is nothing but casual. Or maybe I'm the one storming as indignation flares up inside me. This man. If I could throttle him, I would. I can't even yell something back at him because he's my freaking boss.

"Jerk," I hiss under my breath and then go and change because I'm cold standing here now that he's taken all his body heat with him. The dress fits like a glove, not provocative in the least, but still has something about it that screams sexy.

Lamar is finally waiting for me when I exit and he grabs my arm, dragging me over to hair and makeup and practically shoving me into the chair.

"Why are we still doing this?" I ask as he pulls out the blow-dryer, something I'm more than capable of doing myself.

Lamar's dark eyes meet mine in the reflection of the mirror. "Because a man's blood needs to boil every now and then, and when you learn the secret to keeping his inner fire lit, you don't squander it."

"Am I supposed to know what that means?"

"You're a liar if you tell me you don't. Now let's hurry. The man is waiting on us upstairs."

12

AURELIA

I don't see Zax for the rest of the week. Okay, maybe that's an exaggeration. I mean, I do see him. He's my boss and his office is not even twenty feet from mine. But we have no more one-on-one time and I only catch him in random meetings where he completely and utterly ignores me.

If he has to email me about something, it's still being passed through Thalia or Beth. I help go through the textures and colors I feel will be most eye-catching and flattering and different—I'm going with a sea nymph vibe that will make any tan all the more gorgeous and any hair color radiant. I love this job.

There. I said it.

I freaking do.

It's *everything* I imagined when I decided I wanted to be a designer.

Sure, it's stressful and there is some cattiness and cliques, but tell me a place there isn't. Besides, after modeling for seven years and going to college, I'm more than used to that. In these two weeks, I've helped design clothes that will be on men's and women's bodies next spring/summer. Not to mention, I've made some good friends here.

No one has brought up the photo shoot or the fact that Lamar dresses me for the runway every day. Not one person.

And they like me. They accept me as Aurelia.

Nate, Howie, Iris, and I eat lunch together every day and shoot the shit in between. Now that it's Friday, the four of us are having drinks out tonight. Heaven!

Thalia gave me the schedule for our trip to NYC next week and not only are we staying at the Ritz Carlton, Central Park, but we're eating at some restaurants I never even dreamed of dining in. It doesn't tell me who else is included on this trip, but we have a two-hour long session with the manager and the head physical and elements designer Monroe Fashion has hired to bring their show to life.

I'm excited. I'm stupidly excited and insanely jealous. I've seen some of the mockups of what Monroe has planned for fashion week and I want to walk in the show. I know, I'm trying to be seen as Aurelia Whitlock, serious design intern instead of Lia Sage, fashion model, but come on. We're talking about fashion week and we're talking about stunningly gorgeous clothes I'm personally working on.

And maybe... yes, I will admit... part of me wants to stick it to Valencci.

I want to show her she didn't beat me. That she swung one hell of a sucker punch, but it wasn't a knockout punch.

"What are we cheersing to?" Nate shouts over the rancorous bar crowd as he holds up his shot glass, staring at it as if the thing just grew horns and sharp teeth and bit his finger off. "Wait. This is tequila. I don't do tequila."

"It's good tequila," Howie promises. "It's not bitch tequila. You can do it."

Nate doesn't look so sure.

"Last time I had tequila, I woke up in the emergency room only wearing a diaper."

"Say whaaaaat?" Iris blinks ten thousand times at him.

"It was freshman year of college, and I was pledging for a frat."

"Are you doing that now?" I toss out at him.

I get a *don't be ridiculous* look in response. "No."

"Then slow your uptight roll," Iris shoots back. "No one is making you drink more than you should. It's called adulting and while it sucks Monday through Friday, Friday nights are our playground and we're entitled to have fun. But fun isn't synonymous with dumb even if they do quasi rhyme."

"Right," Howie exclaims, licking the salt off his hand. "What she said. Now drink."

"Shit," Nate hisses.

"Let's go," I squeal, foregoing the salt and wolfing down the clear liquid like a championship hot dog eater on the Fourth of July. I pop a lime into my mouth and do a little twirl in my shimmery gold dress. This isn't a Monroe dress I'm wearing, it's mine, but occasionally I've taken to shopping in the closet. It's been a bonding experience for me and Lamar, and Zax can't complain since it's his clothes. Not that he's complained since that second first day.

He'd have to acknowledge my existence for that.

"Fuck," Nate breathes out. "That... well, I guess it wasn't harsh." He smacks his lips. "Another?"

Howie holds up his hand, stopping him before he can signal the bartender. "One more shot and then regular alcohol. I have to pace myself. If I come home drunk, my girlfriend won't be too happy and then I won't get laid."

"Fuck," Nate groans morosely. "Sex. Remember that? I hardly do. That's how long it's been. Whenever I tell women I work in fashion or for Monroe, they automatically think I'm gay."

"I thought you were gay," Iris admits.

"Shit," Nate breathes out, smacking his hand on the top of our table, rattling our empty shot glasses. "That seriously sucks. Just because a man knows fashion and dresses well, does not make him gay. How am I supposed to ever have sex again with this job?"

"You find the right girl," I tell him.

"Yes. That," Howie agrees, signaling over our waitress and even though he said we were switching to regular alcohol, he goes and orders another two rounds instead of one. Likely thinking Nate needs it. "I used to have the same problem, but then I met Greta and she's great. She assumed that since I was hitting on her, I liked women. You'll find a girl like that too."

"It's been about six months since I've seen action. Miserable."

I pat Nate's shoulder.

"I love sex," he continues, practically leaning on the sticky table. "I'm amazing at it. I always get the woman off at least once before I come."

"Good man," Iris says. "But everyone loves sex. You just have to find the right person, like Howie did."

"Zaxton Monroe doesn't love sex," Nate counters.

And at the mention of his name, I choke on... nothing. Absolutely nothing. I brush it off with a cough, but Iris isn't fooled for a second. I get a raised eyebrow that I immediately return with a wide eye shut it glare. She turns back to Nate. "What do you mean Zax doesn't love sex?"

"Well, he hasn't had it in like eight years, right?"

Iris snorts out an incredulous laugh. "You can't possibly believe that nonsense. No man goes eight years without sex unless they're a priest or a monk or in prison and I'm not even going there with the priest or prisoner thing. He just has to be very good at hiding it."

Howie shakes his head, leaning back in his stool. "No one who gets any sort of regular action is that much of a dick. And why hide it if he is? His girlfriend died tragically. It's been nearly a decade. I think by this point, people would understand. It's weird that he's celibate."

It is weird, but I agree with Iris. I can't imagine a man like Zax, who has so much heat and fire burning beneath his surface, would go that long without sex.

"I'm celibate," I counter.

"But I'm guessing that's your choice. I don't think either of you has problems getting laid," Nate says to me and Iris. "You're hot." He waves a finger at Iris before pointing at me. "And you're a model. Men love that."

Ugh. I roll my eyes. "Now you know why I'm celibate. I will kick you in the nuts where you sit. Then you won't be able to get any even if you have the chance."

He gives me a sheepish look, holding his hand up in surrender. "Sorry. I didn't mean anything bad by that. You must get that a lot then?"

"Ya think?" Iris cuts in for me. "Any place we used to go in New York. 'Hey, you look like a model, wanna fuck?'" she mocks in a dudebro accent and voice. "Such assholes. Used to drive me crazy for you." She looks at me. "You were always too smart and too sweet and too good for them."

"Thank you." I place my head on her shoulder for a beat. "That's why you're a good friend and I love you forever." One of the many reasons. Frankly, Iris is all I've got.

"Again, sorry," Nate says, giving me an apologetic grin. "I didn't mean to be one of those assholes. This round is on me."

"It's fine," I tell him. "I just don't want to be seen as only a model. It's like I have no value beyond my face and body. It's bullshit. You think you have trouble finding women who don't see you as gay. I have trouble finding men who don't only see me as a only Barbie. No one takes me seriously. I can't tell you the number of times people assume I'm dumb as a sack of bricks simply because I'm blond and pose for pictures."

"I get it." Howie lifts his newly delivered shot. "To finding the right person who loves you for you."

"Cheeseballs," Iris whines. "Lord, Howie, that's awful."

"Fine. How about we drink to—" He cuts himself off when the song changes to a Central Square song. A smile slides up his handsome face. "To Zaxton Monroe. Wherever the miserable bastard is, I hope he's getting some."

"Cheers," everyone says, taking down their shots. Only I don't say cheers. I simply drink mine. Because I met Suzie, and she was lovely. Even to me, the girl Zax hated. I don't remember much about her, but I do remember thinking at the time that they seemed very much in love.

Then he lost her and hasn't been the same since. At least that's how it seems.

The song continues to play, and the conversation carries on, but I slip out my phone. I don't know why I do it. We can blame the alcohol or this strange pull I feel toward him or just basic insanity, but I pull up our text chat. Not much is on here other than when he offered me the executive internship nearly two weeks ago.

Feels like a decade has happened in between then and now.

> Me: A Central Square song is playing at the bar I'm in.

I hit send and turn my phone over on my lap. Simple. Basic. No hint of anything beyond that.

Only not even a minute later and my phone vibrates against me. No way I can resist the urge, so I don't even try.

> Zax: Not uncommon for bars in Boston to play us. The real trick is going somewhere without being recognized. I'm with Greyson and it's a good thing we're not there or he'd likely start serenading the bar.

He seems like he's in a good mood for once, so I press that a bit.

> Me: Tell Greyson I say hi. So weird to say that, but please do. If he'll sing for drinks, you should come to The Irish Lady and give everyone here a thrill. I'll buy his round.

> Zax: I'll tell him. Maybe. My cousin Georgia is in town.

> Me: You have a cousin Georgia?

> Zax: Yes. Obviously since I just said I did.

I inwardly roll my eyes at his gruff tone.

> Me: I didn't know this about you. Obviously.

I smirk, returning to the conversation for a minute when Howie asks me a question about whether or not I think they'll pick a color scheme for the show in New York. We talk for a few minutes and since Zax hasn't texted me back, I decide to let it go. I have another shot and then start sipping on a margarita because I started with tequila, and I likely should end with it.

Then of course, I feel my phone.

> Zax: Well now you know. She's more of a little sister to me than anything.

> Me: Yeesh, I feel for her then. You're not known for being kind to your little sisters.

> Zax: You were never my little sister, Aurelia, and I certainly don't think of you like one now.

I reread his words, trying to flesh out what that means. Likely nothing. But that doesn't stop the small flutter in my belly. I like that he doesn't think of me as a little sister. He probably meant he thinks of me as a pain in the ass, but he didn't say that either. And my mind, the hazy, slightly drunk thing, it starts going places. Places it shouldn't.

Especially with my boss.

> Me: Glad to hear it. Your little sister is the last thing I'd ever want to be to you.

There. Cryptic right back at him.

I decide to leave it at that before I do something stupid. The four of us get up and start dancing, having a great time. A few guys try to dance with me, but I'm not in the mood. I'm having fun just blowing off some steam and following the music as it moves me.

Over an hour later, I take a break, polishing off my most recent margarita and asking for a water instead. And of course, another freaking Central Square song comes on. I snicker to myself, dancing (or am I swaying?) as I reach into my purse and pull out my phone.

> Me: Another one of your greatest hits. This town seriously needs to get over its obsession with you.

His text comes in immediately.

> Zax: How much have you had to drink? Please tell me you're not alone or with a random man you just met.

> Me: What? Why would you ask that?

> Zax: Because this is the message you sent me: "Anoer of yer grates hits. This towwn seriously needs too get over itss obslession with you."

I squint, attempting to read that, but it's a little fuzzy, so I hold the phone up closer to my face.

> Me: Oh.

> Zax: Yes. Oh. So answer my question.

> Me: None of your burness and yes. I dink.

> Zax: What does that mean? Yes, what?

> Me: Yes, I'm werth people.

I glance around. Howie is gone. Likely having gone home to be with his girlfriend. And Iris is... I continue to scan and then gasp out a half-screech.

> Me: Holy hell, Iris is marking out with Nate. I don't everen know why I'm telling youu this bercas I doubt you smare, but yeah. That's razy. I wonder if she's go home weth him. Nate was condomplaining he hasn't hat sex in six mouths. Though I likely shouldn't be slaying that to you. You don't never have sex, right?

I hit send way too quickly and gasp again. I just said that. To Zax. And I hit send. And he's reading it. And half of it doesn't make sense or is typos. Oh no. Where is my freaking spellcheck? And brain? God, my mouth. My stupid, drunk mouth. Ugh. I quickly type out more.

> Me: I'm soooooooo sorry. That was insensivie and I didn't bean it. Blame the alcohol and forgot I ever sad anything.

My eyes close and I can't look. Instead of dwelling and freaking out, I order myself an Uber. I need to go home. I need to sleep and detox and hope that Zax ignores what I just said as much as he's been ignoring me this week. I'm drunk. It's obvious from my slurred texting.

I chug down my water, clearly needing something other than alcohol in my system.

Tapping out another—safer—text to Iris, I tell her I'm taking an Uber home and that I want all the Nate details tomorrow. And that she should go for it because he's good people and frankly, very cute. And evidently straight and good at sex. High-fives to Iris. Crap. I need to go home. Too drunk.

My Uber says it's twelve minutes out. Another chalk mark in the how Boston is so different from New York category. In New York, I'd step outside and either flag my hand in the air or have an Uber in front of me in less than two minutes.

I shut off my phone, so I'm not tempted to keep checking my stupid device. "Hey," I say to the bartender. "Can I settle up?"

"Sure. You paying for just your drinks or theirs too?" He points toward smooching Iris and Nate.

"All of them. Why not?" I tell him. I could use the good Karma after what I just texted Zax even if the thought of spending this much money on alcohol has me wincing.

He hands me the slip and my credit card I had on hold for a tab, and I sign my name along with a generous tip—again Karma.

"You want another drink or is it just the water for you?" the bartender asks, resting his elbows on the counter before me and leaning in. "This one would be on me."

"No, thanks. Just the water. It's nearing my bedtime."

I get that all too familiar male grin. "It's almost my bedtime too. In another twenty minutes, it'll be last call if you'd like to wait. I'd be happy to take you home and make sure you get to bed safely."

"That's what I'm here for," a booming male voice calls out that instantly has me shivering in both nerves and pleasure. "And the only one taking her home tonight is me."

13

AURELIA

Chills race up my spine as a firm hand lands on my shoulder, staking a possessive claim. Zax glares scathingly at the bartender, who doesn't seem the least bit put off by Zax's appearance.

"Isn't that up to her to decide?" the bartender smarts, thinking he has any skin in the game.

"No," Zax retorts arrogantly. "Not in this situation. She's drunk. Are you in the habit of taking advantage of women who have had one drink too many?"

The bartender blanches, then looks a little harder at Zax. "Wait. Aren't you—"

"No," both Zax and I say in unison. "He's my knight in shining"—I toss him a quick glance—"blue armor. Now scram if you know what's good for you. I wasn't going home with you anyway."

The bartender smartly scurries off to help other patrons and I swivel in my chair, peering up at the tall, brooding, casually dressed man before me. Then I almost fall off my stool when I get a better look at him.

"That's what you're wearing?" blurts past my lips. I can't stop myself from staring. He's wearing jeans. Dark. Perfectly fitted. Kinda low slung, but not too low on his trim hips. And a pale blue T-shirt that clings like a mofo to every inch of muscle and skin it can. The way it stretches across his biceps is pure lady porn. It's like the cotton is obsessed with its owner, and frankly, staring at him like this, I can't blame it. I haven't seen his arms bare and wow, he's got some fantastic arms. We're talking uppers and lowers. Forearms. Who knew?

Then there's his hair. Begging for my hands to—

"Something wrong with what I'm wearing?" he interjects my drool fest. "You're staring awfully hard." He's smirking at me. Jerk.

"No." Gulp. "You look..." Then I laugh. "Yeah, no. Sorry, but evidently alcohol is like veritas serum and I'm a no-go for launch on speaking the truth. I plead the fifth with that question, Counselor."

"What?"

I point at him. "Exactly. But why are you here?"

"Because your texts were mostly nonsensical, and I was worried. I didn't want you here alone and I certainly didn't want you here with some random asshole all over you as he tried to take advantage."

Oh. Wow, that's...

"You sound jealous, Mr. Monroe," I taunt, batting my eyelashes up at him.

He's unamused, his penetrating gaze on me unrelenting.

"Yeesh. Okay. Keep your shirt on. Or not." I laugh at my own joke. "I'm not here alone. My friends are just making out on the dance floor like high schoolers. I ordered an Uber."

He frowns, giving me the same scrutinizing once-over he's becoming known for. "Your dress is too short again."

"Aw, so cute that you noticed. This time it was intentional." I wink at him. And touch his forearms to make sure they're real. Yep, pretty freaking real and pretty freaking amazing. Firm yet smooth beneath my hand. And warm. "Your skin is so warm."

He snarls. "Come with me."

I don't get a choice as he grasps my upper arm and forces me to rise. I wobble a bit, unsteady in my heels, and am forced to grasp onto his upper arms now—totally not complaining about that either—for support. My head tilts up, his dips down, and our eyes collide.

"Sorry," I murmur.

"For what? For dragging me out to a shitty bar or for insinuating I never have sex anymore?"

"I didn't drag you here."

"No. You invited me."

"In jest. I wasn't serious. And that was like three hours ago. *And* I think it was technically Greyson I invited. Not you."

"You drank too much."

"Thanks, big bro. So glad you came to point that out for me." I pat his chest with my hand because I seriously can't seem to stop touching his fun parts. "Only, I don't remember asking for your opinion or concern or even your appearance as a savior. I can manage myself just like I have been since I was sixteen. Hell, even before that. So, good night."

I reach up and kiss his cheek, toss him another wink, then saunter my way outside into the steamy Boston night. My head spins the moment the stale air hits me, and I stagger a few steps to the right, leaning heavily against the brick wall of the bar so I don't topple over.

Blowing out slow, even breaths, one after the other, I search the street for my Uber. I'm unsteady, my vision swooping and swaying, and I know I did drink too much. It was a stupid rookie mistake. I haven't had a night of drinking in a very long time.

A car slows that I think is my Uber and I manage to push myself away from the wall, making sure I'm steady before I start to head toward it. Only before I reach it, Zax is there, telling the guy the ride is canceled. He tosses him some money for his trouble and then the guy drives away.

"What the hell, Zax? You had no right to do that."

He turns on me, his stormy eyes scowling along with the rest of him. "I already told you. The only one taking you home tonight is me. Not a sketchy bartender and definitely not a random Uber driver." He pulls out a clicker and hits a button. A souped-up, sporty BMW SUV beeps a few cars down. "Come on."

I hesitate. Not necessarily because I'm being stubborn, but I'm annoyed he's being so high-handed with me. I've been the cruise director of my own ship for a very long time, and I don't want Zax thinking this gives him carte blanche on telling me what to do. I'm not at work right now. He's not my boss in this moment.

"Why are you doing this?" I question, unsure of his motives because last time I checked, he didn't care too much about me. And I don't for a second believe this is sexual.

He takes a step into me, towering over me, which is no small feat. Especially in my heels. He has to be at least six-five. "I didn't like the idea of you alone in that bar. Not when—" He blows out a harsh breath, his hands diving through his hair before they land on his hips. "I just wanted to make sure you were safe and no one was taking advantage of you. I know what guys see and want when they look at you. You were obviously drunk and I... I couldn't stand the thought you were alone and vulnerable."

"I'm always alone, Zax. That's not something you can save me from."

"But I can take you home and make sure you're safe."

I shake my head, at a total loss with what to do with that. This man continues to confound me. Just when I think he's one way, he drops a bomb and totally blows my mind. "Fine. Take me home."

I plow past him, heading for his car. I don't make it far. He's by my side, opening the door for me and helping me up and in. I don't comment and I stop overthinking. Mostly because my brain feels like it's on a loop the loop along with my vision. I lean against the glass of the window, ignoring him as he gets in and starts up the car.

The trip-hop beats of Portishead croon through his sound system, and I close my eyes, begging myself not to grow more attracted to this mysterious man than I unfortunately already am.

I WAKE WITH A START, momentarily dazed and confused as I blink up at... a ceiling that isn't mine. I'm also in a bed that most certainly isn't mine. Where am I? For a moment, everything eludes me as I desperately try to put the pieces together through my foggy, muddled memory.

The bar.

The tequila. *Oh, the tequila.* Yeah, that's not so fun right now.

Texting.

Zax. *Oh, Zax coming to the bar and him driving me home.*

But I'm not home and what happened after that is fuzzy to say the least.

Sliding up on the bed, I glance around the room. No one is beside me and hell if that's not a relief. But I wasn't *that* drunk. I mean, I was but not blackout drunk. Then there's what I'm wearing. Zax's shirt and not my dress. But it's not just a regular old T-shirt. It's the same shirt he was wearing last night when he came to the bar.

I pull the fabric up to my nose, inhaling the scent of him, and then it all starts flooding back to me. He was carrying me. Again. I woke up with him doing that. I think I might have yelled at him for taking me to his place instead of mine when he reminded me I fell asleep so he had no choice since he doesn't know my address.

He wouldn't put me down. Again.

The barbarian carried me in here and set me down on the bed. And then... oh! Oh no. Please, please, tell me I didn't do that. My hands cover my face and I flop over onto the pillow. Shit. I totally did. I demanded his shirt to sleep in. He thought I was kidding.

"You want me to take my shirt off so you can sleep in it?"

"Well, I can't sleep in this," I replied, pulling on the strap of my dress.

He stared at me with amused incredulity until I kicked off my heels. One and then the other. "What are you doing?" It was a smoky rasp.

"Getting undressed. I already told you, I can't sleep in this." I waved *down to my dress and then reached around to start unzipping it. The clink of metal on metal filled the room, ratcheting up the temperature along with the heat in his gaze.*

"Aurelia—"

That was it. Only my name on his tongue, but he wasn't leaving, and he wasn't turning to give me privacy. I didn't want him to either. I woke up from my brief nap feeling achy and craving touch, but not just any touch. I was craving his touch and I wasn't afraid in that moment to let him know it. Even if all I was doing was undressing myself in front of him.

"You have two choices, Zax. Either give me the shirt you're wearing or I'm sleeping in only my panties in your bed since I'm not wearing a bra."

"This isn't my bed."

"It's certainly not mine," I countered, and he emitted a low groan. One I don't think he meant to let out. The first strap fell from my shoulder, and he jerked his body, only to catch himself. His eyes were glued to me. All over me like he couldn't decide which part he wanted to look at the most. He licked his lips and then reached behind to pull his shirt up and over his head.

"What are you doing to me?" His pained murmur was so low I had to strain to make it out.

I was wondering the same thing about him. But God, his chest. Golden smooth skin and muscles rippled over every inch down to where his Adonis belt dipped into his jeans. And Adonis is right. He's perfect.

A step and then he was before me, so close I could feel the heat of his body against mine. Smell his skin and cologne. So close that if I reached out, just a little, I could touch him and then what? What would happen then?

He settled that unspoken question for me as he took his shirt and placed it over my head. The soft cotton draped around me, going to my mid-thighs, and I let my dress fall to the floor in a pool of gold.

His gaze held mine until he couldn't resist another second and dragged down to where my nipples were hard, straining through his shirt. A shaky breath and then he took a step back. "Bathroom is through there." He pointed behind him, his voice rough and low. "I'll go get you some water."

Then he was gone. Practically fled the room, and I went into the bathroom. When I came out, I found water and two Advil. But no Zax. After finishing both off, I climbed into bed, squirmy in the worst possible places, but cocooned in all things him, and fell quickly to sleep.

I practically threw myself at him. What was I thinking? I don't even know. Not entirely. No doubt part of me knew he'd reject me. And not simply because I was drunk. There is attraction there. I'm not going to pretend I don't see it in him. But attraction doesn't always mean want and in this case, it doesn't.

Zax doesn't want me.

And I'm not sure I want him back. Not in a real way, last night notwithstanding.

He's not the sort of man who would be good for me. He's too broken. Too in love with Suzie still. A haunted being held captive by a ghost he has no desire to escape. If it were ever anything, it would be sex. I'd grow attached. He'd tear me to shreds. And then everything I've worked for would once again be gone.

No, thanks.

There is nothing even remotely appealing about any of that.

Climbing out of bed, I find my discarded dress hanging over the back of a chair, my shoes upright on the floor beneath it. Damn him. He must have come back in here to check on me. It's still early, dawn only a whisper in the sky. I make quick work of using the bathroom and then slipping back into my dress. But I don't want to go home like this. Not in such a blatant walk of shame when I have nothing to be ashamed about.

Without giving it a second thought, I snatch his shirt and throw it back on, tying the end into a knot so it sits on my hips over my dress. I pick up my shoes, not wanting to walk loudly through his place and risk waking him.

Opening the door, I glance around, taking in the contemporary yet cozy furnishings and high-end finishes I didn't get to appreciate last night. It's a huge place and my curiosity gets the best of me as I meander from room to room, knowing I'll likely never get the chance again. It's all expertly decorated, but only the gym, media room, office, and kitchen feel lived in. The rest are almost as lonely appearing as the man himself.

Then there's his bedroom. His door is open and I'm not sure if that's habit or not. I know it's not an invitation. Peering through the murky darkness, I find him on his back in the middle of the bed, sheets twisted around his bare waist. The man really is a sight to behold. So gorgeous he takes my breath away.

"Thank you," I whisper to him, then spin on the balls of my feet and make a break for it, worried he'll wake up before I'm able to flee.

The last thing I want right now is to talk to him. Not after last night. No, I need more time before I can face him. I have until Monday and then Wednesday we leave for New York.

The rest of this weekend, I plan to spend with my sewing machine watching true crime shows on Hulu or Netflix, eating my weight in sugary carbs to eliminate my hangover. Not thinking of him. Not dwelling on thoughts of last night. At least until Monday comes and I'm forced to see him once again.

14

ZAXTON

I heard her linger by my bedroom door. Felt her breathing even though she was nowhere near me. Then she said, thank you, and ran. Thank you. For what? For leaving my family and friends and showing up like a mad stalker who couldn't handle the idea that his intern was drunk in a bar? A bar where guy after guy would no doubt try his luck with her?

I knew she wasn't alone. I could discern that much in her drunk texts.

But God.

It drove me crazy.

Thinking about what she was wearing. How her hair was styled. What makeup she had on her face. If she was dancing and laughing and flirting with other men. Men who weren't me. Men who got to stare into those eyes with the flagrant interest they no doubt felt. I nearly broke every finger on that bartender's hands when I heard him proposition her.

I knew I wasn't going to fuck her.

But... I also couldn't let her fuck anyone else.

I told myself I was being noble. She was drunk. There was no hiding that.

But my motives were nothing short of selfish. I could have let her go home in that Uber, but at the same time, there was no fucking way I was letting her go home in that Uber. I wanted time alone with her. I wanted to be the one to take her home. And then she went and fell asleep in my car. What choice did I have? I had to bring her to my place. I mean, I could have tried to wake her, demanding her actual address, but no.

The real question. Why does she feel so right when pressed against me?

Why does her body feel like an extension of my own when I get to hold her?

Why can't I stop thinking about her?

Her? Of all damn people. My intern. My ex-stepsister. A woman who might be plotting along with my father against me.

She has me ensnared. A helpless accomplice to her every crime. Resistance is my only weapon, but when she unzipped her tiny gold dress and then put on my shirt—*my fucking shirt*—I nearly lost all willpower in addition to the will to live without one taste. That's what plagued my mind for the rest of the night.

Could I honestly go the rest of my days without one taste of her?

She wanted me. But she would have regretted it. I knew that and she was drunk and that's not my game. I would need her sober, willing, fully cognizant. And likely reticent. My relationship with Suzie was so public once I became so famous. We were hounded. Followed. Photographed. Gossiped about. Then she died and the media storm that followed...

I swore I wouldn't do it again.

I swore Suzie would be it for me.

Random. Meaningless. Faceless. Sex.

But Aurelia isn't random, and she isn't meaningless, and she isn't faceless, and I can't allow her to be sex. Because she wouldn't just be sex. I'd have a taste and I'd need more just the way I need more every time I'm near her.

New York is going to be hell, but not impossible.

"I could always go in your place," Asher teases and I swear, this motherfucker is asking for it. I nearly killed him after I watched him flirt with Aurelia in the office. So easy. It's always so easy for him and she fed right into it.

"Asher, I wouldn't push the man right now." Georgia throws him a warning look.

"That's what you're telling yourself, but yet you're choosing to stay at the hotel with her and not at your place," Grey says to me, ignoring Asher's ridiculous comment. I'm sitting here at Sunday brunch with him, Asher, Callan, and Georgia. And well, I didn't bother with Lenox. He's back in Maine, hiding in his cabin, playing piano for no one and tattooing art on people's bodies while silently taking over the world on his computer.

"What choice do I have? I have to keep an eye on her. Dad could meet her at the hotel and I'd completely miss it if I were at my condo."

I've thought about little else since she left my apartment in the wee hours yesterday morning. I was with everyone who is sitting with me now Friday night. They all know why I left. I could hardly hide it. Thankfully, they didn't badger me about it last night. We were too busy drinking and playing poker. Then Grey had to go and bring her up.

"Tell yourself whatever you want that gets you through, but that's not the only reason you're staying in that hotel, and we all know it."

I flip Asher off because that's my thing with him. He simply begs for it. "I don't have a lot of choices with her."

"Hmmm. I don't know." Georgia taps her bottom lip in mock contemplation. "You could, you know, try *dating* her."

"Do you not remember the conversation Friday night about your less than favorite uncle?" I counter.

"Blah. Boring. You tell me this and yet you still fled the second she started texting you a second time."

"She was drunk."

"So was half the bar," Callan jumps in. "Half my Friday and Saturday nights in the emergency room are spent treating people who have a little too much to drink at a bar. Or women who unfortunately come in contact with the wrong man." He visibly shudders, as do we all.

I point at him. "That. That's why I went. She was drunk and the bartender was offering to take her home."

"But you didn't know that before you got there. Did you?" Asher maintains. "Not to mention, that's her call to make if she says yes. Not yours."

"I couldn't let that happen. Not with how drunk she was. Someone could have easily hurt her."

"Okay," Georgia exclaims, holding up her hand and putting an end to the back and forth. "Fine. You're her hero yet again. But why can't you date her?"

"You mean other than the fact that I don't *want* to date her and the obvious?"

"The obvious?" Georgia parrots, ignoring the first half of my statement while taking a sip of her coffee and planting her elbows on the table like she's about to dig into my argument. She's excited by this. I can tell. Her green eyes are practically glowing emeralds, alight with mischief.

"You can't blow that off, Georgia. I don't date. I have no desire to date. It's the last damn thing I've wanted for the last eight years." When Suzie died, my world stopped spinning. Women all but lost their appeal other than in the most basic, carnal sense. They bored me. They still bore me. They're fake and have agendas I want no part of. Giving that part of my life up hasn't been a hardship after what I had and lost.

"Yawn. Lame." She does the world's fakest, most exaggerated yawn. "You're just scared to meet someone and get attached again. And you never told me what the obvious is."

I roll my eyes at my cousin. "Thanks for the bullshit psychoanalysis. Wrong as usual. The obvious is Aurelia is my intern. She works directly for me and there are rules about that. Do you not remember the main reason my father sits on the rich prick unemployment line? She's also a lot younger than me and my ex-stepsister to boot, which is a bit creepy."

She laughs. "You're a liar."

"Am not."

"You totally are," Asher chimes in. "You don't think it's creepy. Not by a long shot."

"Because it's *not* creepy." Georgia flips her red head in his direction. "It's hot. Can I get an Amen on this? Stepsibling and age-gap tropes are hot."

I shake my head, as do the rest of us men. "Not following," Callan admits for us.

Georgia waves him away. "Whatever. Men are hopeless. Continue."

"He doesn't trust her," Grey answers for me, growing bored with all of this. "Frankly, I'm not sure I do either. She was texting him on her night out with friends and then suddenly she was drunk and alone? I don't know. All this madness seems a bit too coincidental. And maybe it is simply that. I hope it is. I'd hate to think she's doing the worst. And for our father, no less."

"I don't see it," I tell them truthfully. I thought a lot about this too. I realize I don't know her, but from what I've seen, it doesn't seem to be her nature to be that duplicitous. At least that's what my gut is telling me.

"No?"

I shake my head at Grey. "No. I think she was vulnerable, and he took advantage. Do I think she's not a risk? No. I know she is. Because there is no way he got her that internship without planning on cashing in on that huge favor. He will. It's a matter of when. And how will she respond when he presses? That's what I'm unsure of. That's what I don't trust. Because while she just wants a job and to move past what happened with Valencci, she placed herself in the hands of a man who doesn't care if he ruins her on his way to ruining me and the company. Plus, he has someone on the inside besides her. Someone high enough up to get Aurelia in with one phone call. It could have been the woman I just fired, but I don't know, and I won't know until Lenox is able to dig up more."

We fall silent for a moment, our breakfast being delivered.

And while this is a pretty exclusive place, we all know we're being photographed despite our ball caps and indoor sunglasses. Especially Greyson and Asher. Fans go freaking wild for them whenever we're out. Probably because they're still out in the spotlight as a rock star and quarterback.

"On another topic, I'm getting married in eight months," Georgia announces, and I swear, the world comes to a standstill between the remaining four of us.

"I'm sorry," Grey mutters. "What the fuck now?"

"Married. As in, I'm engaged." Georgia holds up a hand with a ring on her finger that she most definitely was not wearing last night.

"Georgia—"

That's as far as I go because none of us like Ezra. He's a pompous douchebag. Something about him has never felt right and Grey agrees with me.

"Knock it off. You're all going to be happy for me because I'm happy for me. End of freaking story."

Grey and I exchange a look. "If you're happy, we're happy for you," I say, even if my tone suggests otherwise.

"Good." She wipes her mouth with her napkin. "Now let's start ragging on Asher before this all gets too serious for us to handle."

CALLAN HAD to get to the hospital for a half shift and Asher had to get to the field for training camp. I left Grey and Georgia outside the restaurant. The two of them were going shopping and as someone who deals in fashion all damn day long, the last thing I want to do is go and look at more clothes. And as much as I love Georgia, she's the type of woman who tries on everything. I can't do it, but that's why Grey's her shopping bestie and not me.

Even if his face will hit every celebrity gossip rag across the planet for it.

The Sunday morning sun is shining high overhead, bright and hot as I walk along the greenway back toward my place. I didn't drive, favoring the walk, but now with the August heat bearing down on me, I'm starting to regret that decision. Up ahead, the canal fountains —a flat, open surface with water jets that shoot out of the ground— are already loaded with screaming, happy children, soaked in both clothes and bathing suits.

I pause for a moment, watching them, watching their parents, feeling that tightness I never allow myself to indulge in when someone catches my eye. Wearing a pink sports bra, cropped gray yoga pants, and a messy bun on top of her head, Aurelia looks way too fuckable as she sits on a blanket, knees half up while she works with focused diligence on whatever she's sketching on her pad.

The dead thing inside my chest does something strange as I watch her, debating my next move.

I could go home and pretend I never saw her, and she would never be the wiser.

That's the prudent thing to do. That's what my mind is screaming for me to do. *Distance, man. We need distance.* Then there's that devil on my shoulder. The one strangling the well-intentioned angel telling me I need distance. The one who is best friends with my dick and enjoys reminding me of my overwhelming desire to be near her.

Even though I don't like her. I don't trust her. And I have no intention of having her be anything to me other than an intern who poses a possible threat.

I decide to leave her to her drawing just as a frisbee lands on her blanket, startling her away from her sketching. She tosses it back to the shirtless guy who originally missed it—probably intentionally by the looks of him and his smile for her—and the second he says something that makes her laugh, my molars gnash and I head in her direction.

She notices me out of the corner of her eye and turns in time to catch me approaching. Blue eyes squint at me and then her lips train up into a small, amused, resigned smile.

"Is there no place in this city that you don't occupy at all times?" she questions as I stand before her, towering over her to the point where she has to lean back, crane her neck, and use her hand to shield her eyes from the sun.

"Very few."

"I'm coming to learn that the hard way."

"Well. Uh." Hippie the Frisbee looks uncomfortable.

"Problem?" I narrow my gaze at him in that blatant male fuck off thing we do with each other. I could be the bigger man and introduce myself while crushing his hand in a shake, but why bother with pretenses.

"Guess not. Nice meeting you," he says to Aurelia, giving her another smile I'm sure he uses every time he tries to get into a girl's pants. Smartly, he returns to his game with his friends, who audibly rag on him, and I sit down beside her, even though I know it's stupid and she didn't invite me to join her.

"You're a bit of a cockblocker, aren't you, Zax? You like this with all your interns?"

"I simply saw you across the lawn and came over to say hi."

"And the look you gave him?" She quirks an eyebrow, a smirk on her lips that tells me she's not put off by my caveman display. Not that I'd care if she was.

"He's not your type."

She falls back on the blanket in an outright mocking belly laugh, her sketchbook sliding off her lap during her antics. "You don't know my type."

I do my best to ignore the smooth, creamy skin of her stomach, the press of her breasts, and the swell of cleavage playfully perked up above her sports bra. And the yoga pants. Those aren't bad either.

I pick up the book, glancing at it to distract myself from her. "Sure, I do. He's not it." *Because I am.*

"And I bet you're about to tell me—hey! What are you doing? That's mine." She flies at me in a rush, but I climb up onto my knees, angling myself away from her so she can't snatch the book back.

"What is this?" I ask, stiff-arming her with my hand pressed into her forehead, holding her back.

"I can't believe you!" she screeches, swatting at me with her kitten claws. "You're not twelve, Zax. What kind of move is this?"

"An effective one."

"Bullshit it is," she shoots back just as she rolls her body out of my hold and grips my shirt at the waist with one hand, yanking on it while her other goes for the book. Only her move throws me off balance and the two of us go tumbling back, somehow pinning her beneath me.

My body notices instantly, even if my brain needs an extra second to catch up.

Pressing my hands into the blanket, I push my face and chest up to find Aurelia's inches from mine, her blue eyes startled wide, her lips parted on a silent O. And fuck, she's *so* pretty. Up close like this, across the damn lawn, it doesn't matter.

My stomach squeezes with my half-digested food as ideas tumble one after the other through my head. Kissing. Touching. Claiming.

Does she feel it? The way my body reacts to her? The shackled passion in her eyes tells me yes and that she's not opposed to it.

The urge to grind up and into the V of her legs—watch her expression as she feels my hard cock rub her exactly where she needs it to—is so compelling, I fist the blanket and lock my jaw. And for a second, all I can do is feel her beneath me. Stare into her eyes and wonder about her lips. I could kiss her so easily like this. A half an inch and she'd be all mine.

Smartly my brain kicks back into high gear, alarm bells blaring in my ears. I shift up into a plank and roll off her. I need to get my head back on straight and remember who I am and who she is. Not someone I should be looking at, touching, or thinking about in any capacity other than in a detached, professional way.

I go back for what started this fiasco. Her sketchbook. It's half on the grass now, its pages still open, revealing what had caught my eye.

"This is your design?" I sit up and she does the same, her knees coming up to her chest as she rests her head on them, peering sideways at me through her dark lashes.

"Yep."

"I didn't kiss you, Aurelia, so why are you suddenly so tense and edgy?"

"Because the last time someone saw my sketches, they ruined my life."

Oh. Right. That.

I take in the image. High-waisted, long, flowy skirt with some sort of ripply shimmery pattern against an ombre of color. Then there's the top. Cropped a couple of inches above the hem of the skirt, revealing a peekaboo of skin. Lace with slithers of the shimmery pattern woven through. One shoulder exposed, the other a full sleeve. It's fancy and trendy and pretty and fun.

"I like it. I like it a lot."

A choppy breath.

"Relax, Aurelia. I'm not stealing your designs. I'm a lot of things, cold, cruel, intolerant—I'm sure I'm missing some from your list of me—but I'm not a thief and I'm not Valencci." I flip the pages, going through her sketches. Gowns and dresses—mostly formal. These weren't in her portfolio from school. These are special to her. These are things she wants to design and bring to life. They're mostly classic with modern twists.

Stunning. Sexy. Smart. Beautiful. Different.

Like her.

I close the book and set it on the blanket by her feet.

"Where do you see yourself in five years?"

"Is this an interview?" she smarts.

"Humor me."

She emits a little annoyed harrumph. "Running my own design house."

I nod. I assumed that. "Why aren't you chasing that now?"

She props her chin up on her knees, staring out at the fountain area and the kids playing. "I'm saving up. As I'm positive you know, starting an endeavor like that and being successful at it requires a lot of capital."

"There are investors."

"I'm aware. I'm not ready yet, Zax. I need more experience inside before I can run my own show. I've heard so many horror stories. People right out of school thinking they had what it took to make it and failed in the first year. I can't fail. Not at this. So I'm learning and I'm saving and I'm sketching and I'm creating."

The breeze catches an errant strand of her white-blond hair, blowing it into her face and I reach for it, tucking it back behind her ear. Lingering there for a second or two longer than I should. She shivers ever so slightly as my thumb glides over her earlobe, only I don't feel the same satisfaction in that as I did Friday night.

I release her, but my eyes don't stray from the side of her face.

Thoughts swirl through my mind, one after the other. Scary thoughts that it's far too soon to be having. Especially with who she is and what she potentially represents. She says she can't fail, and I believe that. That unrelenting grit is what makes her both so dangerous and so vulnerable. It's also part of what makes her so fucking intoxicating and appealing.

All I know is that I'm in awe of her. To be so young and so wise and so persistent.

"I'll let you get back to your sketches. I'll see you tomorrow."

I peel myself up and off her blanket, standing above her. She peers up at me, something in her expression I'm unable to read.

"See you tomorrow, Mr. Monroe."

I frown, hating that tone of hers. Wisely, I walk off, refusing to allow myself to look back. Even if I'm already looking forward to seeing her tomorrow.

15

AURELIA

"Nate, just as there is a boy code, there is a girl code. Iris is my best friend and frankly the only person I have in this world. I can't tell you what she said to me about you."

Nate sags. "She didn't return my texts this morning and I didn't see her on her floor when I went to look."

I shrug helplessly. "You know what they say about the office ink. She's just... more into adventure than settling down right now."

"I'm not looking to place a ring on it. I just want to take her out and try dating her."

"Be persistent without being creepy. That's my best female advice. Let her know you're serious and that you like her, but don't go into over text or call or stalker mode."

"Fine. But if you could put in a good word for me, I'd be forever grateful."

"I can do that," I promise him. "Morning, Lamar," I call out as the man hurriedly marches down the hall, his phone to his face even as he answers me.

"Morning, Madam Liastrange. You look fucking radiant, but why are we not shopping in the closet? I was just there, and you weren't. I already know your skirt isn't at Monroe-approved length and I don't even have to fucking see it. Besides, I had this whole black vamp ensemble going in my head since for some crazy reason I had a dream that you were Bellatrix Lestrange. Hence the new name. Liastrange. Get it?" I open my mouth to say... something to that, when he stops short, glaring at Nate, who is half sitting on the corner of my desk. "Why do you look different?"

Nate blushes redder than my non-Monroe-approved length skirt. "I don't look—"

Lamar holds up his hand. "Bitch, please, don't you dare try to deny it. Spill. Are you two rubbing naked body parts, because if you are—"

Now it's my turn to cut him off. "He was in bed all weekend with my best friend. In fact, if you had arrived two minutes earlier, you would have been privy to Nate begging me for dating Iris tips."

"Phew!" Lamar wipes away the nonexistent sweat from his dark brow. "That would have been a fucking monster truck to park on this floor if you had been."

"You know half the time I have no idea what you're saying."

"That's a total lie. You just don't like my insinuations." He clicks his tongue at me, cocking an *I dare you to try and deny it* eyebrow.

I glance down because damn this observant man! He's not even talking about anything specific because I told no one about what happened Friday with Zax, and I know Nate and Iris didn't see anything when I left the bar. Not to mention I highly doubt Zax said anything either.

No, he's feeding off the hot caramel sauce on ice cream vibe we've had going these last couple of weeks. The decadent dance of hot and cold that Zax and I unfortunately seem to do so well. The one I think we're both determined to stop.

"You. Nate. Intern. Come with me." He snaps his fingers. "It's sample time for the women's power-wear shoot tomorrow, motherfucker. This is a big shoot that in six weeks will be in every major magazine and web publication. We have to make sure that hag who thought she was being cute bringing me a pumpkin orange polyester frock thing on Friday got the fucking message and brought me something real to play with."

Nate hops off my desk, throwing me a wave as he scurries behind Lamar, who sets off once again.

"Liastrange, why are you still sitting there?"

"Huh?" I shout after him since now he's practically down the hall.

"We need a model to help."

Ugh. "I'm not a model."

"Do you not remember that you're an intern and that makes you a company bitch conversation? Move!"

"I hate you." I stand, grab my Diet Coke off my desk, and run after him.

"Another lie. If you're going to make it in this industry, you need to work on your poker face."

Probably true, but he's never seen me actually work my poker face. I'm a queen.

"I have design intern stuff to do," I tell him as we reach his office at the end of the hall. Honestly, I don't fight it too much because that means less Zax time and after my strange weekend that seemed to revolve around him, I need it. He's not even here yet and already I'm tense and edgy simply with the anticipation of him.

I did a lot of soul-searching last night about my situation with him. I'm putting myself at risk. By texting with him. By flirting with him. I'm an intern and he's my boss. I realized last night I came here never viewing him as such. He was Zax to me and not Mr. Monroe, and that way of thinking will only hurt me in the end.

The one bonus was that when I saw him yesterday, he didn't bring up anything about Friday night. Not the fact that I fell asleep, and he had to carry me or that I practically threw myself at him only for him to rightly reject me. So yeah, I need a bit more distance this morning before we leave for New York on Wednesday.

"Honey, trust me," Lamar says without skipping a beat. "This is far more important and fun. Besides, I already texted Zax to tell him you're mine until I say otherwise." He winks at me and then opens the door of his office, only to breathe out a sigh of frustration. "That's what I thought. Fucking moron." He spins to face both Nate and me. "Explain to me why I shouldn't fire this girl this very second. Who in their right fucking mind would think I would want the rack of clothes for a shoot up here in my office and not on the *shoot floor*? This woman is trying to kill me. First orange polyester, now this. I hate to fucking say it, but Martina was better at this." He waves his hand along the massive rack overflowing with at least a hundred suits and power outfits as he put it.

"Do you want us to move it downstairs?" Nate asks.

Lamar taps the toe of his shoe, his hand pressed to his chin as he stares contemplatively at the rack. "I think we have to. I can't ask Aurelia to change in here. My walls are glass and there is no privacy here other than my tiny bathroom. Not to mention the lighting is all wrong for tests." He groans, throwing his hands up in the air. "What is it with Mondays in this place lately?"

Twenty minutes later, the three of us have the rack set on the edge of the closet.

Lamar picks up a suit, shakes his head in dismay, and then moves it to the opposite side of the rack. "Liastrange, go get naked while I rearrange everything and figure out how I want this all to go. I am not a patient man on a good day and today is not a good day if you feel me."

"I feel you."

"Perfect. We'll bring you stuff in a minute. If you could put your hair up on top of your head so it's out of the way, that would help with pictures. There's a robe in there for you to put on. Nate, help me make some sense of this fucking mess."

The two of them set to work and I head for the changing room side of the closet. Polishing off the end of my Diet Coke, I toss it into a recycle bin and then start stripping down in one of the open changing rooms. Just as I'm tying the rope of my robe around my waist, I hear Nate yell, "Are you decent?"

"Yes. You can come in."

"Great." He comes around the corner carrying a black tuxedo-style suit that has a plunging neckline, nearly to the navel, flanked by a wide satin collar. The pants are wide with massive slits up the sides —also with the satin trim—to allow for a peekaboo leg. "He wants you to start with this and then I have a fur and leather strapless minidress for you. He said pick out whatever shoes you think will make the outfit and your legs look the longest and not to worry if your boobs don't fit because the models wearing these for the actual shoot will have boob tape keeping theirs in place."

"Wow. You actually just repeated that to me."

"Just doing my job. And not caring about your boobs now that I've got someone else's to play with." He gives me a cheeky grin.

"This you screwing around with my friend thing is going to be tricky." I snatch the suit from him and sigh. It's going to be a very long morning with these two.

Five minutes later, I'm wearing the tux suit that I have to admit feels like something you'd wear to the Oscars. It's glamorous and sexy and just so wow. I do feel powerful. I step out of the closet to applause. I give a little twirl, mindful of my untaped girls as I do.

"Will you walk it?" Lamar asks, his phone out so he can take pictures. "I want to see how it moves and where your leg pops out as you do. That will help me frame it for the shoot tomorrow."

I start to runway walk across the room and then spin back, only to freeze. Beth is here, standing next to Lamar. She gives me a kind smile and a small wave that I return and then I continue to walk.

"Gorgeous. Love it. Head up higher." Lamar starts snapping pics and then checks his phone when I'm standing in front of him again. "I think this will be our statement piece in the shoot. I want the model shot alone in this with a very simple background. But it has to be edgy and almost masculine because she's mocking that contrast. This needs to say check out this powerful fucking badass woman rocking a tuxedo like a queen. Look at the lines of this. It has to be worn just so by just the right person." He shows Beth, who simply nods and then shrugs. "Liastrange, you need to model this for us tomorrow morning."

"She can't," Beth cuts in. "That's actually why I'm here. There has been a change of schedule and Mr. Monroe asked me to come and get you. He says you need to leave for New York immediately instead of Wednesday."

"Oh. But I don't have any of my stuff."

She waves me away. "He said you should pick out a few outfits from the closet in accordance with the itinerary you've already been given and then you'll make a quick stop at your apartment to pick up anything else you need prior to leaving for the airport."

"Okay then," I say, a little surprised by the urgent turn of events. "Let me get changed."

WITH LAMAR'S HELP, I pick out half a dozen different outfits and shoes that he insists I transport in garment bags because he'll murder me otherwise. Everything from corporate business wear to club wear to cocktail dresses.

"I'll see you Thursday for the fashion week design meeting," he says to me. "Wear those clothes like a boss and don't let the actual boss say anything about them. You're representing Monroe almost more than he is on this trip. You're the model and the executive design intern. Remember that."

"Thanks. Good luck tomorrow at your shoot."

"Bitch, I'm gonna need it. Nate, let's move on to the next outfit."

I wave bye to Nate and then Beth walks me over to the elevator.

"How do you feel your first few weeks have gone?"

"Good," I exclaim with a big, beaming smile I can't help but showcase. "I mean, kind of crazy all things considered, but it's been fantastic. I've learned so much already and have enjoyed getting to know the other interns and staff. Plus, I'm very excited about the projects I've been put on."

"That's great." She reaches out and touches my arm, giving it a squeeze. "I'm so relieved to hear you're getting on in your new role after what happened to the previous person. How are things with Mr. Monroe? Has he been..." Then she laughs. "I don't even know a diplomatic way to ask if he's been a jerk or not."

I laugh in return. "He's been... gruff. How about that?"

"Gruff sounds about right for him."

"Honestly, it's nothing more than I expected. He takes his job and his role very seriously and I respect that about it him. You were right. He's a perfectionist and expects the same from his staff, which again, I like. It pushes me to push myself to the next level."

"Have you had a lot of one-on-one time with him?"

After our initial conversation, I had a feeling she was going to fish about that. "Not much. We had an initial one-on-one and then one or two after that. Mostly, I don't see him or interact with him other than in group meetings." True and yet not true at all.

"But he's taking you early on this trip to New York. Before any of the other interns or staff."

"I know the designer we're meeting with. I used to do shoots for her, and Mr. Monroe believes my relationship with her might help grease some wheels."

"Ah. Okay. That makes more sense to me. All good to hear. Remember, if you have any issues or concerns, come talk to me." She presses the button for the elevator and then turns on me as we wait. "Listen, I want you to feel comfortable confiding in me. I understand your situation is a bit different from the rest. Your history in the industry puts you a step above the other interns who don't have quite the same level of experience. Plus, your direct access to Mr. Monroe has you on the inside of places others aren't. So if you hear anything or something seems... out of line or strange or even concerning, please come and speak directly to me about it first before anyone else."

My eyebrows hit my hairline. "You mean with Mr. Monroe?"

She shifts her weight. "Not necessarily and I didn't mean to alarm you. There has just been some talk and rumors, is all. I can't go into specifics, but please keep what I said in mind."

I blink at her, floored. "I will," I manage just as the elevator dings and the doors open. She gives me a friendly wave as I step on and then I'm plummeting into the bowels of the building, my mind swirling, lost in what Beth said. On everything Beth has said to me thus far. First the warning about not trying to win Zax's heart and now this. Weird.

I'm so lost in thought that when the doors open, I immediately plow straight into someone. The two of us get tangled up and I start to go down, only for him to catch me at the last minute. "Jesus, Aurelia," Zax shoots out as he sets me on my feet. "I thought you said you weren't clumsy."

I shake off his touch from my shoulders and adjust my garment bags. "Mondays evidently aren't my best day," I snap, then take a deep breath. *Professional, Aurelia.* "Sorry. I was lost in thought and didn't expect you to be right there when the elevator opened because who stands directly in front of an elevator without allowing current passengers the social standard benefit of space when exiting." *Professional!* I clear my throat. "I was told we're leaving for New York now?"

"Yes."

That's it, but he lingers on me, his expression unreadable. Only all I can seem to focus on is how we're standing too close. Not only that, he makes no move to change that and I have no path around him as he's bracketed in by two metal railings. Sweet breath fans across my hair while his body heat and heady fragrance infuse themselves into me like a warm bath. His shirt is a crisp charcoal today, and I have no doubt that if I were to peer up, I'd find the same stormy countenance in his dark eyes.

Warm fingers glide along my skin, starting at the edge of my shoulder, startling me so badly I jump and gulp at the same time. They drag along my delicate collarbone until they press in at the notch at the base of my throat. I shiver and close my eyes, frustrated that I can't control my reaction to him or the thoughts that accompany his proximity.

Dirty, dirty thoughts that are nowhere near professional.

Thoughts about what those fingers and hands could do when properly motivated. I stare at the center gray button on his shirt and imagine ripping it off his body, watching those buttons fly in every direction, so I can touch his smooth, muscular chest the way I wanted to the other night.

Two minutes and one not so simple touch and my freaking soul-searching and battle plan are things of the past once again. This attraction I have to him is the pits. I don't even like him all that much. But clearly want and like don't have to be simpatico. Pathetic.

"Your heart is racing," he murmurs in a soft purr, tickling a circle over my pulse point at the bottom of my neck.

"Yes." Because it is. I can hear it and feel it in every inch of my body.

"Is this from me or your near fall?" I don't dare answer that, but I can practically hear the smirk in his voice as he continues with, "I still make you nervous." Not a question. A cocky statement. "Even after this weekend?" A riled tease this time.

I finally glance up, his molten brown eyes intense as they bore into mine, burning with lust and tortured resentment. A war, he's trying to battle through and beat. No doubt my face is an exact replica of his.

"Yes. Even after this weekend. Especially after this weekend."

His fingers trickle up my neck, along the slope of my jaw and then back down, focusing once more on the base of my neck and my undeniable reaction to him.

Nothing and everything about this feels good.

"Breathe, Aurelia. You're not breathing."

His words compel my lungs into action, and I take a deep inhale. "New York?" I squeak, taking a self-preserving step back and forcing his hand to drop.

My motion seems to snap him out of whatever that was, and he too takes a step back, the cloudiness in his eyes clearing. "Yes. Your friend Marie moved the initial meeting to this evening. Typically, I wouldn't abide by that, but I'm willing to make one concession for a schedule change. In any event, we have to go."

"Okay. Beth said I could stop at my place quickly?"

A nod and then he turns and walks toward a waiting Escalade.

A man hops out of the front seat and opens the door for us as he takes the bags from my hand. "I'm Ashley," he introduces. "Mr. Monroe's driver."

"Nice to meet you, Ashley. You're a brave soul and I'm in awe of you."

He laughs. "I've been told something similar on numerous occasions." He gives me a playful wink, taking my hand and helping me up and into the SUV. "What's your address, miss?" he asks when he climbs back in the front. I get myself buckled and tell him, only to see Zax frown.

"What?" I ask, already able to tell where this is headed and not liking it one bit.

"You live in a shit neighborhood."

"Don't judge. It's judgey and no one likes a judger."

He's not amused, but frankly, neither am I.

I glower at him. "Sorry, Mr. Billionaire, we can't all live in penthouses overlooking the water and the skyline."

"Are you telling me you can't afford better? I know your salary. Plus, I assume you did quite well as a model."

"If you recall one of our previous conversations, I explained that I'm saving my money," I say primly, turning my gaze to the window and the sunny Boston morning before I bludgeon my boss to death with my purse.

"You should still live somewhere better. Safer. Your neighborhood is not safe."

"Maybe for you it's not. This is a palace compared to my first apartment in New York, and besides, I know how to take care of myself."

"Aurelia—"

"Drop it, Zax." I flip back around to him, more than done with this. "You're not my stepbrother, my father, or my boyfriend. You're my boss and that gives you exactly zero say in where or how I live. I've been on my own since I was sixteen and the one thing that has gotten me through this world is the assurance that at the end of the day, my life is my own. No one else's."

He shifts on the seat, drawing closer, and I wish he wouldn't do that. Look at me like he cares. It's such a powerful weapon. Especially from someone like him and if I allow myself to falter, even for a second, he could disarm me completely.

"I haven't asked."

I shake my head, willing my chin not to start quivering. I'm stronger than that and I force myself to cling to my miserable indignation instead of succumbing to emotion. Not my strongest suit.

"You won't tell me?"

"No, boss. I won't tell you."

His jaw clenches and his gaze grows stern but immediately softens. His hand reaches out, tucking a strand of hair behind my ear—he likes doing that a lot, I've noticed—and then he's folding his hands in his lap, trying for kind and approachable, but the large, broody man is anything but.

He's a wrecking ball and the Big Bad Wolf all rolled into one.

"How's this?" he asks gently. "For the next twenty minutes until we reach your apartment, I'm Zax and you're Aurelia. And once upon a time, we were quasi family."

"No, we weren't," I hiss, my heart bending and weaving around his jabs but already winded and losing steam.

"Fine. That's my fault. But I'm putting a temporary moratorium on our starting fresh and ignoring our past pact. I want to know what happened that you've been on your own for so long."

Dammit.

16

ZAXTON

urelia stares defiantly at me, but one thing I've learned about her, she's not that good of an actress. My judgment of her living situation hit her on an entirely different level. And she's right. I was being judgmental, despite the seriously crappy neighborhood she lives in. But it's more than that. It's the pleading look in her eyes. The one begging me to back off and never return.

Only I can't do that.

Her body plowed into me right off the elevator and though I told myself a hundred times to remove my hand from her and step back, I couldn't. I couldn't move. Because I wanted her. I wanted to touch her, feel her pulse race beneath my fingers, while I stared into her eyes and feasted on that tiny pout that's so damn sexy I can hardly stand it.

Aurelia only blew back into my life a few weeks ago and I'm already fucked when it comes to her. She exists in the periphery of my thoughts when I'm not with her and at the forefront of my mind when I am. I can keep fighting it, and I plan to, but right now, I'm looking at a woman I want to drag onto my lap, wrap my arms around, and kiss until everything in her world is as perfect as she is to me.

That scared, wrecked, cornered cat look she's glaring at me with is taking an icepick to the frozen barrier around my heart.

"Please, Aurelia. I'd like to know." Even if this level of intimacy with her is killing me, right now, I still need this from her.

A resigned huff. A scowl. A roll of her eyes. And then, "The best decision I ever made was walking into a Starbucks to grab a hot chocolate before school. A woman approached me there and told me I'd be a perfect model. That I had the look she was after and that I could do quite well for myself if I was willing to move to New York. I told my mother when I got home from school that day. Showed her the very official-looking business card. We were living with yet another man I hated by that point. The feeling was pretty mutual, except he too liked the way I looked."

I rein in my temper with a hard swallow. "Did he ever—"

"No. He tried. A couple of times, but I managed to push him off. My mother knew about it and didn't do anything. He was a real estate tycoon, after all, and she wanted his last name. So when this opportunity to get rid of me presented itself, she didn't hesitate. I was a burden by that point. Not young enough to be considered sweet and adorable to the 'daddy' types and old enough to be considered a threat to her or simply unwanted by men who had no desire to deal with a teenager."

"What happened to your real father?" I ask, cutting her off.

She shrugs. "No clue. I never knew who he was, and my mother refused to speak about him whenever I asked."

"Okay. Then what happened?"

"That night, she called the woman and told her I'd do it. By the next day, she had packed all my things up and moved me to an apartment in New York, though apartment is a loose term for tenement."

"Then what?" It's all I can do to hold on. To not have my voice betray the rage bubbling inside me.

"Then she was gone. That was it. She never tried to take my paychecks, which I was grateful for. I needed the money to survive, and I think she knew that. Or she was afraid I'd call the cops and child protective services on her for abandonment if she tried. She'd call to check in with me or my agent every couple of months or so. She told them I was eighteen and they didn't ask a lot of questions. No one checked a birth certificate, and no one cared if was sixteen or eighteen. I had an apartment and a bank account and showed up sober and on time and always with a smile."

"Your mother abandoned you to the modeling industry and New York when you were sixteen?"

She sees the disgust in my eyes, hears it in my voice, and turns back to the window. I'm judging her again. Or more aptly her mother and the life she pushed her down.

"What do you want me to say, Zax? I had it better than many abandoned or runaway kids who live in the city. I had a roof and a good, steady job. I modeled. I finished school. My sob story got me a spot at FIT, and I deferred it for a year so I could model some more."

Then she trusted the wrong woman and was nearly ruined for it, only to have my father pounce on her when she was at her lowest and darkest.

"Do you know how impossible it is to not want to right all your wrongs?"

She laughs, but there is no humor in it. "I am my own hero. Scars are simply souvenirs you collect along the way. They make you tougher and you learn from them. I've learned some lessons the hard way and some the soft way. That's all I could do. But I don't need my boss or his guilt to swoop in and save my day. Frankly, I prefer you when I find you to be an insufferable ass instead of like this." She pans a blind hand my way.

"Why's that?"

Her gaze cuts to mine, visibly calling me out on my baited question. "You want me to say it?"

"I want you to say it."

"Why?"

"Because it's not just you and it's time we address it instead of dancing around it."

She runs her hands over her face and through her hair, only to slap them down on her thighs with a resonating *clap*. "Fine. I like you better when you're an asshole instead of acting like you care—"

"Who says it's an act?" I cut her off quickly.

"Fuck you. Don't you dare do that to me."

Emotion clogs her throat and damn, has no one ever cared about her? No. They haven't, have they? It's all over her, that fear that I'm messing with her and using her before tossing her aside as everyone else has. For all her outward perfection, she is as broken and dismantled as I am. I seize up, having to grip the seat so I don't pull her against me and fucking *hug* her. I'm a mess of a man, but I never lacked love and I always knew where to find it when I needed it most. She's never had that. Not with anyone, I don't think.

"I care, Aurelia."

"I don't *want* you to care," she seethes, though her voice cracks at the end before she fixes it with a simple clearing of her throat. "I don't need to find you any more attractive than I already do. I like not liking you. And I swore, just last night, and frankly every damn night before it, that from now on, you'd only be Mr. Monroe and never Zax to me. I can't lose this opportunity, and frankly, you're simply not worth the risk to me."

"I couldn't have said it better myself."

"Good. Then at least we agree on that."

We do. But her words have me crazed. Slightly deranged.

I want to cup her face and stare into her eyes and put it all on the line just so I can watch that wounded bird determined to fly once again expression disappear for good. Then there's the whole, she feels this too aspect. I knew she did. I'm not blind. Part of me didn't trust her that it was real—or maybe I didn't want to. But now, it's impossible for me to ignore, especially when my body hums, *you asked for it.*

Adrenaline races through my veins as I lean in, my mouth hovering by the shell of her ear. "You don't want me to care?"

"No. I don't."

Shit. Impossible.

"Fine. That doesn't mean I don't want to fuck you, Aurelia,

because I do. And it also doesn't mean I don't want to swoop in and be your hero, because I do. But I'm not going to act on it. That's a promise you can hold on to. So if you believe we can play it safe with each other, that's what we're gonna do. We'll pretend all this other stuff away. But like it or not, every time you see me, you'll know how much I want you. And every time I see you, I'll know you want me back just as much."

My nose grazes her earlobe, and then I right my body just as we pull up in front of her dilapidated building. My teeth set on edge as I take in just how rough this neighborhood is. There are people smoking meth in the alley beside her building, for fuck's sake.

"Go get your things, Miss Whitlock, but please remember, we're on the clock."

"Yes, sir."

Without another word, she flies out of the car, not even waiting on Ashley to help her, though I note he stands outside the car, waiting on her and making his large presence known without my even having to say anything. Ashley Johnson is more than just my driver, he's my security and after this move, I plan to raise his salary.

My finger runs a course back and forth along my bottom lip as I replay all that in my head.

Didn't I say the first step in getting over this attraction is acknowledging it?

Deed done. And knowing she feels the same about all of it might make resistance easier.

She prefers me to be an insufferable ass. I can do that better than anyone. Maybe this time it'll last a whole five minutes before I succumb to her.

AURELIA WAS silent the remainder of the drive and the moment we get through the private airport terminal and over to the plane, my phone rings with the call I've been anxious for. "I have to take this," I tell Ashley, who just gives me a firm nod as I jog up the steps and onto the plane. I throw Carla, the flight attendant, a wave and then head straight for the back, shutting the door in the small bedroom so I have privacy.

"Lenox," I answer, sitting on the edge of the bed, then immediately stand and start pacing.

"Your security guys are morons," he starts, and I drop back onto the bed, elbows on my thighs and hand over my face as I keep my phone pressed to my ear. "That said, I didn't get much further than they did on the insider."

"Are we slacking on our top-notch hacker abilities?"

"I didn't say I didn't get you something. I just said I didn't get much further on that and that's only because there isn't much to get."

"I only spoke to the security guy Monroe uses because he's the same guy my father used when he was CEO. I want him to know I know about his involvement, and I want him to know I'm checking into things on him, but I also want him to think I'm stupid by using a guy he knows how to evade."

"Yeah. I picked up on that. Which is why you called me."

"Which is why I called you."

Only the five of us know about Lenox's skills. The man who dislikes speaking and people even more than I do is an evil genius with a computer. Or phone. Or any electronic device. His hacking abilities got us out of more than a few jams when we were touring, let's just say that.

"I can't tell who he was in touch with in your office because the number he called is a burner phone and so basic, there isn't even an option to track it. Smart. Your father, on the other hand, didn't use a burner number or a burner app. Either he does think you're stupid or he wants you to know he's running the show. Or he doesn't think the security guy will get much, which is likely true. I will tell you, he placed a call last night to the same burner phone that he called the night he dined with Aurelia."

"Last night? How long was the call?"

"Only about five minutes. From seven thirty-two to seven thirty-seven eastern time. He doesn't send texts either, which is smart and annoying. Your father is also back in New York, since I know you were wondering. He flew in last night, getting on a commercial flight about two hours after he placed that call. He's staying in his apartment."

"Marie Marcato's people changed our meeting last night at six. Related or unrelated?"

"I can't say definitively, but again, hell of a coincidence. Could be related and if you want, I can look into her."

I stand again, starting to pace, then pause by the small oval window, peering out at the tarmac. "Yes. Look into her. What about Valencci? Did you find anything on her?"

"There is plenty for you to have some fun with, but nothing linking her to your father. If you want secrets as revenge for your girl, I have those."

The engines rumble through the plane, vibrating the floor beneath my feet, and I know any second they're going to tell me I have to come and sit down. My plane or not, they don't like it when I'm in here during takeoff or landing.

"Send me everything you've got."

"I will."

"Thanks, man. I owe you." I turn, heading for the door.

"We're straight. But you didn't comment on me calling her your girl."

"Lenox—" I cut myself off, freezing in place. Lenox knows I belong to a club for sex, but that's all it is. I haven't been in a relationship or even dated anyone since Suzie. And though Aurelia and I aren't anything more than what we currently are, the thought of discussing this with him...

"I'm fine with it, you know. More than fine with it."

I blow out too many uneven breaths, my throat closing up on me, making it impossible to speak. My hand hits the wall. My body shakes.

"I mean it," he continues. "It's time. You should find happiness, whether it's with this girl or not. I should have said something sooner. Years ago, but I... you never seemed interested in anyone until now. Suzie would never want you to live like this. It would piss her the fuck off if she knew how you've placed your life on hold."

"That go for you too?" I manage, wiping my face and getting my shit back together as I head for the door.

"Love isn't what I'm missing. But you didn't ask."

My steps falter for a half-beat, a frown on my lips as I open the door, and spot Aurelia sitting up by the front, an e-reader poised in front of her face.

I lick my suddenly dry lips. "I didn't."

"Do you want to know?"

Do I?

On an inhale, I make my way up the aisle and take the seat directly across from her, buckling up and staring at her while she ignores me in favor of whatever it is she's reading.

"Yes," I say into the phone, my heart thundering as loud as the engines.

"She's clean as far as I can tell. No contact with your father other than what she mentioned previously to you, and so far everything lines up. Whatever your father has planned, I think she's his pawn and not his queen."

"You're sure?"

A half-chuckle, which from Lenox is the equivalent of a belly laugh. "I'm sure. Does this mean you're fucking the beauty queen already?"

"No. And that's not going to be part of the agenda with this." I continue to watch her.

"Uh-huh. Simply in love then. Poor bastard."

I roll my eyes at his mocking tone but can't help the smile it brings. The unexpected lightness I feel at all that he just said. "Anything else?"

"Just because she's not privy to the scheme doesn't make her less dangerous. It might, in fact, make her more so given her circumstances. In case you weren't aware yet, she's had it rough."

"I know. I plan to deal with that when I can. Is there more?"

"Yes. There's always more, but I'm assuming there are ears near you."

"That is correct. Send me the discussed items along with anything else you feel I should have eyes on. We're about to take off."

"Will do."

"And, Lenox?"

"Yeah?"

"Thanks, man. Later."

I set my phone down on the small table beside me just as the plane picks up speed and we ascend into the air. Aurelia, it seems, is clean, but there are vipers dancing all around her, waiting for the right moment to strike.

"Will we be eating when we get to New York?" she asks without sparing me a glance or removing her eyes from her device.

"Dinner, yes."

"Not lunch?"

"No. Are you hungry? We have snacks and things on board."

She shakes her head and finally sets the e-reader down so she can dig into her purse. She pulls out a bag of granola and then starts quietly munching on it as she returns to her reading, and I can't help but wonder.

"Did you make that?"

"Yes."

"You make your own granola?"

"I do." She glances around her screen with a polite smile. "Would you like to try it? I share." She shakes the bag in my direction.

Yes, but if it's good, I'll like her more. "No, thanks. How come you don't just buy it?"

She shrugs, shoveling another handful into her mouth and crunching on it while returning to her screen, though I know she's not reading anything. "Old habits and I like mine better than the store stuff. It's cheaper for me to buy the ingredients and make it than it is for me to buy it in the store and at least I know what I'm putting into my body this way."

"So you eat?"

She doesn't laugh at my sarcastic question, nor does she roll her eyes or glare at me as I hoped she would. I hate that she's focused on her screen and not me. But after what happened with the last girl in her position and the fact that Aurelia is a model and notoriously they don't have the healthiest eating habits, I need to know.

"Yes. I eat. I eat plenty. Modeling didn't give me an eating disorder. It gave me a cleaner, healthier way of eating. I cooked for myself, and I didn't eat junk food or a lot of sodium or white carbs. Now I eat more like a human, all the carbs, but I still like to make certain things for myself, and this granola is one of them."

"You never starved yourself?"

Finally, my question gets her to set the device down. "Nope. I didn't starve myself and I didn't need to. This is my body." She waves a hand up and down herself as if proving her point. And yep, I take the bait and follow her motion. "A hanger with boobs, is what my agent used to call me. Not the nicest analogy, but that's what models are supposed to be, isn't it? Vehicles to show off clothes and not steal their thunder."

Only she doesn't just steal thunder, she's the storm. The category five hurricane and the F-5 tornado. Destructively exquisite and a force to behold. I saw her walk in that dress she designed, and yes, the dress was something else, but it was her I couldn't take my eyes off of.

I tap out a beat on my thigh. "Did you make that outfit you're wearing now?"

"Yes."

I examine the red linen skirt—short fucking skirt—and matching halter that looks like blood flowing over porcelain on her. She eyes me, waiting for me to comment on the length as I always do—it hits above her knees, and I know that's intentional and all for me. If she knew what the sight of her long, long legs does to me and the accompanying images I have with them, she'd never wear anything short again.

"You don't look like a hanger with boobs."

She smirks. "You're not supposed to notice my boobs."

"I thought we already agreed that I was going to notice your boobs but pretend I don't."

"Is this you pretending?" She folds her arms and quirks that brow, still smirking at me. The woman gets off on challenging me and Lord help me, I get off on it too.

"Absolutely."

She laughs, digging for a piece of her granola and chucking it at me. Whatever it is she threw nails me in the chest and I pick it up, popping it into my mouth. A chocolate chip. Thank God it wasn't a piece of granola, or I'd really be screwed.

She unbuckles her seat belt and stands. "I'm going to use the restroom."

"Aurelia, you might be my intern, but you don't have to ask permission for that."

"I wasn't. I was simply letting you know I was, so you could steal some of my granola while I'm gone. I know you're dying to. *I'll pretend I don't notice*," she emphasizes, sarcastically throwing my words back at me.

With that, she spins around, the bottom of her skirt twirling out around her as she sashays to the bathroom.

"You're swaying your hips and ass," I call out after her.

"Stop noticing."

I smile like a son of a bitch. "Not possible," I murmur under my breath. Then I do, in fact, go for her granola.

AURELIA

"Which one?" I ask the group chat of Iris, Nate, and Howie, holding up two totally different dresses. One is a black, asymmetrical, leather bustier minidress. The other is a periwinkle, silk, ruched one-shoulder minidress. And yes, before you go there, the minidress on both is intentional—*coughs* Lamar—and no, I didn't pick either dress out.

"Leather," Iris says while the two boys say, "Periwinkle."

"No. Leather," Iris argues. "It's fucking New York and fierce and a statement."

"Except this is a business deal we're trying to make, and softer fabrics and colors are less aggressive," Howie insists.

"Agreed," Nate says, only for his phone to be stolen from his hands and Lamar's handsome face to appear on the screen. He pushes his glasses up his nose and gives me the *you better listen and listen good* face.

"Periwinkle, Liastrange. Soft, sweet hair and makeup. You are a nymph who plays with woodland creatures a la Snow Motherfucking White. Your purpose tonight is to join forces and leather is too domme for this crew and dinner. I'm thinking your hair parted in the middle with twin braids going back and thick, soft waves with shimmery eyes and why the fuck am I not there right now?" he barks, turning toward poor Nate as if he has the answer. "Because we're stuck in the office still trying to work out this fucking power suit shoot. That's why."

"Relax," I tell him. "I've got it. I promise. If I send you selfies, will that cool your high heels?"

"It might. Marginally. Be prepared for Thursday."

I snicker. "Fine. But do we have to keep this Liastrange thing going?"

"Give me till Thursday. It will likely have died off by then."

"Fabulous. Okay, I need to finish getting ready." I blow kisses and disconnect the call, dropping my phone on the bed. I love the dress, but there is one major problem with it. The zipper. I get the zipper as high up my back as I can, but no amount of wiggling or acrobatics is allowing me to reach it on the other side. Not to mention the hangers here in the closet are not zipper loop friendly, so I can't even snag it and do my hanger-zipper trick. It's going to have to be Zax and yeah, I like that thought as much as I'm trying not to like that thought.

You know, since we're all about that.

Whatever. I'm not thinking about that because we both agreed nothing is happening nor do we want it to. And I'm *definitely* not thinking about all that he said in the car. That he cares. Jesus. Is he trying to make me fall in love with him while simultaneously ruining me for good? There is only so much I can take before I start to chip away like ancient china and I'm nearly at my cracking point.

I do my hair and makeup as Lamar suggested, because I think he's absolutely right on his style of me for the night, and then I slip into my five-inch matching strappy heels and stare at myself in the mirror. I do feel like a woodland nymph. Very sweet and feminine. I snap a couple of selfies and send them to Lamar.

Then I stuff my purse with my wallet, phone, and room key and head out the door. Zax is on this floor too, though I think he's in some crazy suite I didn't get the benefit of. I glance left and right and thankfully, the hallway is clear since my back is mostly exposed, and the dress is draping a bit in the front since it's woefully unzipped.

I tap on Zax's door and wait a minute or so, only there's no answer, so I knock a bit harder and then ring the bell because yeah, suite. Still no answer. Dammit. He told me to come get him and that we'd go downstairs together. Did he leave before me? I have a key to his room. The woman at registration screwed up and gave me his extra key. I gnaw on the corner of my lip, debating. I try one last knock and ring and with no answer to that, I swipe the flat disc along the circle and the green light flashes. Opening the heavy door, I close my eyes and enter the room.

"Mr. Monroe?"

He doesn't answer, but I do hear some sound in the back by the bedroom. Music. Good music. Wild Minds music. Squinting my eyes open, I meander my way through the living room, hating how it already smells of him in here. Another sound and I follow the trail.

"Mr. Monroe?" No answer. "Zax?" I try a little louder to be heard over the music.

A grunt and a groan. "Aurelia. Fuck." An even louder groan and something isn't right. He doesn't sound like himself. Maybe he's sick and that's why he didn't answer the door? I rush through his bedroom over to the bathroom where the light is on, and the door is partially ajar.

"Zax?" I tap on the wood, but in doing so it slides open all the way and there he is, standing in front of the far sink at the marble double vanity in the massive bathroom, his profile directly in my sight line, his slacks undone, and his cock in his hand.

"Fuck. Aurelia. What the fuck?" His head flies left and our eyes collide for a half-second until mine snap closed.

Flustered and shocked, my head bangs into the wall as I try to spin around to give him privacy. *Ow*. That hurt and better not leave a mark.

I rub my forehead as I start sputtering words. "I'm so sorry. I couldn't zip up the back of my dress and I needed help, and the woman downstairs gave me your room key when we checked in and I knocked and rang, but you didn't answer and then I heard you groan and say my name and I thought you were sick and—" Wait.

"Get out!"

Only I can't move. My legs are jelly, and my heart is racing a mile a minute.

"You said my name. Before you knew I was in your room."

My eyes open and I spin back around to face him. He's unmoved, his fist tight around his large cock, the head purple with how tight he's gripping it. He didn't even try to tuck himself back in or hide what he was doing. He's simply staring at me, head angled in my direction with a hard, unrelenting gaze that sears fire along my skin.

I blink at him. "You were jerking off. To me."

"Get. Out. I can't do this with you here. Out!"

"Zax—"

Now he moves to tuck himself back in and I don't want him to do that. His slacks stay undone, but he's combing his hands back through his hair, angling himself away from me toward the far wall. "I'm your fucking boss. This is not okay. Do you not get that? This is my room, and you should not be in here. Now get the fuck out!"

He's right. I need to go, and I shouldn't be in here and I likely shouldn't have just let myself in. It's not okay and it's not appropriate and he is my boss and yet I'm stepping farther into the bathroom. I'm moving in closer to him.

He sees me coming in the reflection of the mirror and he spins to face me, growling at me, sweat clinging to his brow. "What are you doing? Did you not hear me? Out!" He points over my shoulder to the door behind me.

"No."

"No?" He clutches the counter, bending forward and breathing out harshly. "Aurelia, I'm at my end. You can't be in here right now."

I move in close to him, feeling him shake with his restraint. "You were thinking about me?"

"Fuck," he hisses, closing his eyes and blowing out a breath as his head falls back, chin pointed up to the ceiling. "You know I was. You heard me. Happy now? Go!"

"I want to watch."

"What?" His eyes shoot open, pinning me with a look that is so primal and fierce I tremble, my nipples hardening as my empty core clenches.

"I want to watch you," I repeat, holding his eyes, all that dark brown nearly swallowed by his black pupils.

A slight head shake. "You can't watch me do this."

"Fine." I spin around, facing the door once more. The huge walk-in shower, still coated in steam and drops of water on my left fills the air with humidity that only seems to enhance this. I step back so my unzipped bare back grazes the side of his arm as he faces the sink.

A low, rough sound scratches past his throat.

"I won't look," I tell him. "But I want to hear you. Please, Zax. I want to hear you come while you're thinking about me."

I don't even know what I'm saying or doing, but all I know is I can't leave, and I can't get the vision of him unhinged and hard over me out of my head. I want this man and I know he wants me. But I didn't know it was like *this*. This caliber of desire. Of lust. Of fucking insanity where all you can think about is the other person. Not to this extent where he has to jerk off about me before attending a business dinner with me.

I'm so riled up with this that if he does force me out of here, I'll lie on his bed and get myself off while he finishes in here. Maybe it's just been too long since a man has touched me or wanted me to this extreme, but God, it's doing all kinds of things to me. To the point where I no longer have control.

"Please," I beg, when he doesn't move or speak. "You can touch me or not, and I'll even close my eyes, but just... finish."

His hand clasps my hip over my dress so hard I wonder if it'll leave a mark. I moan at that possibility, my thighs pressing together, my aching pussy desperate for friction, my panties soaked.

"You want this? You really want this?"

"Yes."

"I'm not going to fuck you and I'm not going to get you off. You shouldn't be here. I told you to go and you won't fucking go."

"I can't. Please. I don't care about me. I just want to hear you." Hell, I'd beg him to come on me if I wasn't dressed and ready to go out. "It won't be beyond this. I know it won't and after we walk out of this suite, it will be like it never happened. But please, Zax. I don't even know why, but I need this just as much as you do."

He breathes out a slew of curses, one after the other, and then I feel his body shift until he's right up against me. "Move your hair over one shoulder."

I do it instantly, exposing my back and neck to him. His lips fall to the latter, not kissing, just resting, his nose on my skin as he inhales. My eyes roll back in my head at that, at him *smelling* me, and I swear, I'm so close to coming just from this.

"You can touch me," I repeat because I *need* him to touch me. Even if it's not to get me off. Even if it's just somewhere on my bare skin, I need it like I need oxygen right now. Something I'm gulping in so fast I'm nearly hyperventilating.

"Aurelia, you're killing me. This is so wrong."

It is. I know it is. We've both made a thousand different promises this week, and we continue to break every one. Or maybe that's just me. Maybe I'm the one breaking all the rules while he's trying to do the right thing. I don't even know anymore.

"It never leaves this bathroom," I promise, and this promise is one I won't break. I put this on him. Not the other way around.

His grip on my hip tightens and for a split second, I think he's going to push me out the door and lock it, but then he releases me, and I hear his hand move in his pants. I picture him pulling his hard cock back out and gripping it in his fist. His hand trickles along my exposed back where my zipper is open.

I quake as he dips inside the fabric of my dress, his palm flat as it slides around to my belly, pressing in, fingers splayed.

"No bra."

"Not with this dress."

"What about panties?"

Fucking hell.

"The dress is too short to not wear any."

"I noticed."

His voice is so gruff, sandpaper over polished stone.

"Are you wet for me?"

"Yes. Very."

He groans and I feel him start to jerk himself off, holding me while he does it. His lips and nose on my skin as he pleasures himself. His hand on my belly slides lower at first, gliding along the line of my panties, only to dip just beneath the top, the tips of his fingers tickling my smooth mound.

I bite my lip, my knees weak, ready to buckle beneath me. My right hand flies to the counter so I don't collapse. *Go lower. Please, God in heaven, go lower.* He doesn't. His fingers linger there for a moment, then slide up until his thumb barely brushes the underside of my breast. All the while he's jerking himself. His body thrusts and moves against me, his sounds filling the air. With my eyes closed, all I picture is his large hand working his perfect cock. How thick and long and veiny it is. How good it would feel inside of me.

I want him to bend me over the counter and slide inside of me from behind. I want to look up into the mirror and watch while he loses himself fucking me.

"Zax," escapes my throat before I can stop it because his thumb is moving along the underside of my breast and his sounds are throaty and raw and everything and my thighs are pressing together, rubbing, and I come. I fucking come like this. It's not a big orgasm by any means, but it's enough.

And he feels it. He knows.

It drives him insane, tipping him over the edge. His teeth scrape my neck. His hand on me presses in until my back is flat to his side and then he comes. Loud. Groans and grunts and curses and my name. He's saying my name as he comes on the towel on the counter, and I'd give *anything* right now to see it.

When he's done, he sags against me for a beat and releases me completely. I hear the faucet turn on and then I think he's washing his hands and I hear him cleaning up whatever mess he just made. I haven't moved. I've hardly breathed. He fixes his pants and closes them, looping his belt, the sound of metal jangling through the room.

Then his hands are back on me, on my zipper, and he's zipping me up before he adjusts my hair back in place.

"I need to go change my underwear." No way I can go out tonight with my cold, wet cum in them.

A grunt. "Go. I'll be waiting for you in the hallway."

"Okay."

"And, Aurelia?"

"Yes?"

"Take off the ones you're wearing here."

Is he trying to make me orgasm again?

"Yes, sir."

Reaching up under my dress and not caring in the slightest if it bunches up and he sees me do it, my fingers hook into the skimpy hips of my panties and then I slide them down my legs until they're on the floor.

Then I scurry out of here, my legs wobbly, but I don't care. I need a minute to breathe, and I can't do that with him close to me. Now that the desire has ebbed and the orgasm has swept through me, the gravity of what I just did, what I just put on him, slams into me.

He could fire me. But I don't think he will.

Reaching my room, I tear into my suitcase, pulling out the first pair of underwear I come across. As I slide my new ones up, I can't help thinking about him looking at or touching or smelling my wet ones that I left on his floor, owning the evidence of what just happened. I adjust my dress and a laugh hits the air. Holy shit. I just did that. With Zaxton Monroe. A man who as far as I know hasn't been with a woman in eight years, though I don't see how any of that is true.

I check myself in the mirror. Flushed. But smiling.

Even if I have to go and face him now.

I do a mini freak-out dance and then get myself back together and leave my room. Zax is leaning against the wall, his eyes on his phone, cool and casual as ever. Totally unruffled whereas I'm still a mess.

"I'm ready," I tell him when he doesn't immediately acknowledge me.

He finishes whatever he was typing and then slides his phone into the pocket of his suit pants. He waves for me to go first, and I head toward the elevator. We step on, still in silence, and it's so heavy and thick I'm practically suffocating in it.

"Are we okay?"

"If you feel the need to speak to Beth about what—"

"Beth?" Sharply, I glance up at him. "Why would I want to speak to Beth?"

"Because what I just did was inappropriate."

I shake my head, infuriated by that. Then I remember what Beth said to me just this morning. About rumors. "Have you ever done something like that before with a woman you work with?"

He looks like I just sucker punched him in the gut. "What? N-no. Of course not. And I shouldn't have done that with you now."

I'm far too relieved for anyone's sanity. "I'm not talking to Beth and I'm not mad or upset we did that. That was all me and not you. So if *you'd* like to speak to Beth—"

He laughs. "Aurelia, I'm pretty sure that was me too and if I didn't want it to happen, I would have forced you out."

"Good. So shut up with talking to HR or anything else. We said it was going to stay up there and that's what it will do."

"Fine."

I smirk up at him. "Fine."

"Your dress is too short."

"Yep. It is. Get over it. I'm in New York and this is your couture."

His head dips down to whisper in my ear, "Now you know why I had to make myself come before I could see you. Incidentally, I'm keeping your underwear. And the pretty wet spot you left behind in them."

18

ZAXTON

I f there's one thing I learned today, it's that lines in the sand are just like the sand you draw them in, malleable. Erasable. Far from finite. For every line I cross with Aurelia, I find myself clearing that out and drawing a new one. Scratch. Scribble. Repeat.

I've stopped asking what it is about her that has me so captivated.

I've stopped questioning the extent of my desire for her.

The way I want her is not rational and it's not reasonable. So I've moved on to the acceptance phase of this addiction. Now I have to find my way to the abstinence stage—fucking impossible. It only took a moment. Her eyes on me. The sexy, pleading way she told me she wanted to watch me get off to her. That's all it took for me to finally snap. The way she came, just from the smallest touch—the way she said my name and those goddamn sounds she made as she did that will live forever in my head.

The things this woman does to me.

I had considered going to the club tonight. My club. The one only my friends and brother know I belong to and occasionally frequent with me. There are branches all over the world and the New York one is practically walking distance from our hotel.

But there is no appeal in it. Not that there was ever much, but any that had been there all but died the moment I laid eyes on her. That's how I ended up with my cock in my fist in the first place. Her.

Business dinners are about as appealing to me as sticking my head in a blender and pressing the ON switch. They require peopling and being polite and personable. They require smiles and inane chuckles at ridiculous jokes over small talk meant to put people at ease. All things I not only suck at but don't have the desire to work on improving. This was why I invested in companies instead of running them.

I'm not a gladhander.

But Maria Marcato requires a little finessing and personal attention with her business decisions. Maybe that's why her company is going down the toilet. For such a closed off woman, she needs a lot of hand-holding. I offered to simply view her warehouse and then write her a check, but the woman came back to me demanding I wine and dine her a bit first because apparently, she likes a little foreplay before she gets fucked. Or in her words, she simply can't imagine selling off her business to just anyone off the street.

I think they can feel me rolling my eyes at that from space.

Frankly, it's why I decided to bring Aurelia along in the first place. She is everything I'm not. All bright sunshiney sweet goodness. Not to mention she already has a relationship with Marie when few do.

I open the door of the restaurant, holding it wide for Aurelia to pass through first. It's dark in here in a very New York chic restaurant way. Lots of moody purple lighting and a faint house beat. Not surprising for this place as the back half beyond the curtain is an exclusive club. Not my style of exclusive club unfortunately.

"We're here to meet with Marie Marcato," I tell the maître d' standing snobbishly behind a long wooden desk.

He glances at me, then lingers on Aurelia like she's Kobe beef. "And what name may I use when presenting you to Miss Marcato?"

Is he joking? Presenting?

Aurelia's hand hits my forearm as if she can already sense I'm at the end of my patience. You'd think coming while touching and smelling her would have soothed my savage beast, but nope. If anything, I'm more riled than I was before.

"Please inform her that Mr. Zaxton Monroe and his assistant are here."

The dude's eyes pop at the mention of my name and then everything about this moment changes. "Of course, sir. My apologies for not recognizing you instantly. I'm wearing your suit." He chuckles self-consciously at how awkward that sounds and then collects himself. "Right this way, please."

We follow after him, my hand firmly on Aurelia's lower back in a very possessive way because the number of men who are doing double takes of her is clenching my already clenched jaw tighter. She seems oblivious. It's one thing I like about her. She's not a strutter and she's not a preener. She doesn't care about any of the bullshit every other woman who has ever tried to enter my life after Suzie cared about.

We're led to a small, private room in the back and there waiting for us is Marie Marcato, all chin-length black hair, black eyes, black clothes, and red lips. She's everything that is mod and emo.

"Marie," Aurelia exclaims, stepping away from me and immediately crossing the room to embrace her. Marie stands, hugging Aurelia, who towers a foot taller in her heels.

"My dear girl. You look gorgeous. How have you been? I haven't seen you since shortly before you graduated."

Marie's hand lingers on Aurelia's face, the two of them beaming at each other.

"I'm wonderful. Landed on my feet as you can see. Marie, may I introduce you to my boss, Zaxton Monroe." Aurelia turns to me with those pretty eyes glimmering in the dim lighting. "Mr. Monroe, this is one of my favorite designers I've ever had the pleasure of working for, Marie Marcato."

"Miss Marcato." I step forward and extend my hand, which she shakes, only to immediately sit back down.

"Mr. Monroe, I'm hoping we can skip straight to Marie and Zaxton."

I nod in approval of that and pull out the chair for Aurelia, beating the maître d' to it. I settle in and Marie orders fucking wine and oysters for us like this is a date and the night goes from there. Long. Drawn-out conversations. Very little discussion about business. It's all giving me a headache. Course after course until mercifully Aurelia declines dessert, claiming she's too stuffed to eat another bite.

"Well then, I think I'll retire for the evening," Marie announces. "Thank you for agreeing to this dinner, Zaxton. A man who is serious about his business puts up with such trivialities even when they're not to his benefit or liking. Plus, you've hired on a woman who I consider to be a diamond in a sea of coal. So, tomorrow you can come and see my warehouse and my business operations and then we can talk business."

Savvy woman. I stand, extending my hand to her. "Thank you, Marie. We'll be there. May I walk you out?"

She waves me away, hugging Aurelia, who stands to say goodbye. "No, no. You two stay. Enjoy your evening. It is still early." She winks at me as if she thinks I'm fucking Aurelia and then leaves. Great.

"Well, I need a drink. A real drink."

"Me too," Aurelia states only for her eyes to widen and her to quickly follow that up with, "I didn't mean I was inviting myself to your drink, though."

"And where were you thinking of getting a drink then?" I ask.

"Here? I don't know. The hotel is lovely, but I'm not quite in the mood for that. I was thinking of checking out the club in the back. Maybe having a drink and dancing some of this energy off."

"Alone?"

She rolls her eyes at my no-doubt murderous expression. "Yes, alone. I am a twenty-three-year-old woman, Mr. Monroe. If I want to go dancing by myself, I can. It wouldn't be the first time I've done that in this city."

Jesus. It's like this woman knows how to hit each of my pressure points with fucking precision. She has to know there is no way on God's green earth I am letting her walk into a club alone when she's dressed like this. Forget her being dressed like this, she could be wearing a burqa and I still wouldn't let her do that alone.

Reaching out, I grasp her forearm and give her a good, hard tug into me. My hand hits her lower back and I hold her much the way I did when we did our photo shoot. "I'm coming with you."

"I didn't invite you."

I dip in, my eyes on hers, our noses an inch apart. "I wasn't giving you the option."

"Are you planning on cockblocking me all night?"

"Yup."

She emits a flustered noise, her sweet breath skirting along my lips.

"Like it or not, you're here on a business trip with me. That means I set the rules and call the shots."

"Have it your way. But I plan to dance in that club. You can either dance with me or watch."

IT TOOK LESS than five seconds for us to get into the club and up to the VIP area. Aurelia dropped the name Lia Sage. Not mine. Evidently, in a club like this, model trumps former rock star, billionaire fashion moguls. But as her hand twines with mine and we're led up a back staircase, I can't help but grip it tighter.

Normally, I hate these places.

But there is something thrilling about being here with her. Something hedonistic and forbidden and so fucking sexy my cock is already throbbing in my slacks. More of those lines in the sand being erased and redrawn. She hasn't asked for anything from me, and I don't think that's what she's after. I don't see this as a ploy to climb up the ladder or even crawl into my bed and heart. If anything, I think she fears what this thing between us would do to her job.

She doesn't want to date me.

She's not looking for a relationship or love or commitment.

But that doesn't mean she's not feeling this too. This pulsing need that thrums between us seems to render us both powerless against its lure.

Then something occurs to me. Something bleak and dark and rotten. Lenox said my father is in town. That he flew in last night. Is he here? Is she setting me up? Is that why she said she was coming here and why she dropped her name instead of mine? Every time I begin to trust her, to give in just a few inches...

Her head swivels over her shoulder and she wrecks me with a beaming smile and a squeeze of my hand. This girl. This fucking girl.

"Relax," she mouths, tugging on me as we're directed to a booth, only for her to shake her head at the man. "No. I think we need something smaller. More private." She scans the room and then points to a spot in the back. "There. That's what I'd like."

The man stares at her like she's lost her mind. "But this is the booth I typically put all the models in. It's the most visible."

She slips some cash out of her purse. "If you could move us somewhere more private, I'd be forever grateful. And please, keep it quiet that I'm here. I'll be sure to pass the word along to *all* my friends how accommodating you are."

That smile she was just giving me is all for him now and I almost feel sorry for the poor bastard. He doesn't stand a chance.

"Of course, Lia. I'll remove your name from the list, and you can have whatever booth you'd like for you and your guest."

"Oh, you're so sweet. Thank you." She leans over and plants a soft kiss on his cheek.

A blush lights up his face and then he's seating us in the smaller, darker, back of the room and away from the main VIP floor booth.

"There," she says. "This is much better. Less in the limelight." Settling in on the short, white bench seat, she crosses her impossibly long legs at the knee. The hem of her dress hikes up so high, if she were to uncross those legs, I'd get the most perfect view of her new panties.

I sit beside her but keep a good amount of space between us just as a waitress comes over. I order a bottle of expensive tequila, lime, and margarita mix. Aurelia throws me a side-eye but doesn't comment otherwise until the waitress leaves us.

"You liked me so much on tequila that night you felt the need to recreate it?"

"You're honest on tequila."

She laughs. "Zax, I'm pretty honest most of the time whether I'm drunk or not. You could have saved yourself the bottle fees if you have something you want to know."

I do, but right now isn't the time to start asking questions.

The waitress returns with a loaded tray full of tequila, shot glasses, highball glasses, mixers, waters, limes, and salt. Everything is set on the purple up-lit acrylic table before us and then she's gone, leaving us to ourselves. Shifting forward, Aurelia skirts to the edge of the seat. With the bottle gripped in one hand, she rips the cork on the tequila with her other, pouring us both shots into the high-ball glasses instead of the low shot glasses.

She hands one to me. "You told me you need a real drink."

"Tequila isn't a real drink."

She gives me a bemused look. "Then why did you order it?"

"Because you like it."

"I like everything. I would have had bourbon or scotch or vodka."

"Now you tell me."

"Next time ask." We hold up our glasses and both take our shots, foregoing the salt and lime. Another is poured and tossed down and then one more. And once that third one is down, she rises. "I'm going to dance."

She doesn't wait on me. She's not even inviting me along.

But the moment she reaches the dance floor, her eyes find mine and she gives me the sexiest look I've ever seen. One that tells me she knows I'm watching her, and she likes it. She starts to move her body to the heavy trick-hop and house beats, immediately getting lost in the sound. Whether this dance is for me or for her or for both, I don't care. She has me utterly entranced. Mesmerized by the way she moves. By the way her hands glide along her body and her dress slips up her thighs that much higher. By how her eyes close and her hair tumbles back.

I lose track of time. One song bleeds into the next as I attempt to do some work on my phone but to no avail. And just as I give up the fight, a man comes in behind her, placing his hands on her hips. Her eyes pop open and she shakes her head at him, pointing at me as if I'm her date. Her lover.

And for the first time in eight years, I realize that's exactly what I want to be with her.

It's a startling realization. One that knocks the breath from me.

But also has me standing and moving across the room, straight for her. She catches me coming, a coy smile on her lips as she quirks a come-hither finger at me. My heart tumbles around in my chest, thudding and acting strange. However it's beating it's different and my body feels it.

"I was wondering if you dance," she says to me as I get within earshot, my hands sliding around her hips to the crest above her ass. Her hands loop around my neck, our bodies pressed together, and now I'm moving us, leading because she's letting me.

"I dance. I just haven't in a very long time."

"No clubs for you."

I smirk. "Not this type."

Her head quirks as if she's going to follow that up with the obvious question, only I don't let her. I'm too off right now. Keyed up and edgy and anxious to scratch out another line in the sand. She makes me primal. My body operating on my baser instincts and right now, all I can think about is how she looked when she came in the bathroom. I was watching her in the reflection of the mirror the entire time. Her eyes closed, her lips parted, her cheeks flushed.

But I didn't see her eyes and I didn't get to feel it on my fingers.

My head inclines, my mouth by her ear. "Wanna pretend some more with me, Lia?" I use her model name so she knows what this is. This isn't Mr. Monroe and Aurelia. This is Zax and Lia.

"What did you have in mind?" Her breath hitches when my hand drags down, squeezing and lifting one of her ass cheeks so she's pressed into me. So she feels how fucking hard she makes me.

"Come with me and I'll show you."

I don't give her the option either way. I take her hand in mine and lead her off the dance floor through the miasma of the upstairs club and over to an alcove not far from our table. I spin her around so she's facing me and then I'm walking her backward into the darkness where the arrhythmic strobes don't touch.

Then I attack her.

My hands fly up into her hair and my lips fuse with hers. A groan sears past my lungs because the second my lips touch hers, something inside me shifts, and it feels so fucking good I have no words to describe it because I'm not even sure what the hell it is. Could be because I haven't kissed a woman in... a long fucking time. I don't normally bother with such trivialities as kissing women, but I had to kiss Aurelia.

Her taste. By God, how this woman tastes.

I'm a goner.

Tequila and Aurelia, she's so fucking sweet and spicy my head spins. She moans, her hands up in my hair, clinging to the roots and pulling. I've wanted to kiss her since I first laid eyes on her. Since she first opened that impertinent mouth. And she doesn't disappoint. Her tongue seeks mine, sliding and dancing with me in sync with the beat.

My head tilts and I take her deeper, leading us once again, and she quickly submits. Liking that I'm controlling her. Nips and licks and deep plunges, I'm lost in her. My hands roam, across her shoulders and along her arms, cupping her tits and rolling my thumbs over her hard nipples. No bra, I can feel them through the thin material of her dress.

There are reasons I shouldn't be doing this. But right now, I can't remember a single one. Even if I could, I doubt I'd care enough to stop. Not with her pressed against me, kissing me back like the single source of her next breath lives inside my mouth. Her kiss, her lips, her tongue—hot, delicious, torturous bliss.

I break the kiss, my lips hovering by her ear. "I'm still not going to fuck you. But this time, I'm the one who gets to make you come."

"If we're pretending, then I want to pretend I don't know you."

My dick jerks in my pants and I meet her glazed-over eyes. "You want me to be a stranger? Coming up to you in a club and leading you to a dark corner to have my wicked way with you?"

A breathy whisper. "Yes."

"That a fantasy of yours?"

A head nod and Christ. This woman will be the death of me. I'm wild, crazy and out of control with her.

"Did you see me watching you?" I murmur against her lips as my hand continues lower, finding the silky skin of her legs I'm so obsessed with.

"Yes."

"Did you like that? Me watching you? Knowing you were making me hard as you danced?"

"Yes." She can barely catch her breath as my hand starts to slide up, her body trembling. I take her hand and place it over my aching cock, grinding up into her small palm. She whimpers and I grin against her lips, sucking down her noises, one after the other. The tips of my fingers tickle the edge of her panties, right between her legs. She's so soft. Everywhere.

"I don't want your name and I don't want to know anything about you other than how you look when I make you come."

"Oh fuck, please," she begs as I cover her pussy with my hand, then peel her panties to the side and slip a finger straight inside her.

"Beautiful girl, you're soaked for me."

I pull out of her, gliding my wet finger along her smooth lips, her drenched seam. I glance down between us, hateful of the darkness and the angle. If we were back in the hotel, I'd have her splayed out on my bed. I'd suck on her pussy till she begged me to stop. Till her cum dripped all over my face.

My thumb finds her swollen clit, and I start to rub, only to shift my wrist and plunge two fingers inside her. Her head falls back against the wall as I start fucking her like this. Pumping in and out while massaging her clit in a way that has her gripping my shirt in her fist.

"Oh, God. Oh, yes. Please, don't stop."

My eyes are glued to her face, watching and memorizing her every reaction to my touch. "Open your eyes, Angel. I want them on me." My voice is tight, strung like a rubber band about to snap. Those incredible blue eyes, nearly black with her lust fling open and *fuck*. She is everything. Helplessly, I rub myself against her hip as I start to rub her faster, my fingers quirked, angled in against her G-spot.

Not even twenty feet from us, people are dancing and laughing and drinking. There's a whole club surrounding us. But I can't stop looking at her. All I can see is her gorgeous blissed-out face. All I can feel is her tight pussy clenching my fingers with every slick pass. Her soft tits pressed to my chest.

"So good," she rasps, leaning up to kiss me again, her lips sloppy as she moans and pants. "This feels so good."

"*You* feel so good. I wanted to make you come since I first saw you up there dancing." *Since I first saw you.* "You were cock teasing me. Weren't you? My dirty little slut, you like getting finger fucked by a stranger in the middle of a club?"

"Fuck. Yes. Oh, shit, yes."

I grin against her, biting her bottom lip and dragging it through my teeth. She likes the fantasy. She likes the pretend. She likes me calling her names and making her feel dirty because she knows I think...

"You're fucking perfect."

Does she have a fraction of a clue just how perfect she is to me?

My fingers start to move faster, more urgent as she gets closer. My thumb taps on her clit before pressing in harder, rubbing in tighter circles and she detonates. All over me. Her eyes are almost frantic until she can't take it any longer and they close. Moans tumble past her lips that I greedily swallow.

"So sweet. Such a filthy angel," I tell her as I fuck her through her orgasm. Until she sags against me with a sated, incredulous laugh. I lean her back against the wall and pull my fingers from her, stick them in my mouth, and lick her off them, needing to taste her. She watches me, shellshocked to the point where she doesn't even bother to adjust herself.

I replace her panties and fix her dress before I bring her into me, holding her in my arms.

"You okay?"

"I'm fantastic."

I chuckle against her. "Yes. You are."

"Thank you for that. I've always wanted a random tryst with a stranger in a club but never had the guts to actually do something like that. At least not with any of them who tried before."

I cup her face in my palm. "I liked being your fantasy."

"Too bad that was a one and done. A girl could grow used to playing a little. Especially with fingers as talented as yours."

I give her one last kiss. Because I have to. Because I'm trying to draw this line and for once have it stick. Because I know this can't continue between us. We both have too much at stake for that.

19

AURELIA

Zax holds me close, right up against him for longer than he should. Longer than I should allow him, that's for damn sure. His heart pounds in rhythm with the house beat, his dick still hard, pressed between us, but he's not pushing for more than what we just did. Which I tell myself I'm relieved by.

I wasn't kidding when I said too bad it was a one and done thing, because his fingers and kisses are magic times a billion, but part of that was a reminder for myself. I am considering this a tit for tat situation and while reciprocity was fun, that's all it was.

I won't risk my heart or my job on a man who I know will never be anything more than a good time. He won't love me. He won't date me. Hell, he doesn't even *like* me. I need more than that from a man. More than attraction and heat.

What was left in his suite bathroom is now being left in a club alcove. If we keep this up, no part of Manhattan will be safe. Which is why I pull back and meet his eyes with a smile. He's staring at me, all dark and stormy, a swirl of too many thoughts twisting up his mind.

"I'm going to have another drink and dance some more."

He blinks at me. "You are?"

"Yes. For maybe another half an hour or so. But feel free to go. You certainly don't have to stay and babysit me. I know how it is for you old men when it gets late and you're tired."

He pinches my ass and I yelp.

"One more drink. Thirty minutes. Then we go back to the hotel." He catches himself, his hand now on my cheek as he stares into my eyes. "You're okay with this—"

"Ending right here?" I finish for him. "Yes. I'm okay with it."

"Aurelia. I..."

"Please don't do that. Don't ruin tonight for me. Tonight was perfect. Please don't give me excuses or tell me you like me *but* or say how I'm beautiful *except* or that I'm special *however*. I don't want to hear it. I've heard it all a dozen times before by lesser men than you. We already agreed to what this is and I'm not some heartsick woman who needs you to spell it out for her. I have too much at stake to play games, Zax. Do me a favor? Respect me enough not to play them."

His eyes coast back and forth between mine, his hand on my face, holding me firmly. But it's his expression I can't read. It's not relief and it's not annoyance and it's not even lust anymore. It's... contemplative almost. Frustrated maybe. I don't know. But it's tripping me up and blurring my hardline stance.

So I climb up on my toes and plant my lips to his and when I feel him start to try and deepen the exchange, I pull back and go for our table. Everything is exactly how we left it and I pour myself a big fat double of tequila because he bought the damn bottle, and someone might as well drink it.

He's beside me, watching me, eyes all over me. I pour him the same because why the fuck not and after I hand it to him, I down mine and then without a word, go back to the dance floor. Amazing orgasm aside, I wish he hadn't come with me tonight. I wish I had been able to dance and be free. Just for a night. Unshackled when all I feel is contained.

I start to dance, but then he's there behind me. His hands are on my hips and his chest is to my back. Forever, he doesn't speak a word. We just dance to the music, his hands coasting up and down my sides without ever crossing borders. That is until his mouth finds my ear.

"You're not an except. You're not a but. You're not a however. You're an addiction I don't know how to claim or conquer."

My eyes close at his words, my heart lurching in my chest.

"I have never wanted anyone the way I want you, Aurelia, and that's what's hurting my soul."

Jesus. My hands cover his on my hips and I can't form words. There are no words for that. There is only touch. I take his hands and wrap them around my chest and press myself back against him until he's holding me and I'm holding him.

His forehead meets my shoulder and in the middle of a dance floor, in the middle of a club, this is how we are. Linked. Wordless simply because words aren't necessary between us. He might never have wanted anyone the way he wants me, but I have never felt as connected to anyone as I do to him.

How simply, beautifully, irresistibly broken are the pair of us?

I twirl in his arms and plant my head on his chest, refusing to meet his eyes because while I pride myself on being fearless, sometimes I'm not that brave. He doesn't seem to care. We sway, holding each other, his heartbeat beneath my ear. And when my thirty minutes are up, he takes my hand and leads me out of the club and into a waiting car.

His hand links with mine and that's how we ride back. My gaze out my window and his out his, but our hands hold until we reach the hotel. Then it's all back to baseline. Then I tell him, "Good night, Mr. Monroe. I'll see you tomorrow for the warehouse meeting."

"Good night, Aurelia."

That's it.

I let it go along with the rest of tonight. Stuffing it all into a box in my head I vow never to reopen. I'm not alone in that. Tomorrow is a new day. One where the sins of today are left behind to rot, never to be heard from again.

In the morning, after a fitful night's sleep, I eat my breakfast I don't taste a bite of and drink my Diet Coke that's more precious to me than blood is to a vampire. Halfway through my last sip, a dark shadowy man slides into the seat across from me and barks at the waitress.

"Coffee. Black."

I roll my eyes at him. "You catch more flies with honey than you do with vinegar."

"When did you become a Southern cliché?"

"Rough night of sleep, boss?"

He ignores me in favor of his freshly delivered black coffee. Blowing off the steam, he takes a sip and then another, finishing the mug off with two more gulps.

"I'm going to have to answer for you in the affirmative. Did your tongue just melt from your mouth or is it burned so badly you can no longer speak? Here's keeping my fingers crossed for the latter."

He gives me an unamused look. Even as he orders a second cup. The waitress is savvy enough this time to place a full carafe on our table for him. "How do you not drink coffee?" he questions once he's more human and into his third mug.

"The same way I don't eat fried bugs. Some people are into it and in some cultures, it's a delicacy, but all I see is slimy black shit and in this case, it smells like cat urine."

He blinks at me. Stares down into his mug. Shrugs. And then finishes off his third cup. "You're missing out."

"Clearly since this is the sunshine and jelly beans side of coffee."

He gives me a crooked grin I'm not even sure he's aware he's giving. But damn, he's fine when he does it. "You're a tenacious pain in the ass."

My eyebrows shoot up. "You're just *now* realizing that?"

"No. Maybe finally appreciating it is a better way to put it. Let's go."

I don't get to challenge that before he's on his feet in his next breath, tossing cash onto the table, though he could wait five minutes and sign a check to put it on the room. But nope, that takes too much time and time is not to be wasted for Mr. Zaxton Monroe when he's all business. I was expecting a bit of awkwardness after last night. You know, between jerking off and finger fucking and holding each other in the middle of a club.

But again, nope. Not this man.

Last night was last night and today is a new day and that's how it is. That's the tone he's setting and I'm smart enough to read this for what it is. He's been nothing but straight with me from the start. So where my heart is a bit muddled, the rest of me isn't. I told him he's not worth the risk, which still holds true.

I need this job. A hell of a lot more than I need to chase after a man who doesn't want to be caught.

We ride in silence down Fifth Avenue before we cut west on 35th Street toward Marie's warehouse in the garment district. Zax's face is on his phone the entire ride and since I'm already caught up on everything I need to do, I stare out the window. Incredible to think that only a few short weeks ago, I was still living here. Not far even from where we are now. My life has changed so much and despite how I got where I am, I'm so grateful.

"You good?" Zax asks without taking his eyes off his phone.

"I am," I tell him.

"Are *we* good?"

My head flies left, catching his profile. "Have I given you a reason to suggest otherwise?"

"No. Just checking. Last night was..."

"I don't need a label for what it was. I was there. But that was then."

His eyes finally meet mine. "And this is now?"

I nod. "This is now."

"There should be relief in that."

"I suppose so."

"Good." He grins.

"Great." I up it with a beaming smile.

A flutter hits my chest as he leans across the seat just as the car slows and we come to a stop. "What if there isn't?"

"Sucks to be you then?" I shrug.

He laughs. "Maybe. Still, for the sake of my blood pressure, when we get back to Boston, no more short fucking skirts." His gaze blatantly drops to my crossed legs and then the door is being opened for me and I uncross them so I can get out. He groans. "Tease."

I can't fight my giggle. "You're the one looking." The driver takes my hand, helping me out of the car.

"Because I'm picturing your legs on my shoulders and wrapped around my head," he murmurs, but it's so low and the sound on the street is so loud I'm not even positive that's what he said. And when he's beside me on the sidewalk, New York rushing past us in both directions, he's back to being Mr. Monroe. Stern, no bullshit, hardline CEO.

"Miss Whitlock." He pans his hand in front of me. "After you."

"Thank you, Mr. Monroe."

Marie's warehouse is absolutely enormous. Especially for Manhattan. It's none of my business, but the rent here must be astronomical. It's a four-story brick building, historical if I had to guess by the feel and look of it. It's been renovated and maintained to modern specifications while holding its old-world charm.

"Wow," is what I say because "I love it."

Zax doesn't spare me a glance as he too looks around the space. Right now it's just us standing here. No handler to greet us and I wonder if this is how he designed it so we'd have a few minutes of unobserved time to get a peek around the first floor.

"Can I ask what you want this for?"

"No."

I roll my eyes, though he can't see it since he's too busy looking over everything. "Are you moving the company to New York?"

"Definitely not. But New York is New York and fashion comes through this city, so having a building like this here as a base of Monroe operations in the city is vital for the company's footing. Plus, from what I know of it, we can actually produce some of the clothes and items here in-house if we so choose."

"But isn't that what she was doing?"

"Yes."

I twist to glance up at him. "She has to sell for a reason," I whisper.

His gaze cuts to mine. "That's not why. Some people are excellent with design and shitty with business."

I smirk. "But you're excellent at both." It's a half-question because I already know he is. It's all over the company and the way he runs things.

"I've been known to be."

"Now you understand why I'm doing this instead of attempting to run my own design house. Too much to learn first. Like how not to be shitty with business."

He spins so he's facing me fully. "Aurelia, the mistake Marie and others who have failed at this made is that they believe their passion and designs will be what carry them through and make them successful. They fail because they don't realize that's only half of what makes a company. The other half is business and in order for a company to be successful, the two sides have to be balanced and complement each other. If one side is stronger, the company teeters and risks failure." His eyes hold mine even as we hear footsteps approaching. "The fact that you know you need to have the business as well as the design side tells me you're already ahead of everyone else in your shoes and when you decide to take that leap on your own, you won't fail."

My eyelashes flutter as I absorb his words because wow. That's the most profound thing anyone has ever said to me and it's not even a compliment. To him it's factual and concrete and that's what makes it even better. It wasn't a line or a method to get in my pants. He's not even on that line of thinking right now.

I've been told I'm beautiful a million times, made to believe that's my value and worth, but no one has ever believed in me the way Zax is now.

His vote of confidence in me is everything.

Him seeing me for who I truly am and what I want to be—not Lia Sage, model—but Aurelia Whitlock, aspiring designer and business-woman knocks me sideways.

To him, I'm smart and capable and talented. Yes, he thinks I'm beautiful, I know he does because he's told me. But that's not what he's seeing when he's looking at me now.

He sees *me*.

And nothing... I mean fucking nothing has ever made me feel more incredible than that.

I've never wanted to kiss a man more than I want to kiss Zax in this moment. And despite how buoyant I'm feeling right now, I'm also filled with terminal sadness. I finally met a man who sees beyond my exterior. Who sees my potential and believes in it. Who sees my heart and soul.

But it's a heart and soul he's not interested in keeping for his own.

Marie and her assistant greet us, shaking our hands and showing us around. It's all business and I do my best to learn all that I can. Only I might not be as smart as Zax thinks I am. Because right now, my heart is driven by passion and design for him. For what we could become if we tried. And that part is strong. Stupidly, mentally, I believe it's strong enough to carry whatever this is through and make it successful.

For both of us if need be.

But the smarter business side of me knows that will never be the case. That for all my passion and design, I'd fail. So instead, I shove all that down and focus solely on the smarter business side. The side that knows Zaxton Monroe and I will never be more than what we are now.

No matter how much I'm starting to want to change that for both of us.

20

ZAXTON

"I know the runway is typically white during the shows, but what if we made it black?" Nate asks, staring down at his tablet and then back up at the space where our event will be held.

"You can't do a black runway and dark audience," Aurelia protests. "It's too dangerous for the models walking. It's white so that we can see the clear end of the runway and not walk off into the crowd."

"Huh. That's why it's always white?"

She gives him a 'duh' look. "Yeah. If everything is black and the audience is in the dark and we're keeping our heads up, not watching all that closely, it wouldn't be that difficult."

"But we're saying we want this on a dark background so the colors really stand out."

She throws her hands up and then walks around to where the stage will start. "The only thing I could think of would be LED lighting on the entire border of the stage."

"That could work." Lamar nods, swiping through the images of the final outfits we went over this morning as he paces around. "What do you think, Zax?"

"I think this is why you and Nate are here along with Aurelia. If I wanted to design this thing, I wouldn't have dragged any of you here."

Lamar glances up at me, his eyebrow pinched as he scrutinizes me. "Was that a compliment? Is he being nice?" His gaze snaps over to Aurelia, who does a brilliant impression of an owl.

"Nice?" she parrots the word as if she's never heard it before. "Him? No. I mean, not that I've noticed. He spent yesterday on the phone arguing with the board and then the financial people, only to call one of them a dumb fucking idiot who can't add or subtract more than single-digit numbers."

"Because he couldn't. They were all fucking morons." Aurelia and I spent Tuesday touring Marie's business outfit, especially the warehouse I'm particularly interested in, and then all yesterday morning I was fighting on the phone with my goddamn finance team and board, who were busy trying to tell me that I shouldn't buy her company because it's failing. Dumbasses didn't comprehend that's specifically why I want it.

They didn't stop me. I made Marie an offer that she accepted. Deal done except for the final contracts, which our attorneys are drafting.

"See." Aurelia waves at me. "That's hardly what I'd call nice. If he weren't right in front of me and quick on the firing trigger, I might even venture to call him dickish."

"Are you trying to get me to fire you?"

"That's why I said if you *weren't* in front of me, I'd call you that. But since you are, I won't." She returns my withering stare with an overly sweet, phony smile, and I swear, if I could get away with it, I'd spank her and then fuck the insubordination out of her.

"Hmmm. I don't know." Lamar continues to study me, and I give him my best fuck you face. The one that scares regular humans, but Lamar is far from a regular human, and I already know he can tell something is up between us. I haven't touched Aurelia since Monday night at the club and since then, everything between us has been strictly professional.

While not being professional at all because I live to bicker with her just so I can listen to that smart mouth of hers and see the fire in her eyes when she tells me off. But other than my own personal strange form of foreplay, I've been keeping behind that most recent line I drew and my hands to myself.

"Anyway," I snap, growing bored. "Can you all please figure this out already? We've been standing here for an hour and still, nothing is settled. We've done this twice a year for years. Why is it so difficult?"

"Because every show has to be different from the last, which I know you know."

"Then figure it out, Lamar. We have a plane to catch in three hours."

He's smirking at me. That omniscient asshole is smirking at me and all I can do is pretend I don't notice.

"What if we did black acrylic? Shiny walls as the backdrop and along the floor of the runway but illuminate the entire border as Aurelia said. That way it's bright and the clothes will stand out. Especially if we make the acrylic reflective, so it naturally casts the eye up."

"Nate, I do believe you might have just earned your executive internship," Lamar states. "I like that. I like that a lot. Liastrange?"

She groans, throwing her head back and her arms out wide. "Can we just stop with the Liastrange? You told me you'd be done by today."

"Fine. Apologies, *Aurelia*. So boring. But can you answer the fucking question? Is that too slippery to walk on?"

"Could be." She drops to sit on a wooden crate. "We can always add clear non-slip pads on the bottoms of the shoes or use sandpaper on them if we're really worried. But I think it could work and I agree it will be beautiful. You're going to need a lot of overhead white lighting to cast that reflective glow and also make the room not appear like a cave or a coffin."

"I want white fairy lights overhead." Lamar starts tapping on his screen a million miles a minute, then waves his hand about the room. "Hanging and strung along the ceiling. They'll be such a contrast to all the black while making the room glow. It'll look magical."

They continue on as my phone rings in my pocket. Marie. Oh shit.

"I have to take this."

Lamar waves me away and I swipe across the screen, answering. "Marie?"

"Zaxton. So glad I caught you."

I walk away from the three of them as they continue to go back and forth on the design.

"Is everything all right?"

"Well, this is a bit awkward, but after we made the final deal yesterday afternoon, your father came and saw me that evening."

And just like that, everything inside me freezes. My hand taps out a rhythm on my hip as I stare out the window down at the traffic racing along Sixth Avenue. "My father?" I manage when I think I have control over my voice.

"Yes. He showed up unannounced. The only name that was given to me was Mr. Monroe. I thought it was you again. Otherwise, I wouldn't have agreed to see him. He came in and handed me a check for exactly twenty thousand over our agreed-upon price."

The slimy, sniveling, son of a bitch. How did he know the price we settled on? And what is his game with this? What would he want with her company?

"What did you say to him?" I grit out, trying to rein in my fiery temper.

"I told him I already had a deal going with you. Not to mention, last I checked, he no longer had any design house of his own and doesn't have the best track record with them."

Relief swims through me. "Thank you for that."

"He believed me to be driven by money when I am driven by love, passion, and respect. It was why I chose you when certain others have already tried to buy me out."

"Who else tried?"

"Valencci, of course."

I spin back around, immediately latching on to Aurelia as she laughs with Lamar and Nate.

"Valencci. The same woman who—"

"Who destroyed Lia's career. Yes. In any event, I sent your father away, but I felt you should know."

"I appreciate that," I say into the phone, my eyes still on Aurelia. She senses me watching her and peeks up, curiosity and concern lighting her features when she catches my expression. "And I appreciate you holding to our deal."

"You okay?" Aurelia mouths to me, and all I can do is nod. Even as I'm pelleted with the fierce need to protect her.

"It is how business should be conducted," Marie states evenly.

"I agree. Has Valencci tried to contact you again since her initial offer?"

"No. Last I heard, she is back in Milan."

Could be a coincidence. Marie Marcato's business would be a ripe, juicy apple to any design house willing to fork over the dollars and take on the disaster that it is and it's no secret that Valencci's ultimate goal is fashion world domination. Still, I have to wonder what she'll do when she learns Aurelia works for me and that I now own Marie's business. If she doesn't know already.

"Thank you for informing me of all this."

"I will be in touch once our lawyers get the final draft of the contracts ready for signature. And, Zaxton, take good care of Aurelia." With that, she disconnects the call.

More questions for me to send Lenox to investigate. This is turning into one nightmare after the other. "Come on," I call out. "Time's up. We need to get going."

Aurelia hops off the crate, doing something on her tablet, and I hesitate before deciding I have to know. After what happened Monday with her... once and for all, I have to know.

I grasp her arm and tug her to the side, telling Lamar and Nate we'll meet them down in the car. Lamar gives me a look but doesn't question anything.

"My father is here," I announce once they're gone.

Aurelia jerks upright, her head swiveling around, her eyes wild and frantic. "He is? Where?"

"I don't necessarily mean he's here in this warehouse. But he is in New York."

She frowns, leaning back against the exposed brick wall. "Doesn't he live here?"

"Yes, but he was out of town and flew back Sunday."

"Why? Because you're here to make a deal?"

"You tell me."

Indignation flashes across her pretty face, my accusation wraps around her in the cruelest of ways. "I wouldn't know, Zax. I swear, I wouldn't. He hasn't tried to contact me. I can show you my phone if you don't believe me." She moves to pull out her phone from her purse and I wave it away.

Her phone is useless to me. The person he's been contacting uses a burner phone.

"Valencci also tried to buy Marie out before I did."

"And you think that's me too, right? That I'm working with the woman who *ruined* my career?"

My gaze hits the window and I shift my weight, my hands on my hips. "No. But something is going on and it all seems to revolve around you. Or maybe it's not. Maybe it's all surrounding me, and the other shit is coincidence. I don't fucking know and that's the problem."

"I'm sorry," she says, placing her hand delicately over mine to draw my attention back to her. "I didn't mean to start something between you and your father, but Valencci I had nothing to do with."

"It was likely already started. My father sought you out. He knew your situation, Aurelia. He had to, and then he tracked you down, knowing what you were looking for and how he could help."

She worries her lip with her teeth, her expression grim. "Likely yes. Do you need me to go?"

I step into her, searching her face, hoping it holds the honesty I need. "No. I need to be able to trust you. Even though I was a dick to you when you were a kid. Even though I'm a dick to you now. I need to be able to trust you and I'm not sure I do."

Her gaze holds mine and she's trying to hide the hurt my words just inflicted. "As someone who knows what it feels like to have everything you've worked impossibly hard for taken from you, it's not something I would ever wish on my worst enemy. Even so, I don't think of you that way. Not anymore. You let me stay at Monroe, despite how I got there. You promoted me, even if I don't fully understand why. I get why you feel you can't trust me. But screwing someone over isn't how I operate."

I promoted her because of all this. Because I didn't trust her, and I needed to keep her close. Now everything with her feels different. I don't know when I started letting my guard down with her, but I did and now I can't stop. My phone pings in my pocket, but neither of us so much as blinks or budges. We're glued to each other, as I think this through, and she waits on my verdict.

"I believe you," I say. "I trust you."

"And I won't betray that. Or you," she tells me with a certainty that makes my heart pump out an extra beat.

My hand dives through her hair, cupping the side of her face. I want to kiss her again. I'm desperate for it, in fact. To the point where I step in closer, toe-to-toe and inches apart. I stare at her lips and am hit with something so powerful I'm only now starting to come to grips with it.

I could fall in love with her. I might be halfway there already.

THE REST of Thursday and all day Friday are quiet. They're business as usual, work getting done, people leaving me the hell alone. I don't see or speak to Aurelia beyond my usual visual stalking of her from my office and the occasional dickish—to use her word—comments I toss her way.

I don't know how else to keep my distance from her, and if I don't keep my distance from her, I will touch her again. I will kiss her again. I will do more than simply kiss or touch her because I am a man hanging on by the thinnest of threads. I can't get Monday out of my head. It's all I think about when I'm not working and even then, it's all I fucking think about. I haven't seen her naked, I've hardly seen any of her at all, and it feels like the crime of my life.

But since then, I get no wayward needy glances from her. No emails or texts. Nothing to indicate Monday was anything more to her than blowing off some of the sexual steam that blisters between us.

And it's driving me crazy. All of it.

The insane desire I have for her. How every time her blue eyes cut to mine, I feel a clenching in my chest. The way my skin vibrates every time I get within a foot of her or simply catch sight of her. Or hell, smell her. I'm so close to the edge I'm finding it nearly impossible to hold on.

Which is why I need tonight, this weekend to clear my head of her.

Friends. Distance. Time.

Even if it means I'm stuck at a fucking charity event.

"Bourbon. Straight. Three fingers." The bartender eyes me and makes it a solid five fingers and I drop a fifty into his tip cup.

"Long week, Monroe, or are you just scamming off the free hooch?" I turn to find Oliver Fritz, flanked by two of his brothers, Kaplan, the eldest, and Luca. They're a famous family of billionaires. The brothers all doctors. Oliver does a bit of modeling for Monroe, but you don't live in this city without at least knowing of the Fritz family and in my case, we run in similar circles.

"Both," I tell him, taking a sip. "And it's not bad."

The three of them laugh and then we do the bro hug/shake thing because I haven't seen these guys in a few months. They're older than me. Oliver, the closest in age, is six years my senior. All of them are married with kids.

"Where are Landon and Carter tonight?" I ask, looking around since I don't immediately see the other two Fritz brothers.

"Carter got called in for a patient and Landon is using my house in Tuscany with his wife and their five kids, including Stella, before school starts back up for them," Luca, Landon's twin, explains. "Stella took time away from her restaurant to go and the two sets of twins are apparently tearing the place up."

I laugh at Luca's poor attempt at an annoyed scowl. He'd do anything for his nieces and nephews, and something tells me them destroying his place doesn't bother him a bit.

"I can only imagine," I remark. If memory serves, the two sets of twins—one set is girls, the other boys—are only two years apart. That has to be madness. "Still, I wouldn't mind something like that myself. A week in a Tuscan villa, away from it all. Are the rest of you here stag? I don't see your wives on your arms, and I know they're never far."

"Nah," Kaplan answers. "Our women are somewhere about. Likely talking shit about us and generally getting into trouble. My wife, Bianca, is running this event for the Abbot Foundation, so she's required to be a human, whereas I can simply stay back and drink with these assholes."

"You mean the Abbot Foundation you were the CEO of since it's your *family's* foundation?" I remark sarcastically.

He waves me off. "She's better at it than I am. I don't people nearly as well."

"It's true," Oliver agrees. "He much prefers to slice people open and fix their hearts than play CEO."

I snort, taking a sip of my drink. "If only I had thought of that before I started this gig. Then maybe I wouldn't have to people either."

"It's never too late to go to medical school, Zax. I'll even put in a good word for you at Harvard." A hand slaps my shoulder from behind and then Callan is there along with Asher, both shaking hands with the Fritzes. Callan works in the same hospital as Oliver and Carter, though I wouldn't call them close, and everyone knows Asher.

We shoot the shit for a few more minutes and then the Fritz boys wander off, other people in need of their attention, leaving me with

Callan and Asher, which is frankly how I prefer it. I love those guys, but if I have to listen to any more medical shit, I'll throw Callan at them as a decoy and set the room on fire while I make my escape. I'll leave Asher here to burn since the bastard loves flirting with my girl simply to rile me up.

Wait.

No. Definitely not my girl. That would mean I'd actually have to like her, which I don't. I simply want to fuck her and since fucking her is off the table, she can officially fuck right out of my head. For good. I'm tired of her presence there.

"So how was New York?" Callan asks, sipping on his vodka tonic or whatever he's drinking. "I heard from Lenox you had some issues?"

"I wish I'd had the foresight to stick my father on a raft and shove him out to sea the way ancient Inuit tribes did with their elderly during famines. He deserves senilicide and nothing better."

"Huh," Callan muses. "I see we're in rare form tonight."

"More like done with this week and wishing I had stayed home instead."

"With a certain woman?" Asher grins like the asshole he is.

"Fuck off, Ash."

Only he's just getting started. "Perhaps one with platinum blond hair and stunning blue eyes, a face that makes angels weep and a body built for sin? Too bad she's completely into me and not you."

I clench my fingers into fists, so I don't strangle him and cause a scene.

"I wouldn't be so sure about that," I counter because clearly, I'm an idiot.

That grin grows into a triumphant smile complete with smug, gleeful eyes. "Wanna bet on it?" He juts his chin over my shoulder and instinctively I turn around. Shit.

21

AURELIA

"**A**re you sure we're not party crashing?" I ask, gripping Howie's arm as we enter the swanky palatial ballroom.

"We're fine," he promises, taking my hand and twirling me into the room. "My girlfriend works for the Abbot Foundation. She's the executive event coordinator and is friends with Kaplan Fritz's wife."

"For real?" Iris jumps Howie, practically knocking him to the ground. Nate and I save him at the last second. "Your girlfriend is besties with an official Fritz, and you never told us?"

I grasp Howie's arm since he looks like he's about to call animal control on Iris. "She's just a tad bit obsessed with the Fritz family, is all."

"And the Central Square crew too," she demands. "Don't forget them. They're all equally deliciously hot."

"Thanks for that," Nate grumbles.

"You're hot too and I'm obviously fucking you, but if I ever get the chance with the Fritz or Central Square guys, I'm not saying I wouldn't go there because I would. They're my hall pass."

"Aren't the Fritz men a bit old for you?"

Iris blinks at Howie. "So? Older men are hot. And the Central Square guys aren't as old as the Fritz guys. And they're decidedly more single."

"You realize this event is loaded with Fritz and Central Square people since they all quasi know each other?"

"Oh, Nate, get over it," Iris admonishes in that Iris way of hers, kissing his cheek to try to assuage him. "I'm not hitting on anyone. Jeez. Relax, dude. It's just... you know... a dream. Or whatever. I mean, I wouldn't fuck Zax." And then I get the look. The look that says, *I wouldn't fuck him because I know you are.* Only I'm not. You know, since hot hand action and naughty role-play isn't fucking.

But Iris is up to date on my New York shenanigans. She came over last night and we had pizza and I spilled all to her. Tonight we're here and—

"Wait a sec. You told me that Zax never comes to these things." That's my panic button firing off like a woman playing *Family Feud* slamming the buzzer because she's in it to win it.

"I've been to two of these events and he hasn't been to any of those," Howie assures me. "I've seen a couple of his friends. And definitely the Fritz family. But not Zax."

Okay. That I can deal with. I might even enjoy seeing some of the Central Square guys. It'd be great to see Greyson. Maybe. If he doesn't let on how he knows me since that's far from public information.

"Let's go get a drink," Nate suggests, pointing over to one of the two bars in the massive space. The decor is glimmery silver with lots of candles and floating lights. Very ethereal. I love what Howie's girlfriend did to soften what is otherwise an ordinary ballroom.

"I'm in. Free booze, here I come."

I follow Iris, Nate, and Howie over to the bar, all the while scanning the room and coming up empty. No one I recognize, so I order. "A double of tequila followed immediately by a glass of champagne, please."

"Say what?"

I blink at the bartender's disgusted expression and explain.

"Liquor before beer and you're in the clear. Beer before liquor and you've never been sicker."

"Champagne is not beer. Champagne makes everyone sick regardless of what they have before or after."

I contemplate this for a moment, realizing there might be merit in his words. "Okay. Fine. What do you suggest after my shot?"

He shrugs. "Another shot?"

"I don't know. Let's start with the tequila and go from there."

He pours me a glass and just as he hands it to me, two women step in front of me.

"You're Lia Sage, right?"

"I, um." I'm impersonating a goldfish. "Uh. Yes?"

They laugh at my response, exchanging glances. I know these women. The blond pregnant woman is Rina Fritz, baby sister of the Fritz brothers, and the curvy brunette woman is Bianca Fritz, CEO of the Abbot Foundation, whose event we're currently crashing, and wife of Kaplan Fritz.

"I'm Bianca and this is my sister-in-law, Rina," Bianca introduces as if I needed her to. "We saw you walk at fashion week. Your dress." She fans her face. "It was gorgeous. We had to come over here and tell you that. And meet you since we're both big into fashion ladies and a bit starstruck."

Now it's my turn to laugh. "You're starstruck with me?" I point incredulously to my chest. Meanwhile, Iris makes some sort of strangled noise somewhere behind me. I think she just passed out.

"Well, yeah," Rina says with a laugh, shifting her weight and dropping a hand over her small bump. "Plus, your dress tonight. Wow. I had to get a better look at it up close. Are those... pearls?" She leans in. "May I? I realize how weird and inappropriate this is since we don't know you." Her hand extends, her questioning eyes on me.

"Yes, they're pearls. Not real because I couldn't go there, but sure, you can touch."

Curiosity flickers in their gazes as both women start rubbing their hands up and down my dress and this is how pornos start. I know people are watching because people are always watching the Fritz family.

"It's stunning," Bianca exclaims, turning to Rina. "Right? It's so fun to touch, I'm obsessed. Where did you get it?" She glances up at me.

"I made it."

Both women stand to their full heights, scrutinizing me with new eyes. "You're for real?"

I nod at Rina and take a sip of my drink, suddenly needing a little liquid courage. "Yes. I mean, I work as a design intern at Monroe, but I design and make my own dresses and gowns. It's sorta, okay, not sorta, it's my passion and what I hope to do one day."

"You've made others?"

"Dozens and dozens," Iris chimes in, coming in beside me. "She has racks of them filling her apartment. All gorgeous. You should see them. They're unlike anything else out there."

I'm not much of a blusher, but Iris gushing over my dresses to the Fritz women is, well, making me blush.

"We're always in need of new gowns and dresses and would love to either commission something new from you or purchase what you already have."

Now it's my turn to pass out. "You're serious?" I ask Rina, flabbergasted. My hand drops to a nearby high-top table, needing support before I collapse.

"Absolutely," Bianca assures me, her smile warm if not the slightest bit amused. Likely at my deer in headlights reaction to all this. She sips her champagne. "We know you designed that dress for fashion week and you're telling us you made me this too. We're in."

That should bother me. That they know about what happened at fashion week, but it doesn't. I'm too overwhelmed to care about anything other than these two women wanting me to make them dresses. "Um. Okay. Wow. Sure. I can't speak very well at the moment." They all laugh and so do I, some of the tension in my shoulders releasing with it. "I'd love that opportunity. That's such an honor, truly."

"Great!" Bianca squeals, all excited, knocking back the rest of her champagne and setting the empty flute on the table I'm using as my life raft. "We saw you come in with Howie and we won't monopolize any more of your time. I'm sure we can get your info from him?"

"Yes. And thank you."

"Thank *you*," Bianca says, hugging me. "Sorry, I'm a hugger. Rina is not, so don't worry."

"Yeah. Not a hugger," Rina confirms. "But it was great meeting you and like Bianca said, we'll be in touch for sure."

I throw them a wave and then down the rest of my shot once they're gone. "Oh my God. I'm dead. Like dead, dead."

"Totally dead," Iris exclaims, her wide eyes in my face, her smile uncontainable. "That was so cool. I'm so excited for you!"

"The coolest. I'm so excited for me too!" I emit a close-lipped screech, so people don't think I'm the fire alarm going off. "I need another drink."

"Definitely all the drinks."

I nod, then head back over to the bar. "Can I have another double of tequila, please?" I ask the bartender who gave me my first round.

"That seems like a lot of tequila to ply someone with," comes from behind me.

I spin around to find Asher Reyes, supreme hottie football god there. "Well, if it isn't the donut assassin."

"In the flesh. Or should I say hole?"

"That sounds like more of a golf thing."

"True. It's lovely to see you again, Aurelia." A soft kiss on my cheek, and then he whispers in my ear, "You have no idea how happy I am that you're here tonight." He gives me a charming grin I've seen him flash at the cameras, then his hand is on my lower back, and he's stepping into my side. I likely shouldn't allow it. I mean, I had his best friend's hand there not even a week ago and it ended with his fingers between my legs in a very public setting.

Then again, it's not like I owe Zax anything. It was a moment. A blip. The scratching of a need so great it had no other way of getting rid of it. Unfortunately for me, that itch now feels like a raging case of poison ivy, but what's a girl to do other than get over it and move on.

Not that I plan to do that with Asher, but I don't get the impression he actually wants to fuck me.

I stare up into Asher's eyes. "He—oomph. Ow." A sharp jab to my back has me turning with a scowl, finding Iris, who is giving me the *you've been holding out on me and the only way you can make it up to me is if you introduce me to Asher Reyes immediately* look. "Oh. Right. Sorry. Asher, this is my best friend, Iris. Iris, this is Asher. As I know you know."

"It's a pleasure, Iris." Asher shakes her hand.

"Yes." She sighs dreamily. "Pleasure Iris."

I cough, fighting my laugh, as does Asher. Nate, however, is not amused.

"It seems that responsibility already falls to another man." Asher reaches out and shakes Nate's hand. "And actually, I was coming over to steal away the lovely Aurelia." Those sparkling gray eyes land back on me. "Dance with me, beautiful?"

"Sure."

Asher takes my hand, weaving me past tables set for dinner and over to the dance floor that is sparsely filled with other couples enjoying the band. He drags me into his chest, his hand still in mine as his other goes to my back. He starts to sway us, but his eyes are on mine, serious in a way I'm not expecting.

"I've only got maybe another minute or two before this all comes to an end, so I wanted to ask you something before that happens."

I lick my lips, suddenly nervous. "Okay."

"Are you fucking with him?"

"Am I what?"

"Fucking with him. With his company. With his head. With his heart."

"N-no. I don't..." I trail off as indignation flares within me. "Asher, what the hell?"

He draws me in closer, smiling in a polite fuck off way at a nosy couple who come a little too close to us since Asher is who he is.

They dance away and then he's back on me. "I like you, Aurelia. I do. But I love him. He's my brother even if not by blood. We're a protective group. All each other has in some cases and he's already lost so much. So while I enjoy riling him up and shoving him out of his comfort zone and back into the world of the living, I'm also cautious. Do you know what I'm saying?"

"Um. Kinda, but not really."

"I'm saying I think you're exactly what he needs and exactly what he wants, though he fights it and denies it. But if you're fucking with him in any capacity, it won't end well for you."

I blink about a thousand times at him. "Asher, while I appreciate you playing the role of threatening, overprotective brother to your grown-ass friend, did you ever consider that you're wrong?"

"Wrong?" he parrots as if the word is completely foreign to him.

"Yes. Wrong. I am not what he wants or needs, nor does he fit those roles for me. In fact, he and I have had this conversation already. You know, because we're adults like that." Sort of. Adults who succumbed to a couple moments of pretend, but now we're back in the real world, so I'm not wrong on this the way he is. "He's my boss and I'm his intern. This is not going to be some reverse Cinderella gig where the lowly, downtrodden maiden swoops in and saves the billionaire curmudgeony prince from his life of misery in the palace."

That smug grin returns to his face. "You sure about that, doll?"

"Positive."

"I wouldn't abandon your glass slippers yet, Cindy." He winks at me and then his gaze shifts over my shoulder. "Well, what a surprise. Zaxton Monroe on the dance floor. Sorry, honey, my card is already full."

A shiver of anticipation races up my spine. I should have known what this was all along. Maybe part of me did. I didn't look around all that hard, mostly because I was afraid I'd spot the man now standing to the side of us. But that doesn't mean I necessarily wanted to see him either. Because seeing him makes me want him and wanting him makes my belly flutter and my chest do something weird and then I invariably forget all the reasons I shouldn't want him and end up throwing caution and better sense to the wind while giving in to wanting him. If that makes sense.

"I've seen the way you dance and move," Zax says, his voice a deep, delicious rasp. "Two left feet and always relying on someone else to pick up the slack for you. As in football so is life."

Asher chokes out a laugh. "Now I definitely won't dance with you."

"Good thing you're not the one I'm looking to dance with. *Honey.*" His fierce gaze falls on me. "May I cut in?"

I swallow my tongue. And then search around, but it's impossible to remove my eyes from his magnetic brown ones for longer than a second. "I, uh. I mean. I guess. But you know—"

"I wasn't exactly asking."

Before I know what the hell is happening, Zax moves Asher out of the way. Asher just laughs, giving me an *I told you so* wink, and then he's gone. Leaving me with the guy I should not be dancing with. His hands go to all the proper places and mine follow suit. Then he's moving me around the dance floor and it's nothing like how it was in New York. Or with Asher, for that matter.

"You're nervous with me again," he comments, his voice low and rough, his eyes hooded despite the polite dancing distance he's attempting to maintain between us.

"I'm starting to think you're either the if I can't have her, no one else can type or the insanely jealous and possessive type."

"With you, it's both," he answers evenly, his hand gliding up my back and then sweeping back down. "Your dress is pretty. Did you make it?"

"Yes. I made it." Hand-sewn pearls over white silk. Clearly the Fritz women liked it too.

"I like your hair up. I like how it reveals the soft, silky skin of your neck."

I squint in warning. "Mr. Monroe—"

"I prefer it when you call me Zax." His dark eyes hold mine, intense and broody, hardly budging to so much as blink as he moves us around the dance floor. People are watching. I feel their eyes. Can practically hear their questions and speculations. His power and presence in this town are extraordinary.

This man is dangerous. Every inch of him. From his smile to the soles of his tuxedo shoes. But the danger he presents to me—to my career, to my life, to my heart—is as thrilling as it is terrifying.

I have to swallow twice to get my voice back under control. "Nate, Howie, and Iris are all here and I have no doubt that at least Iris is witnessing this. Not to mention the other guests who know you or at least know your name."

The tiniest quirk of his lips. "I'm dancing with my intern, Aurelia. What's so scandalous about that?"

"Everything. You're you. You don't dance with women."

"And yet I've danced with you twice already. I think that says a lot."

My heart rate spikes as an electric charge ripples between us. "The way you're looking at me—"

His head dips ever so slightly, voice deadly. "And how am I looking at you? Like a man utterly captivated by the woman he's dancing with?"

"It's darker than that."

A smirk. "It is. My thoughts about you right now are darker than that. Because while it's true, I am captivated, I'm also looking at you like a man who knows what you look like when you come. Like a man who is fighting this but deep down knows he's going to make you come over and over, so you'll never come again without thinking my name."

My breath hitches into a gasp as heat unfurls through my body. "What are you doing, Zax?"

"I'm about to ask you the same thing, Aurelia. Did you know I'd be here?"

"No. Howie's girlfriend works with Bianca Fritz. Howie told me you never came to these things."

"You've bewitched me. I'm no longer myself." He takes my hand and places it over his pounding heart, his eyes wild and fierce. "You're all I've been thinking about. Tell me how to make it stop."

I swallow past the nervous lump in my throat. "What have you been thinking?"

"Everything. Dangerous mind-fucking thoughts I can't seem to contain or get a grip on. But this very second? All I can think about is how much I want to fuck you."

Arousal surges hot and heavy between my legs. His thumb drags back and forth on the skin between my shoulder blades, and I shudder against him. "But we said—"

"Tell me you don't want this with me. Tell me you don't want me to take you somewhere and fuck you six ways to Sunday."

I shake my head. "I can't. You know I do."

"Then why are we still dancing?"

"Because I can't go home with you either," I protest, only my voice isn't nearly as strong as I need it to be. "New York was easy to pretend away. To say we got caught up in the madness, but what happens after tonight?"

"I fuck you again tomorrow. I don't just want tonight. Not with you."

"Jesus, Zax." He's going to make me combust right here. I'm trying to stay sane with this, but he's making that impossible. The way he's devouring me with his eyes. The scent of his cologne. How fucking hot he looks in his tux with his dark wavy hair brushed back off his face. "This won't end well for me. I'm lost in you, and I can't lose. Not again."

Something in that registers within him and he blinks, taking a small, self-preserving step back. "Did it ever occur to you that I'm just as lost in you?"

No. Honestly, not really. And still, I'm not sold he's fighting anything stronger than lust with me.

"I'm going to leave and you're going to do the same in five minutes," he tells me when I don't answer. "Meet me downstairs in my car and we'll talk."

"I—"

"Either that, or I'm taking you to the bathroom, lifting up your dress, and fucking you here for all to hear how loud I make you scream my name. The choice is yours. I'm done pretending, Aurelia. I was on my last legs with this and then you walked in that door. Five minutes or I'll come back up here and find you."

With that, he walks away, leaving me standing here alone in the middle of the dance floor with only one option. Follow him.

22

AURELIA

I lied to my best friend. I told her I had a headache and though she was giving me the look—the one that said she saw me dance with my boss—she didn't say anything else to me about it. In fairness, she was standing beside Nate and there was no way I was going to have that conversation with her while he was there.

But now, I'm outside, running like the Cinderella Asher accused me of being. Only instead of running away from the prince, I'm running toward him. This gruff, surly, demanding man. I should have kicked him in the nuts on the dance floor for the ultimatum he dropped on me. But let's be real. It was hot. The whole notion that he wants me this badly is doing things to me.

Treacherous and unhealthy things.

Which is why when I approach his car and the driver I don't recognize opens the back door for me, I enter with a battle plan. One that nearly goes up in smoke when I get a look at him. The dark prince is sitting by the window, hair tousled and run through. White tuxedo shirt open at the collar, bow tie undone, hanging loosely around his neck.

He reaches out, swoops his arm around my waist, and slides me away from the safety of my perch by the opposite window, moving me until I'm directly beside him. Then he buckles me in the center seat.

"Peter, would you mind driving us around for a little?"

"Of course not, sir."

"Peter?" I whisper. "Where's Ashley?"

"Taking his eldest daughter to college. She got into Princeton. Peter is Ashley's brother and has been with me since..." He tilts his head. "How long have you been dealing with me, Peter?"

"Since your first headlining tour, Zax."

"Right." He turns back to me. "Since then. I was about twenty-one, I think."

I stare at this mercurial, complicated man. There are so many multifaceted pieces to him and I'm not sure if I want to rearrange them, piece them back together, or keep them in all their beautiful, sharp, jagged disarray.

"What are we doing?"

His eyes hold mine as he slides up the partition between us and Peter while we drive through endless Boston streets. "I told you what I'm doing. What I want. This isn't just tonight for me. This isn't just scratching an itch. This is me no longer able to deny how I want you. The question is, am I dropping you off or am I coming inside with you?"

"What about my job?"

He almost looks amused. "What about it?"

"You're my boss."

He squints. "Yes. That is a complication. Especially considering one of the reasons my father got ousted. So let's uncomplicate this for both of us. Do you feel coerced in any way to have sex with me because I have a position of power over you in your job?"

I blink. "No."

"Would you feel comfortable saying no to me without fear of repercussions?"

"Yes."

"Are you interested in having sex with me because you feel I can somehow enhance your career or income?"

My nose scrunches up. "Of course not."

"Then what exactly are you concerned about with your job?"

"What people will say."

"Fuck what people will say."

I frown and he lifts my hand, placing a soft kiss on the inside of my wrist.

"Aurelia, I had no intention of spreading this to anyone. It's no one's business what we do as long as it doesn't impact our work."

"Fine, but when this ends..." It will end messy. At least for me. Likely not for him and maybe that's what he's saying. "We keep this separate." It's a question, yet it's not.

I can almost hear his unspoken words, *this is just sex, Aurelia. Not love.*

His eyes hold mine and he does not follow that up. Instead, he watches me work this out for myself, and maybe I shouldn't feel relief in his unspoken words, but I do. My job will not be compromised. It will not turn volatile or ugly because there will be no feelings involved. I'm not sure he's capable of them anymore. Even if he were, he's not interested in having them, so therefore he won't.

That's how Zax works.

I, on the other hand... emotional detachment has been my daily chore since I was a child, and it was never one I enjoyed. That doesn't mean I didn't learn how to be good at it as a matter of survival.

"Okay. Sex."

Instantly, his gaze turns molten, and he intertwines our fingers. I almost pull away from the intimate gesture, but then his thumb starts to drag along the inside of my wrist, and I give up. He lowers the partition.

"Peter, would you mind taking us to Aurelia's?"

"Not at all, sir."

"He knows my address?" I question in a low voice.

"I had given it to him prior to you coming down."

A humorless laugh flees my lungs. "You felt I was that much of a sure thing?"

Zax leans in, his mouth hovering by my ear. "No. Never. But I had hoped you would be. Whether you agreed or not, he was taking you home."

A kiss to my neck, a deep inhale, and then we're riding in silence. In darkness. In swirling tension and barely simmering desire. I feel his want and restraint in every way he touches me. How he uses the side slit to flip my dress over my knees so he can caress me there. How he keeps me close, his thighs and shoulders against mine.

I ignore his frown as we climb out of his Escalade, and I unlock the front of my building. I continue to ignore it as we hoof up the four flights of stairs. He wants to say something but is rightly, for once, keeping his mouth shut.

Hands on my hips as I unlock my front door and then we're inside my apartment and he's peering around. More frowns, but now his wandering gaze is sparked with curiosity and intrigue. Like he's getting a secret glimpse inside me I allow no one else to see.

"You live in a studio." He eyes my bed, a queen stuck in the corner with a nightstand beside it, only separated from the rest of the room by a folding screen that is more for keeping out light than privacy. It's just me here. The small television I watch my true crime shows on and the fabric in rolls and folded piles on the floor. The bins filled with beads and sequins and sewing supplies.

"I told you I'm saving money."

His gaze moves about, stalling on my work area. "How many sewing machines do you have?"

"Three. But they all sort of do different things for me. Honestly, I'd have more if I could afford them and had the space to accommodate them."

A nod. "And these dresses..." He gestures toward the large racks I have filling the tiny living room and kitchen space. "You made all those."

"Yep. I did."

"Hmmm."

"What's that mean?"

"Just thinking, is all."

"Care to share?"

His eyes slingshot back to mine. "No."

I shake my head, crossing the room to my desk so I can put my purse down and charge my phone. I don't offer him a drink. This isn't a date. But then something hits me and hits me hard. A burning thought, a question I have to have answered before any of this can go further.

I turn back around to face him. "Is it true you haven't had sex in eight years?"

He stares at me for what feels like an eternity, likely debating how honest and forthcoming he wants to be with me, and then finally says, "No."

"But that's what—"

"I have the world believing? Yes, I know. If women think you're celibate and completely unavailable, after a while, they tend to leave you alone. At least for the most part, and having women chase after me for whatever their reason is isn't something I wanted to deal with on any level."

"So how do you..."

A step into the room. "I belong to a very exclusive club."

I gasp. "A sex club?"

"Yes."

"But don't they—"

"I wear a mask most times, but even if I didn't, it's private."

"You wear a mask?!" Holy hell. "Do you know who the women are?"

He shakes his head. "I never cared."

"Do you do it in public? Do you tie them up?"

He fights a smile, rubbing his finger along his bottom lip to try and hide it. "Never and rarely. It's not necessarily a kink club, though there is plenty of that there if that's what you're into."

I moan. Something about this is insanely sexy to me. Just picturing handsome, powerful Zax in his tuxedo wearing a mask... "Is that what you're into? Kink?"

"Not with those women."

Jeeeeesuuuuus. I'm burning up. I want to ask him why not with those women, but I'm too keyed up to care at this moment.

"But if you were," I press. "Tell me what you'd do with those women. If I were one of those women, what would you do to me?"

"You want to be my dirty little club whore? My plaything?"

"Yes." And I don't even feel shame admitting it nor do I by his degrading words. I like them. They turn me on and that's the name of this, isn't it? The hottest part is that he knows this about me. I didn't even have to tell him, yet he knows.

He prowls toward me. "Turn around and place your hands on the desk."

I comply instantly, my bottom lip caught in my teeth, my body trembling with every step I hear him take. He stands behind me, his body heat incredible, and my eyes close. Anticipation rolls through me like a freight train, my heart matching its speed.

His fingers are in my hair and then I feel a bobby pin slide out. He drops it on the desk beside me and then continues with the others. Pin by pin, he unfurls my hair from its updo. It's strangely the most sensual and erotic thing a man has ever done to me. The meticulous way he does it so it doesn't hurt or snag. The slow, deliberate nature of it all as he builds this up between us. I'm dying, panting, and he hasn't even touched me yet.

Once my hair is down, the last pin on the desk, he sweeps the heavy mane over, letting it tumble across my shoulder. His nose is on my neck, and he takes a deep inhale of me. The way he did in the bathroom in New York. I bite deeper into my lip to stifle my moan, only he leans into my ear and whispers, "Don't do that again or I'll punish you. I want to hear every sound you make."

"Yes, sir."

I can practically hear him smirking. "That's my girl."

A rustling behind me and then smooth black satin covers my eyes. My breath hitches, holding tight in my lungs as he uses his bowtie to blindfold me. His hands sweep down my neck and along my shoulders until he reaches the zipper at the back of my dress.

"If *you* were the woman I was with in the club, I'd slowly unzip your dress."

He does with such painstaking slowness, I'm not sure I can stand this another second. The dress falls to the floor, and he helps me step out of it, my heels still on. He drapes it on the chair beside me and then his hands are on my ankles.

"Once I had you like this, in only your thong and bra, I'd slide my hands up your legs because there'd be no way I could resist them. I fucking love your legs."

The lightest touch tickles up the inside of my calves and thighs, only to get close to the promise land and then dance back down. He does it again and again, driving me mad with his touch. I whimper in frustration.

"I'd keep doing this. Skirting close to your wet pussy already leaking through your panties, without touching it. I'd draw out your anticipation until you were so desperate for me, you'd beg."

"I'm already there," I tell him.

His mouth is against my right ass cheek. "Then beg me, Aurelia." His teeth sink into my flesh, and I cry out, my hips mindlessly canting forward, my clit needing friction.

"Please."

A smack to my left ass cheek. "Please what? What is it you want?"

"Please touch me."

"Where?"

"My pussy. Please, please, take off my panties and touch me. Or lick me. Or both."

"What is it you need?"

"To come. I need to come."

"Don't move," he whispers by my ear and then he's gone. His heat is nowhere to be found, but I hear him. I hear a drawer opening and some shuffling of things I can't discern and then he's back.

My panties slide down my hips, cool air hitting my wet center, and then I'm stepping out of these too. My bra goes next and now I'm blindfolded and completely bare to him.

"Christ, you're fucking beautiful." A kiss to my spine. "My sweet, perfect girl who likes to play naughty, naughty games."

He runs a finger along my seam just as I hear something click and start to vibrate. Then he's got my wand against my nipple. Fucking asshole went into my nightstand drawer like he knew exactly what he'd find in there. And no doubt he got an eyeful of my toy collection.

A fact he proves as he says, "I didn't grab the pretty plug you have in there, in case you were wondering. You like anal play, Angel?"

"Yes."

"Fuck, baby girl. You're going to be the death of me."

I feel the same way about him.

He moves the wand down the front of me, over my belly, swirling the vibration along my skin as every nerve ending comes alive. Firm lips kiss down my back in the same way the wand moves over my front. I squirm and he nibbles on my hip. I gasp and he sucks on the dip of my waist. I sigh and he swirls his finger around my opening.

Every move or breath I make, he's attuned to. All the while denying me. Sadist.

"Zax, please. I'm losing my mind."

"Patience, Angel. I don't want to rush this the way we did last time. Enjoy the build-up."

"Build-up? I'm so *worked up*, I'm about to hump my desk for relief."

I feel his smile against my skin. "Then do it."

My head flies around, though I'm still blindfolded and can't see. "You want me to hump my desk?" I screech.

He chuckles. "If you need to that badly."

I flip back around, blinking inside the blindfold as I consider this. He thinks I'm bluffing. But am I? Fuck it. He's driving me crazy, I can do the same to him. I part my legs, knowing he's crouched behind me. The wand leaves my skin and I hear him suck in a rush of air as he gets a full view of me. Feeling bold and a touch insane, I find the corner of my desk and grind my pussy on it.

He curses, mumbling things I can't fully make out, and victory surges through me.

I moan as I roll my hips, my clit grinding down on the wood. He grips my ass, almost frantically, spreading my cheeks wide as his foot pushes my legs farther apart. His hot breath fans along my opening, and I whimper at how good that feels.

"You are a filthy fucking woman." His voice is ragged.

"But you like me like this."

"You have no clue how much." His tongue dives up inside of me and I jerk forward, pressing in harder against the desk, only his hands pull me back. "I get to control your pleasure, Aurelia. This is my body, no longer yours. Even if you ask for it."

The wand flips back on and he spits on it before pressing it against my clit as he eats me out from behind. Holy shit. He just spat on my vibrator to lube it. That alone has me spasming—so fucking dirty and yet undeniably hot and deliciously wrong. Pleasure surges through me, both from the wand and his wicked tongue and mouth on me. No one has ever done this to me. Forget using my wand. I've never had someone go down on me from this position. Any exploration into anything beyond the typical vanilla sex has mostly been my own with myself.

But having Zax do this to me, licking me and fucking me with his tongue, growling and groaning into me while edging my clit with the wand is transcending. And being blindfolded only seems to heighten it. I feel lightheaded. Practically euphoric. My skin hot, achy, and tight. Fingers twist into my desk, not finding any purchase to hold me upright as a storm riots within me.

I push back, seeking more of his mouth, rocking forward into the wand.

I feel his nose bump into my asshole, and I squeal and squirm, embarrassed but loving it too much to care enough to stop or pull away. Especially when he grips my hip tighter in his large hand and pulls me back into him. He licks me there, pressing the wand deeper against my clit, and stars sparkle behind my eyes.

"Zax," I plead, only right now, I have no clue what I'm asking for. Just more of whatever he's doing to me. More. More. *More.* My face falls forward, my back bowing as I open myself up completely to him.

"Again, baby girl. Say my name again." Angel. Baby girl. I could live and breathe and die on his names for me alone.

"Zax. Oh God. Don't stop. Please, Zax. I'm so close."

A primal growl rumbles directly into my core and then I feel his fingers. Two of them. Plunging into me and pressing against my inner wall. His tongue flicks my clit as he holds the wand against the top of my mound, right above my lips, and I absolutely fucking shatter.

I cry out in jumbles, moans tearing from my throat. My nails scratch the wood, my body bucking and arching into him without any sort of coordination. His name. I have no idea how many times I say it or scream it, but it's as if I can't stop myself either. He kisses me everywhere. Fucks me without slowing. All the while my body tightens and convulses around him.

The wand switches off the moment I start to sag. Trying to catch my breath and slow my pounding heart, he's kissing back up my body. His chest against my back as he unties my blindfold. I blink and squint, adjusting to the light. Then I smile. A smile I know he can't see, so I let it fly.

"Good?" he mumbles.

"Awful."

A chuckle against my neck as he toys with a strand of my hair. "Don't relax too much," he says in that gruff tone. "I'm far from finished with you."

23

ZAXTON

One hand wraps around her waist, the other across her chest, and I drag her back to me, my face planting in her neck, very similar to how we were on the dance floor in New York. I suck on her skin, slightly tacky with a sheen of sweat, but still so goddamn sweet I can hardly stand it. The feel of her against me, the rise and fall of her every heavy breath, zap through me like music. Loud and resonant, a stronghold of a beat only I seem to be able to hear.

Her pulse thrums against my lips, my fingers absently toying with her nipple, but she's silent. Likely wondering just what the hell I'm up to. I'm losing my mind over her, and I haven't even been inside her yet.

"Do I still make you nervous?" I smile, only it falters. Since when do I smile so much? The answer is obvious. Since her.

"Yes. But keep doing it. Whatever you're doing."

"Licking your pussy?"

"That. For sure."

"Playing with your tits?"

"Won't complain."

"Making you come?"

"I think I'd like to do that the next time with you inside of me."

"Me too," I hum in her ear. "Tell me, baby girl. What does this pretty pussy want?" I stroke her smooth lips, ring her tight, wet hole. In eight years, I never cared about the playing. Only having it on my terms. But the way she eats up my attention and begs me and tells me exactly what she wants me to do to her—I had no clue sex could be this... fun. This soul quenching and freeing.

I'll give this woman anything she asks for and hopefully a few things she hasn't thought of yet.

"Your cock."

And never. In my life. Has a woman ever made me want her as desperately as this one does.

I groan into her, lifting her up so I can drop her down on the edge of her desk. Suddenly, her bed feels too far away. I'm still fully dressed, and this visibly displeases her. With pursed lips, she attacks the buttons of my dress shirt with eager fingers. When she gets to the bottom, she starts to tug and I swat her hand away, doing the last couple of buttons for her.

"You're an impatient little thing, aren't you?"

"So it seems, though I think it's just you doing that to me." Her blue eyes flicker up to meet mine, but then she's back to business, sliding my shirt over my shoulders as she sits here, gloriously naked without a hint of modesty. It's also the first time I've seen all of her and fuck. Just fuck. This woman is indescribably, almost painfully beautiful.

Long legs and curved hips and narrow waist and full, teardrop tits.

I take in every inch of her as her hands explore my chest, shoulders, and abs in return. Her teeth catch her lip as she probes and caresses every muscle I'm comprised of as if she's committing the sight and feel of me to memory. Her fingers are warm and soft as they whisper along my skin, circle my nipples, and then walk lower down the valley separating my abs. Her touch is no less potent than it was the first time I met her when she was all bloody knees and sass.

I never gave touch that much consideration, but hers is electric and distracting. Engrossing to the point where I'm having difficulty focusing on anything other than what she's doing to me with her simple, innocent exploration. My cock strains through my slacks, desperate and hungry for her, jealous of the attention she's paying the rest of me. She kisses the skin below my navel, and I just about die, my blood overheating in my veins.

"I've wanted to do this since you gave me your shirt to sleep in," she confesses.

My hands drag up through her hair, brushing the strands back from her face so I can see all of her. "I think that was the night I realized I didn't stand a chance of resisting you."

Her eyes meet mine, a question as she reaches the top of my slacks and I nearly laugh. Is she kidding?

"Go on. Don't get shy on me now," I tell her, losing my grip, suddenly understanding her impatience.

It's so quiet in here. Just the two of us, breathing and speaking in soft tones.

She undoes my belt, the button and zipper of my tuxedo pants, and then her hand is inside my boxer briefs, gripping me for the first time. I wheeze out a ragged breath as she squeezes me.

She gives me a couple of confident strokes. "This is going to feel so good inside me."

And just like that, my control snaps. My mouth shoots down onto hers, my tongue thrusting in and claiming her. Leaning forward, I angle her back, one of her hands falling to the desk to support her weight. I hold her head where I want it, the other hand pushing her legs farther apart so I can step in between them while touching her at the same time.

For a moment, I debate dropping back to my knees and eating her like this, but she's not having anything other than me inside her. Bold hands tear down my pants until they're around my ankles. My cock springs free, but I can't stop kissing her. Her neck, her shoulders, the tops of her breasts. She sighs and then yelps as my teeth graze her right nipple, followed by her left, only for me to soothe the sting away with my tongue.

I pull back, staring at the angel before me. Lips parted, eyes hooded, pupils blown out with only a ring of blue around them.

"I'm clean, but I don't have a condom." I hardly planned any of this.

She shakes her head. "I don't care. I'm clean and on the pill."

That's all I needed to hear. I knock her hand away from my cock, give myself a few good pumps, spread her legs, and with my eyes glued to her face, I line myself up with her opening and slide inside her. Her back arches, her eyes rolling back, then close as her breath lodges in her chest.

"Fuck, that's a tight fit," she gasps.

I choke on a laugh. "That's supposed to be my line."

Because it is. Holy hell, I can feel every inch of her warm, wet, smooth walls gripping my cock. It's bliss as much as it's torture. I tilt her back, lift her thighs over my hips, and then slowly slide out of her, only to immediately push back in. My gaze slingshots down to where I'm moving inside of her. I pump in and out of her like this, starting at my glistening cock and how her body stretches around me. The feeling is magnificent.

"Aurelia, fuck, look at you. So fucking gorgeous. Look how your pussy tries to swallow me up as I barely fit inside you." I pinch one of her nipples and then cup her breast, loving the bounce and sway of it in my palm. She cries out as I pick up the pace, going in as deep as I can go and circling my hips with every thrust. "Tell me how good it feels when I fuck you. When I fill you up."

"Awful."

"Fucking brat." I smack her tits. "Tell me how much you love the feel of my cock inside you or I'll pull out now and leave you with only the pathetic little dildo you keep in your nightstand to get you off."

"I knew you were a sadist."

I smile against her lips. "Want me to show you how much?" I start to pull out of her.

"Ah. No. Please, more. Sir. Master. Zax. I don't care what your name is, just don't stop fucking me."

"Then you're going to have to tell me, baby girl." I dive back in, roll my hips once more, and she gasps, her nails digging into my shoulders.

Her eyes flash open, blue fire. "You love how my pussy feels with you inside me."

"Is that so?"

"Yup." She grinds up, swallowing me back in as I start to pull away. Her hand grabs my ass, holding me where she wants me.

"And what about you? Do you like it too?"

"Well, now that you're not demanding answers, I love the feel of your cock inside me. I love how big it is and how full I feel every time you do... ah! That. Whatever you're doing, I never want you to stop."

"That's my girl." I suck on her neck, and she shivers, her pussy spasming around me in warm flutters. Fucking heaven. She's pure sensation, unraveling around me with erratic hands and sloppy kisses and gasps and sighs and moans of pleasure.

It drives me wild. Has me upping my pace until I'm slapping into her over and over and over again. Unable to look at anything other than her. Her stunning face and flushed body and I'm clenching my teeth because this woman feels so un-fucking-believable it's all I can do not to come.

"Zax. I need... I need..."

I know what she needs. Sliding my hand beneath her perfect ass, I pick her up with her legs still around me and shift us to the wall. Her arms encircle my neck, her face buried in my chest as I unleash myself in her. I'm practically resting her on my thighs as I pound up, angling in, making sure she feels every powerful surge and inch of me.

"There," she cries, her voice shredding. "Fuck. God." Her head falls back against the wall, utterly lost in this.

"Stay with me," I command, squeezing her ass and roughly gripping her throat with my other hand. I slam us into the wall, in and out as I continue to fuck her like an animal. "Feel me. Feel me fucking you. Feel how hard my cock is for you. How you're dripping all over me."

"Yes. Keep going. Keep going. *Oh!*" With a cry, she seizes against me, grinding herself down on me hard and clinging to me as she spirals into her orgasm.

"Shit," I growl because I'm going to come and I'm not wearing anything even if she is on the pill and fuck. I pull out of her and explode all over her, bellowing out my release as white ropes of hot cum shoot across her belly and the top of her mound.

I fall against her, pressing her into the wall as I attempt to catch my breath and not pass out.

"You okay?" I whisper into her.

"Dandy."

A laugh bursts out of my lungs and I pull back, cupping her face in my hand so I can kiss her. And once I've done that for a minute or two, I set her gently on her feet, making sure she's good and steady before I head for her bathroom. I return with a warm washcloth, and she stares wordlessly at me as I clean her up.

Then I pick her up again, shut off the light so we're bathed in nothing but moonlight, and then carry her to bed.

"Will you take me to the club sometime? I'd like to see it. If you're okay with that."

I hesitate. The club isn't my happy place, but maybe with her, it'd be fun. We could make it something different. "Sure. Maybe."

I position her so she's on top of me, her chest and belly flush with mine, and for the longest time, I hold her. My fingers trickle up and down her spine and eventually, she doses off. Quiet.

This night with her... I'm a mess. I'm confused and agitated and sated and... content.

I haven't gone down on a woman...

I can't do that. I can't go down that path.

The first time I had sex with someone after Suzie, I wasn't sure I was going to survive. I sat on my balcony, staring out at the skyline and the water and the stars and the world stories below, and had the darkest thoughts known to man.

Aurelia asked me if I was kinky. And I know she likes my dirty talk. I haven't been kinky or so much as opened my mouth with a woman because I don't share any part of myself with the women I fuck. I haven't played or toyed or teased or hell, even *enjoyed* the act of it. Certainly not enough to do much more than ensure the woman gets off and I do too.

But fuck if I don't want to do everything with Aurelia.

This exquisite, filthy woman I can't stop watching. Because damn, she's fucking gorgeous. And she's here with me. Not because I'm Zaxton Monroe. Not because I was part of Central Square. And not because I am the billionaire CEO of Monroe Fashion.

I never told her this would be only sex.

I meant to. In the car, I tried. We parried around it, and I watched as she drew her own conclusions to that, but... I couldn't say it. Because I'm not sure it's what I actually want when I get to the truth of it. I'm greedy with the idea of having her as my own. The thought of it sends something sprinting through my chest, and I hold her sleeping form a bit tighter to try and get it under control.

She's the last woman I should be doing this with, yet it feels predestined. As if I had no choice in any of this. She crashed in my path and here we are, only neither of our stories is that simple or easy.

A storm of uncertainty hovers over us.

One that has wind and rain and enough power to potentially blow down my empire and fuck up my world. But is Aurelia the storm or is she as caught up in the flash flood as I am?

I stay awake for a long time, my brain reeling from all that happened tonight. My pulse refusing to settle down. I listen to Aurelia's soft breaths and murmurs, and I can't help but wonder if she'll be another woman I have to fight to survive after she's gone.

My breath quickens and I don't even know where the compulsion comes from, but the words flee my mouth before I can begin to stop them. "If I don't say this now, I'm not sure I'll ever be able to."

She doesn't move. Not really. But instinctively, somehow, I know she's awake and I'm grateful she's pretending she's not. There is no other way I can say these words. Words I've never uttered. Not even to Grey. Words I think are breeding like toxic viruses inside me.

"She was pregnant. Suzie. Eleven weeks. She'd taken a test and then the morning she died, she had a check-up with a random doctor in Switzerland. They did an ultrasound. It was a boy. Our boy and we were... excited. I mean, terrified. But so excited. We were going to tell everyone that night when we celebrated her birthday, but I wouldn't tell our friends, her brother, that I knocked her up unless she had my ring on her finger. I had waited. I wanted it to all be on the same day so we could celebrate it all even though I'd had the ring for weeks and weeks. I was going to tell them that when she hit sixteen weeks, we were going to leave the tour and I was going to quit the band.

"Callan I already knew wanted out, though he never said a word. He was studying hard and had wanted to be a doctor since he was a kid. I knew that's where his head was. And I also knew Lenox was only there because Suzie and I were. Asher wanted to play ball. It was only Grey and Suzie holding us there. Holding the band together. The rest of us had other dreams beyond music."

I blow out a breath, my vision clouding as I remember her. Her smile. Her light. Her energy. And then her colorless, wet face in the shower as she died before my eyes, and I lost my absolute fucking mind. Lost every solid piece of me.

Her. Our baby. I died along with them.

"No one knows about the baby to this day. Not even Lenox, though he did know about the headaches. Those *I* didn't know about." Another breath, this one shaky. "Suzie was secretive and crafty like that. I didn't see the stroke coming. I saw her wince before she went to the shower, and I think part of me knew something wasn't right with that. But... it was a perfect day and I... If I had known about the headaches..."

I squeeze her against me, and I feel her hand grip my shoulder. That's it. No other movement. But that grip is everything. It's exactly what I need to get through this.

I was going to marry her. Suzie was going to be my wife. The mother of my children. So how do I reconcile that? How do I go from that to this? I've never been capable before, which is where the faceless, meaningless women came in. Then the other piece of irony hits me. A week ago, I didn't know if I could trust this woman and now I'm trusting her with the darkest parts of me. But I can't turn back now.

Right or wrong, better or worse, I'm in this with her.

It's been eight years since Suzie died and no one since has even hit my radar until Aurelia.

"You said okay to only sex and I didn't disagree. But you should know, so you can escape now, without repercussions as I promised, that I'm not sure I can agree to those terms. Casual is all I've done for the last eight years, and that casual was meaningless. Those women had no face to me, but you do. I see you, Aurelia. However tragic that might turn for me, I do. So if I take you to the club, you're on my arm. If I'm fucking you, I'm *only* fucking you."

"Okay," she whispers so softly I nearly miss it. "Only you."

Her face pops up, bathed in moonlight, and her eyes hold mine, glassy with unshed tears. I cup her cheek in my hand and lean in to kiss her. Soft. Sweet this time. Full of every thought and emotion that's exploding inside of me.

My cock is already stirring, and I want more of her. Now that I've had her, I don't want to stop. I climb down her body and lick her out with my tongue while my fingers play with her until she comes all over them. But then I'm back on her, over her, slipping inside her as I stare into her pretty eyes.

My fingers knot with hers and I raise our joined hands over her head, her tits on display for me as the moon peeks through her window and hits her just right. I slide in and out of her, slowly at first, feeling her from the inside out. Needing to be closer when there is no such thing as close enough right now. Staring down at my girl, right into her eyes, I lose myself, and for the first time in so long, I don't care if I'm never found again. My control is gone. My heart all over the place as I pump into her body and claim it fully as my own.

Her. This woman.

My reckoning and my salvation.

Before long, I quicken my pace, sweat clinging to my brow. She shakes, her whole body trembling with each drag and draw of my cock. Her grip on my hands tightens, her thighs around my hips holding me solidly against her.

I tell her how sexy she looks when I'm inside her. How beautiful her skin glows. All the things I want to do to it, like tie it up and bite it and mark it. I tell her I want her sore on Monday and to catch her blushing when we're in meetings. I tell her she can have anything. Any fantasy she wants as long as it's with me.

Never have I been so vocal during sex as I am with her. I can't seem to stop myself.

Her orgasm spikes through her unexpectedly, forcing my own to tumble out of me. I come inside her this time—she demands it, promising me it's okay—and it's... fucking hot. My cum leaking out of her is insanely hot and I tell her that too.

When we're both spent, I wrap her back up in my arms and hold her against me, unwilling to give her space. She rolls into me, burrowing her face in my chest and holding me back just as fiercely.

Relief slams into me, knocking me sideways that she's still here with me after all I told her. I close my eyes and settle in. Even as I feel the fear lurking in the darkest depths of the back of my mind. The red flags and the warnings and the what the fuck are you doing. I push it all away. I have to.

Something that is wrong shouldn't feel this right. I hope.

24

AURELIA

O h my heart. Zaxton Monroe, what have you done to it? Where did the gruff, domineering, grumpy, possessive, cockblocking man who danced with me and told me he was going to fuck me go? Him I can deal with. Him I can handle. But the man who confides his darkest, most heart-wrenching secret and then makes love to me?

I've never been intimate with a man. I've had sex, but I've never been intimate.

Everything about last night with Zax was intimate. From the way he took the pins out of my hair and removed my dress to the playing and fantasies to the sex to the way he looked me in the eyes to the way he's holding me now as he sleeps. All of it.

It's so wildly unexpected, though maybe it shouldn't be.

The man is nothing if not passionate and intense. Even when he does his best to keep all that beneath the surface, it leaks through anyway.

Then there's the stuff with Suzie.

When she died, the speculations were rampant. And all of it was wrong. So very, very wrong. There were reports she had overdosed. That she'd killed herself. That she slipped and fell in the shower and hit her head. A hundred different things and he had to hear and see and deal with all of it all the while knowing the horrible truth. And keeping the hardest part of that to himself.

The morning sun dances across his face, and he looks so peaceful like this. So light and almost boyish, though there is nothing boyish about this man with his full, pouty lips and insanely long black eyelashes and rumpled, wavy hair. I could stare at his gorgeous face for hours and when he's like this, it's a hell of a lot easier to do that than it is when he's awake. Something about his eyes on me, no matter what, always gets my heart rate going.

The man truly does make me nervous. In the best and worst of ways.

Then it hits me.

Holy Christmas carols, I had crazy all-night sex with Zaxton Monroe and then slept on top of him after because he wouldn't let me have any space. And I liked it. No. I loved it. My brain is anxious to start going. To start overanalyzing. To start questioning. And for the love of baby kittens, why the hell does the *what does this mean* question have to be part of every woman's genetic makeup? It's like we're programmed for disappointment from the start.

I knock all those bitches away. I am *not* that woman. I will not *be* that woman. And truth, I'm not even sure what I'd want the answer to be. Despite what Zax said in the car last night, this thing between us is a calamitous shitstorm of a fiasco waiting to be unleashed. And let's be honest, when do those things ever end well for the female intern?

Still... I can't find it in me to stop this or walk away. Last night, here now with him, it's filling places inside me that have been vacant all my life.

My lips press to his collarbone.

"Don't tell me you want more," he mumbles, his eyes still closed, but I'd swear his lips are quirked up into a smile. A smile and not a frown and gah!

"That a problem for old men like you?"

Now he's smiling for sure as he squints open one brown eye.

"I think you can tell I have no problems with that." He grinds up into me and yeah, no problems there. Leaning up, he bites my shoulder, and I squeal, rolling off him, only to suddenly be pinned beneath him. "You didn't answer my question," he says menacingly as he hovers over me, dark eyes fierce in the early morning light.

"Actually, I was thinking brunch and then a yoga class. Or a yoga class and then brunch."

"Yoga," he exclaims as if he's never heard the word before. "You didn't get enough exercise and stretching last night?"

"Different kind of stretching. And can a girl ever truly get enough of either?"

He pushes up into a plank and glances down at his naked body and wow. Hard muscles and hard cock and yeah, I'm drooling. And wet.

"I have nothing else to wear other than my tux," he says, still staring down at our bodies.

"Okay. Fine. We can stay here and have more sex," I graciously offer instead. "You know, because I'm giving like that."

His eyes flash up to mine, his grin wicked and wolfish before he drops back down on me, his cock hitting me in just the right place to make me squirm and moan. "I thought you said yoga and brunch."

"Ugh. Who needs food and stretching? Lame."

My hands grasp his shoulder blades as he licks up my neck to my ear. "I could eat you and then stretch you on my dick."

"If you insist."

He thrusts up, gliding through my wet center and pressing firmly on my clit with the head of his cock. Stars flash behind my eyes. "I don't want you too sore, Angel." Another thrust.

"I'll manage," I promise with a breathy sigh, ready to angle my hips up and take him straight inside me.

"Except I wanted to take you somewhere tonight, and believe me when I tell you, you don't want to be sore for what I have in mind."

A rush of wet heat leaks out of me, and he grunts and then groans when he feels it coating him.

"Can you come like this?"

I nod furiously as he picks up his pace, hitting me with perfect precision each time.

"That's it. I could watch you like this forever and never grow bored. Tell me your fantasies, Aurelia. All the filthy, naughty things you've always secretly craved. Tell me so I can make them happen."

"You. This. More." I hike my knees up, seeking more friction.

"I'm going to put you in a mask tonight," he whispers in my ear. "Put your hair up. Have you in a sexy dress. On my arm. And then spend the night letting you explore and do whatever it is you want to do as long as you do it with me."

There's something so freeing in the way he wants me. I can be myself, live out and request all my darkest, deepest, most depraved fantasies. And he's right there, ready to fulfill each one.

I shudder and cry out, gripping him and holding him tight against me as I come all over him like this. He growls and the feel of his hot cum on me sends me spiraling to another level. He groans and so do I, both of us panting.

Deep diving, long, sweet, and soft kisses consume me. It's a kiss unlike any I've ever had before. It's a kiss that says something, as if trying to convey a message, only I can't make out what it is. All I know is that I wasn't lying. I think he might be my fantasy. And I think I want more of this.

"Can your shower fit both of us?" he asks, his forehead pressed to mine.

"It can barely fit me. I have to slouch to wash my hair."

He mutters something impolite under his breath I choose to ignore. "Pack a bag because you're spending the weekend at my place and that's through Monday morning when we go into work together."

"No—"

He shuts me up with a kiss. "We won't be obvious about it and none of this will carry into work. But that's what we're doing. I can't stand you here, Aurelia. I know why you live here and what you're doing, and I respect it. You make hard choices and chase your dreams and that's courageous and admirable. But that doesn't mean I'm going to like the thought of you being here. I want you in my place, in my bed that isn't sitting on the goddamn floor and where we can both fit in the fucking shower."

I glower. "Domineering isn't necessarily one of my fantasies."

"I beg to differ with that. You seemed to like it last night. In fact, I remember you throwing out terms like sir and master to me."

"I would have said anything to come in that moment. That doesn't mean I want that game in my real life."

"Good thing I'm not pretending or playing right now then." Another kiss. "Come on. Let's get cleaned up and go. I also have central air and it's getting hotter in here by the second."

He has a point with that. "That's the only reason I'm saying yes. Otherwise, I *never* take orders. Especially from hot men."

"Work on that poker face, baby girl. Lying isn't your strong suit."

I nearly laugh at that. Nearly.

"Incidentally, no yoga or brunch yet. I need to change."

"I'm assuming Zaxton Monroe doesn't do walks of shame."

He shakes his head.

"Hmm. Well, that's a problem for you."

A raised eyebrow. "You could give me back the shirt you stole from me."

I laugh, because truly, that's a good one. "Not on your life, pal. No takebacks allowed. I confiscated that fair and square just like you did my panties in New York." I return his pointed eyebrow with one of my own, only to give him a once-over and then make an exaggerated huff. "Fine. I *guess* I can let you borrow a pair of my yoga pants but only if you promise to wash them before you return them." I scrunch my nose. "Ball sweat. Yuck."

A laugh vibrates through him, making me laugh in return.

"No teabagging after I've worked out then?"

Now I flat out hysterically laugh. Because Zaxton, the serious, grumpy man himself just used the term teabagging. I think I'm dead. Officially. He starts to tickle me, and I squirm, screaming and slapping at his hands because ticklish is my super-secret middle name.

"Stop! I'm going to pee!"

His smile fills my vision and stops my breath along with my heart. I trace it just to make sure it's real and he kisses the pad of my finger.

"Not my kink," he informs me.

"Mine either, so you need to stop tickling me."

"Beg for mercy."

"Never," I reply, winded. Only I don't think that's a promise I can keep where he's concerned. My heart is already poking me in the ribs, letting me know that danger is on the horizon for us.

"WHAT ARE WE DOING?" I ask as we stroll through the seaport district near his place.

His head swivels to mine and even with the Boston Rebels ball hat and aviator sunglasses he's wearing, I can see his pinched eyebrows. "We're going for brunch," he says as if he's suddenly unsure. "You told me you were hungry."

"I know. I am."

Now he tilts his head. "Did I miss something? You said no to the yoga, right?"

I did say no to the yoga. Peter picked us up and drove us back to Zax's building. I had a bag with me that Zax immediately brought into his massive closet and unpacked, hanging up my dress for tonight for me and everything. That was after he held my hand and introduced me to the weekend doorman, informing him that I'd be staying at least through the weekend.

At least. Such a casual term that is anything but in this scenario.

We showered and made out like teenagers and then he asked if I still wanted to go to yoga. His words were, "I've never done it before, but I'll try if that's what you want to do."

I told him no.

The thought of him going to a yoga class for me is well... yeah. And then there are the other women in the class. Zax in some of those positions would be an otherworldly experience and I'd be swatting them away from him like flies. But he's still holding my hand and we're out in public and I—

"You're thinking awfully hard over there."

"People will see us at brunch together," I rush out, stupidly jittery.

"Yes. And?"

"And I thought we said we were going to keep this private. Between us."

He considers this for a moment. Frowns, only to check it quickly and re-form an emotionless mask. "Would you feel more comfortable going back to my place and eating?"

"Yes. No." I stare down at our linked hands. "I don't know. You didn't want women knowing you were available. It's why you go to the club. It's why you're taking me to the club tonight."

"But I'm not available. I'm with you."

Jesus. The way he says that. So simply. As if that's all the explanation the world would ever need. I'm going to fall in love with him and he won't understand how it happened.

His free hand grasps my chin and then he's tilting my head up to his. He tucks his glasses on top of his hat and stares into my eyes. "Aurelia, I'm taking you to the club because you asked me to. Because the thought of it seemed to turn you on. Did I misread that?"

"No. It does. Honestly, I'm curious about it and I think it'll be fun."

"I'm not taking you there because I feel the need to hide you."

Stop. *Stop!* My heart is blaring like an alarm: Warning. Danger. Crash imminent.

"You're not comfortable being seen with me out in public," he surmises.

"I-I don't know." My face plants in his chest and he wraps his arms around me, holding me against him. "I'm sorry. I don't mean to be crazy, but I feel crazy all the same."

His lips press into my hair. "Now you know how I've been feeling for the last few weeks anytime I'm near you and even when I'm not."

I prop my chin on his chest and stare up at his warm brown eyes. "How do you manage it?"

His thumb brushes across my cheekbone. "I've stopped fighting it.

I've stopped second-guessing and using the easy excuses as reasons not to try. I want this with you. Maybe I haven't been the best at saying it, but for me, this is more than sex. You are more than sex to me. But if you don't feel the same—"

"I do," I quickly interrupt. "I think that's why I'm so crazy. I'm terrified this is too good to be true." Because it always is. For me, it always is.

A smile erupts across his face, eclipsing the sun with its beauty. It's as if twilight is sparkling in his eyes. He bends down and kisses me. Just a sweet pressing of our lips, but it's a promise. A start. I have no idea how we got here from where we were, but I can't fight the rightness of it either.

"How about this?" he murmurs against me. "We keep a low profile as we said we would. Because you're right. When people find out I'm with someone, things will get messy and complicated for both of us, and I'd like to protect you from that as best as I can. We'll lay low. Go to the club. Fuck each other's brains out. Work together as we've been working. And see how it all goes."

"I like that. I like all of that. I like being with you. I've just never had this before, so it's new and scary. I'm in uncharted waters."

"Me too," he says simply. "I was with Suzie for seven years. No one before and no one after. I haven't wanted this with anyone, Aurelia, but I can't think of anything else now that I've thought of you as mine."

It's funny when a moment hits you. When you're going about your day and your life and then something comes out of nowhere and plows through you, knocking your world sideways in such a position where you know never again will it fully be how it was before. Those words were my utter undoing. The final thread pull in my unraveling.

Because I just fell in love with Zaxton Monroe. And I'm not sure if this will turn out to be the best or worst moment of my life.

25

AURELIA

"You're sure this is what you want?" Zax asks, staring directly into my eyes as I sit in the passenger side of the rental car. When he told me that's how we'd be traveling tonight, my heart ached. The lengths this man goes to to hide from the world. To keep his privacy and be left alone. It also endears me to him. That he's willing to take me here, to give me this piece of himself that I'm suspecting he shares with no one, and frankly, doesn't enjoy all that much.

He's fulfilling my fantasies, but I want to be his in return.

I want to resurrect everything that died inside of him when Suzie died. I don't want to try and replace her—that's impossible. But I'd do anything for him to remember fun and love and laughter and heat and passion. I want him to remember what it feels like to not just live but be alive. So while he thinks tonight is only about me, I plan to flip things around on him. Just a bit.

"Yes. I'm sure."

"And you'll stay with me?"

God. This man. He has no clue how fierce and beautiful his heart is. I cup his smooth, chiseled jaw in my hand and hold his brown eyes with mine. "I'm yours, Zax."

He emits a shaky breath and leans in to kiss me. But then the perv sneaks his hand in through the plunging V of my dress and cups my breast. "Damn fucking right you are."

Ah. There's my guy.

"Incidentally, have I told you what a fucking knockout you are in this dress?"

"Nope." I smile against his lips.

"A crime. My apologies." He squeezes my breast again, running the pad of his thumb back and forth over my tight nipple. "This dress is sinful and delicious on you, and I plan to strip it slowly from your body before I lick every inch of your skin."

And just like that, the scrap of fabric I'm calling underwear tonight is soaked.

"I hope you plan to put my pussy where your mouth is."

He smiles on a half-laugh. "Isn't the expression, put your money where your mouth is?"

I shake my head, nibbling playfully on my red lip. "Not tonight it isn't."

"What about my cock?"

I lick the seam of his lips, my hand shifting to his inner thigh without touching one of my favorite parts of him. "Oh, I fully intend to put that where my mouth is. But first, I want to play and explore, Zax. Show me sex club Zaxton. The sexy, dominating man who owns any woman he looks at."

"And yet he seems to only want one."

"He better. I can be a bit possessive too. I almost wish I were wearing a collar that said Zax's cock slave."

He snorts out a strangled laugh and I can't help but gleam at that.

"Come on, filthy girl. Let's go have some fun." He gives me a wink, and just like that, he's out of the car and opening the door for me.

Arm linked in the crook of his elbow, he guides me through a parking lot and along a street lined with very corporate-looking buildings. We enter one and are greeted by a big, burly security guard.

"May I help you?"

Zax pulls out his phone and flashes something at the man, who nods and guides us to an elevator. He presses a button, the doors open, and then we're shooting up forty stories. As the elevator ascends, he twists to me and places one of the black masks he's been holding over my face, careful as to not snag on the tight bun he insisted I wear at the top of my head. Another wink and then he's placing his own over his eyes and nose and suddenly, he is everything dark and nefarious any predator would be.

My heart rate spikes, endorphins slithering through my veins, making me warm and edgy with anticipatory nerves.

The elevator slows, pings, and then the doors part and we step off into a dimly lit anteroom, cloaked in crimson, velvet drapes. A woman in a black corset and leather pants is there to greet us.

"Good evening. Please input your number." She gestures to a large touch screen and Zax walks over and punches in a six-digit code. The screen pings green and then she says, "Room nine is ready for you as requested." She parts the curtain for us. "Enjoy your night, Sir. Ma'am."

"Thank you," Zax says as he guides me into a large open space that is nothing at all how I imagined it would be. I expected sex to be dripping from the walls along with women in cages dancing to hard-core, violent techno. I expected whips and chains and women and men in leather. Hell, I expected the freaking red room of pain on steroids.

This is nothing like that.

This is a classy, chic bar and club. The bar shelves in addition to the shiny black lacquer bar top glow with deep red underlighting. Men are dressed in variations of suits and women in sexy cocktail dresses. Very similar to how Zax and I are dressed. They're sitting on couches or at high-top tables, chatting and laughing, dancing as hypnotic house music plays. No one is openly having sex and is it weird that I'm a bit disappointed by that?

"What is room nine?" I ask softly, leaning into him so my voice doesn't carry.

Zax's masked face dips in my direction. "It's just a room I thought you'd like. We can use it or not. Whatever you want, tonight is about you."

I squeeze his forearm. "Tonight is about us."

"You should call me Sir," he says. "Not because I want you to be submissive to me, unless that's what you want. It's because—"

"I know," I tell him, cutting him off. "I already assumed I would." Zax or Zaxton or Mr. Monroe are too identifying. I mean, who the hell else on this planet is named Zaxton?

"What would you like me to call you?"

I look up into his dark eyes, ringed in black satin. "I like it when you call me angel or baby girl."

A smile curls up his lips. "All right, Angel. Would you care for a drink?"

"Yes, Sir."

Just as we head toward the bar, a gorgeous, curvy redhead intercepts us. "Hello. Are you interested in a third tonight?"

Zax glances at me as if he's asking if that's one of my fantasies and I subtly shake my head. "No, thank you," I tell her politely, and the woman smiles and nods.

"No problem. Have fun."

"Did you want that?" I ask after she walks off. "Another woman with us?"

He smirks at my insatiable curiosity. "No. I want you and only you."

"Would you have if I had said yes?"

"If you had wanted another woman with us, I would have. But it's not what I need or even desire."

I can't help but question, "Is that how it works? I mean, for you in the past?"

"Yes. Sometimes. Women would come up to me or I'd go up to them." He turns to me and cups my jaw until I'm staring straight up at him. "It was perfunctory. Uncomplicated and safe. Boring." His thumb glides along my jaw and he steps in closer to me. "Everything being with you isn't. I never enjoyed being here. It wasn't fun or sexy to me. You are, though, and being here with you is different from anything I've ever had here before."

I angle up onto the balls of my heeled feet and kiss him. This man has a way of making my heart trip over itself. "You keep talking like that and you'll never be able to get rid of me. I'll implant my roots in you like a weed."

"That meant to scare me?"

"I'm a lot to handle."

"So I'm learning. Let's get a drink and then I'll show you around," he murmurs into me. "See what you're interested in doing."

"Sounds good."

We approach the bar and I order a glass of red wine because I don't want to get too drunk and I think it's already been established, I'm a bit of a lightweight. Zax orders a bourbon and then he's guiding me away from the bar and open club area to a long hallway near where we entered.

"It's shaped like a U," he explains, pointing down the hall. "The rooms on the outside are private and reserved. The rooms in the center are more... open and can be communal for watching or participating. The private rooms also have the option of flipping a switch so that the wall becomes two-sided or one-sided glass. So don't be surprised if as we're walking, you're able to look into the rooms and see what people are doing in there."

"Okay." Suddenly, my heart is in my throat and my limbs are shaky. I take a sip of my wine and he holds me close as we walk. And sure enough, the first room we pass has two men and a woman in it. She's in between them, bound with her hands behind her back. One of the men is taking her from behind. The other is in her mouth.

A flare of heat courses through me and my breath quickens.

Zax's hand starts caressing the bare skin of my back, clearly attuned to my reaction.

"Did you ever watch people?" I whisper, my voice tremulous.

"Sometimes."

I can't help but moan. I'm not even sure why that's so sexy to me. Zax watching other couples like this. "I can't tell you how turned on I am being here with you."

His teeth graze my ear, and he shifts against my back so I feel his hard cock straining through his pants. I shiver and moan again as his hand slides through my dress to the front of me, tickling the skin of my stomach while I watch the woman in between these two men.

"Keep going?" he asks.

"Yes."

He's behind me still as we walk. Several more of the rooms on the right are either vacant or their glass is closed off. But then we come upon one of the first open rooms and holy shit. I gasp. The room is bathed in edgy red light with black leather furnishings. Beds, benches, stools. The walls have chains and cuffs and bars and whips and canes. It's Fifty Shades on crack.

There are several people, both men and women, touching and kissing and rubbing and fucking. Some of them are blindfolded and tied up. Some gagged. Some being beaten and flogged and loving it. Some of them are very clearly submissives with their Doms or Dommes. No doubt this is a BDSM room. Some of them are just couples, watching and playing but not necessarily participating.

It's a sex dungeon forty stories up in a Boston skyscraper.

"Is it wrong that I'm questioning the need for Clorox wipes while being turned on?"

"Is it the need for disinfectant that's turning you on?"

I hold in my laugh. "Absolutely not. Just... you know."

"I know. It's all very clean. They take that very seriously here. So you can be turned on and not have to think about... that."

"Good to know. Back to being fully turned on."

Because wow. This is so sexy and hot.

I keep walking. Suddenly a little overwhelmed by it all. But then we come to room nine. And I can't help it. I could keep walking, keep exploring, but I want to see precisely what Zax felt I would enjoy. His breath fans the back of my neck as my hand hits the nob.

Zax punches in a code and the door makes that mechanical unlocking sound.

Holding my breath as nerves fire off like psychotic firecrackers in my body, I twist and open the door.

He flips on the light and a crystal chandelier dimly flicks on. It's the only lighting illuminating the room along with pillar candles. Everything is white. From the large circular bed with satin sheets and pillows. To the chaise with a tufted pleather back and gold embellishments. All the way to the white wood dresser and shimmering wallpaper. The ceiling is a mirror. The crystals of the chandelier and the flames of the candles reflect off the glass, creating prisms of light. It's nothing like I thought it was going to be. It's elegant and pretty.

"Is this okay?" he murmurs.

"It's beautiful." And then I giggle. I'm in a sex club and I just called the room beautiful. But there is no other word for it. "It's a sex room in heaven. You know, if heaven had that sort of thing."

"Now you know why I chose this room for us. *Angel*." He kisses the back of my neck.

I blink about ten thousand times, trying to get my emotions under control. How can a sex room in a sex club where I was just thinking about the need for Clorox wipes be romantic?

Because of the man behind me.

All of this is because of the man behind me. He wanted this to be special for me. He wanted this to be romantic.

My heart flutters.

"Everything in here is new for us," he whispers against my neck. "Nothing from the sheets to the toys has ever been used by anyone else. I purchased everything new."

"Thank you."

Zax takes my hand and leads me to the bed, sitting me down. I glance up at the mirrored ceiling that has the tarnished old-fashioned feel to it and he does the same, both of us staring at each other and the room around us. I watch as he steps between my legs and asks, "Masks on or off?"

I don't know. It's just us in here. But the masks are part of the erotic fun, even with him. "On to start."

"Is there anything you don't want me to do?"

My chin drops and I meet his eyes. "No. I trust you."

"Is there anything you do want me to do?"

I match his smirk, my hands running along the silky fabric of his pants. "Everything."

His mouth comes down on mine, kissing me passionately as he holds my face. "Then let's have some fun."

I smile against him as I reach up to slide his suit jacket off his shoulders. Once that's done, my fingers quickly go for his tie, irritated that he's so dressed up when I need him undressed. I yank on the knot and then decide the buttons might be easier.

"You have no patience," he rumbles against me as he kisses his way down my neck.

"Not my strong suit."

"Do you know why I wore a tie?"

"To torture me?"

He grins against my skin and then licks at my thrumming pulse. "When I was getting dressed for tonight, the idea of tying your wrists up in my tie sent a thrill through me and instantly made me hard."

Oh. *Oh!* He undoes the knot in his ice blue tie, sliding it through the flaps of his collar. I pull back, watching him with rapt attention. Once the tie is undone, he wraps it around his fist and then his hands are beneath me, gripping my ass as he lifts me, positioning me on the far end of the bed by the padded headboard.

"Hands up, Angel."

I comply instantly. He loops the cold silk around one wrist and then the other, tying it to a hook I hadn't previously noticed on the bed. Tugging on my wrists, he tests the restraint and once he's satisfied he has me as he wants me, he stands beside my head and starts to strip out of his shirt and then undoes the button on his slacks without removing them.

I've never seen a sexier man in my life, and I've worked with models.

Zax exudes power and confidence. A fierce predator, he's also a protector and lover. We're here tonight for me. All of this he's done for me, and I can't even begin to wrap my head around that. No one has ever taken care of me. No one has ever worshiped or cherished me. I've been called beautiful countless times—a useless term that says nothing of who I am—but I've never been *seen*.

Until this man.

Nothing about us or our situation is easy, but when I'm with him, it's impossible to care about any of that.

He bends and gives me a chaste kiss, not nearly enough for where my head and heart are. "Don't move," he teases.

"Ha. You're very funny."

That smirk. "Sir. I'm Sir to you right now, baby girl."

"Sir Jokes a Lot?"

"Maybe I should shut you up with my cock."

"Maybe you should," I challenge.

"Hmmm. This first, I think." Reaching behind my neck, he undoes the tie of my dress and slowly peels it off me, his mouth following the trail of fabric as he slides it down and off my body. His fingers loop into my tiny thong and then that's gone too. He emits a shaky breath as he takes me in, staring with wild, dark, hungry eyes. "You truly are an angel. From your white-blond hair to your creamy skin. God. Just looking at you hurts, but knowing you're mine..."

"Yours," I promise him because I can't stop it.

Another kiss to my lips and then he's gone, over to the dresser thing, and I can't see what he's doing from this angle. I hear some things rustling around and then he's back.

"Open for me."

I open my mouth and he slides in a black silicone plug.

"Get it nice and wet. That's it. Suck it like you're going to suck my cock."

Delicious anticipation zaps through my body as I eagerly suck on the plug. When it's wet to his satisfaction, he slips it from my lips and then he's between my legs, spreading my thighs wide for him. His tongue circles my clit at the same time the wet toy circles my forbidden hole. I arch up, tugging on the restraints binding my wrists.

"Has anyone ever fucked you here?" His tongue flicks at me there, getting me wetter and wetter so he can slide the plug into my ass without resistance.

"No," I cry out as he starts to slide it in inch by inch.

"Just you playing then?"

"Yes. God. Ah!"

"You think you're feeling tight and full now? Wait till my cock is in your pussy with this inside your ass."

Jesus. I can't. My mind starts to fracture. To fizzle and grow fuzzy. Especially as he continues to lick me. My opening. My clit. All the while he's pushing this plug inside my ass. But then. "Holy shit!" I scream as pounding vibrations shoot through me.

"Good?"

"Yes. Ah! It's a lot."

"Too much?"

"I don't know."

He licks my clit, toying and sucking and flicking it. The vibration adjusts, more of a pulsing and now I moan, low and loud. Two fingers slide inside me as he continues to make out with my pussy, all the while the plug in my ass is humming through my body, making my core tight and achy and wet.

It feels so good. Unlike anything I've ever come close to experiencing before and the second his fingers hit that magical spot inside of me, I explode around them. Jerking and writhing and tugging on the silk tie around my wrists as I come. Grinding up into his face as much as he'll allow me. His hand on my ass holds me to him while he continues to lick me and finger fuck me, and it goes on and on and on.

Just as I go boneless, he switches the vibration again. This one is three bursts and then a break. Three bursts and then a break. Over and over as he pulls away from me, kissing his way up my body. He licks at my breasts, toying and playing with my nipples, building me slowly back up.

The feel of him over me, pressing me down into the firm mattress, is heady. I want him closer. I want him all over me. I want him to be the only thing I feel. Ever. Always.

Then he's kneeling over me. "Open for me, baby girl. Let's see what this wicked mouth of yours can do."

I open at the feel of his cock bumping into my lips and then greedily suck him in. The taste of him, the smell of his cologne and musk, the feel of his hard, satiny cock against my tongue. I'm high. Shooting full of dopamine as the plug in me continues to pulse. I feel my pussy dripping, my nipples tight and hard.

He pumps into me, his strong thighs on either side of my head, until he hits the back of my throat. I choke and gag, and he caresses my face, clasping my neck and holding me there so he can feel the way my muscles and throat move as I suck him off. A groan sears past his lips when I swallow for him and then he's ripping the mask off my face, followed by his own.

"Fuck, Angel. What you do to me. I'm losing my mind over you." His hips thrust, his cock sliding in and out, picking up speed. Saliva pools in my mouth as I do my best to take all of him. But I'm powerless. At his total mercy. Something that isn't lost on him, his eyes feral as he controls my breathing and gag reflex and the way I take his cock down my throat. All the while he worships me. With his eyes. With his words.

When his thighs start to tremble and he's reaching the point of no return, he pulls out of my mouth and then, he's hiking my legs up over his shoulders and sliding straight inside of me. We groan, the sensation of that with the plug hitting both of us.

The vibration changes again, becoming a steady rhythm as he fucks me. It's so much. All of it. The plug inside my ass as he takes my pussy. I'm full and stretched. Hands planting into the mattress, he bends me in half, upping the pace of his pistoning hips. His face above mine.

"I can't bear how good this feels," he rasps, diving down and nuzzling at my neck, inhaling my skin. "I don't want to stop. Ever.

Fuck, baby. I'm throbbing inside you. Do you feel it?" His fingers grip the sheets by my head.

"Yes. I feel it. More," I plead hoarsely.

"Tell me what you need."

"Harder. Faster. More."

With deft fingers, he unties my bindings and then he's hauling me up until I'm sitting on him, wrapped around him. Blood shoots through my arms, the sensation sending me into overdrive. I squirm on him as he fully impales me, his thigh hitting the base of the plug, pushing it in farther, and I just about lose my mind with the incandescent pleasure of it.

Holding me to his chest, he grips my hips and bounces me on him, thrusting up and into me each time he slams me down. He drags his cock out, hitting just the right angle, making sure I rub my clit against his lower abs each and every time. On and on, he doesn't stop and he doesn't slow. He takes me as he wants me. As I need him to. Hard and rough, but skilled and precise. We're sweaty, sticking to each other, unable to slow the ride or the build-up.

His teeth drag along my neck, licking me, tasting my skin as his mouth whispers a hundred dirty and depraved things that turn me on to the point of madness. I claw at him. Using his thighs and shoulders for leverage, impaling myself on him, needing him deeper and deeper and deeper.

Until finally, my body can't fight it another second. "Zax. Oh God, yes. I—*oh!*" And then I'm coming. So hard I scream and bite his shoulder because it's too much. It's so much. It overtakes me and I can't control it. He continues to push me through it as sparkles of light dance across my vision. And when he can hold off no longer, he splays a hand across my back and stills, roaring out his release, shuddering and gasping uncontrollably.

We tumble down on the bed, his body over mine, and then the plug shuts off. Gently, he pulls it from my body without pulling out of me and then he's back on me, over me, holding me, cradling me against him. He murmurs in my ear. Asking if I'm okay. Telling me how incredible I am and how incredible that was. How he's never experienced anything like it before and that can only be because it was with me.

All I know is that from here on out, I'll never be the same. This man owns my heart, my body, and my soul. I can only hope it's the same for him. And pray this never ends.

26

AURELIA

"I still can't believe you watch these shows," Zax says as I lie on his couch, my head propped up with a pillow as I face the television while he strums on his bass and pretends to watch with me. I don't complain. What is it about musicians? There is something so damn sexy about watching him play, I can't even figure out what it is.

"They're fascinating," I explain. "These things actually happened. How do you not like them?"

I twist to peek at him, his attention on the screen while he absently plays. I have the volume down because I've already seen this one and I'd rather listen to him play.

"I didn't say I didn't like them," he counters. "They're just intense. And a bit disturbing."

"Well, yeah. I mean, that's almost part of the draw. I like true crime documentaries more than when they turn them into movies or TV shows. I feel like the documentaries are more authentic to what truly happened."

He gives me a dubious look.

"You'll see. Soon you won't be able to stop watching them."

"Now I understand why you have two deadbolts on your door."

I snicker. "Those were there when I moved in, and I had three in my apartment in New York. That's where I started getting into it, which I guess is sort of messed up if you think about it since I was a teenager and living alone. I had victim written all over me. I don't know. I never thought about it like that until this moment, so thanks for that reality check."

He rolls his eyes at me. "Now you know why I hate your neighborhood so much."

"Don't remember asking you."

I get a perturbed look and then he says, "You should have been a crime journalist or lawyer or a detective."

I scrunch my nose. "No, thanks. It's one thing to see something on television and know it happened, it's another to see it in the flesh and deal with it as part of your daily life. Fashion is way easier and safer. Plus, sewing is my happy place. I just watch these because they're interesting and addictive."

"You're interesting and addictive." He tickles my feet that are resting on his lap, and I squirm, nearly kicking him straight in the nuts. As it is, it's a glancing blow and he grunts out a curse, falling to his side and half on top of me with a heavy thud. "Ow."

"Serves you right for tickling me."

He bites my butt and I squeal.

"Jerk." I smack at his head. "That hurt."

Only I can't stop laughing and neither can he. "Baby girl, you don't know pain until you get hit in the nuts."

"Oh, please," I taunt. "You men are such babies. We birth children and put up with your miserable asses. You wanna talk about pain? Try being your intern and your lover."

He sits up, bringing me with him and adjusting his bass so we don't crush it. He tucks me in beside him, his lips on my temple as he speaks. "I thought we did pretty well at it this week."

"We did. I guess." I even made it through a Monday disaster free. It was a miracle.

Zax and I kept our distance, and he was his same cantankerous self, complete with growly emails and barky words and heated glares that never fail to give me the shivers—in a good way. We got our work done and no one was the wiser. We didn't flirt or touch—at least not much or where anyone could witness—and even though I was tempted to lock the door to his office and climb onto his desk for a little naughty fun, I heroically resisted.

Last night, I went out with Iris, Howie, Howie's girlfriend, Greta, and Nate. It was a blast, but obviously, Zax couldn't join. I was the fifth wheel and riding solo. Keeping our relationship a secret isn't always fun, but it's a necessity. I don't know what it would mean for my job or my professional credibility if word got out I was screwing the boss. Especially when he already promoted me long before I should have been. Only Iris knows and she's been sworn to secrecy.

After our night out, I came back to Zax's place to sleep, which is where I've been since.

I've hardly been home in the week since we started sleeping together, which is both incredible and problematic. I can't deny being with him is the best time I've ever had. There is no getting enough of him. But I don't like lying or hiding either.

Especially when my feelings are already this intense.

Which is a whole other problem I'm trying very hard not to think about or focus on or obsess over. I'm doing my best to be in the minute with him, but when you've never felt like this before with anyone, it feels unimaginable to hold back when all you want to do is dive in headfirst and see where you land. Even if you end up crashing in the end.

He tosses his arm around me, locking me tightly against him and shifting me so he can strum on his bass. A complicated melody starts to pour out and then he's humming softly in my ear along with it. I don't recognize the song at first and then he sings, "Hey, baby, you got the love I need."

I smile. I think the word is lady, not baby, but he's adapting it for me.

"Maybe I'm not nearly enough."

I can't help the giggle as he continues to mangle the words to "Over the Hills and Far Away" by Led Zeppelin.

"Oh, Angel, Angel, Angel, don't give up on me. Ohh, we've got so much. So much."

His lips plant into my neck and I sigh, unable to help it as I sag into him. I'm so fucking in love with this man. The bass ends up on the floor beside the coffee table and then he's grasping me by the hips and straddling me over his thighs. My arms encircle his neck, and my forehead meets his.

"You have a nice singing voice," I tell him because it's the first I've heard him sing. Usually, he just plays.

"Well, I am Greyson Monroe's brother," he quips.

"True. Ugh, he's so hot." I fan my face.

"Is that so?" A sharp swat on my ass, and then he's flipping us so I'm pinned beneath him on the couch, his body hot, heavy, and hard over me. "You got a thing for my brother?" he growls fiercely against my lips.

"Nah. He's not my guy."

"Better not be. So does that mean you're into Central Square band members?"

"Can you keep a secret?"

He nibbles on my jaw. "Better than most."

I can't stop my smile as I say, "I have this huge, crazy, all-consuming crush on this guy."

His head pops up, his brown eyes dark, but playful. "Oh yeah? Tell me about him."

"Well, he's old. Like seriously old."

"Old?"

I nod exaggeratedly, my eyes round. "Like early thirties old."

"Hmm. That is old compared to you. You don't like older men?"

"Oh no, it's sexy. I get off on it. He also has this incredibly thick, dark hair that I absolutely love running my fingers through." My nails scrape along his scalp. "Oh, did I mention he's gorgeous?"

"No. You skipped over that."

I roll my eyes at myself for my horrific blunder. "Wow. I mean, wow. Easily the hottest man I've ever seen. No contest. He has a chin dimple I love to lick." I mimic my words and he grinds into me, making me breathless. "Then there's my favorite part of him."

"What's that?" he rasps, his voice going low and husky.

Here goes nothing. "His heart." I slide my hand between us and press into his chest. "My crush has the most beautiful heart. I can't get enough of it. He thinks it's ugly and broken, but it's not. One day, I can only hope to call it mine."

His stills above me, eyes searching mine, expression unreadable, though there is something glimmering in there. A light. A heat. Something that has my heart racing harder than it was even seconds ago.

His hand cups my face as he continues to gaze directly at me, into me, intense and thoughtful. "Aurelia," he murmurs, a hint of a smile on his lips now. That is until the buzzer for his door sounds.

I don't move. Because I don't want this moment to end. I want it to stay and grow because it feels like it could. Like it's about to any second, only the fucking buzzer goes off again and then again and then again, followed by loud knocking and what the fuck is so goddamn urgent that someone feels the need to interrupt this?!

"Fuck," he curses, running an agitated hand through his hair. "Don't move. We're not done." In a flash, he's off me, adjusting himself as he runs across his palatial apartment to the front door.

I hear some commotion, lots of voices, and then Zax is saying, "No, that's next week."

"Nope," I hear who I think is Asher argue. "It's this week, bro. We're all in town this week. What, or should I say who are you hiding that you're making us stand out in the hall?"

"Let us in, dickhead. I want to meet her. I didn't get the chance last week at the charity thing." Callan. That has to be Callan.

"Yes, let us get to know your new girlfriend. I haven't seen her since she was a kid." Greyson and now I'm peeling myself up and off the couch. I do a quick fix of my hair and adjust my clothes—grateful I'm wearing some—and then pad over to the door.

Zax hears me approach and swallows down a mournful noise.

Stepping aside, he opens the door wider to allow his friends and brother in.

"Evenin', gentlemen," I greet, trying to contain my excitement. I mean, hello, all five of the Central Square band members are standing before me, all with their gorgeous faces focused on me. Whether you're a fan or not, there is no denying the hotness and celebrity of them. "To what do we owe the pleasure of your company?"

Callan has a large brown bag in his arms. Lenox a bottle of alcohol—one of bourbon and one of tequila—in each hand. Asher has an unlit cigar perched in his mouth, and Greyson is staring at me with what I can only describe as a shit-eating grin.

"Dibs," Greyson yells just as he makes a beeline for me, picking me up off the ground and spinning me around. I squeal out a peal of laughter, my hands planted onto his shoulders so I don't fall. "Hey there, little sis," he calls up to me with a wink. "Nice seeing you again. I hear you've got my big brother all wrapped up."

"Ha, ha, set her down," Zax demands without much heat.

"And what if I don't?" Greyson's eyes flash over to Zax as he twists his body to keep me from him. "What if I decide to keep the pretty lady for myself?"

Zax gives him a look and I exchange quick glances with the other guys.

"I'll just have to steal her back." In the blink of an eye, Zax bolts for me, ripping me from Greyson's clutches and catching me bridge-style in his arms. He swings me about before setting me back on my feet and keeping his arm around me. "There. Back where she belongs." A kiss on my cheek in front of all his guys and yep, there it goes. My heart. And just like his shirt and my underwear, there are no givebacks. Total swoon.

The guys impersonate owls. Likely because this is Zaxton Monroe we're dealing with.

"So, poker?" Callan asks, coughing to clear his throat, cutting the tension as he adjusts the bag in his arms.

"Poker?" I wrestle back a giddy smile.

"Evidently, I screwed up," Zax explains to me. "I thought our monthly poker night was next week."

"Oh. Well, that's not a problem. I can skedaddle."

"Or you can stay and poker with us," Asher suggests. "Do you poker?"

I peek up at Zax, trying to gauge his thoughts on this. I don't want to intrude on boys' night, but he's nothing if not amused, holding me tighter in a nonverbal way of saying he wants me to stay. Which, frankly, I wasn't expecting. Then again, nothing about this man and how things have been with us has gone as expected.

"Depends on where she asks for it."

The guys burst out laughing, Asher clutching his side like I gave him a stitch.

"Fuck, I love this woman," Asher exclaims, wiping away tears from his face. "But I need a real answer, doll."

"When the situation calls for poker, sure," I assure them.

"Then you're in," Greyson announces. "Or at least you're not allowed to leave."

"What's in the bag?" I question, nodding to Callan.

"Food."

"I like food. And I like booze," I say to Lenox, who has been stoically silent, which I won't take personally because that's his thing. Plus, he's Suzie's twin brother and I wonder if it's strange or painful for him to see Zax with someone else. I offer him what I hope is a sweet, friendly smile.

"Now that we've solved the great Aurelia poker debate, let's do this." Asher grabs my hand and drags me from Zax, spinning me around and walking me toward the back where the media room is. "Let me draw this up for you, doll." He grabs the unlit cigar from his mouth. "Poker is serious business. The stakes are high. The alcohol flows. And we men who are typically the epitome of polite, cultured, and respectful, turn into male savages with mouths you wouldn't want your mama to hear."

"Considering I couldn't care less what my mother hears, I'm not at all worried. I'm pretty sure I can handle myself with your savage mouths and high stakes."

"Excellent. Now I need a bit of female advice and since you're, frankly, the only female around, you're it."

Oh boy.

"So, this lady and I, well, let's just say we had a hookup gone wrong several months ago. It wasn't my best night even if it was. That's a whole other story I won't get into. But this lady won't quit my head, and even though I can't find her, I'd like to make up for the bad hookup if I ever did." His gray eyes peer down, his brow pinched as we enter the huge media room that has a full bar, a poker table—for which we are headed—and of course a massive media setup. "Are you following this?"

"Um. I think so."

"Good. Fantastic. So my question is—"

"Enough about the woman, Ash," Grey growls. "Let it go. She's gone to you, bro."

"You're only saying that because you can't have the woman you want."

"Oh, you're going there? You're going to bring her up?" Greyson flips him off, cocking an unamused eyebrow.

"Oh yeah. I'm going there." Asher smirks smugly before turning his gaze to me. "I wonder if Aurelia remembers her. I bet you she does."

"Who?" I practically jump, ready to shake Asher for who Grey's mystery woman is.

Greyson just shakes his head and Asher throws his hands up in the air.

"Ignore them. What are you drinking?" Lenox sets the two bottles down on the bar, dragging my attention over to him. I think it's the longest number of words I've ever heard him string together. Then again, I only met him once before and during interviews, he never spoke.

"Whatever you're pouring," I tell him.

He gives me a firm nod, which I take to mean he approves. For how intimidating Zax can be, Lenox is a whole other beast of a man. Tattoos and rumored piercings and the strong, silent type who lives in the freaking wilds of Maine.

The food is laid out across the bar top and while Callan goes about doling out plates and silverware, Zax is arranging the card table. It's like Vegas as he pulls out a clear plastic-encased set of multicolored chips, setting them out. Then it hits me. They're likely playing for real money and these guys are not short on cash. I mean, Zax is a billionaire fashion mogul. Asher is a big-time NFL quarterback. Greyson is a huge rock star. Callan is a doctor. And Lenox... well... I don't know what he does, but I'm assuming he's not hurting. Not to mention before they were all that, they were Central Square, world's biggest band.

Me, on the other hand?

Is it wrong to play a few hands and see how it goes?

Lenox hands me a glass of tequila with what smells like a squeeze of lime because clearly tequila's my best gal as of late, so I'm thinking it's game on. I raise my glass to him in thanks before taking a sip.

"Five Card or Texas Hold 'em?" Zax asks as he shuffles the cards and accepts a bourbon from Lenox.

"Five," the others say, almost in unison.

"Seven takes too damn long." Asher dips the end of his cigar in his bourbon and then pops it back into his mouth.

"Asher, I swear I'll cut your balls off at the stem if you light that fucking cigar up in my room," Zax barks.

"I second that," Callan states. "I don't want to treat you for oral cancer in ten years." He loads himself up with a plate of buffalo wings, spinach dip, potato skins, and a slider. Jesus, these boys don't mess around.

"Seriously, Cal?" Asher throws him a *you've got to be kidding me* expression. "Oral cancer? I haven't smoked a cigar in months and I'm not going to now. I'm in season. And besides, you're giving me crap about smoking a cigar when you're eating that shit? That's a walking fucking heart attack there, bro."

Callan waves him away as he pops a chip loaded with spinach dip into his mouth. "I'm a growing boy," he grumbles around his mouthful. "And I didn't have a chance to eat today at the hospital. Too busy saving lives and all that."

Asher rolls his eyes at Callan. I wipe away my smirk, watching these guys together.

"Come here, Angel," Zax says, patting his lap. I go over and sit on one of his thighs. "Do you want to watch a few rounds and see how to play?"

I hold my breath so I don't burst out laughing. "How much do you usually play each hand for?"

"It's not exactly about the money, but buy-in is a hundred to start and then it quickly grows from there throughout the night."

"Huh. Okay. Maybe I will watch a few games before deciding if I want to try playing a hand."

"Baby girl, we wouldn't make you pay. It'd just be fun for you."

"That's not fair, though. I wouldn't want that," I tell him. "If I'm going to play, I want the money to be real."

Zax deals the cards to each of the guys, and I lean back against him, watching as he shuffles his own hand around.

"Oh look," I tease, tapping his cards. "You have four hearts. That's good, right?"

Zax hisses something out that isn't all that flattering. The guys crack up, razzing each other and talking so much shit. Even Lenox gets in on it, throwing out a few good diggers this way and that. All the while I sit here, sipping my tequila and lime and soaking up this rare moment between them that I doubt many have been lucky enough to witness.

By the fifth hand, I've seen how they all bet. How they bluff. How they play. "Oh, baby, look. Two aces. That's awesome."

Greyson starts to lose it. "She can stay on your lap all night, brother."

I hop off and take the vacant seat beside him. "But I think I'm finally getting the hang of how you all play," I protest. "Deal me in. If I have to, I'll Venmo you all."

And suddenly, everything grows quiet. Zax's gaze holds mine.

"You don't have to play for money. Seriously, the last hand was over two grand and I know how hard you work to save every penny."

"I'll be fine," I assure him. "I'm a big girl and I don't need to be babied. If I want to gamble my own money, I will."

Something passes around the table between them, a sort of code or unspoken language, only they all seem to understand what I don't even come close to.

"You're sure?"

"Positive," I tell Greyson.

"Then deal her in, brother. I'm fixing us all another round of drinks. And dessert. Why the motherfuck don't we have dessert?"

"Because sugar is bad for you," Callan says.

"Callan..." Greyson stares incredulously at his friend. "You just ate your weight in sliders and wings, and you're talking about *sugar* being bad for you?"

"I can make brownies," I offer.

"Um. No. You're playing poker, doll." Asher gives me an admonishing look. "Women should never serve men. It sets the wrong tone and we become complacent. Just as my single mother. I'll order cookies. I know a place that makes these epic vegan, peanut butter things. I'll get you one. You know, since you're a model and likely don't eat sugar or carbs."

I flip him off. "You're a twat."

"But an endearing one, right?" He bats his long, black eyelashes at me. "One a woman who you didn't blow her mind the first go around might want seconds with?"

"Absolutely not."

"Crap. Fine." I get a glower for my response. "I'm still ordering these damn cookies because I can't eat junky stuff during season. Let's play." He starts tapping away on his phone, likely ordering cookies.

Lenox is dealing this round, sliding out five cards to each of us. I pick them up, shuffling them around in my hand for a moment before taking in the guys as they study their own.

"Aurelia?" Lenox offers me first dish out.

"Age before beauty," I say, making them all snicker.

"Alrighty then. That's you, Zax."

"I'm out." Zax tosses his cards onto the green felt table.

"Me too." That's Callan.

"I'm in," Asher mumbles, shifting his cards around, then flicks two down along with two one-hundred-dollar chips. Lenox deals him two more and then he taps his chin once. Greyson exchanges one card and smirks at his new hand. Lenox doesn't bother saying whether he's in or out. He simply deals himself one card and also throws in money.

"Two," I request, handing him my discarded cards and lifting my new ones from the table. I add my money to the pot and the game builds from there. More betting. Asher especially is building it up, which makes me think he's bluffing since he's refusing to go down and Grey clearly has something, but I'm doubting it's more than two pair by the way he's nervously tapping his fingers on the edge of the table. Lenox is a statue, but I don't think he has much.

"Call."

Asher, Grey, Lenox, and I all show our hands. I have three of a kind—Jacks. Grey, as I suspected, has two pair, tens and twos. Asher has a pair of kings and Lenox has three of a kind too, but it's sixes.

"I'm sure it's just luck." I smile sweetly at them as I pull my winnings toward me. It goes like this for three more hands before Lenox starts to give me the look.

"I have to say, Aurelia, you surprise me. I never would have pegged you for a hustler or a card shark."

I shrug unrepentantly. "I never said I didn't know how to play. Actually, I believe I told you I poker when the situation calls for it and that I could handle your high stakes. You all underestimated me because I'm a woman. You treated me as a helpless little lamb from the start as if I haven't been taking care of myself since I was sixteen. Newsflash: There's a lot of downtime in modeling and always someone around with a deck of cards."

"You're fucking kidding me." Grey bursts out laughing, throwing his cards on the table before the hand even gets started. "You knew how to play like a pro this whole time?"

I throw him a wink. "Always be unexpected."

"Jesus." Zax scrubs his hands up and down his face, though his smile is unstoppable. "I can't tell if you're evil, a genius, or an evil genius."

"Evil genius for sure," Asher says, high-fiving me. "Can I bring you to poker nights with my teammates?" he asks. "You'd fucking clean up there and those boys could use a good knock in their egos."

"Honestly, I think I want to marry you." Grey drops down onto one knee, taking my hand in his. "Aurelia Whitlock. Will you dump my brother and do me the tremendous honor of—"

"All right. That's it." Zax jumps to his feet, grabbing Greyson by the collar of his shirt and dragging him up and away from me. "Everyone out. Now. I need some alone time with my woman. But you all better pay up. She swindled that money fair and square."

The guys hug me, each of them, including Lenox. We tally my winnings and suddenly I'm eight grand richer. It's crazy. I'd almost feel guilty if they hadn't womaned me and then found the whole thing hysterical.

The second the door shuts behind them, Zax is all over me, pinning me to the wall and kissing me senseless. "I think what you just pulled back there is the sexiest thing I've ever witnessed. I don't know whether to keep kissing the hell out of you, spank you, or both."

"Whatever you want, big guy," I sigh against his hips.

"Any other hidden talents or tricks up your sleeve?"

"Why don't you strip me down and see for yourself."

27

A week later, Lamar comes storming into my office unannounced. Only he can get away with that. "What the fuck did you send me?"

"You know what I sent you," I reply evenly, sitting up and adjusting my tie. It's the same one I had wrapped around Aurelia's wrists at the club that night. The one she openly smirked at this morning when she saw me put it on. We've been doing this for over two weeks now and I can't stop. I can't go back. I can only go forward with her—a runaway train with broken brakes I have no desire to fix.

"Okay." He holds up his hand, no patience for my vague answer. "Let me amend that. *Why* are you sending this to me?"

"You can't guess?"

"Oh, I can guess." He slams the door shut with a bit too much force before dropping into a chair and crossing his legs at the knee. "But is this something you're actually considering?"

"Too crazy?"

He purses his lips and glances out the glass window facing the Boston skyline. "I don't know. I mean, kind of, yeah." He chuckles lightly before returning his gaze back to me. "I love it. I won't even pretend I don't because I think it's time you did something like this with this company and I had no clue what you were planning to do with your newest acquisition. I think it will bring Monroe to the next level and I think if done right and done well could be something unique."

"But?"

"Buuuuuuut it's risky. A risky move that could drag your father out of hiding."

"That might be an interesting side effect of this decision, yes."

"*Side effect?* Are you being real with this?"

I can only shake my head at that, chuckling lightly under my breath. "I have to do something. Did you not see the pictures I sent you?" I throw back at him. "Do you not agree that the pictures are everything that would be incredible for this?"

He scoots to the end of his seat, his elbows going to his thighs as he meets my eyes. "They're everything and a milkshake. That's not my worry and you know it."

"The greater the risk, the greater the reward."

"Okay, fine." He waves me away. "It's your call and it's obvious this is where your head is already at, so I will support it. Now, on to more important items, people are asking questions about a certain *other* situation." His eyebrows bounce suggestively up and down.

I smirk, folding my hands in my lap. "Are you people?"

"I am people," he exclaims, slapping a hand down on my desk. "You know I am people, and you better believe I'm asking. I know something is going on, but fuck you both since neither of you is saying anything."

I give him a dubious look. "You know why we're not saying anything. We can't. Is there buzz about it beyond you?" I frown at the thought. Aurelia and I have been careful, but that doesn't mean we've been squeaky clean either.

"No," he states firmly, picking up a pen from my desk and rolling it between his fingers because Lamar cannot sit still to save his life. "I'm the only one and that's because I know you so well and I've gotten to know her so well. Not to mention, the devil is in your eye every fucking time you glance her way. So tell me the truth about what's going on."

I wipe away my smirk with the drag of my finger. "I'm not sure I follow what you're asking."

He rolls his dark eyes at me, growing agitated by my emotionless tone and deadpan expression. "Bitch, please. You're so full of shit your eyes are brown. For real, Zax, does she know?"

"Know what?"

"That you might be so fucking head over heels in love with her there is no hope of recovery."

I blow out an uneven breath. I have not used the words with Aurelia yet. Not because I haven't thought them or felt them. Not because I haven't wanted to say them and kiss them into her a hundred different times in a hundred different ways.

But because the last time I told a woman I loved her, she dropped dead on me seconds later. And I don't know how to do this. Love Aurelia as much as I do. I fucking love this woman like... like I don't think I've ever loved anyone before. And that makes me sick. Because I loved Suzie with all my heart, so how do I reconcile that? It feels like I'm dishonoring her memory and I can't abide that. Suzie doesn't deserve that.

So where does that leave me and where does that leave Aurelia?

Can love be different with different people? Not less true or real, just different?

Aurelia came out of nowhere. A sledgehammer, she demolished the life I had grown uncomfortably comfortable in. I can't go back to the hollow shell I was living in. I can't go back to a time before her.

"Listen, I'm not trying to be a dick about her," he continues when I'm unable to speak through the raging battle inside me. "I'm not. You're happy, Zax. She makes you happy, which is not something I ever thought I'd see for you. I loved Aurelia before, but with you, I love her even more. This isn't about that. This is business, but with that, there are some big fat questions that still aren't answered."

He's right. I know he's right. Lenox hasn't been able to figure out how my father knew the exact amount I offered Marie so he could bid an additional twenty grand over it. There's also how he knew our exact itinerary while we were in New York so that he could make it all as strategic as possible. Plus, we still don't know who originally emailed Beth using my email.

That's the scariest thing of all.

"Aurelia isn't involved with any of that."

"I'm not saying she is, but she's still involved in it because she's here at the hands of your father and we clearly have a *saboteur*," he says in a French accent, "from within."

I stand abruptly. Needing to move, I head for the window, my hands on my hips as I stare out at the early fall day. "As far as Lenox can tell, Valencci trying to purchase Marie's company isn't related. It was a coincidence and happened before my father offered Aurelia the spot here. Plus, Valencci has been in Italy and has had zero contact with my father or Aurelia."

"What about the burner phone or the email?"

"Nothing yet. I haven't tried to call the burner phone because I don't want to tip off that we're onto that number. Lenox is monitoring everything, and all has been quiet for the last couple weeks since my dad tried and failed to buy Marie out from under me."

"What about fashion week? It's in three weeks. Do you think he'll try something then?"

"I don't know." And that's my biggest worry because if he were going to mess with me, that would be the prime time to do it.

"But you want this new stuff at fashion week too?"

"It's all ready to go if we can get board approval and it would make a huge media splash."

"True. And I already told you I love it. Next question, what are you going to do about the fact that you're fucking in love with your executive intern? She works for you."

"She wouldn't if—" I start to argue about the job part of that when a slow, creeping horror washes over me. I spin around and freeze, staring out the glass wall of my office, straight at her as she talks with Nate and Beth about who knows what. "I haven't told her that the reason she's my executive intern is because I didn't trust her. How could I have overlooked this?"

"What?" Lamar asks. "What do you mean?"

I meet his eyes. "I promoted her to be my executive intern because the spot was vacant, and I didn't trust her. Remember? I told you this when I told you about the shit with my dad and how she got here. It was a keep your friends close and enemies even closer. But now..."

"Now she's not your enemy."

"No. She's not." Now she's mine. I'm with her. I trust her.

And yes, she does work for me. And yes, there is a massive conflict of interest with that, but that's why we've stayed quiet and distant here at work and it's also something I'm working on fixing. That's not what has me panicked.

"You have to tell her if you love her, and this is the real deal with you two."

"I have to tell her," I agree. But how? She'll be destroyed. It'll crush her and she'll hate me.

I know he's baiting me with the repeated L-word. And yeah, I do love her. The lovely, sexy, hilarious, feisty, smart, fearless, wonderful creature—how could I not love her? She's magnificent. She's the air I haven't breathed in eight years. She's...

"She's going to hate me." I'd hate me.

"Nah," Lamar promises, pushing up the bridge of his clear glasses. "She's not the hater type. She's the sweet, forgiving, loving type."

"The too trusting type," I counter, running my hands over my face and through my hair before I grip the roots, ready to tear it all out. "I took advantage of that. I promoted her to a position she's talented enough for, but all things being equal should not have received."

A flash of a grimace strikes his features before he quickly shuts it down. "Find the right time. Find the right way. And tell her the truth. All of it. If you do love her, which you have yet to deny so I'm fucking rolling with it, then be honest. It's all you can do."

It's all I can do.

A sweaty sickness swarms through me, making me acutely,

painfully cognizant that even when I tell her everything, despite Lamar's reassurances, she'll leave. She'll feel she didn't earn the job—because technically she didn't—and leave. That's her. I know it is. I'll be yet another person in her life who did her wrong. She's never had anyone walk the line for her. Her world has been not enough love and too much betrayal.

And yet she's all smiles and sunshine and heart. Everything Lamar said.

I don't deserve her. I'm not sure I ever did, but in realizing this, I know that now with one hundred percent certainty. I don't deserve the woman I'm growing more and more unable to go without. I'll never be done. I'll never get enough. She has rewritten me. Every piece of me that lay shattered and broken on that shower floor along with Suzie, she has rebuilt.

I am hers. I. Am. Hers.

Now I have to convince her.

~

THE UNCOMFORTABLE FEELING residing in my chest hasn't just grown in the last two days since my conversation with Lamar, it's multiplied by the thousands like mitotic cells. I was ready—sort of, there is no ready for this—to tell her the other day, but then she told me she was going home that night to sew, and I couldn't interrupt that. Or say anything since I know I've confiscated her time and taken her away from that with my insatiably greedy need to have her near me at all times.

Last night was the same deal and now here I am, sitting in the car beside her, holding her hand, a miserable mess of a man. It's become impossible to pretend I'm not incurably in love with her or that there is hope of any other state of being for me. I already lost a woman who I considered to be the love of my life. I can't do it again. I can't go through that sort of agony twice.

Once again, I'm this guy. The hapless man and I hate no one more than I hate him. Only this time, I did this to myself. It's like I told that kid who tried to mug her. A real man does the right thing even when the wrong thing is easier.

Have I done anything right by her?

Ashley slows, pulling up along the curb outside her dilapidated building, and hating this place doesn't get any easier. I want to move her in with me. I want her sewing stuff taking up one of the spare bedrooms. I want her true crime shows on my television. I want her Diet Coke in my fridge and I want her to drag me out to early-morning yoga, but only after she's spent the night in my bed screaming out my name.

She unlocks the door to her place, and I dutifully follow her, my hands on her hips as we ascend the four flights because not touching her in some physical way right now might in fact kill me.

"You didn't have to do this," she says as we reach her door, slightly winded from the stairs. "We could have stayed at your place tonight. I told you, I finished most of what I wanted to get done last night."

The second the door is closed, I swoop her up in my arms and carry her the three feet over to her bed. I stare into her glowing, happy, impish eyes and then kiss her. Deep. Long. Hard. Unrelenting. I kiss her so she knows. But then, suddenly, kissing isn't enough. I make quick work of her clothes, fabric flying about her tiny studio, until she's bare beneath me.

"Zax," she moans, her fingers up in my hair, clasping me to her, as I suck on her nipple while my hand plays with the other.

"Angel, I have too many things to tell you." My hands clamp her tits, squeezing and kneading them as my mouth continues south, across her belly to the top of her smooth mound where I plant a wet, open-mouthed kiss.

"Tell me." Her breath hitches as I flick her clit with the tip of my tongue.

Peeking up, I meet her eyes. "I'm crazy about you." I spread her legs and slide my tongue up inside her.

"I'm crazy about you too. Oh. Oh, yes. That. Don't stop."

She grinds up into my face, rolling her hips and fucking my lips and tongue. Her hands, still in my hair, hold me where she wants me.

"It's more than that. More than my feelings for you. And I think you're going to hate me when I tell you everything, so I need you to remember what I'm saying to you now."

A breathy laugh. "I can't remember my own name right now."

"Aurelia."

I move to stop, but she pushes me back in. "Please. Make me come. Just… make me come first. Don't tell me when you're doing this."

She knows she's not going to like what I have to say, and I can't deny her.

Her clit becomes my single point of obsession. I'm frenzied. Wild. I suck on her, marveling at how her back arches and her hands fly above her head, slamming into the wall.

"Fuck," she yells, her hips bucking up into my lips. "Fingers, Zax. Give me your fingers."

My hips cant into her bed, grinding and thrusting and fucking her comforter. I want to be inside her. I need to be inside her. I have to fuck this woman, and I can't fuck this woman right now. It would be wrong, and I'd never forgive myself for getting off when only she deserves to. But still, I don't know how to stop my body from flexing, from mindlessly seeking pleasure as I give it to her.

Two fingers slide inside her, her pussy dripping everywhere. She's so wet it would be effortless for me to slide my cock inside her, my dick so hard I can hardly stand it another second. But the pain drives me on. Makes me more ravenous for her. My fingers rub in a circle inside her, right on her spot just as I suck her clit in my mouth, and she comes hard and fast.

But it's not enough.

I continue to pleasure her like this. With teeth and tongue, my finger rimming her asshole as I continue to eat her.

"Zax!"

"One more, baby girl. Give me one more."

She shudders on an exhale as I flatten my tongue against her clit, easing some of the pressure before sliding down. Licking her opening and ringing it in the same motion I do her puckered ring of muscles.

She will come again. That's not even an option for me or for her. I'll make her come on my face and then I'll kiss her and beg for forgiveness.

"Fuck. Push it in."

She likes my finger in her ass when I lick her pussy out. When I shove my other fingers inside her and bang her to erotic bliss. So uninhibited. Such a filthy perfect woman, there is no doubt in my mind she was made only for me. A chasm of endless need, I'll never get enough nor grow tired of her.

My finger pushes into her ass, past the barrier of muscles, and she starts to rock from side to side, her clit sensitive as I lick it. Whimpers and cries and screeches and curses tear past her lips.

"Zax. I need..."

I know what she needs. I up my pace, both of my hands now working inside her, a wet, greedy mess. "You need what, baby girl? To come? For me to make you feel good?"

"Yes. Oh God!" Muscles quivering, she slams her hand into the wall and then comes for me again on a strangled gasp. Her pussy clamps around my fingers, squeezing and pulsing along with her clit against my lips. She comes harder than she did the first time and when she's done, she sags into her bed, limp, but not happy.

Gently, I pull my fingers from her. Hopping up quickly, I wash my hands, only to return and hand her the first thing I find to put on. I can't have her naked when I tell her this. Once she's dressed in her T-shirt and yoga pants, I cover her body with mine. She loves it when I do this too. Only a few weeks together, but I already know her so well. My girl holds nothing of herself back. She loves wholly and effort-lessly despite all she's been through. Despite all that people have done to her.

And because of that, I can't hold it in another second.

I prop myself up on my elbows, staring adoringly into her pretty eyes. "I love you."

Round as saucers, her eyes and lips pop open at my unexpected words. They're no less potent on me now that they've been set free. A shockwave, they rattle through me to the marrow of my bones.

"I do," I tell her. "I love you. I love you so much. I never..." I breathe out. "I never thought I could again. I never *wanted* to again. But then it was you, Aurelia. You." I glance quickly up at the ceiling as I gather my thoughts before meeting her gaze once more. "I fucked something up. Something I'm terrified will change everything about us."

"O-okay." She licks her lips nervously, those fathomless blue eyes turning inward my total undoing. "Just tell me."

"When you told me about how you got your internship, about how my dad helped you, I didn't trust you. You know that because I didn't hide it. There were so many coincidences to things. I knew someone was working on the inside for my father and I knew he was planning something and would use any avenue he could to further his cause." I pause and take a breath, or I'll never be able to say these next words. "I didn't trust you, so I promoted you to be my executive design intern. I felt if you were in that role, working closely with me, I could keep an eye on you and make sure you weren't consorting with my father against me."

The words tumble from my lips and their destruction is instant. Her eyes glass over, and she twists her head away from me, biting into her lip so she doesn't cry, and fuck, I'm a monster.

"I forgot about it," I rush on. "I mean, in these last weeks, that thought wasn't there. After New York with you, the things we talked about, the things we did, I trusted you after that. Maybe even before, I don't know. I liked you working with me. I loved your ideas and insights. You're so talented and you own this job like no one else has and I stopped thinking about it because the job felt like yours. But there are things I want to do. With the company. With you. Things I can't do without you knowing the truth."

She blinks and a tear trickles from the corner of her eye, getting lost in her pillowcase, and I just about lose my mind at the sight of it.

"You lied to me."

"What?"

She turns back to glare at me. "You told me it was on the level. That the job was on the level. You lied to me."

"Yes. Partially. The job was real, and it was available. I did review your portfolio and it was, *it is* incredible. You deserve this job, but yes, originally, that's not why I gave it to you."

I cup her face in my hands and brush away her tears.

"I don't have words for how sorry I am. I never meant to hurt you and I never meant to continue a lie I started. I don't have a way to prove to you that there is no one out there who could do this job better than you. This is what you were born to be, Aurelia. You're a designer and you're so incredibly talented. I'm in awe of you. All of you. And not because I love you or because we're seeing each other or having sex. We always agreed we'd keep our relationship separate from work and I still am. You have to know, every decision I make is business related. I know I lost your trust—"

"Yes. You did." Her expression is fierce and ravaged, her voice sharper than an ice pick. "You lied to me. You used me. You made me the patsy when that's all I've ever been. A tool. Something to use and then toss away."

"No. You're not that to me. I promoted you for all the wrong reasons, yes, but everything after that has been real. This is real." I press my lips to hers, but she refuses to kiss me back. "I love you. Maybe that's wrong to say at a time like this and I swear, I'm not using it as a weapon or a way to keep you if you want to leave me. I'm telling you this now because I should have told you sooner and I'm terrified"—hard swallow—"I'm terrified I'll never get the chance again."

"I don't know what to say right now. My thoughts and feelings are too jumbled. I can't think straight. I'm too mad."

"I know." I almost smirk at that simple word. Almost.

"No. I mean, I'm *mad*." Deep breath. "But I think I also believe you. Part of me always wondered why you promoted me so fast. I just didn't want to think about it. I knew you didn't trust me at first."

"Thank fuck," I hiss, deflating like a balloon.

"That doesn't mean you get to stay and that doesn't mean I forgive you. I need you to go. Now. I need space to think. To figure out what my next steps are. You gave me a job I didn't earn and I'm not okay with that. You did it because you didn't trust me and then you kept it going even after we got together."

"Aurelia—"

"Don't. I'm fucking *mad* at you, Zaxton Monroe. I may not be furious, but I'm sure as shit mad. My heart physically hurts in my chest, that's how mad I am."

I hold her tighter against me, terrified she's slipping through my fingers. "Don't walk away, even if I go now. Don't give up on me and don't give up on this job. There is more here, baby. There is so much more here. For both you and me and us."

"I'm not sure what choice I have."

I swallow past the lump in my throat. "I can't lose you."

She gulps down a sob, blinking back more tears. "I can't lose you either. But I don't know how to keep you right now. Please go."

Everything inside me shatters. Breaks. Rips apart.

"Aurelia—"

"Zax, for the last seven years of my life, it's been only me. I told you this before. I am the one who sails my own ship and charters my own course. Right now, I need to do that. Alone. I'm not saying I won't be with you and I'm not saying I won't stay, but I need fucking space to figure my world out again."

I kiss her forehead and then reluctantly pull myself up and off her. I sit on the end of her bed, staring around her tiny apartment. An apartment overflowing with racks of gowns and fabrics and sewing machines. An apartment filled with Aurelia's dream. And I would give it to her. I would make it all come true.

"Some days it feels like all I'm doing is treading water and then there are days like today when it feels like the water just keeps getting deeper and deeper, and all I can do is just continue to tread water and hope I don't grow tired and drown." I look over at her, sitting up on her bed with her knees pressed to her chest. "I'll never be done with you. I'll get never get enough. For you, I'll keep treading water. Till my muscles burn and my lungs scream and even then I'll keep going. You deserve the world, Aurelia, and there is nothing more I want than to be the one to give it to you." I stand, my heart in a vise that keeps getting tighter and tighter. "Take as much time as you need to figure this out. The whole weekend. Longer. Whatever. I'll be here whenever you're ready to talk."

With that, I walk out of her apartment, make it down to the bottom of the stairs, pause, think for way too long, only to turn around and jog back up. I don't know why, and I don't know what I'll say or even if I'll knock because she needs space and I need to give her that, but then...

My insides turn to ice as I glance up at her door before I turn the corner on the stairs, still out of sight. My father. I can't hear what they're saying, but they're talking. He's at her door and it's open and she's standing there in the clothes I just left her in and they're talking.

And then he walks inside, and she shuts the door behind them.

What the absolute fuck?

28

AURELIA

The second the door shuts behind Zax, I start to fall apart. No, not fall apart. Just cry. My days of letting someone else destroy me are over. But I can't pretend the urge isn't there. That it doesn't feel like someone is poking at my insides with razors dipped in acid because it does.

Invariably in my life, whenever something is too good to be true, it always is. It never lasts. And this is about what I expected when I got involved with Zaxton Monroe. I mean, not *this*, but something that would ruin it.

Life Lessons Aurelia Never Learned: Block it all out and shut myself off the way Zax has.

Or did.

Because, you know, he doesn't seem to be doing that so much anymore. I sigh, wiping at my face, my head resting against the wall as I stare down at my rumpled sheets. Half an hour ago, everything was perfect. Now... now I don't know what it is.

I think I knew all along or at least suspected that that's why he promoted me.

I would have been fine being a simple design intern, working with Howie.

Then Zax went and gave me this whole other side of the pie and now what do I do?

Scrubbing my hands up and down my face, I slide down on my bed, wrapping myself in my blanket. Staring at the spot where his body just was.

That's when it hits me. All of it all at once. He had every right to do what he did with me. I came to his company under less than honorable circumstances, openly disdainful of him, and praying I'd never run into him. His father helped me out, but he did it with motive. I brought this with me when I started there.

And Zax knew me from nothing. Not really. We certainly didn't have a relationship that gave him any sort of loyalty to me. He let me stay when he could have just as easily fired me. Regardless of the reasons for the promotion, he took my suggestions to heart. He listened and made me part of the team, whether I deserved to be there or not.

If anyone here is in the wrong, it's me.

Zax loves me. The man who's sworn off women and relationships. The man who hides himself from the world and has been nothing short of grumpy and miserable for the last eight years. I won his heart, despite what Beth said about that impossibility.

Now he's trying to do the right thing by me.

And I threw it back in his face and kicked him out.

Scrambling off my bed, I slide into my flip-flops and head for the door. I have to catch him. I have to tell him I'm his and I'm sorry.

I fling the door open and a startled gasp slips past my lips. "Mr. Monroe."

A smarmy grin attached to an older dark-haired man, he instantly makes the wrong kind of chills race up my spine. "Good evening, Aurelia. How lovely it is to see you again."

"Uh. Yes. You too." Only not so much. "How did you know where I live?" Because my name is not on the buzzer downstairs. He gives me a funny look.

"Won't you invite me in?"

"I, uh."

"My son just left, so I know you're not expecting anyone."

Crap. "Yeah. Okay. But just for a few minutes."

He pushes past me, and I shut the door, keeping it unlocked in case I have to make a quick escape. "How very gracious of you after all I've done to help you."

There is a very clear and distinct edge to his words and tone, causing my heart rate to shoot through the roof.

"Just give me a moment to put something else on."

"You look fine in that," he tells me, his gaze dropping to my braless chest, and I think I'm going to throw up.

"No. I'm going to change." I run for my nightstand and grab the sweatshirt I keep there. My phone rests beside it and instantly I pick it up, unlocking the screen with my face while I think this all through. I don't have time to call or text anyone, especially with him watching me, so I throw the sweatshirt over my head and slide my phone into the side pocket of my yoga pants.

"You picked a real winner of a place to live," he deadpans, taking in my small space with a crinkled nose and disgusted snarl.

I roll my eyes. "You sound like your son."

That gets his attention. "How long have the two of you been fucking?"

I'd bet my hands he knows exactly how long Zax and I have been a thing. "How long have you been following me?"

A grin that tells me I'm spot-on with that. "I knew he'd never be able to resist you." He waves his hand up and down my body. "Who could?"

"Plenty of people. Why are you here?"

"Do you love him?"

I snort. "Of course not. He's an asshole. I like fucking him and that's about it." Bile rises up the back of my throat at my blatant lie, but I give it my everything so he buys it with little question. I refuse to give him any ammunition against me or Zax.

"Am I supposed to believe that?"

"Believe whatever you want. I don't give a shit either way. I learned a valuable lesson in these last few months. I am in this game for myself. No one else because no one else has my back but me. Your son is hot, and I like his dick. That's it."

"He looked upset when he left."

I huff, folding my arms over my chest. "Sucks for him."

"Care to tell me why?"

"No. I don't give out answers for free anymore."

He studies me, trying so very hard to unravel me, but I won't budge. I know how to bluff, when to hold 'em and when to fold 'em. Now is bluffing time and I'm better than most at it when I apply myself. Try growing up alone as a teenager in an adult world.

"I'm curious."

And of course, he leaves it there.

I laugh in that banal, you're a peon, dismissive way. "Am I supposed to care about that too?" I tilt my head, baiting him, getting him to up his ante. "What do you want, Mr. Monroe? Why did you follow me and Zax to my apartment on a Friday night, wait until he left, and then knock on my door?"

His dark eyes, so similar to his son's, lock on me and my blood runs cold. "I want you to help me regain control of my company."

Oh fuck.

I lean my hip against the wall by the door, arms still folded in a casual way while keeping as much distance from him as possible as he touches every damn surface of my apartment. "And how do you expect me to do that and more importantly why should I? I have a good thing going at Monroe. I'm an executive design intern. Much better than the role you first got me."

He smirks, walking over to my desk and picking up a piece of spare fabric. The silky material slides through his fingers before he sets it down and moves on to one of my hanging gowns. Drawing out the suspense seems to be his game and I'm eating away at it like a TV-binger who can't click the next episode fast enough.

"When I took you to dinner in New York, you weren't this aggressive," he comments dryly. "You were this sweet, innocent, lost little lamb who would have done anything for her second chance."

"And look where being so sweet and innocent got me.

Screwed over. I've grown and learned a lot since then. It's dog eat dog in this industry and I intend to be the Pitbull this go around."

"So it seems. Fine. What's your moral dilemma for helping me versus hurting my son?"

"Depends on the stakes. I won't do anything illegal."

"Commendable and understandable, but likely not your choice to make." He turns to face me fully, his salt-and-pepper hair perfectly coiffed back with pomade, his suit impeccable all the way down to the pristine shine on his shoes. The man is a total sleazebag. "Monday morning, you're going to go to the board and tell them that you've been fucking my son since shortly after you started. You're going to tell them that he promoted you with that expectation in mind and that it became a necessary part of keeping your job, otherwise you'd lose it."

"Even though that's not the least bit true?"

"Does it matter?" he counters, his fingers still all over one of my gowns.

"To me it does. Our relationship has remained separate from work. Nothing of a sexual nature has ever happened inside the Monroe building. Not to mention it's one hundred percent consensual."

"I'm aware. It was impossible for my inside person to know if you were fucking him or not. You were both very good at hiding it. Until I started following you, that is. But that changes nothing. He's your boss. You're his subordinate. And I need you to tell the board exactly what I just dictated you tell them. I also have his emails about your dress length from your first day if they need more than simply your word."

Oh, holy Diet Coke. How the motherfuck did he get those? I swallow and lick my lips, my mouth suddenly feeling like I swallowed burned cotton. "What else?"

"If you do this for me, I will make you an executive designer. No more intern and no more needing to fuck your boss to get ahead."

"Meaning I don't have to fuck you," I retort.

"Not unless you want to, but I don't relish my son's sloppy seconds."

Asshole.

"You'll explain how you agreed out of fear of losing your job," he continues, sitting on the edge of my desk now. "How he was brutal and unkind. Hostile. Not exactly difficult to prove or believe."

"How will I even be able to go to the board?"

"They have their monthly meeting at Monroe on Monday morning. It's already scheduled."

"Hmm. I want a contract. A real contract. Not some hack-ass BS lawyer job. I want this all drawn out for me in writing with your signature on it. I want it promising me the job with a ten-thousand-dollar signing bonus."

He chuckles. "You did learn a thing or two. Fine. I'll have it emailed to you tonight and then Monday at nine, you're there."

"Anything else?"

"That's it. But if you speak to my son before that, I'll know. If you try to tip him off or meet in secret or even call or text him, I'll know. Keep your mouth shut, Aurelia, and you'll get the job you've always dreamed of having. If you fuck with me or don't do what I ask, I promise, you'll regret it. What Valencci did to you will be nothing in comparison."

He leaves that threat hanging in the air, its scent rancid.

Standing, he fixes his jacket that doesn't require any fixing and then wipes off the filth of my place from his pants. "You'll have the contract emailed within two hours. Use the signing bonus to get yourself a better place. Fucking pathetic."

Marching for the door, I scoot to the side, nearly tripping over my bed as the door slams shut behind him. I slide my phone out of my pocket and stare at it, thoughts swirling in a chaotic pattern through my head.

I can't call or text Zax. Or anyone else. And I can't leave here to meet up with anyone because I'm betting he has eyes on me and my apartment and will for the stay of the weekend.

So I'm stuck, leaving Zax to be blindsided come Monday. Especially when the man told me he was giving me the weekend to think. Even if he does reach out to me, I have to push him off.

Other than possibly having mine or Zax's phone tapped by someone...

He can't. Because Zax and I text each other a hundred different dirty things. Even when we're at work. We don't touch in public—much—and we don't make our relationship known, but we're not totally innocent either. If he had that sort of proof, he would have mentioned it since he mentioned the emails. No, my work email is monitored by whoever his inside person is.

But not my phone.

So it's something else.

My eyes scan around my apartment, taking in each surface he touched. I've watched enough crime shows to know that a man as deviant and ruthless as Elias Monroe isn't acting on intimidation alone. He's covering his bets.

He wouldn't be able to plant something on my dresses or gowns. The material wouldn't abide that and I'd notice easily enough. He didn't go into the kitchen or bathroom. My bed is safe too.

My desk.

In a flash, I fly over there, crouching down and searching the wood until I find what I'm looking for. A bug. I don't know how I didn't see him plant it. It's about the size of a quarter and thicker than a pencil.

Wow, that's some poor James Bond crafty business. That took me, what, all of five seconds to find? I give it double middle fingers but leave it untouched. He said he'd know if I was texting with him, but now, seeing this, that has to be his bluff. Still, I can't risk it if I'm wrong about him having access to one of our phones.

Which means I'm stuck like this for the weekend.

But I'll be damned if I make this easy for him. I'll drag whoever his stalker is with me all over town this weekend. I'll shop till I drop, go to farmers' markets, museums, take long strolls. In the meantime, I Google on my phone the most annoying television program and then search through my streaming for it and put it on. Then I turn on music on my phone and play that through my headphones so I don't have to listen to my television.

That's when I start my sewing machine because nothing will kill a silent listening stalker more than obnoxious TV and the sound of a sewing machine on repeat. I do this for now. At least until I figure out what the hell I'm going to do about everything else.

29

ZAXTON

For longer than I should have, I remained frozen on that step, staring incredulously at her door. A flurry of thoughts and second guesses and what the fucks ran through my head. Then came the apprehension. The pangs that he was there to hurt or manipulate her. Those lingered, wearing holes in my brain and leaching toxins in my blood. Admittedly, no part of me felt rational. I was merely a slurry of red haze. Violent, *murderous* imaginations became my closest friends and most favorable allies.

I would end him. I knew that much.

And her? What about her?

No. Somewhere, buried in the depths of my frazzled brain, I knew I wasn't upset with her. I knew she didn't invite him here tonight. It was my idea to come here because I didn't want her trapped at my place if she felt she needed an out after I told her the truth about her job.

Which means my father followed us here.

Likely sat outside her apartment, listening as I tongue fucked her twice to orgasm.

The urge to storm in there, wrap my hands around his throat and squeeze until he either passed out or died was so overwhelming, I nearly caved a dozen times. The fact that I didn't was simply an act of herculean strength.

I should be knighted and awarded the Nobel Peace Prize.

There was no way my father wasn't up to something that wasn't a hundred percent nefarious. And while it might have been easy to revert to the Zax of a few weeks ago—the miserable fuck who outright hated the world and would have stood by to watch it burn— and question Aurelia, I couldn't find it in me to do that.

She loves me.

I know she loves me.

She might not have come out and directly said it, but the girl hasn't been faking anything with me. Her heart is as tied to mine as mine is to hers. I knew if I stormed in there like the mindless caveman I was so tempted to be that it would somehow backfire on me and on Monroe Fashions and probably on Aurelia because I'd likely never tease out what he was doing until he hit me directly with it in the face.

All of this is how I end up lurking in the doorway of the apartment building next to hers, waiting for the motherfucker to go while breathing in the lovely aroma of cooking methamphetamines. I've been texting with Lenox, but I don't have anything to go on other than he's physically here. That is until I catch him strutting out of her building like a king lion, looking far too smug as he searches up and down the street—possibly for me.

Turning in the opposite direction from me, he slips his phone out of his pocket and starts off at a good pace. I slink out behind him, keeping my distance without being too far off.

If he turns to glance over his shoulder, he'll see me. I can't do anything about that, but I need to hear his phone conversation more than I care about him busting me.

"Hey. Yeah. She's in," he starts, only to laugh mirthlessly. "Bitch wants ten grand and a contract stating I won't fuck her over and out of the executive design position I just offered her." He listens for a beat. "Yes, I'm going to do it. She's my strongest weapon since you weren't able to get anything on him other than those stupid emails. I have my guy making sure she doesn't double-cross me. He'll keep watch on her."

No. No, she wouldn't do that. Aurelia wouldn't help my father like that.

"I don't give a shit if he changed his password and they were being careful, Beth. You had one fucking job to do in this."

Beth? As in Beth, Beth? The head of HR and the one in charge of interns? She's his inside person?

"Just write up the contract for her and make it look official. I'll wire the ten grand Monday after she tells the board Zax coerced her into a sexual relationship in exchange for promoting her to a job she shouldn't have been given and that will be that. Zax will be out, and I'll convince the board it has to be me who takes over or I'll make the whole thing public."

I stop walking, no longer able to move or breathe. My father keeps going and somehow I'm back in front of Aurelia's building, staring up at her tiny, crud-covered window that is shining like a beacon. Drawing me in and up to her, only for my feet to stay firmly rooted on the sidewalk.

Doubt is such an insidious monster.

The way it leaches distrust into your mind. The way it infiltrates the softest, most vulnerable parts of us. How it warps and confiscates our minds is nothing short of diabolical. And the way we learn to use it against others is masterful.

I don't want him to make me doubt you.

My gaze latches on the door of her building but just as I put one foot in front of the other, I freeze.

"I have my guy making sure she doesn't double-cross me. He'll keep watch on her."

Fuck. He's having her followed. Likely someone is out here now, and my being here could endanger her. But... is she...

Before I can finish that thought, I'm running as hard and as fast as I can. Up streets and down others until I reach I don't even know where I am. Winded, I press against an old brick building, the sun starting to set, bathing the buildings in a warmth I don't even come close to feeling. I dial up Ashley first because I need to get the fuck out of here and I'm a bit stranded. Then I call Lenox and tell him everything I heard.

"So Beth had access to your computer?" he prods.

"I guess," I lament. "We knew someone managed my password somehow."

I hear him moving in the background and then the telltale sound of keys on a keyboard being tapped at rapid fire. "The call your father just placed was to that burner phone, so we now know it belongs to Beth." A pause. Silence. Then, "We never checked video surveillance."

"What?"

"We have the original email that was sent to Beth. We found it on her system."

"Yeah. So?"

"So we have the time stamp on it, but we never checked surveillance of the building for around that time. We can nail Beth easily enough. Between the phone and whatever I find of her coming and going around the time the email was sent, we can nail her. And we can partially nail your father now that we know the burner belongs to Beth."

"Okay. He's planning this for the monthly board meeting. Monday morning. Nine a.m. I heard him say he'd wire Aurelia the ten grand after she tells the board I..." I can't even finish that.

"I'll come in. I'll be there with you."

"Lenox."

"I'm your computer guy. I'll be there."

That's not why he'll be there, and both he and I know it. He'll be there for me. I swallow thickly, the frog in my throat croaking me. "Thank you."

"Shut up."

"Okay." I smile.

I feel like I'm being snapped repeatedly with a rubber band. "What if Aurelia is in this with him? I hurt her, Lenox. Who's to say she's not helping him to get back at me?"

"Do you honestly believe that?"

"I..."

I trail off, thinking about Aurelia. About all the interactions I've had with her since she started. All the time we've spent together. Our stolen moments. The way she looks at me. Her smile. Her eyes.

"No," I tell him, straightening up as I see the headlights of Ashley in my Escalade up ahead. I wave to him, catching his attention. "I don't believe that. I think she was alone in her apartment, and he threatened her somehow. I think she likely said whatever she had to say to get him out of there."

And I wasn't there to protect her. I should have been. I should have charged in there.

Ashley stops the car and I get in. I give him a grateful nod and then he pulls away from the curb, taking me home and away from Aurelia.

"I can agree with that. But you know, whether she wants to or not, he might have ways of forcing her hand anyway."

I glare out the window at the passing landscape, my jaw clenched tighter than a drum. I may not have stormed in there, but no one fucks with my woman and lives. "Then I'll have to twist his hand behind his back and make the fucker scream uncle first."

I THINK, in fact, this has been the longest weekend of my life. After Ashley picked me up, I had him set up a security detail on Aurelia. If I couldn't be there with her, I wasn't taking any chances on her safety. Who knew what my father's guy was capable of and I had to protect her without tipping him off that I knew what was going on.

I texted Aurelia a heart Saturday night. She texted one back, but that was it. Nothing more. Naturally, I couldn't let that rest because I'm a lovesick sucker and a glutton for punishment who may have had one bourbon too many by that point.

Me: Are we still fighting?

Aurelia: We might be, but I can neither confirm nor deny.

Me: Want me to come over so we can talk it out?

Aurelia: Nope. Cannot do that right now.

I sat there, trying to read between the lines and determine if this was a coded message or not. I decided it was. Because this is Aurelia and Aurelia is my girl and my girl has the purest, most fucking gorgeous heart there is.

Me: I understand. And again, I'm sorry. But so you know, I meant every word I said to you. I'm also sending you cookies from that place Asher ordered from.

Aurelia: I know you did, and those words meant everything to me. I just need some space. And if you send me those vegan peanut butter things instead of cookies with real chocolate, butter, and eggs, it won't go well for you.

Me: I'd never do that. I saw your pretty face when you took a bite of those bricks. Incidentally, I sent you a variety dozen. I think you're supposed to start your period next week so I figured a little chocolate and sugar therapy wouldn't hurt. And just because there is only so much a man can take, how much space are we talking?

Aurelia: Even though I should be freaked out that you track my birth control that closely, I'm very grateful for the cookies and will likely eat them all. I'll be back in the office Monday morning by nine. We can talk in person then. Not before.

And yep. That's when the board meeting is set to begin. My

Angel. I should have killed my father on Friday. You're suffering and I'm not sure the best course to fix this for you other than what I already have planned.

> Me: I track everything about you because I'm so fucking in love with you, Aurelia. I'm consumed in you. So much so that I ache in your absence. Have faith in me as I do in you.

> Aurelia: My heart hurts too. So much. But please, keep your distance this weekend. It's what's best. Monday morning.

> Me: Sorry. I know that was a lot. Anything I should be prepared for for Monday? Not sure my heart can handle you walking away for good.

> Aurelia: With me babe, always expect the unexpected.

And that's how I made it through the rest of my weekend. Sunday, she texted me a pic of her in her pajamas eating the cookies I sent and I texted her a pic of myself in only a towel just after I got out of the shower because I'm shameless like that. At least it wasn't my dick.

Now here it is, Monday morning. Just before nine a.m. I'm in my requisite suit, wearing the tie I tied her up with at the club—my new favorite tie—and sitting with Lenox on my left and the rest of the board on my right, all giving me questioning looks. The kind that ask why the hell is Lenox Ward here?

"I think we're just waiting on a few more people," I tell them precisely as fucking pregnant as hell Beth strolls in the room. Her eyes dart to mine and yeah, I'm not sure what to do about Beth. Other than fire her.

Immediately following Beth is my father and smack dab behind him is Aurelia, who looks like she hasn't slept all weekend. I stand. It's a compulsion. It's only Lenox's hand gripping my forearm that stops me from rounding the table and taking her in my arms.

I turn the full force of my composed fury on my father. "Morning, Dad. It's been a while. Nice to see you looking so old."

Aurelia chokes on the sip of Diet Coke she was just taking. It sprays out of her mouth in a cascade of brown, all of it landing on my father's back, his suit jacket drenched.

"Oh my gosh. I'm so... I mean," she sputters, wiping the spittle of soda and drool from her chin with the back of her hand. "I didn't mean to spit that on you. Wow, what is it about me and Mondays in this place? I'll pay for the dry cleaning. I already owe your son since I bled all over his jacket on my first day."

My father glances over his shoulder, threateningly glaring down at this wet back.

I smother down my laugh, as does Lenox.

"Elias," Brad, the chairman of the board, exclaims, his chair slamming forward into the table with his shock. "What are you doing here?"

"Yes. Morning, gentlemen and ladies. I hope you don't mind me crashing."

"Actually, we do," Pat, another board member, says. She's a no fucking around woman with a wife and six kids. I make it my mission to stay on her good side and I don't care about being on anyone's good side. She's also my favorite of the board members.

"Well, you won't soon enough."

My father takes a seat opposite me, and I reluctantly sit back down. Aurelia's eyes are on her hands in her lap as she sits on the other side of Beth, and I can't read her other than to know she's not okay.

"Care to tell us what this is about?" That's Pat again and bless her.

"I am simply here to help facilitate Aurelia airing her grievances against my son," my father states as if he's a nobleman of the cloth, shepherding his flock to safety.

"What's this, Aurelia?" Astrid, yet another board member, questions, her tone soft.

"She's been involved in a sexual affair with my son for weeks now," my father answers for her. "All of it starting almost immediately after she was inappropriately promoted to executive design intern."

Astrid holds up her hand, stopping my father. "I believe I asked *Aurelia*. Not you." She's back on Aurelia. "Is what Elias is saying true?"

Aurelia clears her throat and squares her shoulders. "There is something I'd like to say, and it is important for everyone here to know the truth about what's been going on between me and Mr. Monroe. Zaxton, that is. But first, I'd like to share something, if I may."

"Go ahead." Astrid waves her hand, indicating that the floor is hers.

"Thank you." Aurelia shifts and then places her phone face up on the table. Then she presses something on her screen and voices pour into the room from the speaker.

"What the hell is this," my father snaps, pounding his fist and trying to reach for the phone the moment he hears his voice saying that he wants Aurelia's help to take back his company. Aurelia is faster than he is, already anticipating his moves, and she slides it toward Astrid and out of his reach.

"This is a recording I took on Friday evening after Elias Monroe followed me back to my apartment. I'd like the whole thing listened to, please, as it explains everything."

My father flies out of his chair, thrusting past Beth and knocking her back. Yelling a slew of half-formed words, he's attempting to cover the sound on the recording, but the damage is already done. Astrid stands, holding the phone in a tight grip, but Lenox and I are there, blocking my father in his pursuit to get to Astrid and the phone.

"Don't even try it, old man," I warn because my father or not, I have no issues taking him down. The audio continues.

"So it seems. Fine. What's your moral dilemma for helping me versus hurting my son?"

"Depends on the stakes. I won't do anything illegal."

"Commendable and understandable, but likely not your choice to make. Monday morning, you're going to go to the board and tell them that you've

been fucking my son since shortly after you started. You're going to tell them that he promoted you with that expectation in mind and that it became a necessary part of keeping your job otherwise you'd lose it."

"Even though that's not the least bit true?"

"Does it matter?"

"To me it does. Our relationship has remained completely separate from work. Nothing of a sexual nature has ever happened inside the Monroe building. Not to mention it's one hundred percent consensual."

"I'm aware. It was impossible for my inside person to know if you were fucking him or not. You were both very good at hiding it. Until I started following you, that is. But that changes nothing. He's your boss. You're his subordinate. And I need you to tell the board exactly what I just dictated you tell them. I also have his emails about your dress length from your first day if they need more than simply your word."

"You fucking bitch," he bellows, spitting at Aurelia while pointing a threatening finger. "You double-crossed me. I warned you what I'd do if you did that. I'll fucking *destroy* you."

Aurelia screams as my father launches himself at her. In a flash, her knee shoots up, connecting with his groin, and he doubles over, but not before he swipes at her. She staggers back a step to avoid it, tripping over a chair, and I catch her, shifting her behind me while letting my fist fly at the same time. With a delightful crunch, it lands squarely in his jaw. His head snaps back, the force of the blow knocking him sideways. He stumbles before slamming the side of his face into the hard wall.

Grabbing him by his suit jacket, I haul him up to me. Eyes dazed and slightly glazed over from the blow, blood dribbles past his lips. I want to see more of it for what he did to Aurelia. I want to bleed him dry and watch as he suffers. Years and years of shit this man put both Greyson and me through and now he's fucking with Aurelia.

He picked the wrong fucking woman to go after.

I shake him because he doesn't get to pass out. That's too easy. Getting right up in his face, I snarl, "You don't touch her. You don't look at her. If you ever come near her or anyone I love again, you will learn firsthand what it means to destroy someone. I will *end* you. It's not a fucking threat. It's a promise. You're done. This is over for you. Run and stay gone, or we'll publish the recording and anything else I can get my hands on that will either throw you in jail or publicly disgrace you."

With a shove in the direction of the door, he tumbles to the ground in a heap of black fabric.

Lamar steps into the room. Not a shocker since there's been shouting and ruckus, a crowd already lingering outside the door. "Good morning, everyone," he says with a chipper gleam. "So sorry I'm late in getting here. Mondays can be a real thing around this place. Am I right, Aurelia?" He steps in and a curse slurs past my father's lips as Lamar steps on his hand. "Oh look." He glances down at my father, who is groaning and grumbling. "The cleaning crew must have forgotten to take out the trash on Friday. Might I have the honor?"

"Be my guest." I flick my hand at the bug on the floor and then Lamar is hoisting him up by the back of his wet jacket, crinkling his nose as he does before literally dragging him from the room.

"Be right back. Don't you *dare* start without me." He throws me a meaningful look and then he's taking my father out, well, like trash. I wouldn't be shocked if he deposits the man in one of the dumpsters out back. Frankly, I don't care what he does with him as long as my father is gone and gone for good.

I turn to Aurelia, cupping her face in my hands. "Are you okay?"

Wide blue eyes search mine in fast, bewildered flicks. An emotion in them I've never seen as she places her hands on my chest. "I'm okay," she finally whispers. "Glad that's over. Your father's a real douchebag."

A mirthless laugh flees my lungs. "You crazy, brave, smart, beautiful girl. I can't believe you did that. I can't believe you recorded him like that and then sat there playing it, knowing how he was going to react."

"I had to do something. I would have told you sooner, but he was having me followed and my apartment bugged."

That motherfucker. I assumed about the following, but bugging her apartment? He got off too easy. I should have pummeled him to death. I move for the door when she drags me back to her.

"Uh-uh. He's not our problem anymore. And, I'm sorry," she says, knocking me sideways.

I nearly laugh. "For what?"

"Because I was wrong. You had every right to do what you did and I'm not mad. I stopped being mad at you almost immediately after you left on Friday. Then your father stepped in and ruined my plans to come after you."

Hope explodes in my chest. "You're serious?"

A nod.

Emotion barrels through me like a flash flood. Anger is replaced by relief, replaced by love. So much love. "Aurelia, I think I fell in love with you the second you glanced up with your knees bleeding and your bright blue eyes glaring at me. I would have waited forever. I would have begged and pleaded and done anything I could think of to win your heart and trust again. I swear it to you now, from here on out, it's nothing but honesty between us."

Without caring in the slightest who sees, without waiting on her to say something in return, I lean in and press my lips to hers. Because I have to kiss her. Because she didn't betray me. She saved me. Over and over again, this woman has saved me.

Now it's time I return the favor.

There is no way to pinpoint all the different jumbled up emotions floating through me at this moment. I'm locked in some strange sort of high. My heart is beating so fast, all quick, rhythmless jabs. It's wild, like I'm on drugs or something. Maybe it's all the adrenaline or that I got a good ball-nailer on Elias Monroe. Whatever it is, I'm flying like a hummingbird in a delightful little bubble until freaking Zaxton Monroe decides this is the moment to burst it.

"We're not done here," he says against my cheek. "Not by a long shot, and I'm not sure how you're going to react to something."

"Oh goody. I love it when you say that."

He smiles at my cheeky retort. "Hopefully, this goes over better than it did the last time, though I'm betting it doesn't."

With that, the man I simultaneously love and want to throttle takes my hand and leads me back over to the damn board table. Everyone is talking in muted tones, shocked and disoriented after what just went down.

"So, now that we sorted out one problem, I think it's time we move on to the next item on my agenda."

All heads swivel in Zax's direction. Especially when he pulls out his phone.

"Oh hell, not another recording," the woman who I think is named Pat bemoans.

"We could show the recording," Zax explains. "We have plenty of proof. Or we can just see what she has to say. Beth?"

Beth turns fifty thousand shades of red and I think half the jaws in the room drop, smacking onto the polished wood table. Mine included. I didn't know what Beth had to do with any of this or why she was even here to begin with.

She nervously licks her lips, resting a hand directly over her large belly. "Elias was blackmailing me." Her expression breaks and then the tears start. "He seduced me shortly after I started here. My husband had just been laid off and... Elias promised me a promotion. We needed the money, and I didn't know what else to do. I couldn't lose this job. It didn't last very long. A few months and then he was gone for doing the same thing to another woman as he did to me. I so was relieved. Until he called me a little over a month ago and explained that he'd tell my husband about the affair if I didn't sneak into Zax's office and send an email stating that we needed to hire Aurelia Whitlock as a design intern. It grew from there, along with his threats."

Jesus. This poor woman. I mean, yeah, she made shitty choices, but I feel for her all the same. How many women have suffered the same thing at the hands of a cruel and powerful man? Too many. Far too many. It all makes sense now. All the things she said to me. The warnings about Zax.

Zax frowns, intertwining his fingers and resting them on the table as he speaks to her, in a gentle tone. "You could have told me, Beth. I would have done what I could to help."

She stares up at the ceiling as more tears drip down her face. "I was scared. He told me if I said anything to anyone, especially you, he'd tell Jared about the affair. He would have destroyed my marriage." Her focus drops to Zax. "I can't lose my husband. I can't break my family apart. I can't."

"You're the one who told him what I offered Marie Marcato."

She nods even though it wasn't a question. "I'm sorry," she cries, wiping at her face. "I'm so sorry. That's all I did. I didn't tell him anything else. I knew you two were together. You tried to hide it, but it was obvious. The way you looked at each other, there was no hiding how you felt. I told him nothing about it."

The members of the board exchange glances. "Beth, if you were us, what would you do?" Brad questions, looking like he doesn't know whether to fire her or hug her.

"Well, she was sexually harassed and then blackmailed."

Brad's gaze casts over to Pat and then immediately back to Beth. "Probation. Six months starting from after you return from maternity leave."

Beth officially breaks down, shaking and sobbing. She thanks everyone profusely, then apologizes once more to both me and Zax. And then smartly flees the room like her ass is on fire just as Lamar returns with a triumphant gleam spread across his face.

"Did I miss it? Am I too late?"

"Right on time." Zax waves a hand at the seat Beth just vacated and then Lamar is there, pulling out his laptop and setting up some sort of presentation. "Ladies and gentlemen of the board, I know it's already been quite the morning and I know you have a dozen questions for me with regard to my relationship with Aurelia. I'm happy to answer any of them, but I'd like, if I may, to explain everything to you first and then propose a business plan for the future of Monroe Fashion that I think will alleviate some of your concerns while drawing in an entirely new market and income stream to the Monroe family."

Brad rubs a weary hand across his forehead before falling back in his chair. "The floor is yours. But Jesus, Zax, this better be good after the morning we've had."

Reaching under the table, he takes my hand, holding it in his. Zax proceeds to explain our relationship to the board, leaving out the dirty bits and focusing on how we did keep it separate from work despite the fact that he's my boss. He explains how we tried to stop it, but it was unstoppable. The phone recording I took with Zax's father corroborates this nicely.

Mental high-fives all around because the board, who doesn't look pleased as punch also doesn't look like the barrel end of a kegger. Plus, you know, there's the whole Zax announcing to the world that we're together and that we're in love. Words I haven't told him yet, but that's just semantics at this point.

Lamar is smiling so wide, his glowing white teeth could navigate sailors into port in the middle of a storm. Lenox looks bored and frankly I'm a bit clueless as to why he's here because other than some unneeded muscle, he hasn't said two words about anything.

"So this leads me to what I had initially hoped to speak to you all about this morning."

The board members stare at Zax, looking like they're ready to shoot up flares in hopes of being rescued. I think they've had it. I can't blame them. After this morning, I could go for a drink, a cookie, and a week in bed.

He leans over to me and whispers in my ear, "Don't be mad at me." Then he addresses the board. "Let it be said from the start, every decision I make here is one hundred percent business. Originally, when I promoted Aurelia, I did so out of distrust. I knew my father would cash in on the favor he did for her, and I wasn't fully sold she wasn't already helping him in some way. But it only took me reviewing her portfolio and listening to her in a few meetings to realize she knows exactly what she's doing in this industry. Her model name is well-known and greatly respected. Then there's this."

Zax nods at Lamar and then the SMART board lights up with... pictures of my gowns and dresses.

"Oh my God." I jerk so hard I half fall out of my chair, only managing to catch myself at the last second. "What is this? What are you doing?" I'm standing. I'm pacing. I'm terrified. "Zax. What are you doing? Those are my designs."

He stands now too. "Aurelia, I'm not stealing them. My proposal is this. You can turn it down, but I'm hoping you won't. Because those gowns and dresses are stunning. They need to be out in the world. Under your name."

"Her name?"

Zax nods at Brad, but his eyes are still all over me, gauging my reaction. "We purchased Marie Marcato's business, which already has the infrastructure to get Lia Sage couture up and mobile within weeks. Given the specialty of this brand and how it is not something Monroe already features, I think it would be a perfect asset to our grander organization as a separate business unit under the Monroe umbrella. Aurelia will be the chief executive designer and officer and she will report to you. Not me."

I think I'm going to pass out. That's how fast my heart is going. The room starts to spin, and I plant my hand on the table for support. "You're giving me my own design house?"

"With the support and backing of Monroe to help it be success-ful," he says. "She already has commissions from Bianca and Rina Fritz. With women like them wearing her dresses, there is no telling how high this can go. Where the Fritzes go, people follow."

"And," Lamar jumps in, barely holding on with his enthusiasm. "We're thinking of revealing the launch of Lia Sage at the end of the Monroe show during fashion week. We're going to change the light-ing." Lamar clicks something on his laptop and then the plans for the runway at fashion week pop up on the screen. "Her gowns will be showcased with her own branding. It will be all anyone will be talking about there. A surprise designer reveal, the media will go absolutely crazy over it."

"You're serious?" I can barely get the words out.

"I think you're ready," Zax tells me with certainty in his voice. "You can do this, Aurelia. You have the talent and the know-how. You have the name. You just need the backing. I think this will be a huge initiative for Monroe that will lead it into the future and diversify the company."

"I love it," Astrid announces, her eyes on the screen. "These gowns and dresses are stunning. We have the baseline set up now that we've acquired Marie Marcato. I say we do it. All of it."

Brad is focused on his screen as well. "Do we have preliminary numbers?"

"I believe that's something for Aurelia to give you. She has a business plan set up."

Jerkface knows everything.

"I don't have it with me," I explain, clearing my throat to stop the tremor in it. "I wasn't expecting this. At all." In fact, I'm finding it nearly impossible to keep myself together. To hold myself back from jumping the man standing beside me. Yes, I believe him when he says it's all business. But it's not. He's giving me my dream and he knows it. "I can walk you through some of the basics. I don't have hard figures."

"Not now," Brad says. "I'm done for today. But I agree with Astrid and Zax. You have some real talent that I think will sell and sell well. It also helps us get out of the whole you're Zax's subordinate issue. I think we'll give this a tentative green light pending a more extensive plan."

That's when I die.

I think. All I know is that I'm floating outside of my body, watching this all unfold around me while mentally dancing and flipping like a cheerleader, complete with ridiculous victory song and pom-poms.

I'm a mess.

The happiest I've ever been, I hardly know what to do with all this glee. I'm shocked glitter isn't shooting out of my ears. What do you do when your dream is literally handed to you by the man you're in love with? Who knew such things were not only possibilities but realities?

He was crass and prickly and so irresistibly broken I had no choice but to fall head over heels in love with him. And while I wanted to save him, I think, in the end, we saved each other.

The room clears out and vaguely I recognize I'm thanking the board members and saying goodbye and promising a hundred different things. I'm not sure if I'm crying or just smiling like a psychotic clown or what, but they leave quickly and without a lot of commentary or fanfare. Could be all the drama. Could be that my boyfriend is now barking things.

"Lamar, Lenox. Out. I appreciate your help, both of you, but now I need to be alone with Aurelia."

"Still a grouch. Fine. But tomorrow, Liastrange, we're brunching. I don't give a fuck if it's Tuesday. We're brunching with bloodies and mimosas. And if you want to hire me to be your right-hand maiden, I won't object."

"I can't lose you."

Lamar flat out rolls his eyes at Zax. "Obviously. Have you met me? I can do everything all at once. It's called multitasking."

"Works for me," I say.

"You got it. Anything you want. Now go!"

Suddenly, I'm alone with Zax, hoisted up and plopped down onto the boardroom table.

"Can people see us?" I don't have time to waste by glancing to my right and I can't remember if this is one of the many glassed office rooms.

"No."

"Perfect."

Before he can so much as make a noise, I drop to my knees, grabbing him by the hips and pulling the crotch of his pants to my face. I take a deep inhale—the scent so fucking masculine I moan and clench and squirm all at once.

I glance up at his eyes. "I'm so in love with you, Zaxton Monroe. And not because you think I'm talented and like my designs. Not because you gave me my dream of running my own design house. Not because you're hot and fantastic in bed. But because I love *you*. All of you. Every broken piece of you I find irresistibly beautiful."

He drops to the ground along with me, sorta spoiling my plans for my mouth and his dick, but the look I'm getting as he grabs my body and hauls it against his tells me this is going to be so much better.

"And I love you," he declares, an electrical storm pulsing in his eyes as he stares into mine. "All of you. The heart you share so openly and freely while carrying it across your body like a suit of armor. The way you love your people with unrivaled fierceness. The passion in which your every breath stems from. The joy you evoke in anyone lucky enough to encroach on your light. Your talent and tireless determination. Your fearlessness." His hands hold my face. "Aurelia, I love you. For all your broken and put together pieces. For all the pieces you left astray, waiting for me to pick up so I can complete your puzzle. I love you because you were always, forever, nonnegotiably meant to be mine."

I collapse into him at the same second his mouth covers mine.

Before he can slip his tongue inside my mouth, I'm climbing onto his lap, straddling him in my dress.

"Someone could see us," he murmurs into my mouth.

"Yup." And for once, I don't care. Our secret is out and pretty soon, he's not going to be my boss. I'm going to be my boss. Besides, after this morning, I don't think anything could stop me from touching this man right now.

"You want this?" he rasps against my lips, his voice hoarse and crackly.

"It's the only room in this building without glass walls. Fulfill my dirty office sex with my boss fantasy, Zax, and I'll happily be your naughty little intern in return." I moan. Why is that so hot? I feel like it shouldn't be, but it's totally getting me going right now.

He groans. "Fuck. You are such a naughty girl. *My* naughty girl."

I don't care. I love the role-play. I love the fantasy. I love how he gives me whatever my brain can cook up and then even things it never began to imagine. I love how he loves me for me, just as I am, just as much as I love him the exact same way.

His tongue skims over mine, hot and wild as he deepens our kiss. I'm so eager and wound up, my hips roll along the hard ridge in his pants. I'm all need, hot and raw.

"Always so impatient for my cock, Aurelia. Naughty girls get punished for that. On all fours now. Ass facing me. Don't make me ask you again."

"Yes, sir."

I'd be embarrassed by how fast I follow his command, but I'm too anxious for what I'm hoping he'll do. The moment I'm in position, my dress is flung up and over my hips, cool air meeting my exposed ass. The cool air is replaced by his warm palms as he massages both ass cheeks.

"How many do you think you deserve?" he rasps.

Oh God. I don't know. A thousand?

"However many you feel I deserve, sir. I've been a very naughty intern."

"Mmmm." He rubs me in a circle once more before spreading my ass wide, his hot breath over the damp material between my legs, and I shiver. "I'm thinking ten. Five on each cheek."

I feel myself dripping into my panties before the first strike even comes, but when it does, there is no stopping my moan. That earns me another quick strike.

"If you're loud and we get caught, this is over. Stay silent, Aurelia, or you won't get what you need."

Silent?! Is he fucking kidding me?

Reading my unspoken question, suddenly his suit jacket is in front of my face. "Bury your face in that if you have to."

Another smack comes and I smother my face in his jacket, inhaling his scent. He runs his finger up my seam, over my panties, and I swear, I'm so close. All the fear and adrenaline of earlier have turned me into a live wire.

He continues to spank me, alternating lighter and harder blows, rubbing my ass in between, and when he gets to ten—I was counting in my head—he slides my thong to the side and buries his tongue inside me.

I buck forward, crying out into his jacket that I know I'm also likely drooling in. He brushes his thumb over my clit, up and down without giving me any pressure. "Please," I beg. "I need to come. Now."

"Wrong thing to say, baby girl."

In a flash, I'm up on my feet, my legs wobbly. He stands behind me, his finger now inside of me, pumping slowly. "See those papers on the table?"

Papers? What the fuck are papers?

"Organize them for me. I want them in a perfect stack. Then I want you to flip one over and write I will never be a bad intern again. And remember—silent."

Holy wow, that's deliciously degrading. Who knew I had a slight humiliation kink? My need to please him right now is off the charts.

I reach for the papers and then he's spreading my legs, crouching between them and licking me again. It's impossible to focus on the papers. Especially when my eyes cross and roll inside my head. His finger finds my G-spot and I try—I swear I do—to organize the fucking papers I'm actually now starting to hate.

I slide them and shuffle them and crunch one or two in my fist. "That's it. Good girl. Now start writing if you want to keep my tongue on your clit and my fingers in your pussy."

He drags his hand slowly up the inside of my thighs and I find a fucking pen, grip the bitch in my fist, and start writing. And as promised, his tongue is on my clit and now he's pumping those two fingers inside my pussy without mercy. I press my lips together, so afraid that if I make a sound he'll stop. But the effort of not making a sound propels this up to an entirely new degree. Outside the door, people are there. Working and talking and drinking coffee.

Someone could open the door any second. Someone could come looking for either one of us. The thought of them finding Zax kneeling behind me with his face and fingers in my pussy is enough to make me spasm and rock back against him.

"Zax," slips past my lips in a gritty, pleading way.

I get a hard slap on the ass for that and then I'm coming. The pen goes shooting across the smooth wood top and I'm biting into my fist to fight the sounds desperately clawing up the back of my throat. His fingers and tongue don't stop. They circle and flick and suck and pump and I'm dying. Grinding against his face like the shameless hussy this man makes me.

He wrings every ounce of pleasure out of my body before I slump forward, the papers askew. A hand slides my hair from my face, fanning it across the table, and then he picks up the piece of paper I wrote on. Staring at it for a brief moment, I hear his warm chuckle at the same time I hear the metal teeth of his zipper as he unzips himself.

"I will continue to be a bad intern because I like pissing off my asshole boss," he reads.

I grin, twisting my neck and catching his eye. "I'm not even sorry."

He smiles before his mouth covers mine from the side. "Never change. I love you so fucking much. Never change, Aurelia. You're my goddess. My queen. My Angel. Now tell me, Angel, do you want me to fuck you like this or do you want to ride me in my big, office chair?"

Oh. Decisions, decisions. And both of them so very tempting.

"Both."

"I was hoping you'd say that." I feel him line the head of his cock up and then he's thrusting inside me. Hard. "I'm going to take you like this, Aurelia." He pumps in and out of me at a fast clip. "And then suck on your sweet tits while you ride my cock."

"Oh God. I might not make it." He's at the perfect angle, hitting my spot with the head of his cock before sliding against it with every deep thrust. It's out of this world fantastic and all I can do is lie here and take it.

"How's this then?" he groans, and I can tell he's hanging on by a thread too. "We'll make this quick and dirty." Thrust. "We're on borrowed time as it is." Thrust. "Then tonight, after everyone leaves for the day." Thrust. "I'll fuck you in my office for real." Thrust. "Any way you want." Thrust.

"Yes. That. All of that. All of this."

"Shhh," he admonishes, his hand covering my mouth and fuck, I start to go wild from that. My whole body quivers, every muscle clenching and seizing as pleasure skyrockets through me. I come so hard stars dance behind my eyes and my vision goes fuzzy. He's relentless, pounding into me, dragging every last drop out of me, and then he still, his face falling to the middle of my back where he growls against my dress.

I'm panting for my life when he peels himself up and off me.

Tucking himself away, zipping up, and then he's helping me up, fixing my underwear and dress and kissing my lips. Murmuring, "I love you," in my ear over and over again. "Let's go get you cleaned up and then tonight after we celebrate in the office, I'm taking you out. On a date. With you as my girlfriend. We're going to celebrate Aurelia Whitlock and her new company."

A girl can seriously get used to the sound of that. All of it.

EPILOGUE 1

AURELIA

Let it never be said that what goes around doesn't come around. Or, that when you find the right people to have and keep in your corner, you hold on to them for dear life. Then there are your loved ones who you want to fucking strangle. That's where I am right now.

"Yeah, he bought her a ticket," one of the models for Monroe murmurs to the model directly in front of her as they're lined up, ready to walk. "That's like, the lowest blow ever. Do you think he's trying to break up with her like that? Because if he is, I'll totally nail him tonight at the after-party."

"No joke. You think Zaxton Monroe does threesomes?"

Laugh. Laugh. Laugh. Giggle. Giggle. Giggle. So fucking funny.

"Why else would he invite Valencci to this show and give her a front row ticket if he wasn't trying to stick it to Lia and get rid of her? Oh sorry," she mocks in a snooty voice. "*Aurelia.*"

I smirk. No one knows about the second act of this show. Not even the models walking in it. I wanted it all to be a surprise. A true designer reveal. But at the same time, did I hear that correctly? Valencci is sitting front row? What in the Wide World of Sports could

Zaxton Monroe, the man who claims to love me, have been thinking with that move?

He wouldn't have... unless—

"Lia, you've got two minutes to hair and makeup," one tech informs me. I throw him an acknowledging wave. I'm not walking for Monroe. I'm walking as the final piece in my show. A piece that won't reveal my new brand banner until I start to walk.

"Thanks," I reply, making sure my voice carries. "I'll be there in a second."

The two models' heads whip around at light speed. Their looks of panic quickly reform into plastered plastic smiles.

"Hey, ladies," I say, tossing them a wiggly finger wave, making sure they know I heard them and not letting them know their words have any effect on me. "See you out there. Have fun tonight. Break a leg."

"Thanks." Air kisses from both of them. "You too!"

I'm tempted to peek my head out through the curtain and see if they're right, but I don't have the time. And truth, do I want to know? I'm liable to fly out there all ninja style and kick her chair out from under her. Or rip out her hair extensions. Or slice up the back of her dress so that when she stands, her ass will show.

The lights morph, and the music starts, and the handlers—many of them FIT student volunteers—are rushing models over to the entrance of the stage and there is no longer time to think about anything other than tonight.

Than this show.

The show that's about to change my life.

And didn't I once say that I hoped I could walk in this show at fashion week so that I could show Valencci up? Prove to her that she didn't get me. That must be why Zax invited her. So I could get my coup de grâce on her boney ass.

"Showtime," Zax whispers in my ear as he wraps his arms around my waist from behind. "You're going to be brilliant. I can't wait to sit out there and watch you shine. I'm so proud of you, baby girl. You're going to take the fashion world by storm with what you've created."

I spin in his arms, twining my fingers up into his hair. This man. Who knew Zaxton Monroe had such a sweet side? I love his gruff, unpolished side too, but the gem beneath is nothing short of breathtaking. And mine. All mine—cue maniacal stage laugh. Okay, I think I'm a touch crazy right now.

"I heard a rumor."

His eyebrows shoot up, eyes wide, though he's not selling me on this feigned innocence thing. "Oh?"

"I heard a certain Italian witch is present. And by witch I actually mean bitch."

A smirk. "Like I said. You're going to be brilliant, and I can't wait to sit out there and watch you shine."

Yup. Knew it.

"I love you," I tell him. "Tonight I plan to show you just how much. But for now, you need to get your hot ass moving since it's your show that's on and I need to—"

"Lia, now!" Lamar comes flying over, shaking my arm. "Hair. Makeup. Dress."

"That," I finish. Reaching up on my toes, I plant a kiss on Zax's cheek. "For luck. Go get 'em, big guy." I give him a wink and another kiss, this one on the lips, and then Lamar is extricating me from Zax's arms, dragging me along the back space of the show where my models are now getting ready.

"Okay." Lamar shoves me into a chair, right in front of a lighted mirror. "So, I know we talked about having your hair down and flowy, but I'm changing everything up."

I groan. "No. We can't! We already did a trial and loved it."

"Yes. But I changed your gown, too."

"You what?" screeches past my lips. "No. No!"

"Yes." He's grinning like the devil. "Why do you think I saved it for when we have five minutes left before you walk?"

"What?!" I point an accusatory finger, squinting at him. "What do you know that I don't?"

Lamar snaps his fingers and then Eloise and Sonia come flying over, carrying...

"My dress. What the fuck, Lamar?! Where did you even get that?" Only, it's not my dress for tonight. It's the dress I wore for Valencci. The same dress she later claimed as hers before proceeding to try and ruin me in this industry for good.

"It's yours, Aurelia. You designed it."

I shake my head. "I can't wear that. She'll sue me. She's freaking sitting out there now."

His dark eyes meet my panicked ones in the mirror. "She won't. Trust me. Trust Zax. We've got you on this."

I nibble terribly on my lip, my eyes creased with worry, even as hope slithers through my veins like a drug. Eloise and Sonia are all smiles, looking excited. And like vultures, waiting to attack my hair and makeup.

"You're sure?"

"Positive," he swears. "Wear the dress. Make the statement that this is *your* brand."

I blow out an uneven breath. "Okay. Let's do it."

And like roadkill, the vultures attack. My makeup is dark and smoky eyes with red lips. My hair is up in a high, tight, sleek ponytail. The gown, black satin. Long. An insane slit up the side. Backless. The neck, ropes of black twisted fabric with filigrees of gold threaded through them to yes, look like rope.

Nerves skate through my body and I shake out my hands, wanting to jog in place but resisting the urge. My stomach churns, but I force myself to get my shit together and go to each of the eleven models lined up, adjust their dresses and make sure it's all as it should be. The last of the Monroe models, a six-foot curvy goddess of a woman, comes up to me, a slightly embarrassed expression on her face.

"Mr. Monroe just walked to take his bow, but he asked me to give you this. Sorry!"

She presses a kiss to my cheek, and I smile, fingering the skin she just touched. "What was that for?"

"Luck and mental diversion, he said." Then she shrugs as if she has no clue what any of that means.

I laugh. That man. "Thank you. I needed that."

The man knew exactly how to pull me out of my head and get me to calm down and smile. It worked.

"Okay, everyone." I clap my hands, drawing everyone's attention. "It's time. We've got this!" I whisper-shout so my voice doesn't carry. "Listen, I'm tricking you a bit. You think you're walking for Monroe, but you're not. You're walking for me, or more accurately Lia Sage, which are the gowns you're wearing now as part of my new design house. This is my debut and you're a part of it. So from one model to another, please give this one your all and I'll be happy to return the favor."

I get a few hugs and congratulations and excited flutters. But all that quickly dies as they get in line and ready to walk.

The lights go black outside in the main show area and then the music starts to pulse. The overheads come back on, the stage flipping to white from black thanks to different lighting through the acrylic stage and here we go.

A hand holds mine and I glance to my left to find Lamar, vibrating beside me. Silently, he gives me a squeeze and I squeeze back as the handlers start moving the models. I can hear the curious and confused mumblings of the audience from back here. That quickly morphs when the first model starts to walk.

"You can't be out there. But I know Zax is. And I also know what they're seeing. They're seeing art, Aurelia Whitlock."

"I love you," I tell him.

"I know. That doesn't mean I'll fuck you."

I laugh, the sound cackling past my lungs. "Thank God for that. Then we couldn't work together." I wink at him.

"Lia, you're next."

A deep breath. "Here goes nothing."

Lamar releases my hand and I cast my body to muscle memory. I start to walk. Hips popping to the beat of the music. One foot crossed over the other. Head up high and eyes straight ahead. I don't look to my left as I make it to the middle of the runway, though I can feel the instant Valencci realizes precisely what this is. I can almost hear her hissing out who knows what.

I ignore it. She's not important and she no longer has power over me. I have to have faith in Lamar and Zax that they wouldn't put me in this dress if they didn't already know something I don't.

The banner with my brand name falls behind me and applause erupts.

I complete my walk and then all the models wearing my gowns are there, spinning me around and drawing me back into the center of the stage. Thunderous cheers fill the room. Everyone is on their feet. Tears threaten like weapons ready to start a war, but I hold them at bay. Giving a bow—never a curtsy—and thanking everyone with kisses blown and personal hugs.

Just as the applause starts to die down and I plan my retreat, someone is before me. Zax. All tall, gorgeous man in his suit with his wavy hair in perfect disarray. "We're not done yet," he says, loud enough for the room to hear.

"What?" comes out baffled and messy.

He spins around, facing the audience. "Thank you all for coming to our show. As you can see, Lia Sage has created a fantastic new line of formal dresses and gowns. Her brand will no doubt lead the industry from award shows to galas to charity events to weddings. Her work is stunning. But not as stunning as she is."

He glances over his shoulder and meets my eyes, holding there as he continues to speak to the room.

"In the last few weeks, you've all heard about our relationship because keeping it a secret became an impossibility for me. I loved a woman years ago with all my heart. But I was foolish. I waited to show her just what her love meant to me, and she died without ever wearing my ring on her finger and knowing just how deep I went for her. A mistake I'll never make again."

He pivots to me, my hand in his, just as he lowers himself onto one knee in front of the entire fashion world, press included. He's got a small black jewelry boxy in his other hand, his serious eyes all over me as he opens it to reveal a Titanic-sinking pear-shaped diamond. Tears well in my eyes, my free hand over my lips. What in the hell?

"Aurelia Whitlock, from the moment my eyes met yours, I tried to resist you. My efforts were in vain as immediately I knew you were unlike any woman I had ever known. My love for you is boundless. Pure. Forever. But so beautiful because it has your love in return. We are it for each other, baby girl. And I can't wait. I can't take it slow. I can't live another day knowing how much I love you and attempting to hold that back for the sake of it might be considered too soon. It's not too soon. You were brought into my life right on time. I love you." He licks his lips nervously. "Marry me?"

I collapse to my knees, falling on top of him, right in front of everyone. "Yes."

Tears pour from my eyes, likely followed by my dark makeup, but who cares?

"I love you so much," I murmur into his lips as he kisses me, consumes me right here on stage without a second thought. He slides the heavy ring onto my finger and then kisses my knuckles one by one until he reaches that finger and then kisses right above his ring.

"It looks good on you."

"I can't believe you did this." I stare down at the massive, sparkly thing. "We've been together a hot second."

"And we have a lifetime to figure out the rest." His brown eyes crinkle at me. "Second thoughts?"

"Not one," I promise him. "So long as you move into my place."

"Brat." He laughs the word and then he's kissing me again, holding me so close and so tight against him.

My hero. My prince. My biggest fan. That's what every woman needs. Their biggest fan to be their best champion.

That's my guy.

And I'll always be the same for him.

His lips fuse with mine and absently I hear some sort of commotion. Applause and happy cheers and even a lot of surprised murmurings sure, but then a shrill screech. Then a few curses in Italian.

I blink open my eyes to find Zax's beaming face before mine. "What in the Hell's Angels? How am I wearing this dress and what just happened?"

He glances left and I follow just in time to find Valencci storming off, throwing random things as she comes across them and making a dramatic scene until she's out of sight. Truth, in all the nerves and excitement and then this, I had forgotten all about her. I turn back to Zax.

His hands cup my face, and he kisses me again. "She's made a lot of enemies. It wasn't difficult to find a few witnesses who were willing to testify against her to intellectual copyright infringement."

"What?"

"You're evidently not the only one she stole from. Just the biggest name and the most vocal about it. There are also others willing to testify that Valencci called the gown yours prior to you walking in it. You didn't know this, but Lenox discovered that since spring fashion week when she claimed the dress as hers, though everyone knew it wasn't, her business has had a sharp decline. Investors and celebrities and magazines have left her because they know what she did to you, and no one wanted to be part of that. So just now, our lawyers presented her with an option. That was the screaming and fit you just witnessed. A class action lawsuit against her for intellectual property theft or something resembling a hostile takeover of her business where she walks away with not a whole lot other than her worthless name."

My eyes pop out of my head. "What?" This time it's a half-scream.

"We'll see what she says, but she'd be a fool not to take my deal. Valencci's business will be Monroe's. Or more likely yours if you want it."

"I can't even with that. I can barely with today."

He wipes the tears from my happy, smiling face.

"Thank you."

His nose rubs along mine and he speaks against my lips. "Thank you, Aurelia. Thank you for reminding me what it is to live. To love. To have passion. To believe in happiness. To look forward to tomorrow. To want forever. All with you."

EPILOGUE 2 - IRRESISTIBLY PERFECT

** U NEDITED AND SUBJECT TO CHANGE!

Greyson

"CAN I HAVE YOUR AUTOGRAPH?" the waitress who unsnapped the top two buttons of her uniform after recognizing both me and my brother asks with a smile that tells me she'd give me anything she could including her body if we wanted.

"Sure," I say with a tight grin, mournfully setting down my coffee mug and casting a longing glance at my breakfast. I'm starving, having woken up at five a.m. with a song in my head that wouldn't quit until I got it out on paper.

"Great!" She jumps up and down, practically screaming. "You're my absolute favorite artist. I have all your albums including the Central Square ones." She laughs, batting her eyelashes. "Which I guess means I have your albums too." She points to my brother, Zax with her pen.

"Thank you for that," I tell her genuinely. Hungry or not, a fan is a fan and I fucking love my fans. "That's very sweet of you." I take the pen from her outstretched hand. "Where would you like me to sign?"

"My cleavage for sure so I can show my boyfriend later and well…" She searches around as if something is going to materialize before her eyes. "I guess my guest check pad?"

"Um." I have no judgment that she wants me to sign her tits for her boyfriend—that's between them—but we're in a public restaurant, not an after-party or a club. "You're sure about this?"

"Absolutely," she exclaims with a fierce head bob. I shrug and do as the lady asks before handing her back her pen. She eyes my handy work. "Thank you so much. This is amazing. It reminds me of this one time when I came to—"

"We'd like to enjoy our breakfast now," Zax says with a gruff yet somehow slightly polite tone.

"Oh." She blushes like a virgin on her wedding night. "Of course. Sure. Enjoy." She shakes her head in a self-deprecating way and then skulks off.

"Thank you," I say to him, finally slicing into my omelet and shoveling a piece into my mouth, stifling my satisfied moan. My stomach was about to start a revolution if I didn't eat in the next ten seconds.

"You have to be harder with them or they think you're easy pickings and drape themselves all over you."

I nod, as I chew. "I know," I garble around a mouthful of eggs, spinach, and bacon, washing it down with a sip of my coffee. "But I'm not good at it. Suzie used to tell me that fans are fans and without them you're nothing—which is true—and that if you start blowing them off or making them feel unimportant word spreads faster than chlamydia at a frat party that you're a dick.

Zax chokes on his benedict. "Did you have to use the word chlamydia while I'm eating?"

I give him an amused look and then continue to devour my eggs.

"You know, if you had a steady girlfriend women would back off you."

I laugh, because truly, that's funny. "You know that's not true. You were a rock star once and had women all over you even though were you with Suzie at the time. It was even worse after she died, and you were mourning. The women who want to fuck a rock star for the sake of fucking a rock star don't care if you or even themselves are coupled up already. That waitress just had me sign her tits and she has a boyfriend. Besides, there is no one out there I'd want to date."

"You sure about that?"

"Which part?" I retort cheekily and he rolls his eyes at me. "Yes, matchmaker Jane, I'm sure. What is this? Because you've found someone again you have to make sure the rest of us do too? Monogamy doesn't fit with my lifestyle right now," I tell my brother, around a mouthful of toast this time. "I just finished recording my latest album a few weeks ago. Eden Dawson and Lyric Rose told me it's the best yet." (They're my producer and record company exec.) "But who knows if my songs will register that way with fans. I have to play them live, which means I'm traveling for weeks or months soon. Dating doesn't jive well with that. As it is, I spend too much time getting hit on for simply being Greyson Monroe. That's not what I want in a woman and until I meet the perfect one, I'm a big fat hard pass on dating."

Zax laughs. A real laugh, which for Zax is saying a lot. He lost Suzie and that destroyed him for over eight years until our ex-step-sister Aurelia became his intern in his fashion empire, Monroe Fashion. After some serious drama, they fell in love. Now it's a lot of smiles and laughs, which seriously make me smile and laugh in return.

He was the grumpiest fucker on the planet before she came into his life.

"Except we both know there already is one perfect woman out there for you."

And just like, my world shuts down.

"You could look her up," he continues casually as if he's not scrambling my insides and frying them in searing hot butter like the eggs I'm eating.

"Fuck you." I practically snarl the words at him, my hand fisting around my butterknife. He knows better than to bring her up to me like this. It's one thing when our friend and former bandmate Asher jokes around, but Zax? No. Not cool.

A nonchalant sip of his coffee. "I'm serious. You could."

I glare and I do it hard so he knows just what level of a dick he's being—it's a twelve out of ten in case you were curious. "I can't. You know I can't."

Zax's eyes cast over my shoulder toward the exit of the restaurant in a contemplative wander. But there is no contemplation with this. With her. My best friend—or was. An obsession I haven't been able to shake in the fourteen years since I first laid eyes on her.

But the last time I saw her...

"Where is she living now?"

"Fuck you!" I repeat, not even bothering to temper the octave of my voice. We're getting looks, I'm positive about it, but right now I don't care. "Stop, Zax. I'm not kidding around with this. Not her, brother."

The one woman I will never have as mine and he knows it. We were impossible from day one, but that didn't exactly make it easier. Especially as we got older and had our stolen moments.

He sighs. Then he stands, wiping his mouth with his napkin before dropping it onto his half-finished plate. "I have to make a call. Then I likely have to go. So..." Eyes up high toward the exit. "Yep. See ya. Call me. I'm here for you. Remember that."

With a crinkle in my brow and a what the fuck expression, my brother waltzes out of the restaurant with a meager pat on the shoulder, leaving me here alone. Only, it takes less than two seconds to realize why he did that. What his motive was for leaving me was.

A woman takes the bench seat diagonal from me at the table beside mine. I stare. My breath gone. My lungs completely empty. My mind frazzled. My heart, a rave...

Then I blow out a breath. Even and slow. Warmth creeps slowly through me like drugs and I smile like the devil I have occasionally been known to be.

When I was fourteen, I met a girl I instantly knew would give me all the come to Jesus moments I'd never want but always need. She was the girl next door, her family moved in without having any clue about the fucked-up nightmare that lived beside them in the pretty old mansion. One night, I was sitting on my rooftop, staring across the Charles River at the twinkling lights of Boston while strumming on my guitar when she climbed up and joined me, introducing herself as the girl I'll never be friends with but will always regret not knowing.

That's what she said, and I was instantly intrigued.

Plus she was fucking beautiful.

There was no denying that part of it. I looked at her and my heart spun wildly in my chest. She sat there with me for hours that summer night, listening to me play and sing, talking to me about the books she loved to read and how one day she wanted to see the world country by country by getting lost in each one. She wanted to be a doctor, she wanted to save lives and make a difference—the one thing she did actually manage to do for herself.

It wasn't until the next day that I realized the reality of our situation. I met her twin brother and instantly became best friends with him—well, at least until a life-changing accident made us enemies. He I could talk to. He I could be friends with because every guy has that one friend that your parents hate but overlook because they know you will outgrow him soon enough.

Her, not so much.

The daughter of an extremely wealthy and influential senator and an old money heiress, her life had already been mapped out for her. A good girl who was not allowed to spend time with let alone get wrapped up in the bad boy filled with rock star dreams.

I left Boston when I was sixteen. That's when our band Central Square hit it massive with a YouTube video gone viral and we scored a record contract. She and I had our night before I left. A first for both of us and then every few years after that she'd come to see me play and we'd have another night or sometimes even two.

By that point, her family hated mine. Montague and Capulet, Hatfield and McCoy—they had nothing on us. If the accident with her brother didn't start the war, my father sure as hell did.

The last time I saw her was three years ago. She came to my concert in Chicago where she was finishing up medical school. We spent the night talking because she told me nothing else could happen, and in that talking, the woman whom I considered to be my best friend, the person who I told all my darkest secrets to, who knew me inside and out, who I was likely insanely, disruptively, terminally in love with, told me that would be the last time I'd see her.

Except now here she is, back home in Boston sitting across from me in a random cafe.

Without hesitation, I climb out of my seat, toss some cash on the table, and then drop down onto the bench directly beside her.

She jumps, her head snapping in my direction, caught off guard by some random weirdo creeping in on her personal space until recognition lights her features. Purple eyes—never seen anything like them on anyone else—grow wider than Fenway Park, her pink glossy lips parting on a surprised breath. Her hair, much shorter than the last time I saw it, flows like ribbons of black ink around her shoulders. On an inhale, I'm sideswiped by her intoxicating fragrance and I find myself inching in just a tad closer, anxious for more of it.

"Hi," I say. "This seat taken?"

"Greyson."

"Fallon," I mock her exaggeration of my name, especially when we never use each other's full names. "Shocker of shockers seeing you here. You don't even like breakfast food."

A hard swallow. "I... I do now."

"Really?"

She lets out a remorseful laugh, her gaze flickering over to me briefly before it playfully bounces around the restaurant. "No. Not really. But that has to stay our little secret."

"We're good at that," I chide, nudging her. "Having our little secrets and even some bigger ones. How are you, Fall Girl? You look beautiful."

Her eyes sparkle and a smile curls up the corner of her lips as we fall back into our old routine. "I'm good. How are you, Grey? Handsome as ever I see."

I wink at her and take her hand from her lap, trying not to think about how smooth and soft it is, and set it down on the seat between us. Then I loop our pinkies together. The way we used to.

"When did you get into town?"

That question does something unexpected to her and suddenly she's staring at me so intently I can see all the flecks of purple and lavender and even touches of blue in her eyes. Her eyes are fucking wild and so beautiful it pains me that I've gone so long without looking directly into them. I squeeze her finger, but I can feel her resistance, her need to pull away.

She blinks and then blinks again. And in those blinks, I catch her oh shit moment and it hurts. It hurts a lot.

"I... um." She licks her lips, giving me an apologetic look. "I've been here, Grey."

"Here?"

She sags a bit. "Boston."

"For how long, Fall Girl?"

Her gaze plummets to the empty place setting before her. "Since I finished med school."

Sucker. Punch. Everything inside me freezes over. Like holding an ice cube in your first, it hurts and it's brutally cold all the while numbing you from within. "Wow."

"I know."

"Do you, babe? You told me you were doing your residency in Chicago. You lied to me."

"Yes. I lied," she admits, shame consuming her features even as she leans ever so slightly against me, shoulder to shoulder now. "I did my residency at Boston Children's Hospital and at Hughes Healthcare."

"Jesus." I run my free hand across my face. "I don't even know what to say to that. All this time? Why? Why didn't you tell me?"

"I'm sorry. I hated myself for the lie and I've hated myself for being back in Boston and not telling you, especially any time I knew you were here. It hurt like hell. Not seeing you, not telling you, keeping something like that from you. I didn't have a choice though, Grey. I didn't."

"You could have told me the truth."

"No. I couldn't have," she says adamantly, but her fierceness crumbles before me. Suddenly she looks wrecked, exhausted, her weight falling heavily against me, her head on my shoulder, and fuck it if anyone is taking pictures or not. She squeezes my pinky back and tilts her head, staring regretfully up at me. "If you knew I was here, we would have seen each other, and I couldn't see you. It was difficult enough for me to hold back." A hard swallow and then her gaze falls to our joined pinkies. "I told you the last time I saw you..."

"But you wouldn't tell me why," I accuse. "I woke up in that hotel room on the sofa and found the bed you were supposed to be sleeping in empty. A simple fucking note on hotel stationary saying goodbye."

"I'm engaged," she blurts out, righting her body.

I stare at her, positive I did not just hear those words from her sweet lips. "Engaged? Since when?"

"Two weeks. The notice is going out publicly this week. We waited for political reasons since the mid-term elections are coming up and both of our fathers are running for senatorial re-election." She emits a mournful sigh. "I should have told you. I know this. I thought about it so many times, but I..."

She trails off just as the door of the restaurant swings open, and in walks a dude who screams aristocrat. His blue eyes sparkle, his short blond hair expensively cut and perfectly coiffed, his Monroe suit—which inherently makes me want to kill him since it's my family's brand—perfectly tailored. He does a sweep of the restaurant, not immediately finding Fallon, but I know that's whom he's searching for.

I know it the same way I know how to play any song I hear once without sheet music.

"To him?" I point incredulously. Fallon's other hand covers mine, lowering it back to my lap and I take her hand, holding it firmly, touching the ring on her finger. My stomach sinks like lead. It's a big diamond, I'll give the prick that much.

"Yes. Grey... I..."

Finally he locates Fallon and the smile that erupts across his face has my jaw clenching. Why didn't Zax drag me out of here when he saw her enter? Why didn't he save me from this? I should—could—get up and walk away. Walk right out of the damn restaurant, but I can't seem to make my legs move. Engaged? How in the fuck did that happen?

She's going to marry this guy? Marry him? She can't.

"Bacchus," she murmurs, her hands releasing both of mine as she stands.

I choke on a laugh. Bacchus?! For real?

"Dumpling!"

"Dumpling?" I repeat and she kicks my shin under the table before she rounds it and greets him with a kiss on the cheek—not the lips I note—and then sits back down beside me.

"And who is this?" he asks, setting his napkin down on his lap and eyeing me with a look I'm all too familiar with. One that says he knows exactly who I am and he doesn't like it one bit.

"Greyson, this is my fiancé, Bacchus Hastings Astley the fourth. Bacchus, this is Greyson Monroe—"

"The original," I cut her off. Fallon coughs out a laugh but quickly stifles it. I stretch out my hand and he grips me, but it's limp compared to the death grip I'm giving him. I smile. He does too and for a few moments, we do the male sizing-each-other-up thing.

He releases my hand first. "It's nice to meet you, Greyson. Fallon never mentioned you before. How long have you two known each other since I assume you didn't just meet now?"

"Funny, she never mentioned you to me either."

He makes a displeased noise in the back of his throat and Fallon pinches my thigh.

I redirect. "I imagine she wouldn't have told you about me. Her family doesn't like me too much. Fallon and I used to be neighbors growing up. I was friends with her brother Dillon before the accident."

Fallon shifts beside me, her foot rubbing mine. She hates it when I blame myself for the accident with Dillon. I want to throw my arm around her shoulder or retake her hand, but I restrain myself. Just barely.

"How long have you two been together?" I toss back at him, though I'm pretty positive I already know the answer. I never looked her up. I never had the stomach for it, but now I feel foolish for that.

"Three years," he tells me arrogantly, and yep, it's all coming together now.

"Interesting. That's exactly how long it's been since I saw her last."

Another pinch, this one harder, and yeah, I likely shouldn't have said that. Or still be here since her family can't know we've kept in touch after I left when we were teenagers.

"Hmmm," he says appraising me with a tilt of his head and narrowing of his eyes. After a beat, a smug smile twists his lips, and he snaps his fingers in that 'ah ha' way as if he's just figured out who I am and didn't already know. Douche. "You're one of those boy banders, right? From that band that broke up all those years ago after that girl died." Fallon stiffens beside me at the mention of Suzie's death, but her dirtbag fiancé doesn't catch it before he continues with, "What was it called again... Harvard Square?"

"Central Square," she corrects for me.

His gaze snaps sharply over to hers. "Were you a fan?"

"You know I am, Bacchus. I listen to their music and Greyson's all the time."

That shouldn't give me as much satisfaction as it does.

"Well, now I know why."

"It's good music," I cut in to take the heat off her. "You should give it a listen. Though technically we were never considered a boy band. Now I play as a solo artist. What do you do?"

He squares his shoulders and sets his folded hands on the edge of the table. "I'm a partner in a law firm."

I grin. "Of course you are. The Lark's wouldn't have set their daughter up with anyone else."

"How did you know they set us up?"

"Greyson," Fallon hisses under her breath, and I need to stop this before it ends badly for her.

"Lucky guess, but what a small world that I ran into Fallon here." I turn and take her in, wanting to continue being angry and hostile, but it's impossible. I know Fallon. A hell of a lot better than this douchebag does or ever will. I know why she didn't tell me she was doing her residency here and I know why she's engaged to this guy. I also know that other than being a doctor, this life that her family has forced her into is never what she wanted but had always resigned herself to.

I want to ask her if she actually loves him. If he's the guy for her and if she's happy. If she's happy, well, at least then this would be easier to swallow. I always swore I wouldn't be another person in her life to demand things of her. Especially things I know she can't give me.

Like herself. Like her time. Like her heart.

Now... now she's going to marry him and there is nothing I can do to stop it. No matter how much the thought feels like someone is stabbing me with a jagged knife and twisting it around and around in my chest. I have to protect myself. She tried and now I'm looking at this guy and I'm an open, bleeding mess of a man.

"Well, I'll let you two enjoy your breakfast." I stand and her eyes follow me, saying so many things to me. Things like I'm sorry and this hurts and I miss you and I wish, I wish, I wish. "Take care of yourself, Fall Girl." I turn to her fiancé who is watching us carefully. "Nice meeting you, man."

I smack his shoulder and head for the exit, my heart in my feet making my steps heavy. I stop short, blinking at the rays of sun as they shine through the glass door, thinking. Before I can talk myself out of it, I slip my small notebook and pen I use to write song lyrics from my back pocket and scribble down a quick message. Then I tear the sheet from the spirals and fold it in quarters and tuck it into my palm.

Turning back around, I realize she's still watching me even as she speaks to him. I smile because damn, she takes my breath away, and then I return to her table. "How rude of me. I forgot to congratulate you on your engagement. I hope you're as happy as you look."

I lean in and press my lips to her cheek at the same time I clasp her hand and slip her the folded piece of paper. She takes it, her brows pinched questioningly even as her breath catches. Her hand closes around the paper and I release her.

Walking away.

This time I don't look back. My message was delivered. It's hers now and I feel better for her having it. Even if I know, I'll likely never see her again after today.

THE END.

END OF BOOK NOTE

Thank you for taking the time to read Irresistibly Broken. If you're new to me, welcome! If you're not, thank you for sticking with me. You are who I do this for!

I had so much fun writing Zax and Aurelia. They were complicated and messy and heartfelt and deep. Both individually and together. My whole purpose with Aurelia was to demonstrate how perfection is an illusion. So many times we associate someone's external appearance with the state of their lives. Like, oh, she's so beautiful I'm sure everything in her life is perfect. Wrong. Aurelia felt this misassumption every day and I think that's part of what makes her such a unique character.

Zax, well, he's suffered. But even in his suffering, he was never anti-love or anti-relationships or any of that other stuff we frequently see with our heroes. He just didn't want to be bothered. He loved and lost and kind of called it quits.

But when these two came together they were instant fire. Just so much passion between them that I couldn't stop writing them. I'm so excited for where their journey will take them next and for you to get to know the rest of the Central Square crew.

Big, fat special thank you to my family. To my three girls who are growing up way too fast and to my guy, who is the best husband and father on the planet. I am so grateful for you!!

To my incredible team: Danielle, Patricia, Kelly, and Joy. I would be absolutely lost without you. Because of you, I'm able to do this and thank you hardly ever feels like enough.

Thank you all! Love you!!

XO,

J. Saman

Made in United States
North Haven, CT
06 January 2023

30686988R00205